ACE OF SHADES

A HUMOROUS PARANORMAL WOMEN'S
FICTION

DEBORAH WILDE

te da media inc.
vancouver

Book Cover Design by ebooklaunch.com

Issued in print and electronic formats.

ISBN: 978-1-988681-75-7 (paperback)

ISBN: 978-1-988681-74-0 (epub)

ISBN: 978-1-988681-76-4 (Large Print)

1

"Celestial beings are colossal dicks," Dumah, the angel currently presenting as my cousin Goldie, said. Her plastic clogs slapped against the rough-hewn paving stones of an enormous courtyard and orange blossoms fluttered into her frizzy gray hair from surrounding trees. "Present company included."

One second, I'd been in my living room, having the shock of my life realizing that the three angels Senoi, Sansenoi, and Sammaneglof had been the ones who killed my parents and Fred McMurtry. The next, Dumah-Goldie had appeared in a blast of trumpets and was ushering me into Gehenna. If only solving my jigsaw puzzles earned me this same kind of fanfare.

Hummingbirds in a rainbow of iridescent colors dipped and soared between patches of swaying wildflowers, while the air was fresh and sweet. I spun slowly, eyes wide. This was the land of the dead where wicked spirits resided?

"Stop." I pinched myself, half convinced this was some go-into-the-light scenario, especially since my magic was gone. A distant part of me freaked out at my helplessness, but most of me fell into line with the chill vibe exuded here.

Not once in my life had I been described as chill.

"Are you compelling me into being calm?" I said, abruptly becoming even less calm.

"Compulsions are so passive-aggressive. If I wanted you calm, I'd say so." The older woman tugged up her shapeless jeans with a little hip wriggle. It was such quintessentially Goldie behavior that I squeaked, plowing my fingers into my hair. Though my real cousin, who lived in Florida, veered less to jeans and more to floral capris these days.

At least the angel didn't smell like tea tree oil, that fresh camphor scent from my cousin's favorite lotion. It might have sent me over the edge.

"You look like you're gonna plotz." Dumah-Goldie jerked her chin at two elaborately carved chairs on the grassy bank overlooking the water. "Sit. Take a load off."

Fumbling for the armrest, I crashed into the seat then squinted up at the sun, shielding my face with one hand.

The storm clouds and fog that were visible every time Laurent tore open a portal to this place were notably missing, and the fluffy cloud drifting overhead looked like a bunny rabbit. Not even a bunny rabbit with fangs or rabies of the damned. Huh. I peered into the crystalline depths of the meandering river, but unless the fat koi sunning themselves were repositories for especially malevolent souls who'd been terrified of water, I had nothing.

Where were all the tortured dybbuks? It was one thing for Dumah to assume my cousin's image to accommodate the limits of my brain in looking upon the angel, but either the angel had done a massive cleanup campaign before I got here, or... I shook my head. Nope. I had nothing.

"Shouldn't it be black and ringing with tortured screams?"

She scoffed. "Oy. Who wants to listen to that 24/7? This is Ḥaẓarmavet, the Courtyard of Death, also known as my happy place."

"Wait! So, I *am* dead?" I half rose up off my seat, feeling for a heartbeat.

She lowered herself into the chair next to mine, leaned over, and smooshed my cheeks with her hand. "Ah, matzoh ball, always with the worries. Stress and lack of fiber: they'll do you in far too soon."

I wrenched free, massaging my aching cheeks, because for a celestial being, she had a wrestler's grip. "Please don't call me by Goldie's nickname." My cousin's way of keeping my real initials—M.B. for Miriam Blum—alive after I took her surname; this was the second time the angel had used it in our brief acquaintanceship, and it was getting weird. "Also, being dead is a pretty fair thing to worry about."

"You're alive and kicking." She snapped her fingers and a black smudgy shadow appeared.

The demon was both too large and too small, had too many horns and too few limbs, but mostly I couldn't process the sight because its utter malevolence was causing my brain to curl into a quivering lump. I looked away.

It growled something, to which the angel replied, "Prosecco, I think. Thanks, Tad."

The air pulled taut and Gehenna's stench of rotting onions that had been missing from this courtyard suddenly wafted in, then with a sproingy snap, all was serenity and orange blossoms once more.

I cautiously looked back, but we were alone. "The demon is called Tad?"

Was that the most important question right now? Of course not, but my mind was screaming at me that I was in Gehenna and that angels had murdered my parents, and I could grasp only the low-hanging fruit of knowledge.

"No," the angel said, "but if I said its full name, along with all its titles, we'd be here forever. Also, your ears would be bleeding." She shrugged. "Easier to use names of people Goldie likes."

3

I furrowed my eyebrows. "Goldie doesn't know any Tads."

"Disagreeing here, since she checked in on him every day for years."

It took me a second, but then the penny dropped, and I stifled a snort. The angel was talking about a soap opera character. "Right. That Tad."

Speak of the devil. I hurriedly dropped my gaze to my feet, because the demon was back. Glass clanked softly, there was another growl, more onion disgustingness, and that same air stretch and pop.

I cautiously raised my eyes again.

A table with a white cloth held two champagne flutes and a bucket with a bottle of chilled prosecco. There were a few scorch marks in the fabric and something had taken a bite out of one side, but in the face of much-needed booze, I was willing to overlook a few minor horrors.

As the angel poured our drinks, a blue and green butterfly flew over and settled in her hair.

"L'chaim." Doubting I'd been brought here to be poisoned, I clinked my glass to hers and took a healthy slug. Fruity, light, and fizzy. Setting the glass down, I bolstered my courage. "We should talk about..." I lowered my voice. "The three."

Dumah-Goldie boomed her laugh, and startled, the hummingbird zipped off. "The schmuck trio. You can say their names, though I refer to them very differently." The angel's eyes morphed from Goldie's warm honey brown to an unforgiving gold with black vertical slits for pupils, cold-blooded as a snake.

I shivered, but in the next blink they were Goldie's familiar ones. The abrupt shift was more unsettling.

A small tin containing hard lemon candies appeared in the angel's palm, her nails bitten to the quick, just like my cousin's. She popped a candy in her mouth with a pleased hum before offering one to me, but when I shook my head, the tin vanished.

"I've been watching you, matz—Miriam."

"I gathered." I clasped my fingers in my lap to keep from downing the rest of the booze, since I required a sober head right now. "You don't want to be freed, do you?"

The angel topped up our prosecco from the bottle. "Big fish, small pond. No politics. I've got a good life here." She belched and covered her mouth with the same half giggle as when Goldie got tipsy. "Tell me what you've figured out, I'll fill in the blanks, and we'll go from there."

Go from there? To where? What more was there? An icy tendril danced down my spine. The angel could serve me delicious drinks and take on Goldie's appearance, but the fact of the matter was that I was in Gehenna and at her mercy. I didn't think she'd hurt me physically, but I had a history of supernatural beings cornering me into doing their dangerous bidding. If this self-admitted dick of a celestial creature requested something, I was in no position to refuse. She got points for self-awareness, but given the whole angel thing, that was only mildly reassuring.

"Okay." I twisted my old engagement ring around my finger, slotting my thoughts into the correct order. Taking a leap of faith that the three other angels couldn't hear this conversation, I spoke.

"Senoi, Sansenoi, and Sammaneglof wanted a Banim Shovavim to use the Ascendant to free you. Why?" I rubbed away a smudge on the ring's band. "I'm torn between them either wanting to kill you or exile you like they did with the Leviathan. But what I don't know is why they'd go to all that effort."

"Because they hate that I've found a measure of peace and satisfaction here. Should I jailbreak out of my fine prison, freeing the dybbuks and causing death and chaos, they'll swoop in and play winged avengers, finally putting me in my proper place."

"They don't care about the Ohrists who'd be inhabited, just that you'd damned yourself." I saluted the angel with my glass. "Joke's on them since you don't want to leave."

The puffy clouds flickered and darkened, their edges sharpening like razor wire, and Dumah-Goldie's smile had a strained quality to it before she drained her glass. It was the same expression Eli had worn when he'd arranged a picnic dinner for our anniversary one year, eventually admitting that he'd forgotten about it until his partner, Detective Rose Tanaka, had reminded him at the eleventh hour.

Was it because Dumah enjoyed their life here even though it involved torturing dybbuks? Those wicked spirits had earned their damnation and, in my opinion, Dumah had nothing to feel bad about. Not like Gehenna's former visitor, Kian, who'd enjoyed the pain she'd inflicted, even if it had been payback for—

I gasped. "If I use the Ascendant on you, you won't have a choice about whether to stay. Kian was forced to leave and you would be as well."

"Yes." She opened her mouth but took another sip instead of speaking. Why was she acting cagey?

"Destroy the Ascendant," I said. "Problem solved."

"Why didn't I think of that?" She set her glass on the table and leaned back in her chair, her face tilted up and her hands linked behind her head. "It was once believed that angels were the souls of stars."

Goosebumps broke out on my skin. Stars meant ascendancy, and worse, mazel. Every choice I'd ever made, every path taken, curled in on me in tighter and tighter coils leading to this moment. I rejected the concept of mazel, but I'd been sure that I'd made the decision to destroy the Ascendant out of free will, and not because all the possibilities had narrowed down to an inevitable set of options.

6

"You can't destroy the artifact, can you?" I said in a dull voice. "Is that why I'm here?" Forget it. I'd hide the Ascendant away and take my chances on it not being found before I became anyone's pawn.

"That's not why I brought you, so put that stubborn face away. Only an angel can destroy the Ascendant." Her lips twisted wryly. "Look at you, all disappointed. Well, join the club. By 'only an angel' I mean 'only a true, unfallen angel,' which means I'm shit out of luck myself. The Ascendant was forged in stardust, the ultimate light relic to combat the forces of darkness. Ironically, only Banim Shovavim can wield it as part of darkness balancing that intense light." She plucked one of the four-leaf clovers that sprang up around her feet and twisted it around in her fingers. "Any supernatural being with even a hint of darkness is helpless to its call."

Like Kian. Something shifted in the pit of my stomach. "Was the estrie happy here?"

"If I say yes, will you torture yourself?" The angel pulled off the first of the four leaflets. "She was happy." Pluck. "Not happy." Pluck. "Happy." She handed me the clover with the remaining leaflet.

"Unhappy." I shredded the clover. "Except she wasn't."

"You have no more proof of that than what a clover tells you is true."

"Why won't you give me a straight answer?" I demanded.

"Because what's done is done. Is knowing going to give you closure? Straight answers aren't always the right answers, Miriam. Sometimes lies are. Or not having any answer at all. Sometimes it's best to make your peace with remaining in the dark."

That was annoyingly inscrutable. I wiped my hands on my yoga pants. "Why don't Senoi, Sansenoi, and Sammaneglof like you? Is it truly as simplistic as you're, uh, fallen?"

"I besmirched our kind with my actions." The angel spoke in a haughty, mocking tone. "They've killed weaker angels for lesser infractions. But then again, to a purity complex, all morally ambiguous entities are worthy of destruction as soon as they stop toeing the line." She paused. "I stood up for Lilith, you know."

"No way."

"Way." She nodded. "They ran tattling and I got a slap on the wrist." She tipped the bottle into the glass, but when nothing came out, tossed it onto the grass. "But nooo. That wasn't good enough for the schmuck trio and they pushed for me to be exiled." She lifted her glass, which had magically refilled itself. "The smug bastards were fine until it got out that I was getting a bit too comfy here."

There was a ringing in my ears and something wet trickled down from my nose. When I touched it, my hand came away red. I screwed my eyes shut, realizing the demon had returned.

"I told you before, *Tad*, this isn't a union shop, so no, I'm not overstepping by refilling my own glass, and if you have a problem with that, you can take it up with the boss." She snapped her fingers. "Oh, wait. That's me."

As the angel spoke, ice formed under my feet, a layer of frost crawling up my legs and along my torso. I wrapped my arms around myself, my teeth chattering and my eyes still very much closed.

Tad's growls intensified and an acrid smoke tickled my nostrils. Okay, the demon wasn't responsible for the ice. That was less comforting.

"Well, I don't like your attitude either," the angel said, "and I always win."

Meaty chunks rained down on me, whapping me over the head. Screaming, I slid off my chair and pulled it over myself like a shield.

"Jeez, Tad," Dumah-Goldie said, "where were you hiding that gut?"

Spitting demon bits out of my mouth, I white-knuckled

the chair. If I died from ingesting demon blubber, I was going on an afterlife rampage starting with this batshit angel. What was I thinking coming here? I mean, it wasn't like I had a choice, but still. Angels, all of them, were clearly unstable.

Silence fell.

Wiping goo off my face, I opened my eyes.

Dumah-Goldie stood in a splash-free zone, the one remaining circle of pristine lawn. Sadly, the rest of the courtyard hadn't fared as well, because the grass that wasn't stained black and red had acquired an oily texture, and oddly shaped bits floated down the river.

A knot of hummingbirds swooped down to feast and I gagged.

The angel placed her hands on her hips. "And here we were, almost at a week with no turnover," she said. "Erica!"

This new demon was an enormous cube of red eczema'd skin, its eyes on stalks drooping off the top. Stumpy arms with terrifyingly sharp claws covered the cube, each claw stabbing a writhing, yowling dybbuk. She looked nothing like the glamorous character from the same soap opera as Tad.

"Holy shit," I muttered. The demon didn't melt my brain, but it still vibed evil. I scrambled back on my ass, landing in a puddle of Tad ooze, which stung mildly through my clothes. *Please don't let me grow a third ass cheek like the fish with extra eyes in polluted waters.*

Erica beeped out some sounds.

"Tad's gone. Congratulations. You're my new personal assistant."

The demon chittered excitedly and disappeared.

The angel motioned impatiently at me. "Did I tell you to stop speaking?"

"No?" What was the topic? *Think, Feldman.* Righting my chair, which immediately fell over again thanks to a broken leg, I envisioned my office whiteboard with all my notes. "Almost thirty years ago, Senoi, Sansenoi, and Sammaneglof convinced Arlo Garcia to steal the Ascendant and use its magic to free you. He used it for himself instead, resulting in his eternal torture in the Kefitzat Haderech. The schmuck trio was none the wiser that you didn't want to leave Gehenna."

"Keep going." The angel cocked her head and narrowed her eyes.

I flinched, but all that happened was she restored the Courtyard of Death to its former glory. She'd even fixed my chair and put me back in it, nice and clean.

A hummingbird flitted in front of my face, but I waved it away, positive there was a lethal glint in its eyes that the ones on earth didn't have. Or at least didn't show.

"Arlo had already turned the Ascendant over to his subcontractor," I continued, "and as angels aren't omniscient —" *Thank fuck, because I'd be in a shitload of trouble with the three for this conversation.* "The trio had to track it down, which brought them to my parents, another couple of Banim Shovavim with the amplifier." I bit the inside of my cheek, needing the sharp pain to keep my voice steady. "But my parents had given it to Calvin Jones, the Ohrist who hired them. Why didn't the three leave Mom and Dad alone?" My voice cracked. "Why kill them?"

"They refused to help." Dumah-Goldie eyed the river, changed the koi to octopi, shook her head, and switched them back. "You don't say no to those angels."

"Mom and Dad didn't refuse," I argued. "There was nothing they could have done even if they wanted to. They didn't have the Ascendant anymore." My stomach twisted into a knot; semantics wouldn't matter to the trio.

Dumah-Goldie waved a hand like that was of no concern. "They'd stolen it once, they could have stolen it again. Your parents wouldn't free me, allowing dybbuks to flood the world, and that's why they were killed."

I rubbed a hand over my chest, a single ray of sunlight breaking through the morass in my heart. My parents may have been petty thieves, but they'd died for their line in the sand. They were good people. I swiped at my damp eyes, conscious of the angel's fidgeting.

"One thing you should know," Dumah-Goldie finally said, "is that it wasn't angels. Hunters killed your parents."

I flinched. "Not a fire demon and an Ohrist?"

She made a raspberry noise. "Like they'd trust demons to carry out their orders. Besides, they founded the hunters, and even though Lonestars had banned them years before, some were still around."

I stood up abruptly, wanting to kick something, or throw my chair, but I took deep breaths and walked it off until I was calm enough to continue. "The three lost track of the Ascendant after Mom and Dad," I said. "Cut to years later when James Learsdon starts chasing after it. Maybe they turned him on to the artifact, but I think he learned of it through his archaeology pursuits, and they latched on to that, whispering to him, and eventually connecting him to me."

"The Blank who wasn't so Blank." Dumah-Goldie snorted. "The schmuck trio did not appreciate you showing them up in the Kefitzat Haderech by solving the riddle. That's when I took note of you."

The breeze picked up.

Dumah-Goldie licked the pad of her finger, held it up, and nodded. "Erica! Time for walksies."

The ground shook and I whipped my head around, expecting some Cerberus-like hellhound to come bounding out, but it was so much worse. The river bubbled, heat rising off it, and the far bank exploded, unleashing a tornado of pulsing, howling, furious slashes of crimson and gray.

I reached for my magic, but as it hadn't miraculously reappeared, ducked behind the angel's chair.

The tornado grew until it blocked out all light. Wind lashed my hair around, its force driving me to my knees. I scratched at my skin, trying to tear it off—anything to get away from the fury and evil emanating from the other shore.

The angel whistled sharply, and the gale stopped.

Erica popped into view, all her claws pointing left, and the dybbuks streamed into a relatively peaceful line flowing in that direction. The demon kept pace, bobbing along next to them like a guard overseeing the prisoners' time in the yard.

Shaking, I pushed to my feet and mopped my face with a sleeve. Dizzy and nauseous from this many dybbuks, I couldn't stay here much longer, and I rushed through the rest of my summation.

"The three angels bribed a Lonestar into covering up my parents' deaths, then killed him when he was going to rat them out to me." They could have cured McMurtry them-selves, I bet, but used a demon parasite as a red herring. "I found the Ascendant and handed it to you. In turn, you pursued me with that engraved amulet and here we are."

Dumah-Goldie cracked her knuckles. "They almost killed you after you found the Ascendant, did you know that? They didn't want to risk another member of the Blum family having their own agenda for it. But you gave me the orb in the nick of time and got to live. They probably think I'm convincing you to free me right now."

I wrapped my arms around myself. "Will they murder me if I don't?"

"Not immediately." She sounded so blasé about my immi-nent death. The angel whistled again, and Erica and dybbuks switched direction.

"You have a plan, right? You're going to protect me?"

She chuckled. "I can't interfere."

A muscle ticked in my jaw. "Then what?"

The angel leaned in close. Her eyes were snake slits once more, but this time they danced with a deadly arctic chill. "You're going take Senoi, Sansenoi, and Sammaneglof down."

2

No wonder she'd been cagey if that was her plan. I fell back into my chair, her fervent gleam pinning me in place. "I can't kill three angels. They'd spot me coming a mile away." I longed to slap those snake eyes off my cousin's face but didn't dare.

"Obviously. You wouldn't last a second. A half second." She tapped her lips. "What's less than a half second?"

"A quarter second?" I suggested weakly.

"Smaller." She motioned for me to keep going with one hand, drinking prosecco from the flute.

"An eighth?" Another head shake. I went down another couple of measurements.

A tiny cluster of dybbuks broke free and charged toward me in a funnel cloud.

I slapped uselessly at them. "Help!"

The angel chuckled, her eyes reverting to human. "Dybbuks will be dybbuks. You're a host, they need a body."

"Then give me my magic back!"

She looked at me like I was a silly child and drained her glass.

One of the dybbuks slithered partway into my ear. It felt like a shard of molten glass burrowing into my head.

Cursing, I violently shook my head to dislodge the spirit, which landed with a *plop* in the angel's flute.

Dumah-Goldie plucked it out. "Oh no you don't, you little bastard." She closed her fingers into a fist, and the dybbuks swarming around us blew back across the river.

For a single second, each one assumed a very human and terrified face, their eyes darting to me in plea.

My heart twisted, but there was nothing I could do. There was nothing I *would* do. These were dybbuks, wicked spirits who'd ended up here for a reason, and one of them had tried to inhabit me.

Still, their scared human faces haunted me, and I had to look away.

The large brown stones of the courtyard wall on the other side of the river tore open into a jagged portal of toxic orange and red swirls, the stench of rotting onions making me gag. With a single soul-piercing cry, all the dybbuks were sucked into the rift and the stones resealed to the sound of thunder.

Erica's eye stalks swiveled to the angel and she beeped.

"Good idea. Extra torture for everyone."

The demon vanished and the angel turned to me with a pleasant smile. "Zeptosecond."

"Huh?"

"It's a trillionth of a billionth of a second. That's how long you'd last." She screwed up her face. "Maybe."

I ground a layer of enamel off my teeth. "Then why suggest it?"

"I didn't." The angel shook her head. "Taking the trio down is not killing. For someone who loves facts as much as you do, I'd expect you to listen better. You're going to unravel them."

I dug my nails into my thighs to keep from screaming. "That's different how?" When the angel merely gave me the same "I'm waiting" look that my university math professor had turned on me many a time, I ran through my Miripedia of facts. "Is an unraveling similar to stars being devoured by black holes and crushed into nothingness?" After all the mazel BS I'd faced, I'd brushed up on astronomy, immensely enjoying the fact that even stars had predators.

"Oh no." A cruel smile flitted over Dumah's lips. "Devourment, nothingness, that is too good for them. This is an eternal and endless unspooling." The angel deepened the pitch of Goldie's voice, suffusing it with a gravitas matching her expression.

"Torment forever and ever." I bobbed my head. "Got it."

"On a celestial scale." She licked her lips, her eyes glistening.

I did my best to repress a shudder.

"They'll no longer have magic or be able to take on any physical form, reduced to sentient dust motes crashing and breaking like waves across the heavens, yet aware that they crossed the wrong being." By the end of that sentence her voice was a harsh growl that was almost unintelligible, her cheeks were flushed, and her chest rose and fell in ragged breaths.

The sight of my cousin getting lady hard was bad enough, the fact that it was really an angel who relished this kind of suffering and could easily mete it out on any human had me holding myself very still, like a gazelle in tall grass not wanting to catch a nearby lion's eye.

She blinked back to Goldie's natural good humor. "You get the gist."

"O-kay, but *you're* the one they shouldn't cross, thus you are the one who should unravel them."

"Don't be ridiculous. They'd sense any attack from me, not that I can do much from here. But you? They'll never see you coming because they'd never expect a weak, pitiful, abomination of a human to target them."

"When you put it like that," I said snarkily. I took a deep breath to compose myself. "I can't do it. If they catch me, *which they will*, I'll last less than a zeptosecond."

"Untrue. They'd keep you alive forever."

I bent over with a moan.

"But should you do it right," the angel said, "they'll never know it was you until it's too late." She chucked me under the chin. "Don't you believe in yourself, Miriam?"

I smacked her hand away, not in the mood for one of Goldie's pep talks, then froze, my eyes wide. "I—I—" Had I just hit a celestial being who could also keep me alive and tortured forever? I dropped to my knees, my head pressed to the grass. "Forgive me for striking you, O merciful angel."

She prodded me with a plastic clog. "Jeez Louise. Get up. You were finally showing some of that backbone that I'd seen in you. Don't ruin it."

I took my seat, my body tense.

The angel shrugged. "If it makes you feel better, I wouldn't have chosen you if I didn't believe you could pull this off, but I can't force you."

"You can't?" *Yes!* I mentally fist pumped.

"I mean, obviously I can." She tossed her hair, but frizzy as it was, it didn't move much, just sort of clumped up in a different configuration. "But I won't. I want your cooperation and not just because people tend to do a better job out of inspiration than fear."

Could I actually attempt this and win? I'd get vengeance for Mom's and Dad's murders. Plus, if Senoi, Sansenoi, and Sammaneglof were unraveled, that lie about Banim Shovavim's wickedness wouldn't be sold to us anymore and no one else would be damned in the Kefitzat Haderech.

Those were pretty strong arguments. However, they were up against the more compelling counterpoint of "ARE YOU INSANE? IT'S ANGELS!"

"Could I get some more information to base my decision on?" I said. "What exactly would I be expected to do?"

"That's easy. Destroy the Kefitzat Haderech."

My mouth fell open. The KH gave me freedom to go anywhere in the world. It had broadened the cases I could work, and while I hadn't yet jaunted off to Vienna for an afternoon of eating my body weight in pastries, the point was that I could so long as the KH existed. I'd be taking away one of the best perks of being a Banim Shovavim, for myself and all my kind. "I can't do that."

"Why not? Air travel has come a long way. Sure, the security lineups are a bitch, but—"

"It's not because of its travel benefits." I brushed an orange blossom from my hair. "Though that is pretty great."

"Right? I've never used it myself, but from all reports, mere minutes to anywhere."

"No overpriced bad food or being squished into a seat." I ticked the items off on my fingers. "Forget surplus luggage charges."

"Not to mention new homes for all those lost socks."

"But that's not why I can't destroy it." Pyotr could go home—though if he was in Russia, how often would he visit? —but I'd be destroying his livelihood. And sure, I'd free the Leviathan first, but what about Neon Sign Face and all the Banim Shovavim stuck there in damnation? Would they cease to exist? I twisted my fingers together, thinking of Arlo. It might be a mitzvah to end their torments, but I'd still be killing them. "There are living beings in there."

Dumah-Goldie shrugged. "Red shirts. You always did get so upset whenever an away team went to explore a new planet, and just like I explained to you on TV date night, sacrifices must be made for a higher purpose."

How much loss was acceptable for the greater good? Senoi, Sansenoi, and Sammaneglof's narrow and bigoted view of the world had caused untold harm for centuries. Stopping them was the right thing to do, but I'd felt a stab of remorse not ten minutes ago when I saw a dybbuk with a human face. When push came to shove would I be able to disregard all emotion and do what had to be done?

What if the angels came after my loved ones? Every step of this magic journey had involved me checking and double-checking and cutting crazy deals to ensure they all stayed safe. But there'd be no safety net here.

I picked at a cuticle. I'd been so proud of myself for casting off Zev's protection and finally standing on my own two feet and look where it had gotten me. I was completely at a loss as to what choice to make. "Why would destroying the KH unravel the three?"

"It's the same as lighting a fire." Off my blank stare, the angel made an exasperated noise. "What about this do you not understand?"

"All of it."

"Would flash cards help? You like those." A stack of index cards winked into view, fluttering down to the sound of a card-sorting machine. When it finished, the stack was chair height.

I took yet another very deep, very composed breath. "A brief explanatory paragraph will suffice."

The angel held up the top card. "Are you sure? I used color-coded bullet points." She singsonged that last bit like a dog owner asking their pet if they wanted a treat.

There was this new age shop near my place with a large selection of goods devoted to angels, including the classic angel pocket token ("I choose to let the angels guide me"), the regrettable framed quotes ("Angels are everywhere"), and my personal favorite, a chunky metal tumbler inscribed with "I am open to divine inspiration."

Dumah-Goldie was certainly inspiring me in all kinds of creative and possibly anatomically impossible thoughts.

My eye twitched. "I'm sure."

She regarded the stack with disappointment, then the cards vanished. "The schmuck trio infused their magic into the Kefitzat Haderech. That's what made it possible for them to send those Banim Shovavim into their lost, wandering damnation, as well as imprison the Leviathan."

"I know that."

"Then what exactly is so difficult about the fire analogy?"

I swallowed my sarcastic retort. "Humor me."

She wriggled her big toe out through a hole on the left sock. "Fire. How do you—"

"Oxygen, fuel, and heat," I said.

"There's no gold star, Miriam," she said dryly. "But yes. Those three elements combine to trigger a chemical reaction. Take any one of them away and poof." She snapped her fingers. "No fire."

"Extrapolating then, there are three elements that trigger a magical, rather than a chemical, reaction to unravel the angels."

"Very good. Light magic dismantles the foundation of the Kefitzat Haderech, because as a Banim Shovavim space, it was built with your dark magic."

"Balance," I mused.

"Exactly. Those schmucks are so bound to the Kefitzat Haderech now that any destabilization to the structure also destabilizes them."

I drummed a finger on the armrest. "As celestial beings, they're the ultimate expression of light magic. Which means they're vulnerable to Banim Shovavim magic." I shook my head. "Wild. I can unravel angels."

She smiled with a mouthful of sharp teeth. "Don't be getting ideas. It only works in this case because so much of their power is tied to the Kefitzat Haderech. Otherwise, you'd need every Banim Shovavim in existence working together."

I stopped myself just in time from asking where I could

find other Banim Shovavim—to befriend, not for angel-killing purposes.

"When the KH goes," she continued, "the shock wave will ripple through that connection to them and your magic can do its work and unravel them."

That was only two elements. "Light magic plus dark magic plus what? What's the match, so to speak?"

"You said you didn't want flash cards." The angel's eyes flitted back to snake form.

I held up my hands placatingly. "The Ascendant, right? We need its amplifying abilities to achieve the strength to accomplish this."

The slits morphed back to human pupils and I sighed.

"Open the Ascendant," she said, "funnel both types of magic through it, and big bam boom. Everything will be groovy."

"Regardless of whether I do this, and I'm not sure yet that I will, I want to leave here today with the Ascendant so I can free the Leviathan."

The silver orb appeared in the angel's hand and she threw it to me. "A gesture of goodwill. This won't do the trick, mind you, as the sea monster is angel-cursed. But you take it with you."

I curled my fingers around the cool artifact. "He can't escape unless I destroy the KH, can he?"

The angel booped me on the nose. "Bingo!"

I tossed the Ascendant up and down. For the first time, I had a hot home (partially, but I was slowly transforming it), a hot job, and a hot lover. I'd never dared to aspire to more than two, and even then I'd managed only one and a half at best.

If I walked away from all of this, I'd let down the Leviathan and the trio would continue on their merry way, but I'd keep my fabulous life. After years of living under the radar in such a tightly contained ball, I'd burst free of my self-imposed restraints and the freedom felt glorious.

But I'd promised to help the Leviathan, and making those angels suffer appealed in a deep and primal way.

Dumah-Goldie patted my knee before I could decide. "The schmuck trio doesn't care that you've been asking questions about your parents because they believe you'll never figure it out. Think about it, and if you decide to move ahead, we'll plant rumors about when you're planning to free me. That'll keep them off your back and keep you under their radar."

"I don't know."

"It's a big decision, but here's one more thing to make your life easier," she said, "should you choose to accept this mission."

I sighed. "What?"

She made the sound of a trumpet fanfare and tossed me a gold ring. "Wear this when you strike and the agent of the Kefitzat Haderech will remain unaware of your actions."

Agent? For a second I thought she meant I had yet another minion to worry about until it hit me. "Neon Sign Face?" It was my guess based on the fact that it was higher up the food chain than Pyotr.

"You and your nicknames. Yes, Neon Sign Face. It acts in the best interests of the Kefitzat Haderech."

I closed my hand over the band. Unless Neon Sign Face had a death wish, the less it knew, the better. "Thanks. If I go ahead, this will be useful."

A crooked smile of light cracked through the courtyard, revealing my living room.

I stood up. "How long do I have to decide?"

"You deserve a fair period of time to consider it. Get back to me in two days."

Before I could protest that wasn't long enough, an invisible force grabbed me around the waist and tossed me back into my house.

I hit the carpet, stomach first, with a grunt, the Ascendant bouncing on the ground beside me. By the time I'd turned around, the rift and the angel were gone.

Eli and Sadie, however, sat on my sofa with a large bowl of popcorn on the coffee table and a superhero movie on TV, their eyes wide.

Scrambling to my feet, I examined my precious baby for butter stains. The sofa, not my kid. "What did I say about laying a towel down if you're going to eat on her? Why are you even here?"

My child and ex demonstrated they were clearly of the same gene pool by crossing their arms at the same moment to glare at me with identical expressions. Huh. She really did inherit her father's brow.

"You have Disney+," Sadie said.

Eli shot her a "seriously?" look.

"She asked," Sadie muttered. "Where the hell were you, Mom?"

"And why did your living room just light up like *Close Encounters of the Third Kind*?" my ex-husband said.

I sat cross-legged on the floor. "If I were to wonder what day it was—"

"Are you serious?" Sadie screeched.

"Wednesday evening," Eli said evenly.

"It's the same day I left?" I said. "Great. I figured I'd have lost way more..." At their deepening scowls, I smiled. "What's new with you, my beloved family?"

Sadie flung a pillow at me, which I stuffed under my butt. Ah. Much more comfortable.

"Here's the thing," I began.

Eli picked up another pillow, his eyes narrowed.

My stomach rumbled, and I helped myself to some popcorn. "Look, when an angel summons you to Gehenna, you go. I'm back and no one's going to be smote."

"That's your new benchmark, is it?" Eli said in a hard voice, but he lowered the pillow.

Sadie scratched her nose. "Angels exist? Do they have big wings and flowing white robes? Otherwise, I've got some cosplay props to update."

"You're as bad as your mother," Eli said.

One converted, one to go. "I have no idea," I said. "Their true form would have melted my brain, so they drew from my memories and presented as Goldie."

Eli quirked an eyebrow. "Like Goldie in that 1970s minidress and go-go boots?"

Sadie covered her face with her hands. "Ew, gross, Dad."

"Your cousin was a gorgeous woman in her youth," he said.

"For a gay man, you're suspiciously attracted to that photo," I said.

He stretched his arm out along the back of the sofa. "I am a connoisseur of beauty in all forms."

I snorted. "To answer your question, they were Goldie as we saw her on her last visit."

His face fell. "With the clogs?"

"And purple socks."

Sadie swallowed a mouthful of food. "What did the angel want?"

Between bites of popcorn, I explained the choice I faced. It was a testament to how far we'd come that Eli's bald head didn't turn rage red, nor did Sadie's leg jitter. The buttery treat, however, was turning into a greasy clump in my stomach, so I grabbed one of the paper towels lying beside the bowl and wiped off my fingers. "Thoughts?"

Sadie swiped her finger along a trail of salt in the bowl then licked the crystals off. "This almost sucks harder than what that vamp had me do."

Eli and I exchanged looks. Less than two days ago, Sadie had fulfilled a bargain she'd made with Zev Toledano— formerly BatKian—Vancouver's master vampire, after sneaking her friends into Blood Alley. He'd set her nulling magic on his great-great-something-granddaughter Celeste BatSila after she'd betrayed him. Both Sadie and Celeste had expected it to be a death sentence, since magic kept vampires animated. Even Zev hadn't been certain Celeste would survive.

It had been an incredibly traumatic moment for all involved, but Sadie refused to discuss it. Until now.

I grabbed the blanket that had slipped off the sofa and tossed it next to my daughter. "Why do you think that?"

"Do it and you're manipulated by an angel, don't do it and you miss your shot to get back at the ones who killed your parents." Sadie could switch emotions at the drop of a hat, and she had a predilection for melodrama, but bitterness was a new and unwelcome entry in her repertoire.

"Dumah isn't manipulating me," I said.

"Wake up, Mom. People in power do that." She threaded her fingers through the loops in the knit blanket. "Even using Ohrist magic is like playing this deadly game of 'I dare you.'"

Our friend Juliette had been conducting a healing session at the funeral home where Sadie had to null the magic and the young Frenchwoman had almost been killed by a blindspot. Seeing the consequences of magic use was very different from being told about it, and my daughter had been rattled.

Eli rested his hand on the back of her neck. "If you don't use magic, you're safe from blindspots."

"I don't want to be safe. I want to use my magic without worrying that I'm going to die every time." She crossed her arms. "It's not fair."

She was finally opening up, which was great, but her timing was...*selfish*? Less than ideal when I had this decision to make.

"What am I supposed to do?" she said.

"That's a risk you have to assess for yourself," I said. "It terrifies me to think of you and blindspots, but I also don't want you to wake up one day and realize you could have lived a much fuller version of the past thirty years of your life if you hadn't been scared to use your magic. Either way, I won't be the one to tell you not to use it. I know what that's like, and I won't make that decision for someone else."

"It'd be easier if you would." She sighed.

I hadn't allowed Sadie to get out of her bargain with Zev. It had been a terrible and valuable lesson to learn about magic and consequences, but protecting her from it would have been the worst thing that I could have done as a parent.

At the time, she'd indicated that she understood why I had backed the deal, but we hadn't explicitly discussed her feelings toward me after that.

"You don't get to make me the bad guy," I said with a lightness belied by my aching stomach.

"Oh? Isn't that what you signed up to be when you started talking about the consequences of my actions?" she said.

"Sades," her dad said sternly, "enough. You got yourself into trouble and you had to pay the price. That's life, kid. Every choice has consequences. Some are awful and some are unfair but that's the way it is. Even in the magic community, there are checks and balances. You may not see the consequences that more powerful people face, but they do face them."

As a seasoned homicide detective, Eli spoke from experience, and I appreciated him weighing in.

"Here's a thought," I said. "Why don't you call Juliette and see if she's up to getting together with you? This way you'd have a friend to talk to instead of your parents."

"That's a good idea." Sadie stood up, taking the popcorn bowl with her as she left. She paused in the doorway. "Mom?"

"Yeah?"

"Whatever you decide, make sure you don't regret it." She tucked the bowl under one arm and held up her other fist. "Team Feldman Chu for the win."

Eli and I both held up our fists until Sadie was clomping up the stairs.

"Guess she's staying here the rest of the week," he said.

"That's okay." My ass had fallen asleep, so I flaked out on the sofa with a cushion behind my back and my feet propped in my ex-husband's lap.

"That kid." He shook his head before massaging my foot. "Why do you think this angel is on the level?"

"I can't be one hundred percent certain, but what's the hidden agenda? They're clear about wanting the three unraveled and all the dangers to me. If Dumah meant to be free, they'd have forced me to use the Ascendant while I was in Gehenna, not handed it over making them vulnerable to the trio's plan."

Eli made a noncommittal noise, pressing his thumb into my instep, while I quietly moaned in bliss. "This angel thing trumps meeting Ryan Reynolds at the Greek restaurant, doesn't it?" he said glumly.

"I'm so glad you have your priorities straight. And no. Ryan still wins."

"What was the angel like?" He switched the massage to my other foot. "I can't believe I just asked that question. Oh, for the days of vampires and shifters."

"Bet Tatiana's even looking pretty good now." I wiggled my foot so he'd work on the arch.

"Nah. She still scares the crap out of me. Getting back to the angel?"

I blew out a breath. "I can't decide if Dumah is a subtle precision instrument or a blunt object with sharp teeth."

"That describes most of the magic people we know."

"Including your boyfriend."

Eli grinned. "He does have teeth."

I kicked him. "Seriously, though, what do you think I should do?"

He took a moment before replying. "In my experience,

vengeance doesn't make anyone happier. It only fucks up more lives."

"It's not just about my parents. The three angels will eventually find a Banim Shovavim happy to use the Ascendant to force Dumah out and release the dybbuks. Humanity will be doomed."

"When? Next week? In five hundred years?"

I shrugged.

He dropped my feet onto the floor and stood up, stretching. His sweatshirt rode up over his six-pack, and I took a moment to reminisce fondly about those abs. "As much as I want to tell you it's crazy to contemplate this, it's not for me to say. Sorry, babe." He dropped a kiss on the top of my head. "Only you can decide this one."

I buried my face into the sofa with a groan. "I hate when my advice bites me in the ass."

"Adulting is a bitch." Chuckling, he left.

After locking up after him, I headed upstairs into my bedroom, dumping my clothes on the floor before stepping into a piping-hot shower. This was the biggest decision I'd ever had to make, with the most on the line, and I wasn't about to rush it, but damn would it feel great to outwit and outplay those three fucking angels.

Thursday started off promising. I slept late, waking up to find a note on the kitchen counter from Sadie saying Juliette was busy today so she'd just come home after school. It was signed with an "xo." Smiling, I spooned espresso grounds into my stovetop Moka pot.

Enjoying a leisurely breakfast, I cracked open a new jigsaw puzzle. On the smaller side at five hundred pieces, it was a single rectangle of ombré orange, and a challenge to assemble. Sifting through the pieces was a soothing and familiar motion, while finding matches occupied the front consciousness of my brain.

Often I used lists to work my way through a decision, but this was one of those situations where I let my thoughts percolate. Licking croissant crumbs from my finger, I slotted the corner piece next to its neighbor.

My life had been stuck on full tilt for too long. Dumah's two-day deadline loomed, but it required thought, not action, and sitting here recharged me. I even savored a second cappuccino before getting dressed.

Still in my pajamas, I opened my underwear drawer where I was met with a plethora of beige and black. There were a couple of cute items, but most of the undergarments screamed "I've given up on having sex ever again." Grimacing, I flung open my closet, revealing what Emmett termed my "sad clothes."

I had a hot younger lover, I was cavorting with angels, and I was a badass magic fixer. I fired my disco classics playlist up to eleven, and by the time the last song faded out, every single drawer was upended, my closet was practically empty, and my mattress sagged under the weight of discarded items.

In the ensuing silence, I snapped out of my manic trance. Shaking my head ruefully, I picked up a perfectly nice blouse and a hanger. I couldn't just get rid of my entire wardrobe. I would replace a few pieces at a time. Be sensible—

My rib cage constricted and I placed my hands on either side of my chest to force down a deep breath. My appearance had been the last remnant of my "blend in at all costs" self. Time to rip off the Band-Aid. I flung the blouse back on the bed and ran downstairs to grab a box of extra-large garbage bags. Each one I filled took more and more weight off my shoulders until I had eight bulging bags, a ton of empty space in my room, and I felt as light as a helium balloon.

After throwing on a pair of black trousers that made my ass look amazing and a sexy yellow top that had been slightly too snug when I'd first bought it, but now fit great, I lugged all the bags down to my car.

I made a trip to the recycling plant with the clothes that were too ratty to pass on, then I donated my pricy corporate and nicer casual clothing to a store where the proceeds supported a local women's shelter. I slammed my empty trunk closed with a laugh, spun my keys around my finger, then headed downtown for the mall like a woman possessed.

Four hours later, I stumbled into my home laden with shopping bags and a credit card balance that didn't bear thinking about. I'd also had my hair cut, chopping off several inches into a flapper bob that made my curls super juicy, my eyes pop, and took ten years off me.

"Mom?" The front door slammed as I entered my bedroom. "I'm home."

"Up here."

Sadie wandered in, and eyes widening, she motioned for me to spin. "No way. Your hair. I love it." She took in the rest of the bags. "You're going after the angels and you think you're going to die." She flopped backward on my mattress. "Moooom."

Her tone was teasing but her tight features said otherwise.

I pushed her off a bag she was crushing. If I did go after the angels, of course she'd be scared and anxious. Sadie's mental well-being was an important consideration, but all the considerations were important. "First of all, I haven't made any decisions and I'm not dying for a very long time. I just wanted a change. Like painting the walls."

Sadie hauled herself into a cross-legged position. "In that case, fashion show time." She was already pulling out her phone to provide the music, so I changed into the first outfit.

My choices were met with overwhelming approval and the occasional "I am so borrowing that," to which I replied, "Over my dead body."

I hammed my modeling up, pulling my best duckface and catwalk strut, while Sadie howled. It was the most fun we'd had in ages. She even snipped off tags and put each outfit away.

"It's a giant yes pile," she said. When she was little and I had to go clothes shopping, I'd seat her on the bench inside the change cubicle and tell her she was the yes pile. If we agreed on the item, she'd hang on to it. It kept her from squirming and ducking under the cubicle wall to run wild in the store. Ask me how I learned that lesson.

As I finished putting the last few items away and set the musky perfume I'd always meant to buy on my dresser next to my jewelry box, Tatiana called to invite me to the Bear's Den for dinner. I'd hoped to see Laurent this evening, but I could phone him afterward, so I agreed that I'd see her in a couple of hours.

While tonight may not have been one of the formal nights that Vikram, the speakeasy owner, threw at the Bear's Den, that didn't mean I couldn't dress to impress. I intended to wow my boss so she'd never diss my appearance again. Same with that smartass golem. Game on.

———

At 7PM sharp, I stepped out of the parking garage elevator into a grimy concrete foyer with a broken payphone. I lifted the receiver, depressed the switch hook twice, and the wall swung away, a funky cover of "Suspicious Minds" singing out from the hidden space.

Vikram, whose large human stature hinted at his bear shifter form, greeted me with a slap of a drinks menu against his meaty palm. His usually bushy eyebrows had been trimmed and he sported a neat goatee. "Very elegant, Miriam."

My stiletto heels clicked on the wide wooden floor planks as I entered the speakeasy proper and the wall behind me slid into place. I brushed a hand over the black pencil skirt and white filmy blouse that I'd paired with black sheer stockings with a seam up the backs. "Thank you. You're also looking very fine this evening."

He scowled, a flush hitting his brown skin. "My wife said that if I didn't clean up, she was going to make me into a rug."

I covered my laugh with my hand.

"Yes, yes," he said impatiently. "Very funny. Go. Tatiana's in the back room."

I froze. The one time I'd seen Vikram drag a couple of

shifters into a back room, they hadn't come out again. "Do you have more than one back room?"

He frowned. "I have lots of back rooms." That didn't make it better. When I didn't move, he pointed toward the far-left corner. "The private dining room."

"Oh. Okay."

The art gallery to one side of the large restaurant was closed while a new show was installed. An Ohrist woman in sharp tortoiseshell frames floated an entrancing painting of lovers glimpsed embracing through a window over to one of the white walls, while two younger workers marked the spot in pencil.

Making a mental note to find out more about the new show, I wove between packed tables set with sparkling gold tablecloths, turning sideways so a server could deposit two plates of heaped pasta in a creamy cheese sauce at one of the curved leather banquettes. My stomach rumbled, and I blushed at the server's smile, but I was totally ordering that.

Under the pressed tin ceiling tiles, I continued until a stray diner getting drinks at the bar jogged my elbow accidentally. He apologized and I recognized the voice.

I spun around. "Hello, partner mine."

Emmett jerked back hard enough to slosh the contents of his two drinks over his hands, but he didn't notice, too busy sputtering at me. "When did you become a real girl?"

"Very funny, asshole." I pointed at the highball glass. "Those better be nonalcoholic."

"7UP for me." He licked off one hand. "Toots, you're positively va-va-voom."

"Thank you." I preened.

He nudged me with one hip. "Come on. Let's show you off to the boss."

Sconce lights set evenly into the gold brocade wallpaper and crystal chandeliers bathed the space in a rich glow as I followed Emmett past the small stage where a five-piece band was serving up groovy pop covers over the wash of conversation.

He stopped in front of a closed door and held up his drinks. "Get the knob for me, will ya?"

Once inside the intimate space, the music fell away. It was decorated much like the rest of the speakeasy, with the addition of this gorgeous black-and-white framed photograph of a woman in 1920s attire on a fainting couch.

Tatiana didn't immediately notice me, speaking with Juliette and a dark blond man, maybe in his late forties, with rugged good looks. Dressed in a simple navy sweater, he gestured with strong, elegant fingers as he spoke. Juliette was in a cute yellow sweater that fell off one shoulder, her hair in a simple twist, while the elderly artist wore a shirt that resembled a crimson pincushion along with a spiky blue necklace and her trademark oversize glasses.

I hadn't expected to see anyone other than Tatiana and Emmett. Was this work-based or social?

Emmett plonked the drinks on the lone table and pushed the cocktail glass with a swirling blue liquid to Juliette. "Miri's here."

The group turned as one to me.

Juliette clapped her hands. "Très chic, Miriam."

My boss narrowed her eyes. "What have you done?"

I touched my short, curly bob self-consciously. "Uh, got a haircut and went shopping for a new wardrobe?"

Emmett dropped onto the banquette beside Tatiana.

The unfamiliar man said something in French, and Tatiana waved him off.

"It was a question, not a criticism," she said. "I like it. Don't revert back." With that pronouncement, she motioned for me to take a seat on one of the wood chairs with red velvet seat cushions.

"It's a pleasure to finally meet you." The man extended his

hand, revealing a dimple in his right cheek when he spoke. His accent was stronger than Laurent's.

I shook, feeling like a flustered teenager in the face of his good looks and French charm. Remembering that I had a Frenchman of my own didn't help, because as much as I adored Laurent, he was hardly charming. After a beat too long and the realization that he resembled Juliette, I dropped my hand with an "Oh. You're Gabriel." Her father.

"Yes. I hope you've not heard too many bad things about me."

"Not at all. I'm delighted to meet you as well." I set my clutch on the table and moved my chair in closer.

"Oh good." He slung an arm around his daughter's shoulders. "Between this hellion and Tante Tati, my reputation could have been in tatters."

"Maman is the exciting one," Juliette said with a grin. "You're just a boring scientist."

Gabriel pressed a hand to his heart with an exaggerated wince.

I smiled at their playfulness to hide the fact that my head was reeling. Tatiana was Gabriel's aunt. I wasn't usually this dense. She was Juliette's great-aunt, Delphine was her niece, and Gabriel was Delphine's brother.

My cheeks pinked. Oh God. What had he heard about *me*?

And wait. Why was I here tonight? Was I invited to family dinner because Tatiana considered me mishpocha or because of Laurent? I cough-choked. Were they going to interrogate me the way Goldie had when I brought Eli home? Did I not even get Laurent in my corner to keep me safe? Also, this was way too soon to be introducing me, the new girlfriend, to the brother of Laurent's dead wife. A decade or so from now might be appropriate. Still coughing, I thumped my chest.

"Drink?" I twisted around in my seat and locked eyes with Laurent opening the door.

His camel-colored trench coat flapped behind him as he

walked. He'd thrown a dark blue plaid scarf artlessly around his neck over a light blue pullover, and combined with his long, loping strides and dusting of dark stubble along his jaw, he looked like he'd stepped out of the pages of a French fashion magazine.

Stopping in front of me, he raked a very slow, very thorough gaze from the crown of my head, along my smoky eyes, red lipstick, and every curve. His green eyes heated to a luminous emerald.

I swallowed. Forget charm, just give me more of that.

"Wildflowers," he said in a husky voice.

I swayed in toward him.

"Ah-hem," Tatiana said loudly.

I glanced down at the ground, but when it didn't helpfully open up and swallow me whole, I cringed. Gabriel had just caught another woman macking on his dead sister's husband. I dropped my napkin into my lap and twisted it into a pretzel. We were all adults, and it's not like her body was still warm before Laurent replaced her. *Not* that he'd replaced her.

I blotted my brow. Could I fake a heart attack?

Juliette regarded me with a twinkle in her eye like she could hear my thoughts, but Gabriel stared at his estranged brother-in-law with wide eyes and a stiff posture.

Laurent nervously toyed with his scarf. "Gabriel. I—" It fell to the floor and he stumbled backward over it. I grabbed his hand to steady him, and while his fingers closed tightly over mine, I wasn't sure he registered the motion. "I didn't know you were in town."

"I asked Tati not to say anything," Gabriel said.

"Oh." His face fell. "I should…" His brow furrowed and he took another step back.

"I love you to death, but you are such an idiot," Juliette said. "He didn't tell you because he doesn't want you to avoid him like you always do. If you leave and upset Papa?" Juliette gripped her fork, prongs up. "So help me, I will rearrange your organs."

Laurent blinked twice rapidly, his mouth falling open.

Emmett saluted her with his soda. "L'chaim to that, sister."

"I should have—" Gabriel began.

"No, that's on me," Laurent said, making no move to sit.

Tatiana slammed her hand on the table. "Get it together."

"Laurent?" I murmured, picking up the discarded scarf and draping it over the chair beside mine.

He looked down at me, then slid free from my grasp and moved around to the other side of the banquette where Gabriel was. "It's good to see you again." He held out his hand, his expression uncertain.

Gabriel stood up, said something in French, and hugged Laurent. My wolf shifter stood stiffly for half a second then hugged the other man back tightly.

Tatiana stirred her dirty martini with a small smile.

Gabriel clasped the back of Laurent's head, speaking quietly. I caught only "mon frère," but whatever he said made Laurent close his eyes briefly, and when he opened them, they were damp.

He shrugged out of his coat, his shoulders flexing as he hung the garment on a hook, then he took the chair beside mine, feeling under the table for my hand.

"Is that mishegoss finally over?" Tatiana drained her martini.

My stomach rumbled again, and she glowered at me, but it broke the tension, because the others laughed. I was fine with that. "Drinks and food, stat."

"Good idea," Juliette said.

Tatiana tugged on an old-fashioned bellpull complete with a tassel, and barely a minute later our server was there to take our orders. How very *Downton Abbey*. I approved. My boss eyed Laurent the entire time.

"Quit it, I'm fine," he said.

"Are you sure?" Juliette said.

"I promise." His annoyed expression softened for his niece, and he turned to me, sensing my puzzlement. "It's coming up on the anniversary of Delphine's death."

"I'm sorry. When?"

"September 8." On Monday, four days from now. I opened my mouth, but he cut me off with a gentle smile. "I'm at peace with it. No fussing wanted or required."

There was no tension in his body or strain in his voice, and I believed him. He was no longer a ball of sorrow, rage, and guilt, throwing himself headlong into danger. He'd found closure and contentment with his life now.

I smiled back.

Gabriel bounced a curled knuckle against his mouth, studying his brother-in-law and Laurent rolled his eyes.

"Eh, leave the wolf alone," Emmett said. "If he said he's good, he's good."

Laughing, Gabriel held up his hands.

Emmett had gone from hating Laurent to adoring him like a big brother. It was heartwarming—and would get annoying incredibly fast if the golem picked his bro-crush over his partner.

Our gathering carried on, and when no one interrogated me as to my intentions with Laurent, my stomach gradually unknotted enough so I could enjoy their chatting about mutual friends in France. Some words seemed easier for them to find in French, but they kept their conversation in English to include Emmett and me.

Laurent and Gabriel hadn't quite found their conversational rhythm, one or the other cutting over top or apologizing, but they were trying so hard to get in sync, and it was incredibly sweet.

I learned that Juliette's mother, Léa, was more than just a badass wolf shifter; she was strong enough to challenge

Laurent's successor for pack alpha and had won. Her duties kept her busy back in France, but I admired the cunning, intelligence, and strength she had to exhibit to gain and hold one of the largest packs in Europe. Hopefully I'd get to meet her one day.

After devouring half a roll, I checked in with Juliette on how she was doing and if she'd heard anything else about Sabrina Mayhew, the lawyer who'd been turned into a vampire without her consent.

Vincenzo, Sabrina's vampire fiancé, had whisked her back to Vegas once she'd woken from her coma, and Juliette had had no further contact.

"What about—"

"As *enlightening* as it all was," she said with a pointed look at her father, who was filling Laurent in on what a cousin was up to, "I'm still processing it."

Message received. She didn't want to tell her family about her close encounter with the blindspot.

"Is Sadie okay?" Juliette's question landed in a lull in conversation.

"Why wouldn't my girl be okay?" Emmett gripped his empty glass so hard that cracks appeared in it.

I sighed in annoyance. If everyone had kept talking, no one would have heard Juliette's question, since she'd asked it in a whisper, but I hadn't shared the details of that night or thought about when—or if—I was going to, given my visit to Gehenna.

Juliette bit her lower lip, looking chagrined, and I patted her hand. This wasn't her fault nor was it a secret.

"Tattele." Tatiana tapped Emmett's knuckles, and he released his death grip on the poor glass.

Laurent set his butter knife down on the plate. "Yes. You didn't tell me what happened."

"I got busy yesterday." I took a large gulp of gin and tonic.

He didn't push, but from his narrowed eyes, there would

be follow-up questions on that matter. Precisely what I'd hoped to avoid tonight. "And Sadie?"

"Zev had her use her nulling magic on his vampire granddaughter." I spread my hands wide.

"Bastard," Emmett said. "Why?"

"That's not mine to share," I said.

Laurent rested his hand against the small of my back, and I leaned into his strength.

Tatiana sank back against the leather with a wary expression. "Is Celeste dead?"

"No. She had the wits scared out of her, though."

"Did BatKian know it wouldn't work?" Laurent growled.

"Not exact—ow." I rubbed my shin. "Who kicked me?"

"Me. I was aiming for the wolf," Emmett said. "You're not going to let BatKian get away with traumatizing kids, are you?"

"Toledano," Tatiana said.

"Get real." Emmett snorted. "The vamp forced a minor to commit heinous acts. I'm not giving him the courtesy of using his new name."

"I'm not Sadie's parent, Emmett," Laurent said in a resigned voice.

"Toots can't do it. Her position with him is precarious enough."

"There's nothing precarious about it." I slathered butter on the other half of my roll with angry strokes.

The golem shot me an "oh please" look.

"Emmett, while I appreciate your concern for my daughter, she got herself into this. And now it's done. There is no payback or stopping Zev required. It was a one-time, very specific situation, though if I did want to follow up, I would. Thoroughly." I dropped my butter knife to my plate with a clatter.

"All right. Don't get touchy," he groused.

I took a deep breath. "That said, it would be great if you could meet with her," I added to Juliette.

"Of course. It would be good for me as well."

Our food arrived and I took a bite of that cheesy pasta dish. "Oh my God, this is delicious."

Laurent peered at my food hopefully, creeping his fork closer to my plate.

I smacked his hand. "Eyes on your steak, wolf."

Gabriel laughed. "Now I really like you. And I know I made the right decision, because anyone who has the guts to refuse a wolf shifter food is the person I need."

Juliette stole a slice of grilled zucchini off her dad's plate before he had a chance to try it and he mock scowled at her. She flashed him an innocent smile, her cheeks bulging.

"Need?" I wiped my mouth with my napkin. "For what?"

"I want to hire your people, Tante," he said.

"And here I thought you'd come to visit me for my good looks and witty repartee," Tatiana drawled.

"That's a given." He winked at her, and while she rolled her eyes, she blushed faintly.

"What's the case?" I raised my eyebrows in question at Laurent, but he shrugged.

Gabriel poured the last few drops of red wine into his glass, then set it down carefully and leaned in. "To stop a vampire contagion."

4

My brow furrowed. "How do you know about the contagion?"

Tatiana pushed her glasses up her nose. "How do you?"

"Why stop it?" Laurent said. "The world would be better off without bloodsuckers."

"What are you all going on about?" Emmett frowned at his empty glass and leaned across Tatiana to summon the server.

She swatted him and rang the bellpull herself while I tamped down a grin. Don't get between the queen and her show of power, Emmett.

"Is this contagion just limited to vampires?" Juliette said.

Gabriel held up his hands. "I'll answer all your questions, but I want your promise that nothing we say goes any further. Even mentioning that you're aware of the contagion could have dangerous consequences."

"Of course it does," Laurent said in a deceptively mild voice. "Mitzi and our aunt don't know any other type of information."

Tatiana speared a piece of salmon and swirled it in the

lemon butter sauce. "After Zev was so desperate to get his hands on the Ascendant, I had a chat with Yoshi."

I ate another bite of cheesy heaven, my eyes on my food to hide my surprise. Yoshi actually spilled details to Tatiana? I'd never seen them interact, but with Zev such a huge presence in both their lives, there had to be some relationship between the two. Ooh. A new mystery to pry out of my boss.

Tatiana flicked her gaze at me and then stabbed another piece of salmon with a shake of her head.

Laurent poked my side. "That's what the estrie was for, wasn't it? To use her blood to heal the infected vampires?"

His intelligence and ability to put pieces together was incredibly sexy. That combined with his many teasing comments about being book-learned when, given his huge bookshelf with a variety of complex subjects, he clearly enjoyed seeking out knowledge, made me want to kiss him hard.

Usually.

I crunched a piece of ice. "Got it in one."

"Estrie?" Gabriel scratched his jaw. "That would certainly be a faster cure than science."

Zev could have the benefit of the doubt about his compassion levels for all vampire-kind, but I'd bet my house that he'd have sacrificed them all if that was the condition to Yoshi being healed.

Juliette had been silent, pushing her risotto around her plate, but she turned to her father. "If it's so dangerous, why are you part of this? Have you been asked to stop it or is it your scientific curiosity?"

"It's both." He ate another piece of chicken marsala before launching into his tale. "I'm a geneticist."

"Wow," I said. "That must be fascinating."

"He's not just any geneticist," Laurent said with pride. "He was one of the youngest scientists to ever have a

42

published paper in a top medical journal, and he's considered one of the preeminent minds in the field."

Our server came in with another round of drinks, and after checking we didn't need anything else, departed again.

"You work in the Sapien scientific community?" I'd switched to Coke since I had to drive home, and the cold, sugary bite made my teeth tingle. "Are you Ohrist? Is there even an Ohrist scientific research community? Sorry, I don't know much about this."

"I wouldn't expect you to," Gabriel said. "I am Ohrist but there are very few avenues to use my magic for scientific advancement. However, the combination of my experience and powers was why I learned of the contagion. Zev sent me several vials of infected blood to thoroughly study."

"How helpful." Laurent's expression soured. "Following in someone else we know's footsteps, are you, but for the good of all mankind?"

With a loud snap, Juliette broke her breadstick, interrupting me before I could ask him to explain, because I did not copy. Tatiana sighed, and Gabriel tossed down the napkin he'd been cleaning his hands with.

Emmett, refueling on sugar with his third 7UP, didn't care that the mood had turned sharp and sad, but I curled my hand around Laurent's hip, stroking my thumb along a sliver of exposed olive skin.

I forwent my curiosity about whoever he was referring to. "Did taking time to analyze their blood cause problems in your Sapien professional life or something?"

Gabriel shook off his steely expression. "Au contraire."

It's not as if I leaned in drooling with hearts in my eyes. I ran my hand through my curls because I was still getting used to the cut, not because of Gabriel's whiskey-infused voice and the way he rolled his Rs.

I felt Laurent's gaze on me, then he teased his foot up the back of my calf.

Lust throbbed through me, starbursts of tight need. I ate another piece of ice, and when my boyfriend huffed with quiet satisfaction, I subtly scratched the side of my neck with my middle finger, almost missing Gabriel's explanation that Zev started funneling money into finding a cure about a year ago.

Had Zev attempted to find the Ascendant on his own before bringing me in? Is that why he'd never followed through on any of his many threats to hurt me? Had he known who my parents were from our first meeting and were all our dealings one long con that would lead him to the Ascendant?

There was no hot flare of rage at this possibility. Zev was who he was and he'd never pretended to be my friend. Besides, it hardly mattered now. I set myself on this path when I chose to find my parents' murderer. Still, I dragged in a deep breath, every second closer to Dumah's deadline landing on my chest in a crushing weight.

"Zev knew about the contagion for that long?" I said.

"BatKian plays all the angles." Laurent snapped his fingers. "That too reminds me of someone we both know."

"Then they deserve each other," Tatiana said. "You can't change him, Lolo."

I swung my head back to Laurent for his parry, dying to shake him and yell, "Who?"

"Gabriel," Laurent implored. "Be careful."

His brother-in-law replied in French, and whatever he said mollified Laurent somewhat because the shifter nodded reluctantly.

"Zev's funded many important projects within the scientific community," Gabriel added. He reached for the glass container with the breadsticks, helping himself before passing it to his daughter to take the last one.

"Did you work on developing synthetic blood?" I asked.

"No, this analysis was the first time our paths had

crossed," Gabriel said. "But regardless of who asked me for assistance, I'd have a moral imperative to stop the contagion."

"Why?" Emmett tossed the last remaining drops of pop into his mouth. "They're undead assholes. It's not natural." He shrugged. "Let them die for good."

Laurent bestowed the golem with an approving smile.

"Some would say that about you, Emmett," Juliette said, not unkindly. "Is all life sacred or is none of it? Where do you draw that line? I'd hope on the side of all."

Laurent snorted and Emmett chortled at the shifter's reaction.

I admit that I struggled with Gabriel and Juliette's moral imperative stance as well. I'd fought to let Sabrina live as a vampire, but I also killed the undead, and would again if necessary. Hell, I'd sanctioned Sadie keeping her end of the bargain, fully believing that Celeste wouldn't survive.

"It all matters," Tatiana pronounced. "With notable exceptions at my choosing." That pulled a smile from Laurent. "Otherwise," she continued, with a pointed look at me, "we're no better than hunters."

"Hunters have a higher esteem of vampires than Banim Shovavim." I struggled to temper my bitterness. "Did your investigations yield any interesting results?"

Gabriel nodded. "One in particular."

The server came in to clear our plates, taking our coffee, tea, and dessert orders. As soon as the door shut behind her, I raised my eyebrows at Gabriel.

"The contagion is a virus," he said. "One created with both science and magic."

Our incredulous responses to this varied in intensity, but all of us were shocked.

"How?" Juliette said.

"The short version is that a vector created with scientific means was used as the base to dispel magic toxins."

Tatiana toyed with her spiky necklace. "That's a disturbing

development. There's technology advanced enough to weave with magic like that?"

"Not that's applicable on humans," Gabriel said. "Remember, while vampires can heal, they don't have active white blood cells to fight off pathogens like we do."

"But if you suppress their magic healing with other magic?" Gabriel nodded at my guess. "Then once the virus is implanted, it has free rein," I said. "Yikes."

"That would be part of it, but it's not that simple. Whatever magic this is must both override a vampire's innate healing abilities and create the lethal infection. If they were merely having their immune systems destroyed, there could be any number of elements attributed to their deaths, but the symptoms are the same across all victims. I cannot fathom a magic that could accomplish this."

Tatiana looked faintly nauseous. "Me neither."

Juliette's eyes gleamed, as she hung on her father's every word. "Could you have created the delivery mechanism?"

"No. The skill it took to tailor it to a vampire physiology surpasses even mine."

Laurent whistled softly. "Then who?"

Our server returned laden with a large tray.

"I'm positive it was Dr. Justine Eversol, an American geneticist." Gabriel waited for drinks and dessert to be served. He added sugar to his black espresso, stirring it vigorously, the silence growing more and more tense as we waited for him to finish dropping this bombshell on us. "What bothers me about all this," he finally continued once the server had left, "is that I'd swear Justine is Sapien."

"You know her?" Laurent said.

"We've spoken on panels at conferences together, but she retired a couple years ago."

Tatiana dumped cream in her coffee. "Then someone in the Ohrist community made her a very sweet offer to come out of retirement and work for them."

I swallowed my lemon meringue pie, my mouth puckering at the sharp citrus flavor. "As a scientist, would she have been intrigued to create something for beings she previously didn't know existed?"

"Despite her brilliance in our field," he said, "she struck me as a very conservative woman. I thought she'd be disgusted. That aside, I've tried to find her but can't, and that worries me." He motioned to the rest of us. "That's where you come in."

"Do you suspect foul play or just deep in hiding for her own safety?" Tatiana said, nibbling on her cherry cheesecake.

"I've found nothing to suggest the former," Gabriel said. "But anything is possible."

"What do we do with her when we find her?" Emmett pounded a fist into his palm.

I lowered his hand. "Give her to the Lonestars?"

"Present her with an award?" Laurent said with a bright smile.

"None of the above," Gabriel said. "Have her explain the specific Ohrist magic she paired with her genetic editing. That way, I can reverse engineer a cure."

"It's terribly difficult to do unless you know the magic type," Juliette explained, "as there's no way to differentiate Ohrist magic. They all feel the same. Unless Papa has the exact type and strength, he could be trying variants for decades before he found the correct one. And it's ten times worse if he doesn't even know where to begin."

Gabriel ruffled his daughter's hair. "So you haven't forgotten all your training since you fled across the ocean?"

She groaned and elbowed him.

"My team will find Dr. Eversol," Tatiana assured her nephew.

Emmett cracked his knuckles. I really had to ask him how he pulled that off without bones. "We'll work her over and make her sing like a canary."

Sighing, I shook my head.

"Who's hiring them?" Laurent rubbed his side where Zev had left him with a long, nasty scar. "You or BatKian?"

"Toledano," I murmured.

To Gabriel's credit, he met Laurent's eyes when he answered. "I am. They'll report to me, though I'm paying them with discretionary fees from the budget Zev originally allocated to me. I'd like you to be part of the investigation as well."

"As what expense line item?" Laurent said. "Incidental?"

"We're taking the job," Tatiana said. "You can join or not as you wish."

He pushed away from the table and stood with a jerky gesture. "What is it with everyone in my family so willing to jump into bed with that vampire? Especially after all your bitching about him recently, Tatiana. I should be shocked that you'd work for him, even indirectly, but..." He grabbed his scarf. "I'm not."

"Sit down, Lolo. Ho nisht kein koyach." She was telling him she didn't have the strength to deal with this. Goldie had used the Yiddish phrase more than once when dealing with some of her activist colleagues.

Laurent quirked an eyebrow. "Je m'en bats les couilles."

Juliette sucked in a breath. "Don't talk to Tante Tatiana that way."

"Miriam." He nabbed his trench coat off the hook. "Allons-y."

Caught between his expectant look on our side of the table and everyone else's on the other, I hesitated.

"It's Tatiana's call on which clients—" I began. The door shut behind him, though at least he didn't slam it. "And he's gone. One of you should talk to him."

"It won't help." Tatiana shook her head. "If anyone can get through his thick skull, it's you. Go. We'll meet tomorrow."

Her approval—backhanded as it was—was appreciated,

but you know what would have been more appreciated? An explanation for all the sub- and not-so-subtext of this whole evening. Even better? A detailed brief on the particulars of this precise family dysfunction, explaining the animosity between Laurent and Zev. But nooooo. Send out the girlfriend with zero facts to draw upon.

"We will be adding some amendments to my terms of employment to cover future similar situations." Grabbing my clutch, I went to calm the beast.

5

LAURENT SAT ON THE HOOD OF MY SEDAN IN THE parking garage, his motorcycle parked a couple of stalls away. He'd stayed and waited for me to talk to him. I'd hoped he had enough faith in us to do that, but I'd also half expected to chase him back to his hotel and corner him into talking.

I slid onto the hood next to him, but he didn't lift his head, his fingers threaded through his dark curls.

"If you've come to berate me," he said defeatedly, "you won't say anything I haven't already thought. It was very poorly done of me." He glanced up, his expression wistful. "Especially with Gabriel..." He shook off his musings. "I will apologize. Tomorrow."

"That made my job easy." I nudged his side. "You're not hurt I didn't come with you?"

"I was until Vikram asked me on my way out why I was leaving when he had an excellent cognac ready as a digestif to round out the family reunion. Then I felt terribly ashamed of myself, but I couldn't slink back into the room with my tail between my legs."

"Poor wolf." I took his hand and we sat in companionable

silence, listening to the distant sound of traffic and the occasional slam of a car door.

"What's the deal with you and Zev?" Shivering, I leaned
into his side.

Laurent picked his coat off the hood and draped the camel-
colored trench around my shoulders.

I stroked the warm fabric, his cedar scent imbued in its
lapels. "This is cashmere." I frowned, pulling it tighter around
me. I was used to seeing Laurent in T-shirts and jeans, or the
occasional suit, not Mr. Parisian Catwalk with his carelessly
draped scarf and cashmere coats. "Do you have an entire
French wardrobe that I'm unaware of?"

His brow furrowed. "I am French. I have bought clothes
there."

I patted his leg because I suddenly yearned to play dress-
up with him. "We'll be revisiting this. For now, back to you
and Zev."

Laurent wound the scarf around his knuckles like a
boxer's wrap. "I've told you about my father and the financial
management firm he founded."

"Yes, and that he values intellect over magic. Is that why
you don't get along? Because you took on extra magic to fight
dybbuks? Or is it just the Banim Shovavim part that upsets
him?"

"It's not that he dislikes magic, he considers it cheating."

"There's no other way to fight dybbuks."

"Yes, well," he said bitterly, "that's hardly a worthy pursuit
in my father's eyes." He slid the scarf free. "Our mutual
disdain didn't start with my chosen path, but his. It is very
difficult to create a financial firm and achieve the success that
my father did without powerful backers. One in particular."

I startled, catching the coat before it slipped off my shoulders. "Zev helped him found the business? Did he give your
dad a loan or did the vampire's connections help get it off the
ground?"

"Both, indirectly. My upstanding father, that pillar of the financial community, has been laundering money for Ba—" He eyed me warily. "Toledano for decades. A fact I believed appalled Gabriel as much as it did me."

"Whoa. Okay, there's a lot to unpack here." Zev was obviously wealthy, but it wasn't like he could stuff Blood Alley's profits under his coffin. I swallowed my snicker at that mental image. Laurent's father, Jacques, must have been very talented, if that was the right word, to have cleaned all that cash, probably helped the investments grow, and not gotten caught.

Not that I was about to share any praiseworthy thoughts and rile my boyfriend.

"Did Zev connect with your dad through Tatiana?"

"Obviously." He narrowed his eyes, searching my face. "You know about them, don't you?"

I narrowed mine right back. "As do you, apparently. I asked you about the two of them before and you said you had theories but didn't know the truth."

"Technically, I don't," he said innocently. I swatted him and he laughed. "It was never discussed in front of me, but were I to guess, I'd say they were lovers for a very long time until she chose Samuel over him." He bumped my shoulder. "Which you were aware of and didn't share, right?"

I inspected my fingernails. "Technically, I'm still in the process of gathering informa—" Laurent tickled me and I yelped. "Yes. All right. Stop!"

He fell still but left his hand resting on my hip. He sighed. "It never made sense to me. My father disparaged magic when he'd never have become this esteemed businessman without the most magical of beings."

"Perhaps your father doesn't understand your commitment to rid the world of dybbuks, but he had to respect your intelligence in running one of the largest shifter packs in Europe."

"Not everyone sees the good in people the way you do, Mitzi." He hopped off the car. "When I moved to Vancouver, I demanded that Zev stop using my father. He laughed and said Jacques wasn't doing anything he didn't want to."

"Do you think he's been coerced all these years? Compelled?" I shrugged out of Laurent's coat, but he stopped me.

"Keep it. Easier to ride the bike without it. To answer your question, I don't know, but Tatiana was different when I was younger. Lighter. And when Maman speaks of my father when they first met..." He shrugged, scrubbing a hand over his face. "Compulsion or not, Zev changed them. Hardened them. I saw him as a parasite eating away at our family and I told him as much."

I whistled softly. No wonder the vampire lashed out and gave Laurent that scar. That accusation had come from one of the "normal humans" that Tatiana loved and remained close to, when Zev had been scorned. "You're lucky to be alive."

He nodded, his expression somber.

Fishing my keys out of my clutch, I stood up. "Will you work the case with us?"

"Let me sleep on it." He tugged me close by the lapels. "Thank you for coming out here and staying with me."

"Always."

He inhaled. "What's that scent?"

"New perfume. You like it?"

He gave me a crooked grin, walking me backward until I hit the car door. "It's been driving me crazy all night." He skimmed his hand along my hip. "That and this skirt. I want to ride it up inch by inch, laying you bare for me."

My lips parted in a breathy sigh, my core tightening and pulsing.

His nostrils flared, his pupils dilating. "Do you know how hard I get when I smell your arousal?"

"Hmm. Let's check." I ground against his erection, a delicious shudder running through me.

"I can't get enough of you," he murmured, nipping my bottom lip with his teeth. "I crave you. Your body, your mind. I imagine your laugh before I fall asleep." He gave this small, dreamy smile that I'd never seen on him before, and I pictured that look on his face as he lay in bed, thinking of me.

Sexual desire was heady, but Laurent knew all of me, a new experience in my romantic relationships. I didn't have to hide or pretend to be anything other than exactly who I was; Laurent craved it all, even the parts I'd hidden in the shadows.

Gazing at him with the same adoring expression formerly reserved for my teen celebrity crushes, I rocked forward on the balls of my feet, my heels putting me at the perfect height to crash my mouth to his.

He threaded one hand into my hair, the other interlacing with mine. He tasted like whiskey and kissed like he was sealing a promise, his tongue tangling with mine.

A car with a loud muffler drew closer and I leaned back, reality bursting through my haze, but Laurent squeezed the hand he held, gentling the kiss before stepping away.

"Wear that more often," he declared. "And model all your new things for me."

"Sounds good." I caressed his cheek with my hand. "I wish you could come home with me, but Sadie's there." I cringed, hearing how that sounded. "Not that I don't want you around her, but sleeping over is a big step, even if she is sixteen, and I'm sure she's been at Eli's when Nav stayed over." I frowned. "Why am I holding myself to a different standard than Eli is with her?" Sure, I was her mother, but why should that matter?

Laurent kissed the crease between my brows. "We can ease Sadie into getting used to our relationship as slowly as you like. You lead and I'll follow."

54

He spoke sense; Sadie was my kid and it was up to me to determine the pace, but it felt like yet one more thing to add to a to-do list that now included a decision on whether to unravel angels—*angels!*—and finding Dr. Eversol. For the first time in forever, I longed to rip up every single list and just exist in the moment.

"I miss the simple days of the Jabberwocky and the Vorpal Blade," I said, "when dybbuks were the scariest thing out there."

He raised an eyebrow. "I think you mean when *I* was the scariest thing out there."

I chuckled and mimed claws slashing through the air. "Snicker snack."

He heaved a pained sigh, then winked at me before striding to his bike and unlocking the helmet. "Sweet dreams, Mitzi."

"Sweet dreams, Huff 'n' Puff."

Once I was in my car, Laurent followed me down the ramp, turning left to my right with a wave. I drove home with the windows down and the radio blasting, yawning every few minutes, and resolved to go to bed early tonight. Luckily, traffic was light, and I made it home in no time.

The wind picked up, rattling branches as I parked at my front curb, and the streetlamp on the sidewalk flickered and winked out, throwing our duplex into a myriad of shadows. A light shone through Sadie's curtains, so it wasn't a power outage. The back of my neck prickling, I beeped the fob to lock my car, scanning the sky.

A dark shape swooped across the moon. It could have been any bird, but I thrust my hands into the pockets of Laurent's coat and hurried up my walk.

Something small plummeted out of the sky to land at my feet. I bit my bottom lip, tempted to step over it, but curiosity got the better of me, and I picked the item up between two fingertips like it was radioactive, frowning at the ace of spades.

"Fuck off, Poe." I flung the card on the ground.

Another card drifted down, but I ignored it, striding up the stairs, my house key at the ready. However, the front door swung open of its own accord, and I jumped.

Sadie caught my arm to steady me, peering outside. "Were you talking to someone?"

"Poe." I pushed her inside, locked the door, and tossed my keys into Jude's ceramic bowl on the small foyer table.

"What did they want?"

"Don't know. Don't care."

Thump!

The two of us froze, our eyes darting to the door. I hung up my coat. "Ignore—"

Thump!

"Is that Poe?" Sadie whispered.

Motioning for her to stay put, I opened the door a crack, leaving the security chain on, ready to give the shifter a piece of my mind.

Two more aces of spades lay on my stoop.

A raven cawed.

"Go. Away."

Another card flew out of the darkness and hit the door, before falling to the ground and revealing yet another ace of spades.

I slammed the door, but the thumps grew faster.

Sadie and I ran into the kitchen and all fell silent. All except my heart, which beat like a timpani in my chest.

"They must know we're not standing there anymore," I said.

Sadie pulled the kettle out of the cupboard. "Tea?" she said in a squeaky voice.

"Please."

She turned on the tap as a succession of cards slammed

into the window over the sink. Screaming, she dropped the kettle, the water still running, and fled.

I shut the tap off and followed her into the living room.

Cards battered the window in there now, the assault worsening as they rammed the roof, shaking the house down to its foundation.

Sadie covered her head with a pillow. "Mom, do something or we'll end up like the Dursleys with nowhere to run."

My front window rattled so hard, I feared it would shatter, and I clenched my fists, my teeth grinding together. Shadows swam over my skin, my scythe half manifested, even though it would do nothing against the raven shifter. I stormed into my foyer and threw my door open. "Enough!"

My fury ebbed and goosebumps broke out over my arms.

Cards littered my lawn like the aftermath of a tornado while ravens sat shoulder to shoulder along every conceivable surface on my street: lampposts, telephone wires, cars, and trees. There must have been hundreds of them.

I could practically taste my thudding pulse, but my footsteps were steady as I strode onto the porch. "Show yourself, Poe."

They appeared on my lawn in human form, draped in shadow and ruffles, and fixed me with a beady eye.

All the other birds swiveled their heads as one to focus on me and I shivered.

"The cards call you," Poe said in a raspy voice.

"Then consider them sent to voice mail." I waved my arms to shoo the birds off, but they didn't move.

The cards lifted off my lawn in a funnel with a whooshing sound so loud and forceful that it plugged my ears, before firing into Poe's hand in a perfectly straight deck.

The multitude of ravens stared on in eerie silence, not a single feather ruffled by the disturbance.

"You're paying for any damages." I wiggled a finger in one ear to pop it. "Now listen up, because this is the last time I am ever going to say this. I will never play games with a raven shifter again. Find another victim."

"Not a game." Poe rapidly shot each card from one hand to another in an arced flourish. "A resetting."

I braced a hand on the doorframe. "Cut to the chase because I'm tired."

The inoperative streetlamp flicked on, the glow reaching into my yard to spotlight the games master. Poe fanned the cards out, revealing each one to be an ace of spades. "My deck changed this evening."

Nope. I wasn't going to ask. I didn't care. I'd gone down this road before and that way lay ruin. Not today, curiosity. I crossed my arms.

"Why?" I blurted out.

Damn it.

6

"I DO NOT KNOW," THEY SAID, "BUT WHEN I SOUGHT an answer, I was guided to your house."

I crossed my arms. "This isn't my fault."

Poe shrugged. "Whether it is or not, I require your assistance to reset the deck. One game. I vow that it will not bring anything into existence."

"Will it take something out of existence?"

He sighed as if put-upon, but I wasn't the trusting woman I'd once been. "No."

"And if I decline?"

The shifter's eyes turned downcast and their body hunched in on itself. "I cannot force you."

Life was a lot easier when bad guys acted like bad guys. This "choose for myself" shit was the worst. I kicked at the ground. If I didn't help Poe, their deck would be stuck in this weird form instead of the way it should be.

This wasn't my problem, but with a decision about the angels looming over me, I didn't want to be complicit—even inadvertently—for something remaining out of balance. That was a fast track to karmic payback.

Not that I believed in karma.

Except when it was bad. And directed at me.

Generations of Jewish ancestors nodded in approval.

I rubbed the back of my neck. "What's the game?"

The raven shifter brightened. "War."

"Fucking hilarious, universe." I shook a fist at the sky. "Come onto the porch. We'll play here."

Poe hopped up the stairs in a side-to-side gait like they still had raven's feet. They flicked their tuxedo jacket tail out before easing onto the chair beside me and setting the deck on the wide armrest, face side up.

"How is this going to work if all the cards are the same?"

They produced an unopened deck from their inside jacket pocket. "I have extra. Nonmagic."

"Goody."

They dealt the regular cards evenly between us, and we flipped the top card over. My ten trumped their four, and I took both cards, stacking them on the bottom of my deck.

I hadn't played this game since Sadie was a child and it was as boring now as it had been then. "Couldn't we play Go Fish?"

"That is not what the resetting requires." They added my five to their pile.

I gave an aggrieved sigh. "Can we at least put a limit on the rounds? We could be here for ages." I flipped over a seven at the same time as Poe.

"War!" We yelled it in unison.

The top card on the magic deck, which sat on Poe's armrest, changed from an ace of spades to a three of diamonds. Poe clapped their hands in childlike glee.

Well, one of us was a happy camper.

"Mazel tov," I said. "Are we done?"

They sorted through the magic deck, only about a third of which had been restored. "Not yet."

"Awesome. Let the battle begin." As per the rules of the game, I set one nonmagic card facedown and the other faceup.

Poe did the same.

Before I could determine the winner, my porchlight swam, the wood boards under my feet turning to mud.

My eyes watered at the acrid smell of burning wood, smoke hanging over the churned-up field like wraiths. Smoldering piles of rubble were my only company, my feet squelching through the muck.

Arms outstretched, I sprinted forward, desperate to find someone, anyone.

A single black feather with an iridescent sheen drifted down, and I jumped away from it with a pained moan, further startled by a loud trumpet blast.

"Dumah?" I waved away some of the fog. Okay then, what new game had Poe thrust me into with this desolate wasteland? Spinning around, seeking friend or foe, I whacked my foot.

"Fuck!" I hopped on one foot, having bashed my toes on one of the porch slats.

There was no smoke, no angel, and even the other ravens had flown away, leaving Poe on my porch watching me with a bemused expression.

I grabbed them by the shoulders. "What was that? What did I see?"

"I have no knowledge of this vision."

"You gave me your word," I snarled.

Feathers erupted on their head as they pried my fingers off. "My promise stands. Whatever you beheld was not connected to this game or me, and thus, not a portent of anything. I swear." The shifter was too upset to be lying.

I sank into my chair on wobbly legs. All this unraveling business had unnerved me and I was imagining worst-case scenarios. That's all it was. Swallowing, I focused on the game. We'd tied that last round.

Once more, I lay a card facedown, but when it came time to place the second card faceup, I hesitated, my hand trembling, certain a trace of smoke danced on the breeze. Steeling myself, I slapped the card down.

The world remained stable and Poe won the hand.

We both played fives next, necessitating another round of War. There were no visions, and I won with an eight.

Again and again, we played, each time hitting War with a statistically impossible frequency. I was about to call an end to the game when I played the ace of spades. Convinced this was the sign that the game was finally, blessedly over, I put my hand on Poe's stack before they could draw again. "Check your magic deck."

Poe riffled through it, every number and suit accounted for. "It is reset. Thank you, Miriam." They gathered up the nonmagic deck we'd been playing with and stilled, fanning them faceup for my perusal.

I took a breath through a rib cage that felt as fragile as glass. Every single card save for the ace of spades that I'd played was blank. "Why the ace of spades?" I croaked out.

The raven cleared their throat. "It's the death card."

"My death or the death I bring to others?" I took the card from them.

"Not yours, though you have brought death before." The shifter pocketed both decks.

"That's not helpful." I paced along my porch.

First, Poe's magic deck changed to only aces of spades cards, which led them to me. I wasn't sure if that was a compliment or the saddest accomplishment I'd earned so far. Then, midgame to cleanse the cards, I'd gotten a vision of a battlefield, followed by round after round of ties, resulting in hand after hand of War. A thought prodded at my brain and I teased it out. "If I'm connected to the death card, why did you win as many times as I did? Shouldn't I have trounced you on every round? What does it mean?"

Poe tilted their head, their shrewd gaze framed by inky black feathers. "It means nothing. A resetting, no more. If you seek some answer, you will not find it tonight in these cards."

Dumah's words came back to me. *Straight answers aren't always the right answers. Sometimes lies are. Or not having any answer at all.*

The only good thing to come out of this fakakta game was the answer to the question weighing me down. I *was* an instrument of death. I killed dybbuks, I'd killed vampires, and no doubt would do both again. That was my choice but that's as far as it went. I wasn't some great savior, hoping to fly with the angels. I was a very human woman, content with her life.

Poe held out their hand for the ace of spades, but I ripped it up and stuffed the halves in my blouse pocket.

I was about to say no to an angel; annoying this raven shifter hardly rated.

"You got what you came for, now leave." I pointed at the sidewalk.

Poe opened their mouth as if to argue, but with a bow, strode down the stairs and into the night.

After checking that Sadie was distracted in her bedroom, I drew my living room curtains shut and pulled out the Ascendant, holding it in my palm. Dumah wouldn't be pleased when I turned down the unraveling, but hopefully they'd respect my decision like they'd said they would.

My happiness lay in the rich bloom of present and future love, not the charred corpse of past deaths.

That still left me with the problem of what to do with the Ascendant. Senoi, Sansenoi, and Sammaneglof hadn't found it in all the years that Tatiana had it. *I* had, and since I couldn't destroy the artifact, I'd bury it even deeper now. Except, I had no idea where. Well, I'd find a place. It wasn't a perfect plan, but it was the best I could do. And sometimes, I'd learned, I didn't have to totally solve a problem for all time.

Sometimes that fell to someone else.

Should those angels find a Banim Shovavim willing to

unleash dybbuks on the world, they wouldn't have the means to do so. That was enough.

My magic swelled and rose to my skin like a gentle tide, and I depressed the tiny groove in the silver orb. The artifact fell open into two perfect halves. "Dumah? You around?"

The rift of crooked light careened across the room, eclipsing my sofa.

My heart dropped into my stomach like I was on a roller coaster. "Oh shit! I'm not calling you forth! Absolutely not." I waved my hand in front of the rift like I could physically stop the angel from flying out. "I'm just giving you my answer about you-know-what."

An invisible force grasped me gently around the waist and whisked me in through the blinding light of the portal. By the time my vision was clear again, I stood in the courtyard.

Dumah-Goldie, in a battered straw sunhat, was on her knees, wearing a pair of gardening gloves as she snipped dead blooms off a patch of wildflowers. She had a smear of dirt across one cheek and a beatific smile on her face.

"This isn't drawn from my memories," I said. "My cousin despises gardening." She'd been responsible for weeding her parents' garden as a teen, and when she grew up, had allowed herself the "bougie" privilege of hiring a gardener.

The angel tenderly brushed some dirt off a slender shoot. "Even the smallest tendril of life provides beauty in the face of constant death." White expansive wings shimmered in the air for a moment as if quivering in joy.

It was the first true glimpse of Dumah that I'd been given and the perfect segue into announcing my decision, for I too was choosing life. I touched the card halves in my pocket.

The angel hummed under her breath, clearing some weeds to let her flowers breathe. What other life might Dumah have cultivated had she not been forced here by the trio? Was that why she'd defended Lilith? She'd seen the value of that fierce woman whose love of her children made her stand up to the angels themselves?

A hose appeared in Dumah-Goldie's hand, and she watered her flowers, tiny rainbows appearing in the spray.

I clasped the orb tightly. The three weren't merely avenging angels; they fancied themselves God, passing judgment on life and worth, while driven by a deep and twisted hatred.

As with the Leviathan and countless Banim Shovavim, damned to eternal torture not for crimes of their making but a failure to fit the trio's purity worldview, they'd pronounced judgment on Dumah and were desperate to carry out their chosen sentence.

They wouldn't stop until they'd torn Dumah from Gehenna, giving the angel no say in the matter.

Exactly as my parents had done when they tore me from my childhood.

I shook my head. That wasn't fair. They were pawns in a long game devised by beings who had no regard for their lives or the trauma and upheaval a young girl would carry with her for years.

I struggled to find my breath. My emotions now weren't the drowning swell of grief that I'd experienced for months after I lost Mom and Dad. No, I'd found a steady drip of sorrow beating within me. The result wasn't a rocky canyon fortified by time; it was a fathomless hole that hurt to contemplate because the happy, trusting kid I'd once been lay at the bottom of it.

God, I'd been so young.

I'd grieved my parents, but I'd never grieved myself.

Dumah-Goldie smiled up at me, one hand shielding her eyes. "What's your decision?"

I swear the universe chuckled when I pulled out the torn ace of spades halves and ran my thumb over them. This wasn't destiny or some written in the stars BS, it wasn't even about Dumah.

Senoi, Sansenoi, and Sammaneglof had killed my childhood in so many ways, but I was culpable as well. Every choice I'd made out of fear or to survive had destroyed me a little more, and while I'd reclaimed my adult life, this was my opportunity to make it up to that lost and scared girl.

"I'll do it."

7

"GABRIEL SAYS I'M A MARVEL. THE MOST PERFECT example of a golem he's ever seen with the most advanced intelligence." The overhead kitchen light winked off the 1970s gold satin short shorts that Emmett wore with a red velour crop top. "He's a smart guy."

I smiled at how Emmett took full credit for his own creation. Poor Jude. "Those of us who love you knew that already."

Rain and wind battered the windows this gloomy September morning, and even though I did my best not to flinch, the memory of the card assault on my poor home last night was too fresh.

Emmett propped a hip against my boss's counter and blew on his freshly painted gold nails. "Why so jumpy?"

"Poe encounter." I retied my crimson scarf for the thirtieth time this morning. French women made it look so easy, whereas I looked like I had a droopy noose around my neck. Eh, it still topped off my slouchy black T-shirt and mint-green wide-legged trousers, even matching the sparkly barrettes holding back my hair. Miriam Feldman, embracing color with a vengeance. "Were you waiting for me to start the meeting?"

"Nope." The kettle on the stove whistled. "Tatiana had to run to the bank and the wolf took Gabriel out to breakfast to grovel for his behavior last night. I told Gabriel he should hold out for dinner, really make the wolf work for it." Emmett filled two mugs with boiling water and deposited a small, round tea infuser filled with rich black loose tea in each one.

That was thoughtful of the golem to make me a hot drink on this cold day. "What happened to Laurent being your new bestie?" I said wryly.

"Did he call me a marvel? I think not. He's dropped to…" Emmett counted off on his fingers, muttering under his breath. "Sadie, Pyotr, Juliette. No, wait, Tatiana should be higher."

"I'm going to cut you off before you forget to stick me in the top five."

"I wouldn't be forgetting," he said with a cheeky grin, picking up the mugs.

"Can I get milk in mine?"

"In your what?" He stopped, already halfway across the kitchen.

I pointed at the drinks. "That wasn't for me, was it?"

"Marjorie has been on the phone with gallery owners all morning," he said. "She's probably parched. You've got two working hands. Help yourself." With that he left.

His concern for his *girlfriend*?—their exact status was unclear—was adorable. That attribute kept me from cursing out the little shit while I made my own tea and then sat in the living room drinking it by myself and waiting for someone to appear.

Luckily, Tatiana arrived home shortly, followed by the men. Laurent didn't even notice me at first; he was in the foyer chatting away in French and laughing with his brother-in-law. There was a lightness in him that I'd never seen, even at his most playful with me. It was an ease born of love and familiarity, and my smile over the rim of my cup stretched from ear to ear.

"What did that poor scarf ever do to you?" Tatiana marched up to me with the resolve of a general taking down opposing troops on the battlefield. With three quick motions, she'd knotted the fabric into my desired style. Stepping back, she surveyed the rest of me with a critical eye. "Do I spy a color palette not found in industrial carpeting?" She wiped away an imaginary tear and I shot her the finger.

She smirked.

"I had an idea for your memoirs." The coffee table book was progressing nicely, with a solid balance of showcasing her artwork and her personal life. "If we could figure out the logistics of putting out an edition that only Ohrists could purchase, what do you think of doing one for that community that includes your love affair with Zev?"

"No."

I blinked. "You don't want to think about it?"

"I don't need to. And before you bombard me with arguments about how it would fly off the shelves, of course it would. But I worked my tuchus off to become the artistic legend I am. Zev is a well-known patron of the arts, and I refuse to let people say that I slept my way to the top." A purple bulb in one of the hanging baskets burst into thick spikes.

Her vehemence surprised me, because in my experience, she'd never cared what anyone thought, but she wasn't wrong. "Say no more."

"Thank you." She adjusted my scarf one last time. "Give me five minutes, then we'll be off."

"Where?"

"Zev needs to be looped in. No need to trouble yourself finding your keys—I'll drive." Leaving the room, she told the men we'd be heading out in five minutes for Blood Alley.

I groaned, dropping my head in my hands. Trips to

Gehenna where I was divebombed by dybbuks were a lovely jaunt compared to being that woman's passenger. Plus I hadn't gotten over my desire to punch Zev in the throat for what he'd put Sadie through. This visit did not bode well.

"Hey, you." Laurent sank onto the sofa, nudging me with his shoulder.

"Hey yourself." I leaned into his side. I was here for work so I wouldn't kiss him, but his steady presence combined with his easy grin and dancing eyes lit up something bright and vital inside me. I wanted to doodle our initials together in hearts, which made me kind of want to smack myself but also made me painfully aware of the many things I stood to lose if the angels caught me.

Jokes about the schmuck trio aside, they were the deadliest foes I'd ever taken on. Not that my résumé of villains faced was particularly extensive, but even with a surprise attack, the idea of overpowering the three seemed impossible.

My facial muscles hurt from the strain of maintaining my happy façade. At some point, I'd have to speak with Laurent, Tatiana, and Emmett because there was no doing this alone, but today we were here for Gabriel.

"Are you going to work on the case?" I said.

"Oui. You're stuck with me."

Setting my mug on a coaster, I wrinkled my nose, earning another nudge from my boyfriend. "Why'd you change your mind? Did Gabriel guilt you into it?"

"As much as I dislike vampires, I dislike people bioengineering viruses even more. What's to stop someone from hacking this virus and turning it on the magic community?" He shook his head, his expression grim. "It's best that Gabriel get a handle on it now."

"Good reasoning. How was breakfast?" I said.

Gabriel dropped into the seat across from us. He wore narrow rectangular glasses that focused the shrewd intelligence in his eyes to sharp points. "Eggs Benedict taste much better with a side of 'forgive me, mon frère, for I am the worst and will spend the rest of my life earning your absolution.'"

Laurent draped his arm along the sofa at my back. "How Léa has not divorced you yet remains one of the world's great mysteries."

"The Naumovich siblings are something else. I believe *you* said that about Delphine and myself." Gabriel pulled his bulky sweater off in a fluid motion.

Had I noticed his broad shoulders and flexing biceps, I'd have proclaimed that he was more muscular than I'd expect of a scientist, but as I had eyes only for my charmingly rumpled boyfriend, that revelation went unseen.

"Yes," Laurent said, "and it was not a compliment at the time."

"That says more about you and Léa for marrying us than about my sister and I." Gabriel caught himself and winced. "Miriam, are you all right if we discuss Delphine?"

"Absolutely. I like learning more about her. Just because we've lost someone or our relationship changes doesn't mean that our love for them does. My ex-husband, Eli, is one of the people I'm closest to."

Laurent gave a grumpy huff.

"Has Eli not fallen for your abundant charm?" Gabriel raked a lock of hair off his forehead. "Quelle horreur."

"He disrespects le football," Laurent said.

Gabriel crossed his arms, all good humor gone. "Well, that is an uncivilized and unforgiveable attitude."

"He's a proper Canadian boy with a deep love of hockey, not Conan the Barbarian. Besides, all sports are equally boring," I said.

Gabriel gaped at me. "Non. Now I must find someone else to hire."

Tatiana returned wearing psychedelic purple rubber boots and a raincoat. "Oy vey. Miriam, did you disrespect soccer?" Both men flinched at the North American term, and my boss winked at me. "Tough titties, Gabriel, we have a verbal contract, and I am very litigious. Now let's go."

"It's too early for Zev to be awake," I protested. "Let's meet here and I'll stop by Blood Alley later." In my own car, which I could drive blindfolded and have a higher chance of surviving.

"Emmett," she bellowed, "we're going."

His footsteps thudded overhead, and then the golem jumped down the stairs, joining us in the foyer. He handed me a small, sealed container. "Marjorie made cookies."

Oh wow. "Tell her thank you." I pulled up the corner, inhaling butter, sugar, and ginger before pressing it to my chest. "I'm keeping them," I told Tatiana.

"Obviously," she said. "I wouldn't have asked her to put some aside for you otherwise."

I jammed the cookies in my purse. Was this because Tatiana loved me or was it a bribe?

Emmett jerked his chin at Laurent. "Did he grovel enough?"

Gabriel tied his shoelaces. "It was spectacular. He brought the restaurant to tears."

"I hate you," Laurent said, stuffing his feet into sneakers.

Gabriel clapped him on the shoulder. "Methinks he doth protest too much."

Laurent did his best to maintain a curmudgeonly expression, but his lips quirked. It must have been agony for him to lose this relationship for so long, even if it was largely of his own making.

"I'll stay and help Marjorie," Emmett said, already backing up the stairs.

"Good idea." Tatiana dug her car keys out of her jacket pocket.

I paused, halfway into my coat. Damn it. The cookies weren't a bribe, they were my last meal. "We could all help."

"Get over yourself." Tatiana sniffed. "I'm an excellent driver."

"You're driving?" Gabriel said in a strangled voice.

"I have my tru—" Laurent swallowed, cowed into silence by his aunt's glower.

Tatiana rattled off a list of items for Emmett and Marjorie to tackle, then sailed out the door, jingling the keys. "Allons-y."

She strode to her giant gold behemoth from a bygone century like the rain would part for her, but the rest of us hopped puddles, grimacing at the freezing water running down our necks.

I headed for the back door, but Tatiana pushed me around the front of the car. "You're with me."

"The men have longer legs, though. I'm sure one of them would really—"

"I'm not going to send you through the windshield." With that she got into the car and slammed the door.

I turned to the guys, hoping one of them would offer to switch, but they were already in the back, seat belts on, and one hand on each of the "oh shit" handles.

Fine. Be that way. When Tatiana crashed us and we were hanging upside down, unable to escape because the paramedics hadn't yet arrived with the jaws of death, see if I share any of the cookies with you two.

I slid onto the passenger seat and twisted around to sarcastically thank them for their concern, but they became engrossed in a conversation so vital to the world that they couldn't even glance at me.

"Netflix isn't a French word," I said with a grunt because Tatiana had just dumped her huge purse on my lap. "You're discussing some TV show?"

"We're exploring a very important ethical question," Gabriel said.

Tatiana jerked the bench seat back and forth.

"About what?" I braced my hands on the dashboard so I didn't get whiplash.

"Zombies." Tatiana tsked at them through the rearview mirror. "Use all the French slang you want, I do still get the gist."

"Humph." I faced front.

"You are in so much trouble," Gabriel said to Laurent.

"I wasn't the one who lied to her," he hissed.

"You were the one who started the stupid zombie conversation so she couldn't ask you to switch seats," Gabriel retorted.

Laurent gasped. "Again, you lie."

It would have been funny, except instead of pulling away from the curb, Tatiana drove backward over it so hard that I jolted against the seat belt before my head bounced off the headrest.

"If you could not dash my brains out in the first fifteen seconds," I said, "that would be appreciated."

She flicked on the wipers. "Save dashing Miriam's brains for later in the ride. Noted."

"Hilarious." I put my hand over hers on the gearshift. "Wait. Are you wearing your driving glasses?"

"Yes, Mother," she snarked. She changed gears, peeling out onto the street with enough force to send us careening into a neighbor's motorcycle, which toppled to the ground with a crunch.

Laurent yelped in sympathy, while Gabriel slid farther down in his seat, one hand over his face.

Tatiana merely smirked. "Maybe now he'll fix his muffler." She turned the windshield wipers off then on again. "Walk us through the relevant points, Gabriel."

"Attends. My life isn't finished flashing before my eyes."

"Please," she said. "You're not that exciting."

Laurent snickered.

"Just for that," Gabriel said haughtily, "I will include all the science stuff."

Tatiana and Laurent groaned, but I sat up, excited to learn new facts. "If you determined that there was magic involved, how did you figure out there was also science?" I said.

"Alors. A virus is a parasite that infects a cell. Geneticists can tell whether a virus is created in a lab by identifying any insertions. Those are mutations involving added genetic material. We compare them to viruses existing in nature. If any have the same mutations then voilà, they are natural."

Tatiana reached into her purse while running a stop sign.

I shoved her hand away. "Whatever you need, I'll get it."

"My driving glasses."

I pried my fingers off her purse strap. I bet if I got the schmuck trio in a car with her, they'd unravel themselves. Hello, plan B. I pulled the glasses out of their case and thrust them under her nose, and she switched out the pairs.

Gabriel cleared his throat.

"Please carry on," I said, putting away her original frames.

"It was a fairly basic hypothesis I wouldn't find the virus in nature given I was dealing with vampires," he said, "but one must keep an open mind."

"So that hypothesis was proven correct," I said. "How did you further break it down?"

"The fastest way to create a virus is to use an existing virus backbone, an existing genetic sequence. One means of doing this is via serial passage, where scientists force a virus to repeatedly mutate into a different form."

"Like evolution," Laurent said.

"Exact—" Gabriel's voice ended in a pitchy cry. "Red light!"

Tatiana slammed on the brakes in the middle of the inter-section, but they locked up and we slid right through. She steered the wheel back and forth, sending the car into a spin.

The world outside the window blurred, cars honked, and the vehicle filled with angry French screaming.

With one final spin, we drifted to a stop, miraculously untouched.

"Happy now, Gabriel?" Tatiana did a thirty-seven point turn to reorient to the correct direction. "You almost got us killed with your hysterics. Even Miriam remained calm."

No, Miriam's jaw was locked together so tight that it might never unclamp, and I'd broken a nail digging my fingers into the seat belt.

Laurent massaged my shoulders. Okay, he massaged them, then gave up, and more or less shoved them down from ear level.

"Why?" Tatiana said, finally driving like a normal person.

There was confused silence in the car.

"Why what?" I said.

"Why would scientists want to force a virus to mutate?" Tatiana made a tsking sound. "Aren't you listening?"

"Yeah, Mitzi. Don't be rude." Laurent would pay for the thread of laughter in his voice.

"Uh." Gabriel took a moment before he continued. "Certain vaccines are produced through this method by weakening the virus, but you can do the opposite and strengthen one to transmit it more effectively."

"That's not scary," I muttered.

"If it reassures you," he said, "there's a limit to that process. I quickly ruled it out, returning my attention to studying added or deleted genetic material. Checking if they matched any known man-made viruses. Or at least, if the backbone did."

"I read something about that." Tatiana slowed to a stop at a yellow light and the vise around my chest temporarily eased. "Biohacking, right?"

I relaxed further to the comforting swish of the wipers.

"Yes, it's a trendy topic in the media." Gabriel's disdain

was evident. "But CRISPR, the gene editing tech, is one of the most influential developments in life sciences because it allows us to rewrite portions of the DNA genome through addition and deletion. However, those leave easily detectable traces, which is how I narrowed down what I was dealing with."

"If it's tech, why are you so certain that a specific geneticist is involved?" Laurent said.

The light turned green, and Tatiana pulled forward smoothly. I crossed my fingers and toes that the rest of the journey would continue in the same manner.

"There is a scientific precision required to use this technology, especially since there is also magic involved," Gabriel said. "I had two scenarios to test once I ruled out this being a virus found in nature. Either the magic was the delivery system for a scientifically made virus or vice versa."

"You're right," Tatiana said. "The only way that this virus could be purely magic would be if the Ohrist was personally infecting every single vampire."

"Yes," Gabriel said. "Since it was too widespread for that to be the case, there had to be a scientific means of transmission and reproduction. Back to your questions, Laurent, it's one thing to edit human genomes and quite another to do so with vampire DNA. As humans age, the ends of our chromosomes, the telomeres, shorten. In vampires, that process is frozen, leading to immortality."

"There are rare Ohrists with the ability to make people rapidly age and die," Tatiana said. "Excellent assassins." Her approving tone was the scariest part of this entire ride.

She pulled a U-turn across two lanes of oncoming traffic.

"What the hell?" I screeched, careening into the door. Note to self: never underestimate Tatiana's ability to make things more terrifying.

"Assassins reminded me of that mishegoss in Budapest, which reminded me that I had to pick up my red jacket from the dry cleaner's." She pulled into a small strip mall and parked diagonally in two spaces. "Back in a sec."

"She's gotten better at driving," Laurent observed.

"You've got to be kidding," I said.

"No." Gabriel sighed. "You couldn't convince her that her house was haunted so someone else had to drive?"

"She wouldn't have bought it now," Laurent said.

"Hang on." I twisted around to face them. "You convinced her she lived in a haunted house? Why would that affect her driving?"

"Her apartment in Paris," Gabriel said. "The building was three hundred years old and very creaky, so it wasn't a stretch."

Laurent grinned. "Samuel used to pay me to hide her car keys so we could blame it on the ghost."

Gabriel slugged his arm. "You got paid? Delphine and I didn't."

"I know." Laurent nodded loftily. "That was very stupid of you. It kept me in candy and comics for years."

"Yeah, that was poor negotiation on your part," I said, chuckling.

Tatiana exited the shop. A young employee held an umbrella over my boss's head, while another carried her plastic-wrapped garment.

They placed her laundry in the trunk, escorted her to the car, making sure she didn't get wet when she took the driver's seat, then waved her off.

I recognized their looks of relief.

Tatiana managed to merge in the correct direction without killing us, and I whispered my thanks to the universe.

"Where were we?" she said.

"Ohrist assassins who kill people by aging them up," Laurent said. "Let's hear more about them."

"Gabriel, continue," I said. "I'm finding this discussion fascinating."

"Thank you. Those Ohrists you refer to, Tante, manipulate life force energy, which vampires don't have," Gabriel said. "Plus, the magic implanted in the vector that delivered the virus also had to suppress the natural healing ability of vampires."

"Which brings us back to an unknown power." I ran a finger through the condensation on the window. "Aside from delivering the magic virus to vampire DNA, was there anything about the science that made you think Dr. Eversol was the one involved?"

"Bien sûr." Gabriel leaned forward over the bench seat. "While vampires' telomeres are frozen, they are, ironically, very delicate to work with, so the geneticist who created the backbone would have to be incredibly knowledgeable about the telomere landscape." He spread his hands wide. "Hence, Justine, who spent decades researching that very topic."

"If she's involved in something this illicit, it's not a great sign that you can't find her," Laurent said. "What if someone else came to the same conclusion as you and took her out?"

"It's doubtful," Gabriel said. "I'm the only Ohrist who could have analyzed the vampire blood and successfully deduced these findings to make her the top candidate."

"What if a vampire went after her because she helped create the virus?" I said.

Gabriel made a sound of disagreement. "It would be incredibly rash to kill the person who holds the key to their species' cure."

"Vampires don't always think before they act," I said.

Now a couple of blocks from Blood Alley, Tatiana pulled up behind a parked car that was leaving, but when it failed to move in ten seconds, leaned on the horn.

"Oh my God!" I yanked her hand away, giving an apologetic wave to the mother whose baby had just begun to scream from its car seat in the back.

"It worked, didn't it?" My boss jutted her chin at the dejected woman getting into her vehicle.

"You won't even fit in that space."

Tatiana narrowed her eyes. "Oh, I'll fit."

"Nope." I opened the door and got out. "I'll meet you at Zev's."

Laurent and Gabriel scrambled out as well.

"Cowards," she snapped.

After shutting the door, I gave her a friendly wave. Coward? Perhaps. Alive? Barely. Still, these days when I was fighting angels and investigating vampire viruses, barely alive was a win.

8

LAURENT, GABRIEL, AND I RAN FROM AWNING TO awning, doing our best to stay dry until we made it to the demarcation line into Blood Alley. Thinking fondly of the umbrella in my car, I splashed through the spiky metal gates under the watchful gaze of the gargoyle statues on the corners. At least the rain hadn't followed us into the hidden magic space, though the sky here was filled with black storm clouds, and the air had a metallic bite.

Gabriel's mouth fell open. He wandered slowly up one of the center lanes, shamelessly rubbernecking.

As I squeezed water from my hair, I caught a flash of a godawful gold-braided chauffeur's cap.

Reality fell away, replaced by Emmett's mangled face and Rodrigo's dead eyes. I shivered, extending a trembling hand to shake the Undertaker's shoulders, his presence so immutable that I couldn't comprehend his sprawled body lying so still.

"Mitzi?"

Laurent's face swam into view, wavering and flickering. Hair sprouted, his teeth elongating to fangs before grinding back to human, his bones cracking and breaking and the plates of his skull a shifting, slithering mess. I clapped my hands over my ears against the sound of his broken wail.

"Miriam!" Laurent shook me.

I snapped out of my trance, my heart racing, searching for any sign of a shift. I pressed my palms against his cheeks, which were pink from cold, but solid. Stubble scratched my palms, and there was no trace of white fur among the dark, wet curls plastered to his head.

"I'm okay." Those last icy tendrils didn't fully retreat until the fear seeped from Laurent's wide eyes.

"What happened?" he said.

"The cap." Shaking free, I ran past Gabriel to a tall man wheeling a dolly loaded with cardboard boxes and tapped his shoulder.

As impossible as it was, I expected to find the Undertaker ready to give me grief, and I blinked stupidly at the unfamiliar employee in his red shirt with the word "Rome" embroidered in black over his heart.

"Can I help you with something?"

I pointed at the black hat with its gold braid, holding myself back from snatching it off his head. "Where did you get that?"

He patted the top of it. "Mr. Toledano added it as part of the human uniform." He paused, trying to find a good customer service solution. "I can ask my manager where they buy them if you like?"

Zev was commemorating the loss of his human friend.

I swallowed, my chest heavy. "I'm good. Thanks."

"No problem." He opened the nearest door with three red light bulbs on it and disappeared inside.

"Trouble?" Gabriel caught up with me.

I felt that odd clarity you got after a long time crying and something settled in my chest. "The opposite actually."

Laurent's reasons for coming on board this investigation had resonated with me, since getting the jump on a virus that could be tailored to affect humans was vital. However, Zev's small gesture meant more in terms of swaying me to the cause. Toledano wasn't speciesist—he disliked most beings equally—but the unexpected benefit of that was his capacity to cherish a handful of individuals regardless of what they were.

Who's to say he wouldn't help were it Ohrists or even Banim Shovavim facing this virus? I'd initially agreed to do this job for money, but my commitment hardened into something more tangible and resolved.

Laurent had waited by the gate for Tatiana, keeping pace with her, his expression thoughtful. With his enhanced shifter abilities, he would have overheard my conversation with the employee, and as a victim of the same attack that killed Rodrigo, he understood the significance of the wardrobe update.

Perhaps his stance toward vampires would be softened by one vamp's mourning. I smiled as he and Tatiana joined me alongside Gabriel.

Zev strode down the hill in workout gear and Laurent's lip curled. "BatKian."

Or not.

"It's Toledano now." The vampire stopped beside us bereft of pit stains, pink cheeks, or the faintest sign that he'd been exercising. "I've reclaimed my human surname."

"Bully for you," Laurent said.

There was nothing so pedestrian as baggy sweats and a sweatshirt emblazoned with a university logo for Vancouver's master vamp. His gray shirt caught the light in a manner that suggested it was not only high-tech enough to repel sweat, but in a pinch, you could use it to light a fire and signal for help. His mottled gray pants, on the other hand, draped off his hips and strong thighs so perfectly they may have had their own gravitational field calibrated to his ass.

I snorted, earning an arched eyebrow from him.

"A penny for your thoughts," he drawled.

"They're worth infinitely more than that." I wagged a finger at Zev. "You can't afford them."

My boyfriend laughed at the vamp's dour expression.

"Was it necessary to bring the riffraff?" Zev said to Tatiana. "You and Gabriel would have sufficed."

"Miriam has to earn her salary and there was room in the car for Laurent."

I planted my hands on my hips. "Thanks for defending your prized associate."

"And your favorite nephew," Laurent huffed.

"Second favorite." Gabriel offered his arm to his aunt, who took it with a fond smile.

Zev accompanied them up the lane, chatting with my boss about the art opening of a mutual acquaintance.

"I get enough workplace abuse from the dybbuks." Laurent's brows furrowed together. "Room in the car? Is she even paying me?"

"Take it up with HR," I said.

Laurent draped his arm over me, the two of us strolling up toward Rome. "There's HR now?"

"Of sorts." I laughed. "Tatiana is so upset about making Marjorie cry that she's caving to anything her assistant asks for."

"That girl is too sweet." Laurent got an evil look on his face. "She'll need guidance exploiting my aunt properly."

"Yeah, I figured that Emmett would have jumped on that, but he gets all gentlemanly around her."

"Eh. He'll stop caring about impressing her soon en —omph."

"Oh dear." I batted my lashes. "My elbow slipped."

Once inside Rome, Zev led us to a boring conference room straight out of any corporation. The one striking detail was the large monitor set up for teleconferencing, and the image of all these powerful vamps on Zoom made me snicker.

Sadly, unlike other meetings, I was not treated to an array of coffee and pastries. He didn't even fulfill minimum host duties and set out water. Had I not known how much he reveled in my presence, I might have taken offense.

The vamp signed off on this investigation with a mean smirk at Laurent's involvement. "Joining the other men in your family and working for me? And here I thought you'd simply come to bristle. What an unexpected delight."

"I'm working for Gabriel," Laurent said through gritted teeth.

Grabbing his hands before he could follow that up with an expressive—and bluntly direct—French gesture, I told Zev that given the urgent nature of this case, he should be grateful for the tracking expertise Laurent brought.

Zev made a noncommittal noise, then informed us that both he and Gabriel were to be informed immediately of developments. Such a darling control freak.

Gabriel seemed surprised but wisely kept his musings to himself, while my boyfriend smirked and kicked his brother-in-law under the table like a little brat.

At my stern look, he shrugged and muttered, *"I'm Tatiana's favorite nephew."*

The vampire sat back in his leather chair with his hands steepled under his chin. "Is there anything specific you require of me?"

I half raised my hand. "Can you reach out to other master vampires and ask about any of their crew who have gone missing in the last few years?"

"That's rather sensitive information." Zev's voice held a warning note. "Some might perceive it as probing for weaknesses."

I rolled my eyes. "Dr. Eversol couldn't have created this virus without studying vampire genetics, and it's not like she could have conducted trials on substitute beings and achieved usable results. Where did she get the vampires who were experimented on?"

Zev's gaze sharpened and a hint of fang peeked out from his top lip. Good. Get angry and help us.

"Plus, if Gabriel is right," I said, "and Justine is a Sapien, how did she capture and imprison vampires to study and administer the virus until she had the winner?"

"A surge in any single location of missing vampires would be a strong indicator of Eversol's location," Tatiana said. "Even with an Ohrist partner's assistance, they wouldn't want the added hassle of transporting their subjects too far."

I nodded. "Don't forget that she had to keep them alive, which means a blood supply. I could circulate Dr. Eversol's photo among distributors. Would you introduce me to some?"

"That's a good idea." Gabriel turned to Zev. "The private detective I hired initially found no trace of Justine since her retirement. No credit card use, no bank transactions, no real estate in her name."

"She's being funded somehow," I said. "Maybe by the Ohrist who provided the magic for the virus?"

Laurent wasn't contributing anything to the conversation. He wasn't sulking, in fact he was listening quite intently, but his silence was odd.

Zev had been replying to a text, but he glanced up. "I'll put you in touch with a few of the bigger blood suppliers, but I won't pry into missing vampires." He pocketed the phone. "It's not wise to show too much interest in those things."

"Not even if it leads to a cure for the contagion?" Laurent snapped his fingers. "Are you aiming for another monopoly on the cure or do you just need to replenish your own stockpile now that the estrie's blood is in limited supply?"

I pressed my foot on his. That was what he chose to chime in with?

Laurent ignored me. "That self-serving aspect wouldn't

surprise me, and honestly, I'd put my people first too, but the thing that does bother me?"

Zev examined his nails. "If I don't ask, will you still subject me to your tedious thinking?"

Laurent slouched insolently in his chair, one elbow braced over the back. "No one has claimed credit for unleashing that virus. A bioweapon like that would put someone in a formidable position and very few would have the restraint to keep from bragging." He stroked his chin, his expression thoughtful, and I pressed my lips together against my snigger. The balls on that boy.

"You think *I* created the contagion?" Zev slammed his hands on the table, sending up a shower of splinters.

I flinched.

"Out of respect for Tatiana," Zev said in a deadly purr, "I've given you a lot of leeway, Amar. Do not insult me further."

"Or what?" His eyebrow cocked, Laurent raised his shirt on the side that the vampire *hadn't* scarred years ago. I couldn't decide if that was hot or psychotic, so I went with psychotically hot and didn't beat myself up for it.

Zev pushed to his feet, and smiling coldly, gripped the table. The wood in his hands was crushed, falling to the floor in a powder. "I'm sure I'll think of something," he said, brushing off his trousers.

Gabriel, Tatiana, and I gaped at him like fish floundering for air, but Laurent actually snorted.

"Nice show," he said, "but you won't. Do it again and you lose your minion and all that wonderfully clean cash."

"Would I?" Zev pretended to think it over. "I doubt that's the case."

"We all know that dealing with you changed the kind of person my father is, but even he has his limit, and you hit it with your previous attack on me."

Zev mimed wiping a tear from his eye. "You do so love

making me out to be the villain where your father is concerned."

Laurent's hands shifted to claws. "Not just with him."

"Lolo." Tatiana's voice quivered. "Stop. Je t'en prie."

"Listen to your aunt, Lolo." Zev toyed with his sharp-bladed letter opener. "Jacques has always been a willing participant in our relationship. Can you honestly say the same about yours?"

Laurent lunged and the vampire hissed.

Gabriel grabbed his brother-in-law by the shoulders, holding him back and murmuring to him in French.

My stomach was in knots. Not only did I have no idea how to help, if Zev was provoked on this topic—yet again—Laurent could end up with far worse than a matching scar.

He finally calmed down enough to shoot Tatiana a contrite look before addressing the vamp. "Regarding the virus. I don't believe you created it. That's beneath you."

"I have standards now?" Zev placed his hand on his heart, his eyes wide in exaggeration.

Laurent held his finger and thumb a smidge apart. He paused and then narrowed his eyes. "Let's make a bet."

Gabriel hissed something at him in French, but I watched him in curious wonder.

Despite what Tatiana and Gabriel appeared to believe, this wasn't Laurent's death wish surfacing. The shifter was leading this conversation somewhere to catch the vampire off guard.

Zev clenched his jaw, his eyes trained on the shifter as if searching for Laurent's angle. "About what?"

"Should my deductions prove correct," Laurent said, "you'll give me your Dantora painting."

Tatiana's face scrunched up. Join the club, lady. Why did he want a piece of art?

The vamp sat down. "Not Chopin's original copy of his military Polonaise?"

Laurent waved a dismissive hand. "Hearing music, playing it, that is the only joy. Its ownership means nothing."

"Which Dantora do you have?" Tatiana said.

"*In Pursuit of Wisdom*." Zev watched her reaction carefully, but if he was hoping for some insight into Laurent's motives, he was disappointed.

Tatiana frowned. "That's not even one of the good ones. Not that there are many Dantoras of note."

"Are you taking the bet or not?" Laurent said.

"I'll take it," Zev replied with a dismissive wave of his hand. "Go ahead."

"You know who provided the magic for the virus," Laurent said.

I clenched my fists. "Did they meet with an unfortunate accident or was their murder more of a statement piece?"

"Zev doesn't like to brag, remember?" Tatiana wagged a finger at Laurent and me. "That body will never be found."

Her former lover laughed.

"They're not dead," Laurent said, wiping Zev's smile away.

Gabriel turned to Zev. "Then why not tell me what magic was involved so I can create a cure you desire? Unless I'm being used." Up until now, I'd have described Gabriel as good-humored, but the menace rolling off those last words took even Zev aback.

Laurent made a placating motion at his brother-in-law. "He doesn't know because the bloodsucker was turned long ago and has kept their Ohrist magic secret."

Talk about a record scratch moment. Tatiana pursed her lips, her eyes huge, while Gabriel nodded slowly as if given the key to unlocking this puzzle.

"A vamp?" I sputtered.

"What's their name?" Laurent said. "Where are they?"

Zev reached a hand to the notch at his collarbone like he intended to adjust his tie. Not finding one, his hand dropped into his lap, and he ran his tongue over his bottom lip before rising slowly to his feet. "Her name is Imogine, and as to where she currently resides, I have no earthly idea." He paused, his fingers tightening into a fist before he released them. "I'll have the painting delivered to you."

With that he walked out of the room.

The second the door closed, Tatiana leaned over the table. "Good guess or did you know something we didn't, Lolo?"

"Educated guess," he said.

"Book-learned," I murmured, earning a faint smile from him. I propped my head on his shoulder. "Are you okay?"

"Yes." *Liar*. His body was tight with tension.

"Why wouldn't he be?" Tatiana said with pride. "He just won himself a mediocre painting, after all."

That made Laurent chuckle, and the rigid line of his shoulders eased.

Gabriel watched Laurent but kept his thoughts to himself. Just as I did. For now.

"Circulating a photo to blood suppliers was a smart idea, Mitzi," my boyfriend said. He rolled his neck from side to side, his body relaxing into a more languid posture. "But it would take too long to go down the chain, and it occurred to me that Dr. Eversol wouldn't need large numbers of vamps to experiment on."

"One at a time would suffice," Gabriel said. "Which isn't enough to cause a spike or raise suspicion."

"Plus, Imogine could easily provide them," I added.

"I didn't test for vampire magic in the blood analysis I did. Just Ohrist powers." Gabriel clapped. "Bravo."

"But why that painting?" Tatiana said.

"Okay, I confess." Laurent threw her a charming grin. "I did have some information coming into this meeting."

"You only decided to be a part of the case this morning," Gabriel said.

"Weelll," Laurent hedged.

Tatiana held out a hand. "You owe me two bucks."

"Yeah, yeah," Gabriel said.

Laurent looked affronted. "I'm only worth two dollars?"

"Focus," I said.

He saluted me. "The bragging rights angle occurred to me last night, and I assumed that Toledano had been trying to track down the one with the magic for some time. A powerful Ohrist with an incentive to stay under the radar would be difficult to find."

"But an ancient vampire could be nigh impossible," I said.

"For most, yes, but for someone who deals in information?"

Tatiana laughed. "*In Pursuit of Wisdom*. Which one wanted it?"

"Hiram," he said.

"The Wise Brothers? Oy." I slapped my hand to my forehead.

"We'll offer a trade." Laurent rubbed my back. "No games. I learned that from you with the raven shifters."

"Glad to be your cautionary tale."

"Nicely played." Tatiana stood up and held out her arm to Laurent. "My favorite nephew may escort me back to the car."

He smirked, making a show of accepting.

Gabriel huffed, so I tugged him to his feet. "Come on," I said, "I'll be your consolation prize."

"You are far too much of a treasure to be anyone's consolation," he said in his melty accent and swept me from the room.

Laurent's mock jealousy was going to be so much fun.

9

After surviving the ride back to Tatiana's place, we split up. Tatiana co-opted Emmett to put out feelers among her connections for any info on Dr. Eversol or intel on Imogine.

Gabriel was concerned about her mentioning the virus, but she assured him that everyone she dealt with knew how to keep secrets, and he left soon after, because he and Juliette were catching the ferry to Vancouver Island to sightsee together for a few days.

I would have checked in with Laurent to discuss what had happened at Zev's, but he volunteered to get hold of Hiram and Ephraim to propose trading the painting for information, which surprised me. After our last encounter with the Wise Brothers, I expected him to leave all contact to me, but he assured me that he'd handle this without escalating things and left.

Gee, wonder why he didn't want me to get him alone. He didn't need to discuss his feelings about his dad with me, but continuing to bottle up all that resentment would only continue to hurt him.

We'd be revisiting this.

Assuming we'd have to deliver the painting to the men in Los Angeles, I took it upon myself to speak with the Leviathan about giving Laurent safe passage. I also had to break the news that the Ascendant wouldn't free the sea monster and share the bigger plan of destroying the KH.

Since the team also had to be filled in on that last part, I invited them out for drinks at the Bear's Den, but Tatiana was busy, and we scheduled it for tomorrow. She promised to bring Emmett.

After scarfing down an early dinner and most of Marjorie's cookies, which were incredible, I retrieved the Ascendant and stepped into the KH. Pyotr wasn't around and Smoky didn't answer my call, which left me at a loss as to how to find the sea monster, since generally, it contacted me. I plucked a sock from the pile, hoping that "Leviathan's grotto" counted as a location, and headed along the dim path outside the reception area.

After a few minutes of what felt like aimless wandering, I turned a corner and smacked into a shadow.

It was too dark in here to summon Delilah, and I didn't understand how another Banim Shovavim could animate theirs or what danger they were reacting to.

"I'm not a threat," I said. "Show yourself."

There was a low moan and the shadow shuffled closer.

I gasped because it was one of the damned Banim Shovavim, his transparent skin stretched so tightly over the vast darkness inside him that his body was wrinkled, as if the eternal cosmos was in need of ironing.

The old man stared through me with rheumy, milky eyes that no longer bore any trace of humanity. They were the only discernable feature on his entire body. Unlike the one other damned Banim Shovavim that I'd met, he didn't speak. He didn't even move, like he no longer had the brain function to go around obstacles.

He simply stood there, rippling darkness. Is this what I'd

come to if the trio caught me? Humans could burn so bright. Yet to those angels, we Banim Shovavim didn't have any of that. To them, we were a void, a place where beauty went to die and sparks were snuffed out, more than deserving of being ruthlessly eradicated.

Unable to help myself, I touched his cheek and frowned. He wasn't hot or cold or reeking of evil. In fact, there was no sensation at all, to the point that I pressed harder, trying to feel anything.

I might as well have been pressing against air. He was tangible but that was it. It was the most disconcerting feeling. Was this the final stage of damnation?

Had the three angels devised this suffering as a twisted inversion to what they themselves faced with unraveling? Where they would remain eternally aware and unmade, we were damned to no longer thinking, feeling, or even seeming to exist?

I dropped my hand with a heavy heart, and the man's eyelids fluttered.

For one brief second, his eyes shone brown and clear, tears pouring from them. "Don't leave," he whispered brokenly.

I sucked in a breath, but before I could reply, his eyes filmed over once more.

Pressing my lips tightly together, I stepped to the side, allowing him to pass. I couldn't fathom the trio's hatred of my kind. Eternal torment wasn't enough, they'd arranged it so that any physical contact with another Banim Shovavim resulted in a split-second reminder of what that human had lost.

A wave of nausea hit me, and I braced one hand against the rock wall.

"Miriam?" Pyotr gently squeezed my shoulder.

"I hate—" I swallowed the angels' names for fear they'd hear me.

The gargoyle nodded. "Come with me." He led me a short

distance down the path to a door in the rock. "Don't go in," he admonished before opening it and revealing a huge cavern.

Hot, sticky magic leaked out, coating me like I'd been dipped in a cotton candy machine, but before I could ask where we were, Smoky, the phantom skeleton face made from the Leviathan's nasal exhaust, appeared. The door to the cavern slammed shut, and with a sickening lurch, the world tugged sideways.

I sucked in a breath and sputtered, flailing my arms in water and choking. Seconds later, I was deposited on the thin strip of rocky ground in the sea monster's grotto.

The Leviathan's scaly armored head rose from beneath the turquoise waters, regarding me with its ancient gaze, while Smoky hovered above it.

Still coughing, I wrung out my shirt. "What. The. Actual. Fuck."

"You should not have been there."

"Been where? What was that place?" I wiped water off the back of my neck, glancing nervously at the ceiling.

"Speak freely here," Smoky said brusquely.

"Was it a prison for someone like Arlo Garcia? Someone who transgressed badly?" My stomach formed a giant knot in anticipation of that answer.

"Not like."

Really fond of the cryptic answers, this one. Oh wait. "That *was* Arlo's prison? Where is he?"

"He is no more. The angels bled him dry, reabsorbing all the magic to reinforce that cell."

"No." I shook my head like I could dislodge those words, and in so doing, change the past. Arlo was insane with no possibility of redemption, but he was Banim Shovavim, and at least he existed. Had existed. There was no way his death had been merciful. "Why?"

"They require his prison."

Shivering, I wrapped my arms around myself. "Me or

Dumah?"

"The fallen one. Though, they have spoken of using it for another, if that person does not free the angel from Gehenna quickly enough for their liking."

"Got it. The cell is for Dumah unless I take too long. How much time do I have?" The trio wasn't getting either of us, but that was for me to know and them to painfully find out.

"Fortifying a prison for an angel is a far more complex magical procedure than containing a human. It is only about a quarter done, but how fast or slow the rest will take, I know not. Did you bring the Ascendant?"

I pulled the silver orb from my pocket, holding it up for the Leviathan's inspection. "Yes, but—"

The monster surged from the water, rising over me.

My eyes bounced from its pointed scales to its claws and razor-sharp teeth, looking for somewhere soft to land. Barbed wire was cuddlier. Its breath heated my skin to an angry, painful red.

"Wait." I held up a hand, my pulse fluttering wildly in my throat. "This artifact won't free you. You're angel-cursed."

Smoky flew at me, swirling faster and faster around my body, and I threw my arm over my face to protect against the pebbles pinging off me. An earsplitting howl steeped in misery bounced off the walls.

"There's another way!" I screamed.

Silence fell like a guillotine. I opened my eyes and yelped because Smoky was all up in my face.

After blotting my forehead with my scarf, I stuffed the orb back in a pocket, explaining that for the Leviathan to be free, I had to destroy the KH and take down Senoi, Sansenoi, and Sammaneglof.

Smoky didn't comment after I finished. I fidgeted, waiting for either a stamp of approval or useful directions on proper use of the Ascendant to achieve my goal.

"My escape has to be carefully timed," it finally said. "The angels will be alerted the moment I leave."

"Yeah, you have to go within zeptoseconds of us nuking the place." I kicked a couple of pebbles away. "We'll need some way to contact you and give you the signal. Maybe Pyotr can help with that."

"We can have code words," Smoky said excitedly.

"I don't think that's nec—"

"Pyotr can say, 'The yellow bird rises at dawn.' And I will reply with, 'My aunt loved yellow birds.'" While Smoky spoke, the sea monster's dark eyes glittered, and it slapped the water giddily with a huge talon. "Just like in the movies."

"Riiight," I said. "That won't sound suspicious to anyone listening." Like Neon Sign.

Smoky nodded vigorously.

"Okay, well, there's a more pressing issue," I said. "You can't attack any Ohrist I bring in to help."

Smoky gave an off-the-cuff laugh. "Impossible."

I crossed my arms. "Do the three angels force you to attack Ohrists or is this your initiative?"

The monster sank under the waves, and Smoky floated up to the ceiling like it was fascinated by the stalactites.

"That's what I thought. I get that you don't have a lot of opportunity to take out your frustrations, but attacking people who want to help is not conducive to the bigger picture."

Smoky pouted.

"Do you or do you not want to be free?"

"I do," it said sulkily.

"Good." I beamed my best mom-approval smile. "You can show me how great you are at restraint when I bring the wolf shifter in here. Hopefully tomorrow. Count it as practice."

Smoky was again all up in my personal space. "Wolf is abomination," it roared. "It sullies Banim Shovavim magic with Ohrist."

I raised an eyebrow. "Wow. Now you're sounding as

closed-minded as three other someones."

"Am not."

"Yes, you are." I shook my head sadly. "I thought you were better than them, but maybe this is too much for you to handle. Maybe you aren't the grown-up sea monster that you seem to be." I spun around like there was a door I could march out.

Smoky zipped in front of me, blocking my way. "I am a grown-up."

I shrugged and clasped my hands on my chest, as if I wanted to agree with Smoky but circumstances were preventing me. "Then prove it."

"I never get to have any fun," the Leviathan grumbled, slapping its tail against the water.

Before I could get out of the splash zone, an exit opened to my living room. I darted through and closed the door, just as tons of water crashed down behind me.

What a day. Mom-ing supernatural creatures could be *such* a pain in the ass.

Sadly, Saturday didn't start off any better. Laurent showed up before I'd finished my first cup of coffee. He'd already run about five kilometers from his place to mine and wasn't even perspiring as he jogged in place on my porch.

"Aren't we visiting the Wise Brothers today?" I blew on my drink.

"Not until Zev delivers the painting. We will use the time to train."

I took another sip, making an exaggerated sound of pleasure and hoping he'd get the hint that now was the time for caffeination, not torture.

The stubborn shifter badgered me until I threw on some workout clothes.

"You know," I said casually, tying the laces of my sneakers. "If you have energy to burn, I can think of much better exercise."

His brows drew together. "Better than a run?" I shot him the finger and he laughed. "Your stamina isn't where I want it."

I smiled sweetly. "Are you speaking as my boyfriend or my trainer?"

His return smile was equally as saccharine. "Take that how you will."

I put up my dukes. "Suddenly, I'm in more of a fighting mood."

"Good, because the run is the second part of our training." Whistling, he jogged into my living room and started pushing furniture aside.

"You say that like it's a reward." I eeped when he grabbed one end of the sofa. "Watch my—"

"Yes, Mitzi, I will be gentle with her. So," he said in an extremely casual voice, moving the couch to the wall, "I called Léa."

It took me a minute. "Your sister-in-law? How come?"

He rubbed a hand over the back of his neck. "I want to meet with the shifters left from my pack. The ones who stayed after I abandoned them to the stress and the violence of a sudden leadership vacuum. I owe them answers and apologies. It might never be enough but…" He shrugged.

I hugged him. "That's huge. I'm really proud of you."

He pulled away, blushing, then gave a grumpy huff. "Enough chitchat. It's time to train."

I tamped down my grin.

Once we had enough free space, Laurent drilled me in dirty fight moves. I dutifully practiced the proper finger positions to scoop out eyeballs even though the very idea made me gag. However, I enjoyed the groin and knee strikes more, and throat punching was super fun.

Laurent shook his head, giving me a wry grin when I did extra practice rounds of the latter. "I've created a monster."

"A monster who can totally punch you in the throat," I said, "so you should be nice to me and not make me run."

He kissed the tip of my nose, the only part of me that wasn't sweaty. "Nice try."

Sadie had deigned to wake up since it was almost noon. I marveled—and despaired—at her ability to sleep through anything. She glanced into the living room, muttered "Nope," and trundled into the kitchen.

Laurent accompanied me upstairs while I grabbed a hoodie for the dreaded run. The lid of my jewelry box on the dresser by the door was open, and he did a double-take, his face contorted in a horrified grimace.

I shrugged into my sweater. "What?"

He held up a tiny clear plastic box, shaking it and making the contents rattle. "Are these trophies from a spree of killings?"

"Would that be a deal breaker?" I snatched the box away.

"I'm not sure," he said, peering at it. "But really. What is that?"

"Sadie's baby teeth. And the wisdoms she had pulled when she was twelve." I dropped it back in my jewelry box and firmly shut the lid.

"You keep these mouth rejects like some kind of offering?"

"They're mementos."

His eyebrows lifted well into his forehead and he raised his hands mollifyingly. "That is what serial killers say."

I patted his cheek as I swept out of my bedroom. "Then don't tempt me to add to the collection."

In retaliation, the mean, mean man hustled me out the door for our run. I locked up, before tossing my keys into a small backpack, along with a water bottle and a granola bar.

We headed over to Queen Elizabeth Park, a jewel of a place popular with brides and tourists located near my home, and Laurent led me onto one of the trails in the woods. This wouldn't be too bad since these paths were designed for leisurely strolls, and with all the tree cover, they weren't too muddy considering the rainfall earlier.

Laurent flung off his shirt and shoes, placing them under a bush.

"You're sending incredibly mixed messages about this next part," I said, my eyes widening as his shorts hit the ground. "Oh, commando. Nice."

A stripe of fur bloomed down his spine.

"Hang on, you're shift—" I winced at the crunch of breaking, morphing bones. I didn't hear anyone else nearby, and Laurent would be able to scent them long before someone showed up, but what exactly was the plan here?

Clamping my hands over my ears to drown out the worst of his transformation, I kept my eyes closed until a cold wolfy nose nudged my belly.

My boyfriend trotted back and forth on four legs, his tongue lolling out of his mouth, while I considered the life choices that had led me here.

"Not seeing the fun part, Huff 'n' Puff."

He nosed me again, and when I didn't move, butted me with his shoulder.

"I can't keep up with you when you're two-legged, never mind four."

The wolf butted me again then sat back on his haunches expectantly. When I still didn't get it, he gave a very French and annoyed sigh, then he growled at me, baring his canines.

I stumbled backward. "What is your problem?"

He stalked me.

"Oh no." I shook my head. "I am not being prey for you to chase. I mean, we can definitely circle back to that idea for sexy role-play time, but not here. What happens if your wolf side takes over and you eat me? And not in a good way. You be prey and I'll catch you."

The dumb animal snorted and shot me a look of "Fine, we'll do this your way." He turned tail and ran off.

Mentally berating myself for letting him set the pace, I raced after him, following flashes of white through the trees. I lasted about five minutes before yelling out that I couldn't go that fast.

Either he was so far ahead that he didn't hear me with his enhanced abilities, or he was ignoring me. Conscious that I did need to build my stamina, I went as fast as I could sustain, which was slightly better than speed walking.

When I finally found Laurent, he was dozing in a patch of sunlight. The wolf made a big show of stretching and yawning, waiting for me to catch up to him.

"Tortoise and the hare, wise ass." I chugged from my water bottle. "Slow and steady."

He barked at me, but I shrugged. "Sorry, I don't speak wolf. If you want to shift and speak to me, go right ahead."

The animal held my gaze in challenge.

"Since I have your undivided attention," I said, "how about a different game?"

He immediately sat down and thumped his tail.

I put on a bright smile. "It's called Laurent Goes through the KH with Me to Visit the Wise Brothers and Comes Out Unharmed."

The fur on his body bristled and he growled, but I wasn't afraid.

"It won't be the same as last time," I said. "Besides, it's faster than a plane, which you hate anyway, and I swear nothing will happen to you."

He shot me a long-suffering look, then dropped his head in acquiescence.

"Excellent." I paused. "Could you shift so we could talk about Zev and your dad?"

Just over the copse of trees came the excited chatter of kids' voices.

The wolf perked up a furry ear then charged in their direction.

Hiding behind children? Brat. I drank more water, flinching at a child's shriek. He wouldn't have hurt one, even inadvertently, right? Jamming the cap on with a curse, I sprinted in that direction, burning sweat dripping into my eyes.

Laurent sat at the tree line. Two moms, both pushing strollers with babies in them, kept their other five- or six-year-olds from going apeshit over the big animal.

"Is the dog yours?" one mom said. "Is it safe to pet?"

"Mr. Fluffington is a sweetheart," I said. "He adores kids."

The wolf's eyes narrowed, promising payback, but he didn't bite any fingers off as three screaming children rushed him. He was incredibly patient with their attention and even played a game of fetch with them.

I stood with one of the mothers and a reticent girl, watching Laurent with a fuzzy, warm feeling.

"He's very well trained," the mom said.

"He has his moments."

The little girl pointed. "He's as big as a wolf."

"Well, he's mostly mutt," I said, knowing that Laurent could hear me, "but he is part Russian wolf."

The other munchkins overheard her and growled at Laurent in glee. He twitched his ears and shot me a look to get him out of this.

Eh.

"Really?" The mom studied him.

"Oh yeah. Bit of an inbred species but strong like a bull. Or wolf, as the case might be."

One of the munchkins pet him a little too forcefully, and the wolf swung his head my way, glowering.

I stifled a grin. "Okay." I strode over, clapping my hands. "Mr. Fluffington has had enough excitement for today. Thanks, kids."

Chorusing goodbye, they headed back to their moms.

"Did you like that, Mr. Fluffington?" I cooed, unwrapping

a cheese stick I'd brought. Sadie had never outgrown her love of the snack and we always had them on hand.

He whined at me.

"This is mine. Go hunt a mouse or something." I yelped, because he'd snatched the cheese out of my hand and swallowed it in one gulp. "Hilarious. I'm going home without my snack." I placed a hand to my forehead theatrically. "If I fall to the ground in starvation, just leave me there. My body will eventually decompose and I'll be one with nature."

With that, I pivoted on my heel and marched off.

Laurent caught up to me before I'd even left the park, fully dressed and human again. We walked in silence for a bit.

"Thanks for attempting the KH again," I said. "It's important, not just for this Wise Brothers visit, but I'll explain why at the Bear's Den."

"Is it connected to what happened with Poe?" His intel no longer surprised me. Much.

"Not exactly."

"I'll give you this, but, Mitzi?" He shook his head. "There's nothing more to discuss about my father, okay?"

I nodded, though this was clearly a hot-button issue for him. Maybe it would be better to ease him into the topic once he'd gotten through the anniversary of Delphine's death. I slid my hand into his. "Do you want me to stay with you on Monday or would you prefer to be alone?"

"I'd like to be with you, but not because of Delphine's passing." He raised our intertwined hands and kissed my knuckles.

My insides melted into a goopy puddle. "You got it."

Let's see. My stamina was still pretty crap, our KH venture might not pan out so great if the Leviathan couldn't restrain itself, and I had yet to break the news of unraveling the three angels, but the quiet contentment Laurent and I shared brightened this overcast day. Sometimes the little things mattered more than the big ones.

10

———

Laurent texted me when I was getting out of the shower to say that one of Zev's minions had delivered the Dantora painting. I drove over to Hotel Terminus after an important stop, snickering to myself. In retaliation for Laurent inhaling my cheese stick, I'd purchased a "Mr. Fluffington Lives Here" sign with a cartoon picture of a dog on it at a local sign shop. It was worth every penny of the rush job.

Once the sign was nice and secure on the front lawn of the property, I strolled over to the side door and knocked.

Laurent's welcoming smile turned to a narrowing of his eyes. "Why do you look so pleased with yourself?"

I stuffed my hands in my trouser pockets. "I survived the run and I won't have to be a contestant on a messed-up game show to get answers."

He didn't totally buy it, but he didn't push, and I managed not to smirk. He'd see the sign soon enough.

The Dantora painting *In Pursuit of Wisdom* was carefully wrapped so I didn't get to examine it, though it was smaller than I expected.

"Hiram and Ephraim agreed to a straight trade?" I crossed my fingers.

"I couldn't get hold of them, but the art broker they've been working with assured me they were very interested in acquiring the piece. I figured we'd do the negotiations in person."

Even with a strong hand, any dealings with the Wise Brothers would take champion-level poker faces, strategy, and luck. The sooner this visit was over with, the better.

I stepped into a shadow, holding out my hand at Laurent's hesitation. "I'm not asking you to blindly trust me this time. I've arranged safe passage." I better have or our relationship was going to hit some serious rocky ground.

Tucking the artwork under one arm, Laurent took my hand and we stepped through. His grip tightened for the long moment where the ground turned spongey, and his lids were screwed shut. While he opened his eyes when we arrived in the cave, his body remained stiff and tense.

Pyotr was watering his plant Scarlet, but upon seeing us, the gargoyle's eyes widened, and he watered his foot instead of the plant. Shaking his leg to cast off the droplets, he shooed Laurent away. "Go. Quickly."

Smoky popped into view, and Pyotr ducked under his rickety table, his wings and lower half sticking out.

Laurent jutted his chin up, but he remained in human form, and I gave a relieved sigh.

"We good?" I said to the phantom.

Smoky eyed us, weighing its decision.

The neon sign lit up with a jaunty *ping* and I tensed. I hadn't brought the ring that Dumah gave me because we were merely transiting, but the last time Laurent had come through, it had gone haywire. Even though its glow was steady and calm, as an agent of the KH, would it object to the shifter's presence?

What do you call a wolf with a fever?

I groaned. "No one invited you to this party," I admonished.

A hot dog.

Though still human, Laurent's snarl was very wolflike. The neon sign flashed us its smirking face. Great. It was going to kill us with puns.

Smoky dissolved into a puff and then another puff as if the Leviathan itself was snorting repeatedly in protest for letting Laurent through, but the narrow green door opened in the far wall, so I grabbed a sock and we bolted.

The skeleton face followed us along the path, my boyfriend darting glances back at it every few seconds and muttering under his breath in French, while the neon sign flicked on at regular intervals to torment us with more horrible jokes.

What do you call a wolf that you have trouble finding? A where wolf. Which animal has four legs, howls at the moon, and wears glasses? A wolf. I added glasses to fool you.

Between the muttering, the stalking, and the bad jokes, my patience grew thinner and thinner.

I spun around. "Enough!"

Laurent, Smoky, and the Neon Sign froze.

I jerked a thumb at the sign. "You. Get lost."

It pixelated a tongue to stick out at me and vanished.

Next, I rounded on Smoky. "You, stop menacing."

It bared its razor-sharp teeth at me but also disappeared.

"And you." I pressed a kiss to Laurent's mouth. "Relax. I've got this covered."

"Mmm. Should I be worried about how?"

"Not till later," I said cheerfully. "Oh, look. There's the exit. LA, here we come."

We were far calmer than the last time we'd shown up at the Wise Brothers' Lair of Lore and Learning and our magic was intact. Very important differences. Still, the two of us slowed down as we approached the bookstore, located on the ground floor of an older three-story apartment building with cedar shingles painted a faded purple. My librarian side once more recoiled at the windows jammed with piles of books with no rhyme or reason, their covers bleached by the sun.

Laurent opened the door to the chime of a tinkly bell, and we stepped inside. I inhaled, breathing in the scent of sun-warmed paper, old glue, and linseed oil from the dozens of crowded wooden bookshelves forming narrow aisles. Dust motes danced through sunbeams that made the tarnished bronze chandelier glitter, and an elderly dog with mottled gray and tan fur and a sweet face looked up from the thread-bare Persian rug with cloudy eyes.

It was kind of perfect.

The dog growled at Laurent, who quirked an eyebrow at the mutt. Instead of the dog submitting to an alpha, it growled harder.

"Theo!" The lone employee snapped his fingers, but when the dog didn't stop growling, he grabbed the dog's collar and coaxed him behind the small glass counter. "Sorry about that. He's usually chill."

His owner was chill too, with chin-length blond surfer hair, loose board shorts, and a floral-printed button-up short-sleeved shirt.

"Are Hiram or Ephraim around?" Laurent said.

"Who?" The man cracked open a roll of quarters and dumped them in the open cash drawer of the old-fashioned metal register, which occupied most of the space on the counter. The rest was taken up by a large travel mug and a stack of books on WWII.

"The owners," Laurent said.

"I'm the owner." He slammed the drawer shut.

Did one of them have a son who was part of the business? "You're one of the Wise Brothers? Is this the Lair of Lore and Learning?"

The man grinned sheepishly. "I always wanted to run away and join the circus, so I figured I'd give the name a carny feel."

"Look, we know Hiram and Ephraim Wise, and we don't have time to be jerked around." Laurent set the wrapped painting on top of the books. "Just tell them we have something they're interested in."

"I'm sorry, man, but I have no idea who those people are." Fake Owner tucked his hair behind his ear. "Like I said, I made up the name."

I animated Delilah, making her pounce on the counter in front of the owner, but he didn't flinch or recognize her existence at all.

He gave us a friendly smile. "Anything else I can help you with?"

There was no trace of dybbuk inside him.

"Yeah, one other thing." Laurent retrieved the painting, headed for the door. "Could you point the way to Ventura Boulevard?"

"No problem." Fake Owner stepped outside with us, coffee mug in hand, rattled off a set of directions, then retreated into the store.

Laurent glanced up at the bright sun. "Not a vamp."

"Not a demon either," I said. "Unless he's also a brilliant actor because he didn't react at all to Delilah. Which begs the question of what the hell is going on?"

Stumped, we returned through the KH to Hotel Terminus. There were no issues, though Neon Sign kept appearing to shake its head at us.

Boo scampered over to me when we stepped through into Laurent's place, and I picked up the cat, cuddling her against my chest, while my boyfriend contacted the art broker.

His side of the call didn't sound encouraging, and he hung up with a frown. "My contact hasn't heard directly from them in a couple of weeks."

Boo tilted her head up, directing me with her paw to the precise spot under her jaw I was to scratch. Bossy cat.

It was a good distraction from the mild ache in my stomach. Were Hiram and Ephraim alive or had they crossed the wrong person, their fate to be erased from the face of the earth? The Wise Brothers' form of quid pro quo was cruel, yet Hiram was a fellow Banim Shovavim. There were so few of us, plus he and Ephraim, an Ohrist, had a tender relationship, and I didn't want to see them hurt.

"How did you find out that Hiram was interested in this painting?" I said.

"I dug into them after we met." Laurent set the painting on the dining room table.

"Looking for leverage?"

"To put it politely." He shifted one hand to claws and carefully tore through the first layer of wrapping. "I discovered that Hiram and Ephraim had a private art collection. The art brokerage firm working for them gave me a heads-up a couple weeks ago about Hiram's interest."

I slid the string out from under the painting and tossed it to Boo, who immediately tussled with it. "Did you do a job for someone there? Why'd they share that information?"

"Everyone has their price."

I forgot that Laurent had money. How rich he was remained a mystery that I was happy to leave unsolved because our income disparity would feel weird.

He removed the last of the packaging and I leaned in.

In Pursuit of Wisdom portrayed a tableau of an escritoire, its cubby holes stuffed with rolled-up sheafs. The desk sat by a window whose delicate lace curtains were open to the night beyond. Half-melted candles on porcelain holders covered in wax splotches bathed the scene in an intimate glow while a fountain pen tipped with dark ink rested on an open manuscript, its rough cream-colored pages partially filled with scribblings.

"It's so evocative," I said, ghosting a finger over the fine brushstrokes. "Like the author is just beyond this frame, getting more ink."

We appreciated it in silence for a few moments, then Laurent frowned. "It wasn't hard for me to find out that Toledano had this painting," he said, "and he just handed it over, so it's not like he was averse to selling it if he'd been asked."

"Hiram and Ephraim didn't contact him then," I said. "Did someone or something get to them before they could ask Zev?"

Laurent drummed his fingers on the table. "Check the painting with Delilah's vision."

It took me all of two seconds in her vision to see a hidden image and jerk back with my hands thrown up. "Jesus! There's a face in the window."

My boyfriend immediately flipped the artwork facedown on the table. "What kind of face?"

"It's in shadow so I can't identify it, or tell if it's even human, but its eyes are wide and the mouth is open as if crying out in pain. And…" I wrapped my arms around myself. "I swear it saw me."

Nav once told me that one reason Jews covered their mirrors while they sat shiva was because demons and evil spirits are attracted to grief, to an emptiness in the soul. Not that I was in mourning right now, but nothing good came from shadowy sentient figures sussing me out.

Laurent had already wrapped the piece up and was halfway across the large space to the elevator where he chained up the dybbuk-possessed. There was the sound of the doors closing, then he was back at my side, examining my eyes. "Do you feel strange in any way?"

"No. Just freaked out. What if that thing got Hiram and Ephraim?"

"Or if that's why they wanted the piece," he said.

"Why did Zev happen to have it? Can he see the face?" I was already dialing the master vampire, but the call went to voice mail, so I left a message asking to speak to him as soon as possible.

Laurent said he'd check in with his contact at the brokerage firm and offered to pick me up tonight and drive me to the speakeasy. I'd been hoping to lubricate the news of unraveling the angels by plying Tatiana and Laurent with booze, and Emmett with enough sugar to amp up a woolly mammoth, but maybe it was better if I was the one who could drink.

I accepted the offer.

Jittery over how the night would unfold, I barely ate dinner, and changed outfits four times before settling on an indigo jumpsuit with a deep V-neck. I pulled my curls back with sparkly combs, swiped gold shadow over my lids, and finished it off with some pale pink lip gloss.

Since Caleb was hanging out with Sadie, there was an odd moment of introducing my boyfriend to my daughter's boyfriend, especially when Caleb took one look at Laurent, all badass in dark Parisian casualwear, and adopted the same broody stance, which didn't quite play the same with his Rubik's Cube T-shirt.

The fanboyness got worse when Laurent invited him out to see his motorcycle, Caleb practically skipping behind him, telling him all about the bike he planned to get one day.

I'd stayed in the foyer to grab the leather jacket I'd bought specifically for these rides and find closed-toe shoes. "No riding motorcycles until you're thirty," I teased Sadie, who stood in the doorway watching them.

She frowned and turned away, heading for the living room.

"Hey. What's wrong?"

She shook her head. "Do you ever wonder if Dad hadn't come out, whether your marriage would have survived all the magic stuff?"

I zipped up my ankle boots. "I was so busy hiding from

anything magic that it becoming a problem didn't occur to me. But honestly? I don't know."

"I mean, I don't want to marry Caleb or break up with him, but do I only have to date Ohrists?"

I ruffled her hair. "Date whoever you like. If you decide to get serious with a Sapien, then you tell them. Marriages are allowed and partners can know. Is that what you're worried about?"

She bit her bottom lip, her gaze on her feet. "I really screwed up."

"With Caleb?"

"Tovah. I've been thinking about it a lot."

Laurent was still occupied showing Caleb his bike, so I stayed with my daughter.

"Yeah, I imagine you have been. The two of you seemed to click."

"Totally. She was really cool and talking about magic was just a bonus." She picked at a loose thread on her hem. "I wish I could tell Caleb everything, but I've accepted that I can't. It's just that I see you with Laurent and it seems nice not to have to hide a big part of yourself."

"It is." I gently tilted her chin up. "How do you think you could have that?"

"Do you think…" She gnawed on a cuticle. "If I apologized to Ava and Romi about Blood Alley, would they help me talk to Tovah's parents and convince them to let me be friends with her again?" My friend Ava, owner of Stay in Your Lane bowling alley, and her wife Romi, were Tovah's aunts.

I'd expected Sadie to suggest meeting other Ohrists, not take this level of responsibility for her actions. My awesome kid had given me a lot of reasons to be proud of her, but this newfound maturity rocketed to the top.

"I think they absolutely would."

Sadie nodded and blew out a breath. "Okay." She skipped

over to the door. "Caleb," she called out, "I'm restarting the movie."

He waved at her. "Coming, Sparky."

When we passed on the front walk, he told me to have a nice night. My happiness that Sadie had a great first love was tempered because he was cut out of an important part of her life.

When I reached Laurent, he handed me a helmet then ran his hands over the collar of my jacket, lingering on my hips. "Nice, but I like you better in my jacket."

I curled my toes under. "I like you better in yours."

"Then I wouldn't want to deprive you." He checked that my straps were properly adjusted then kissed me.

The connection that came from being with someone for a long time was a sturdy anchor, appreciated all the more for having weathered the currents of a relationship, but I'd missed the potent headiness of a new relationship. That giddy rush of constant flirtation and desire flamed hot and tight inside me.

His own helmet securely on, he swung a leg over the bike.

I sat down behind him and wrapped my arms around his waist, snuggling closer than I'd ever allowed myself, my cheek resting against his leather jacket.

There was nothing like the rush of motoring through the city on the back of a bike. I still got nervous flutters in my stomach and screwed my eyes shut every time Laurent leaned the bike too far to one side, but my senses were at full throttle. The red of an awning I'd passed a million times was suddenly a brilliant bloom against the night sky, while every flex and bunch of Laurent's muscles was the beat of a booming timpani over the constant percussion of vibrations shuddering up through the bike.

This was the first time I'd ridden on the motorcycle since we'd committed to our relationship, and by the time Laurent parked in the lot where the speakeasy was hidden, I was ready to tell him to turn it around and take me to his place.

He laughed at me when I scrambled off the motorcycle. "Getting handsy on the ride there, Mitzi. You made it very hard to focus."

I licked my lips, a shiver dancing through me, and stepped back. Fun later. Angel unraveling talk now. "Right. I have something important to discuss."

"Then I shall pay close attention." After quickly locking up the bike, he grabbed my waist and rocked into me.

I moaned and reached for his jacket, but my fists closed on empty air.

Laurent was no longer in front of me and smiling hungrily down, but on the ground, fighting barbed shadows that swooped over him like liquid glass.

I swung around. Shadows commanded by another person. I knew that trick.

And sure enough, there was a scarred man in Mad Max-esque clothing made of strips of leather and gray cloth controlling the shadows. A man who had just stepped out of a doorway in the parkade.

A doorway that hadn't been there before he'd exited.

A doorway from a place that could take you anywhere you wanted.

The Kefitzat Haderech.

Our assailant was Banim Shovavim.

11

I SWUNG MY SHADOW SCYTHE AT MY OPPONENT, BUT it dissolved into wisps, as did Delilah.

Laurent struggled to his feet, his face and hands scratched up, but luckily, his leather jacket took the brunt of the injuries. He used his wolf claws to attack the shadows biting into him. "Run," he growled at me.

I wasn't leaving without him. The garage was filled with regular shadows that would get us back into the KH, and yes, the Banim Shovavim could follow, but I had Smoky on my side. I backed up but every time I stepped into an escape shadow, it moved out of range.

The attacker prowled closer.

My back hit the parking garage wall. Nowhere to run, my magic wouldn't stay corporeal, and there was nothing to throw at him. "Why are you doing this? We're the same."

He held up a hand, barbed shadows curled around it like a mace, and swung.

Screaming, I ducked, the weapon whistling overhead to slam into the concrete wall. While he yanked it free, I jumped on his back and slammed my fist into his throat. It would have been more powerful as a front strike, but it caught the assailant off guard.

The barbed shadows disappeared, the man coughing and spinning around to dislodge me. I hit him again and again until he crumpled to his knees and I was thrown off.

I scrambled to my feet and kicked him in the ribs, knocking him prone onto the ground. "Booyah, motherfucker!"

Laurent pounced on the Banim Shovavim, his eyes feral, and raked a claw across the man's chest.

On a lower level of the parking garage, a car beeped, and I jerked my head up. We had to get out of the open.

"Don't kill him." I punched the elevator button and the doors slid open.

Laurent dragged our attacker into the car and slammed him up against the wall, his claws digging into the man's bruised throat. "Who sent you?"

"Kill me," he rasped. "It doesn't matter. We saw you and more will come."

Laurent furrowed his brows. "Saw me?"

The man looked at me then his eyes rolled back in his head, and he went limp.

Laurent caught him. "He's still breathing."

I depressed the broken payphone switch hook twice to enter the Bear's Den.

Vikram took one look at us, sighed, and hit a wall panel, which swung open to reveal a hidden room. I flinched, but concern, not anger, marred his features. "Inside," he said. "I'll get Tatiana and Emmett."

One wall of the small space held a green metal cabinet, sorted into multiple slots with first aid supplies like bandages, gauze, ointments, and hot and cold packs.

The moment that Laurent lay the unconscious man on the narrow cot, my adrenaline rush left me, and I crashed onto the lone plastic chair.

I stuffed my trembling hands into my armpits. "The painting."

"Quoi?" Laurent washed blood off his now-human hands in the stainless-steel sink.

"'We saw you.' That face in the painting. I'm sure that's how they tracked me."

He dried his hands off and tossed the paper towel in the trash. "Who is 'they'?"

I had no idea, but they were coming for me. I shook my head, my teeth chattering.

Laurent patted the man down, but he had no identification. "Help me get his jacket off so I can check for any identifying marks."

I wrestled the injured man out of his shredded jacket, frowning at the Hebrew letters tattooed on his uninjured pec. "Do you know what that says?"

"No. Try searching online for it."

The task kept me focused enough to stay calm until Tatiana and Emmett arrived.

Emmett shook his head at the injured man. "No wonder Vikram handed us that booze."

My boss swore in Russian and pressed shot glasses into both Laurent's and my hands.

I slammed mine back, the vodka a smooth, sharp burn.

Emmett kneaded my shoulders as Tatiana fired questions at us. She was horrified to hear about the missing Wise Brothers and the painting, but she didn't have any ideas on who the unconscious man worked for. The fact that he was Banim Shovavim threw her for a loop.

"Wait. He has a tattoo," I said. "It's in Hebrew, which is doubly weird because Jews aren't supposed to ink themselves. Not that he has to be Jewish to be Banim Shovavim." I was babbling.

Tatiana frowned as she read the letters. "Shad-dai. That's written on the backs of mezuzahs, from the letters shin, dalet, and yud. But what significance does it have here as a tattoo?"

Puzzle solving. I could do that. I hit the web. "Apparently, it's an acronym for 'Shomer Daltot Yisrael' or Guardian of the Gates of Israel. Kabbalists believe that the letters shin and dalet form the word 'sheid' for demon, so writing 'shad-dai' wards off the forces of evil." I rested my phone in my lap.

"You're not evil," Emmett teased. "Mildly annoying some-times, but nowhere near demon-shield level."

"It still doesn't explain who this guy is with or why he attacked." Laurent rummaged through the supplies. "But there's one way to find out." He cracked the cap on a small glass bottle, the smell of ammonia filling the air, and waved it under the man's nose.

Our assailant's eyes fluttered open and he touched his battered throat with a hiss.

I smiled coldly, leaning over him. "Tell us who sent you or my friend will rip your balls off."

Laurent helpfully shifted a hand to claws again, waggling them.

Our target turned an interesting shade of green but refused to answer, placing his back to us.

Laurent raised his eyebrows in question at me, and I shook my head. We'd have to find a different motivation.

"Did you find a wallet?" Tatiana said.

"You that hard up for cash?" Emmett cracked a cold pack, placed it on his own head, and shivered. "Brain freeze," he said gleefully.

Okay, weirdo.

"Identification," Laurent replied. "And no, I didn't, but there's a phone in the left pocket."

The man didn't react to us handling his personal property, still stonewalling us.

Tatiana removed it from the jacket that was tossed on the chair. "You think people could disconnect when they go on a hit, but no. Humanity is in a sad state." She tried to open it with facial recognition, even going so far as to have Emmett pry the man's eyes open, but it didn't work. Nor did forcing his thumb against the home key.

To be fair, I had the same problem with mine.

"It's time to visit the foremost authority on Banim Shovavim," I said.

"Who's that?" Laurent said. "The Leviathan?"

"The what?" Tatiana smacked her forehead. "Oy vey."

Wait until I told her about the angels.

"No. If you needed to know what was going on at the law firm, you didn't go to the senior partners, you went to the executive assistant, the gatekeeper."

"Pyotr," Emmett said.

"Exactly." I prodded the stranger. "Get up." When he refused to move, I sighed and motioned to Emmett.

When the man fought back, the golem shot me a hopeful look. At my nod, Emmett decked him with a clay fist. That made the guy compliant enough to be hauled up and dragged into a shadow.

"Back in a sec." I jumped the three of us into the KH, where Emmett immediately let go of the attacker to do a complicated handshake with Pyotr, the likes of which I hadn't seen since Sadie was in seventh grade.

The Banim Shovavim stumbled into a low part of the cave and whacked his head, then woozily crashed onto his butt on the large rock containing the socks.

Pyotr urgently motioned me over.

"Yes?"

He leaned his large stone head close and whispered, "Why you with bad man?"

Good, he did know him. "He attacked me. What's his deal?"

Pyotr glanced around the cave and bit his bottom lip. "Big boss," he called out. "Must speak privately."

All of us were whisked to the Leviathan's grotto, where I got the lowdown. It made my mind reel.

After asking the Leviathan for an update on Dumah's prison and learning the magic fortification was about halfway complete, I left the Banim Shovavim with the sea monster to do as he pleased.

I returned to my friends, wondering if time was running out to unravel the angels or if it was on our side. I'd been working on the premise that when the three angels completed fortifications on Dumah's prison, they'd be spread thin and maxed out in terms of their magic, but what if it gave them a secure place to retreat to when we attacked?

"Drinks first," I said in answer to their questions. Not only did I have to still share news of the unraveling plan, the information I'd just learned about the Banim Shovavim was enough on its own to warrant booze.

Tatiana flung open the door and marched across the speakeasy to her favorite banquette, which was occupied by four men, their muscles straining the fabric of their dark suit jackets. "Move."

A bearded man gave an ugly laugh and elbowed his neighbor. "Yeah, right."

The biggest and baldest one stood up, motioning for his seatmates to stay calm. "You always do this, Tatiana. Look, the booth right there is empty. If you don't want that one, we'll be done in a little while."

My boss stood on tiptoe and leaned into Baldy's face. "I like this one, Matteo."

Two servers were already moving the meals to the new table, while Vikram presented the men with a nice bottle of wine.

Bearded Guy batted Vikram's arm away. "Put the old bitch in her place."

Oy vey. I motioned at Harry, the gargoyle tending bar, to pour me a drink. Whatever paired well with bloodshed.

Emmett, bouncing on his toes, swung his head to Tatiana, and Laurent pressed his lips together, his shoulders shaking.

Tatiana gave Bearded Guy a crocodile smile.

Matteo hauled his companion out of his seat. "We'd be happy to move."

At the other man's curse-laden protests, Matteo murmured, "Remember Jacob?" and jerked his chin at Tatiana. The color drained from Bearded Guy's face, and he scrambled into the new booth so fast, he knocked over a water glass, mopping the spill up with a napkin and apologizing to Tatiana for any inconvenience.

My boss settled herself at the banquette like a queen, reacting to the blatant inquisitive stares about this Jacob from Laurent, Emmett, and me with a shrug. "A mishap."

Vikram snorted, not backing down at Tatiana's eyebrow raise. That bear shifter had balls, which he further demonstrated by scowling at her. "You know," he said, "my life would be much easier if you'd let me permanently reserve this table for you."

"There's no need." Tatiana snapped her fingers, and yet another server handed her a dirty martini, along with a gin and tonic for me. "Everyone can use it."

Laurent barked a laugh, and I almost smiled because this interlude had made me steady enough to share what Emmett and I had learned from Pyotr.

"That Banim Shovavim was a hunter."

Tatiana coughed, spitting her half-chewed olive onto the table, and Laurent's eyes bugged comically out of his head.

I held up my water glass. "L'chaim."

Emmett clinked his against it.

Flippancy was the only way I could process this horrific treachery, but honestly, it's not like the other Banim Shovavim I'd met were famed for their strong moral stances. My list included my parents (petty criminals), Frances Rothstein (assassin), Hiram Wise (manipulative trickster), and now this hunter. Oh, there was Pyotr's friend Malorie who gave him books, but she was the exception.

Were I prone to fatalistic thinking, I'd say that as Lilith's descendants, we were more susceptible to the darker side of human behavior, further evidenced by our shadow magic. Except at that point, I might as well accept the schmuck trio's views on my kind as fact.

Fuck that. I rejected mazel and I rejected any thinking that Banim Shovavim were inherently bad or flawed. We were what we made of ourselves, but damn, did I wish I had more examples like Malorie on that list.

Tatiana crumpled her partially masticated olive in her napkin. "Are you positive about him being a hunter?"

"Yes. The proof is that Hebrew tattoo. They all have them. Banim Shovavim hunters are super rare, thank goodness, but they do exist."

"That's impressive self-loathing," Laurent said.

"It wouldn't have happened without the trio's brainwashing that we're all horrible people," I said hotly.

He held up his hands. "I don't disagree."

"Sorry." I sighed. "I just can't fathom hunting my own kind."

"Why not?" Emmett crunched some ice from his 7UP. "You've done it before." He shrugged off my glare. "Frances Rothstein?"

"I wasn't hunting her to kill her," I said waspishly. "It's not the same thing and you know it."

He shrugged and I ground my teeth together.

Tatiana wagged a finger at him. "Stop provoking. Miriam is right."

"Did the hunters get the Wise Brothers?" Laurent said.

I shook my head. "Doubtful. The man at their bookstore believed what he said about making up the name. If hunters got Hiram and Ephraim, all they had to do was close the bookstore, not make up some elaborate story where the Wise Brothers never existed."

Laurent ate the orange garnish served with his juice, refusing any more alcohol after that one shot earlier since he was driving. "It just raises more red flags."

"It's quite brilliant actually." Tatiana tapped her head. "If I feared hunters were closing in, I'd cause as much confusion as possible to cover my tracks."

Hiram and Ephraim being responsible for their own disappearance was the best-case scenario, but if we couldn't trade the painting for information, it didn't help us find the vampire Imogine. Zev couldn't locate her, Tatiana's informants had nothing—the Wise Brothers were our only hope. Except I had no idea how to root them out.

Yet.

"Moving on." I stirred my drink. "The Banim Shovavim confirmed that I'd been found via that painting. Hunters implanted a number of artifacts with magic tracking devices over the years for that very purpose."

Laurent swore under his breath.

Emmett looked intrigued until someone kicked him under the table and he muttered, "That's awful."

"How did you get him to talk?" Tatiana said.

"Let's just say that sea monsters and waterboarding are a very persuasive combination."

"Interesting," she murmured.

Emmett snickered. He was spending way too much time with her.

"I wonder if Hiram was collecting these artifacts." Laurent sipped his orange juice. "Or if Toledano was." He placed his hand on my jittering leg. "Why are you so nervous?"

"Well..." I took another big slug of my drink for fortification. "Hunters were founded by the three angels Senoi, Sansenoi, and Sammaneglof. While they were pretty hands-off after they started the hunters, those humans got exceedingly creative in finding and killing Banim Shovavim to please their celestial masters. Who knows what other devices I might come across?"

Tatiana narrowed her eyes. "Is that what the summons in Vegas was about? It was from the angels?"

"Not exactly," I said.

A muscle ticked in Laurent's jaw.

I pried his hand off my thigh. "The three weren't the ones summoning me. That was a different angel." I paused. "Dumah."

"As in Gehenna Dumah?" The edge in Laurent's voice made me squirm.

"Got it in one!" I flashed him a thumbs-up. "But Dumah doesn't want to hurt me. We had a very nice chat in the Courtyard of Death—"

Flowers all across the speakeasy exploded into petals, stems, and multiple disparate parts, sending customers and staff into a tizzy.

"You went *into* Gehenna? Your conversation didn't take place with the angel on its side and you on yours?" Tatiana's tone was deceptively calm. If I wasn't spitting out rose petals that had blown into my mouth from the vase on the table, I'd have said this chat was going swimmingly.

Laurent wasn't even attempting to lose his sharp canines, so perhaps "swimmingly" was a stretch.

"The important thing to focus on," I said, "is that this hunter incident wasn't an order from the three angels since I need to stay under their radar until we unravel them."

Silence wasn't so much golden right now as pointy, lethal, and stomach-twisting.

A server replaced the bouquet in our vase with a fresh one made of gerbera daisies, mercifully whisking away the detritus of the poor dead flora.

Emmett shook the last few drops of soda into his mouth. "What's the plan?"

I gave him a grateful smile. "According to Dumah, the schmuck trio have so much of their magic tied to the KH that if we destroy it—"

"No!" The golem pounded the table so hard with his fist that the rest of us grabbed the rattling dinnerware.

I set a glass back down, and Vikram glared at me, pointing from his eyes to mine.

Great. Emmett causes the damage and I'm the one the big bad bear shifter eyed warningly. "Pyotr won't be hurt and neither will the Leviathan. They'll both have plenty of time to get away, and if I can help Neon Sign, I'll do that too. I promise."

Tatiana patted his shoulder. "Trust Miriam, tattele."

He nodded reluctantly, but his outburst had drained the others' tension at my news.

"How do we destroy it?" Laurent scratched his stubbled jaw.

"Think of igniting a magic fire, but instead of oxygen, fuel, and heat to trigger a chemical reaction, we channel Ohrist and Banim Shovavim magic, amplified by the Ascendant, to set off a magic one. We need the combined force of the two types of magic amplified by the Ascendant to send a shock wave through the KH. That will nuke it and unravel the angels into sentient dust motes that will be powerless yet aware of their helpless situation for eternity."

"You've been busy," Tatiana said with a nod of approval.

Laurent tapped a finger on the table. "Don't you need the artifact to free the Leviathan?"

"The sea monster is angel-cursed," I said. "This plan is its only hope."

He nodded. "Bien. Give me the Ascendant and I'll do it."

"Do what?" I said stupidly.

"Destroy it. I have both types of magic." Laurent pushed his empty glass away with a shrug. "That's why I could travel through the KH safely, wasn't it? You cut a deal with the Leviathan to allow me there without consequence."

I crammed my mouth with ice to buy time for my reply. My admission that I hadn't considered him at all for the job—that honor was to go to me and Tatiana—wouldn't go over well. His Banim Shovavim magic was acquired, not a birthright, and I doubted it would work. It would probably be akin to a spark that quickly died out, instead of roaring to life as a full-blown blaze.

On the other hand, why damage his ego—and my chances for sex on a regular basis—when it wouldn't hurt to let him try? Worst-case scenario, we'd consider it a practice run, and if I was proven wrong and it worked, I'd happily take the loss.

I swallowed the crushed ice. "You're correct, but in case your magic combo doesn't work, we should plan for Tatiana and me to go in as backup."

Tatiana smirked, but Laurent, bless him, simply announced with alpha confidence that it wouldn't come to that. He would shift so his Ohrist magic was at its most potent and then deploy his Banim Shovavim magic.

We decided to strike in the morning after a good night's sleep, hoping that the hunters wouldn't have time to attack again. My boss informed me that afterward I was to review the information that she and Emmett had gathered on Dr. Eversol.

Her certainty that there would be an afterward was appreciated.

I was more subdued on the motorcycle ride back home. In less than twelve hours, I might finally get vengeance and closure for my parents' murders. It was almost incomprehensible. That event had ruled my life, and the fact that it could be so quickly and definitively resolved was almost anticlimactic.

Though, I suppose anticlimactic was good, given the alternative. Still, it would have been nice to look the three angels in the eyes (metaphorically) and pull an Inigo Montoya as they unraveled.

Laurent pulled up to the curb at my house, and I handed over my helmet with a quiet "Thanks."

"It's a lot, yes?" he said.

"Yeah."

He swept a lock of hair from my face and leaned in.

I closed my eyes, my lips pursed, but he bypassed my mouth to whisper in my ear.

"I saw the dog sign, Mitzi. You realize this means war."

Locking eyes with him, I grinned. "Do your worst, Mr. Fluffington."

"Oh, I will," he said arrogantly, gave me a toe-curling kiss, and drove away into the night.

12

I WAS BACK ON THE BATTLEFIELD THAT I'D SEEN while playing War with Poe, but it was a sunny day, and instead of standing in the mud I looked down on it from above.

What I'd taken for smoldering piles of rubble in the first vision became bodies. I swooped down to identify them, but I couldn't get any closer.

A raven flew past at eye level. "You're focusing on the wrong things," it croaked.

"Poe?"

It caught me in its beady-eyed gaze, then flapped a wing.

The cushion of air I'd been floating on slipped away, and I fell. I flailed my arms and legs in a pointless attempt to fly, but as I plummeted, screaming, the reason for my fears changed, because I finally identified the bodies.

All of them were me: as a child with a remnant of my favorite red headband, a teenager with one of my battered Converse overturned in the mud by my ankle, and a half dozen versions of my adult self.

I jolted awake, sweaty and twisted in my blankets, lying still, and trying to calm my racing heart while I hung on to the details of the dream. Raven shifters didn't affect dreams, but even if there was Ohrist magic that could influence them, it would still require a line of sight to the victim.

This was all me. My subconscious had taken bird form to warn me, but what was the *right* thing to focus on?

I pulled the covers up to my chin. This was not the relaxing Sunday morning I'd hoped for before the unraveling. Was this dream about that or was it about Dr. Eversol? Maybe my vision of war wasn't about a battle with the angels but one with the vampires for getting involved in their business? I wouldn't have thought so, considering I was attempting to help Gabriel find a cure for the contagion, but then again, I wouldn't have thought that a vampire would be Dr. Eversol's partner in creating the virus in the first place.

I sat up. Perhaps this dream was evidence of self-loathing? Brainwashing? A desire for vengeance?

How could I possibly focus on unraveling the angels today with all these questions poking at me like a sore tooth? My skin felt like it was poorly tailored and ill-fitting, and my insides were a mass of churning knots.

I untangled myself from the blankets and hopped in the hottest shower I could stand, unable to shake off the multiple versions of my dead self. Was this not about an external war but an internal one? Over what? I let the water run over me until I was bright red and steam wafted off my skin, but it didn't thaw my icy core.

A terrible thought hit me while I stood shivering and damp in my bedroom. The first time I'd been on that battle-field, I'd been alone except for a raven feather. This time, I'd seen multiples of my dead self, once more alone except for a raven.

I threw on some clothes for warmth. Did I keep envisioning these birds as a symbol of knowledge? I sat down on my bed, pulling on socks. What had these visions imparted?

That I was alone and dead many times over? That was so bleak.

I grabbed the ring that Dumah had given me to keep Neon Sign Face in the dark, and slid it onto my thumb before hurrying downstairs into the kitchen.

Sadie's eyes widened when she saw me. "Floral print and houndstooth. Bold choice, Mom." She squeaked as I bundled her into a hug.

"I'm going to take down the angels today," I said.

Even if everything went right, how would this change me? I hadn't considered that ramification of destroying the Kefitzat Haderech. Did the dream represent change and the death of self from one stage to another? I could handle symbolic death.

Sadie dropped the cereal box in her hand and crispy rice puffs spilled across the counter. "Already?"

"We're meeting at Tatiana's to go into the KH." I paused. "Do you want to be there?" I'd have called Eli, but he was working this weekend and Jude was out of town and off-grid at a yoga retreat.

"Obviously." She hurriedly cleaned up the cereal without eating. "Let me get dressed."

While I waited, I wrote two letters, one to Eli and one to Jude, both with essentially the same content: I loved them and look after Sadie. There wasn't time to rehash our lives together and they knew how much they meant to me, but it didn't hurt to hear it one last time.

Sadie would give them any details, and waiting for them to be available when we took down the KH wouldn't make anything easier. Meantime, I wanted my daughter by my side until the last possible second in case anything went wrong.

She took the letters without comment, placed them on her desk, then shrugged into Caleb's jean jacket that he'd left the other day. At the last moment, she grabbed Phoebe, her mini flamethrower. The weapon wouldn't help, but if she needed it as a security blanket, it wouldn't hurt either.

Our drive to Tatiana's home was tense. First thing Sadie did was shut off the radio, an unheard-of action, then she spent the rest of the ride braiding and rebraiding her hair while I swallowed a lot to moisten my dry throat and made sure we didn't get into an accident.

My boss answered her door in yoga pants and a hoodie.

I pretend to spit three times with a "pu pu pu."

"Really?" She jabbed a bony finger at me. "You wear that mismatched atrocity and have the gall to treat my outfit as evil?"

"You wouldn't wear sweats unless you thought you were all going to die." Sadie crossed her arms. "That's a total bull-shit defeatist attitude."

I placed a hand on her shoulder, but honestly, what other takeaway was there?

Tatiana snorted. "Mamele, I have a fabulous death outfit planned, and trust me, this isn't it. But the combination of your mother and magic tends to result in ruined clothing and I didn't have anything else I'm willing to sacrifice."

My child shrugged. "Fair."

"Hey!" I snapped.

"Is that Sadie?" Emmett called out. "Come in the kitchen. Marjorie made cookies last night and I'm putting tea on."

"Go," I said. "I'll join you in a minute."

She headed down the hall.

"Can I talk to you?" I motioned to the living room.

Tatiana followed me over to the sofa. "Is there a problem? Other than with your fashion choices?" She clucked her tongue. "For a brief shining moment, you showed such promise."

"I was understandably distracted. Get over it. And that's not what I want to discuss." I told her about the vision and then dream I'd had of the same battlefield.

"It's an omen." She folded a knit blanket that had been tossed on the couch cushions.

"Maybe?"

Tatiana was silent for a bit, the blanket in her lap, and a distant expression on her face. "Do you know how to be happy, Miriam?"

"What kind of a question is that? Of course I do."

"I'm sure you've been mostly happy, but have you ever fully forgotten about the wound in your soul and closed that gap?"

I opened my mouth and then shut it immediately.

"You've been focused on fighting, *surviving* for so long that maybe your subconscious is alerting you to the most important battle you face as this chapter of your life draws to a close."

"Being happy?" I crossed my arms. "Come on. Why do you think I'm going into the KH today to begin with? To move forward and enjoy my life."

She patted my knee. "Intellectually wanting it and understanding emotionally what it's going to cost you are two different things."

"If happiness costs me, then how is it happiness?"

"Only you can answer that. And I hope you do, otherwise that gap will always be there." She took off her glasses and rubbed her eyes, her frail body sagging and her wrinkles more etched on her papery skin.

I placed my hand over my purse, feeling the lump that was the Ascendant. Tatiana had ended her decades-long affair with Zev, which sounded as tumultuous as it had been passionate, though she'd deeply loved her husband, Samuel. My boss was a complicated woman, and I doubted her happiness was merely tied to romantic love. What had it been like straddling fame in the Sapien world with her art and infamy in the Ohrist one as a fixer?

What had been the cost of her happiness?

What was mine?

There was a brisk rap at the front door, and then it opened, Laurent calling out hello.

Tatiana smiled and rose to greet her nephew, while I hovered in the doorway, forcing away costs and futures. Right now, I had to keep my wits about me in the present and successfully unravel the angels.

She patted Laurent on the shoulder. "Join us in the kitchen."

He nodded, already heading for me like a magnet to metal, and kissed me.

Sighing happily, I slid my arms from his neck. "Ready to nuke the KH?"

"Ma chère tante does not believe I am fit for the job." Laurent narrowed his eyes and studied me. "You don't think I can do it either."

Had my finger guns given it away? My supportive smile faltered, but on closer examination, his lips twitched so he wasn't actually upset. Or he'd gotten over it if he had been.

I spread my thumb and index finger apart. "It's a bit presumptuous to assume that an Ohrist with a touch of Banim Shovavim magic can pull this off."

He flexed his biceps. "My Banim Shovavim magic is mighty."

"It is, and I'm sure your prowess will irrevocably weaken the KH, allowing us women to deal the final blow." I pressed my hands to my cheek. "Thank you, O manly one."

"You will pay for your lack of respect," he mock growled and threw me over his shoulder.

Shrieking with laughter, I pummeled his back to put me down as he jogged into the kitchen.

"Have you no dignity?" Emmett said.

"They're kind of cute," Sadie said. "For old people."

Laurent set me on my feet.

Tatiana threw a cookie at my kid. "Watch it, infant."

I strode over and grabbed the treat away from Sadie, leaving her to bite into empty air. "No cookie for you."

She brushed crumbs off her shirt. "Wow. I compliment you and get grief." She snagged my gaze and the twinkle in her eyes faded.

"And you'll continue to get it for many years to come." I set my purse on the counter and pulled out the silver orb. "Dumah wants those three angels to pay and so do I. We have the Ascendant and two different combinations of light and dark magic to test out. We've got this. Laurent will go first."

"Pointless," Tatiana coughed.

"Some people have supportive families," he said.

"Ah, but I build character, Lolo." She ruffled his hair and he ducked away with a scowl.

"I am going to shift."

I appreciated that he removed himself out of Sadie's earshot so she didn't hear how painful his shift was, but her eyes almost bugged out of her head when he returned. He was a majestic creature, prowling toward us, his superior strength evident in every step. His fur was as white as newly fallen snow, and his eyes, while familiar to me in any form he took, glowed with excitement that could be misread as a predatory lethalness.

"Whoa." Sadie held herself very still, her breathing shallow.

Laurent and I realized at the same time that she'd never seen his wolf form before. He sent me a questioning look and I nodded.

Tail wagging, he slowly approached her.

Sadie relaxed a bit and held out her hand. "Can I..." She glanced at me. "Does he understand me in this form?"

"Yup."

She crouched down, careful not to make eye contact with him, just like her dad had taught her with aggressive dogs. "Can I touch you?"

He licked her hand, making her giggle, then pushed his muzzle against her palm.

"You're incredible." She scratched his head.

Tatiana rolled her eyes. "Don't add to his ego."

Sadie screwed up her face, brushing off wolf fur. "Bristlier than I thought you'd feel. I figured you'd be like a big dog."

"Just like that lovely Mr. Fluffington." I snorted a laugh, and the wolf swatted me with his tail. "On that note." I put out my hand, palm down. "Operation Angel Take Down for the Win."

Sadie placed her hand on mine, followed by an enthusiastic Emmett. The wolf shook his head, but added a paw, leaving Tatiana frowning.

"I despise shows of peppiness," she said.

Emmett grabbed her hand and placed it on top. "Go team!"

Echoing him, we threw our hands up. Okay, Tatiana made a sound of disgust, but inside she was totally cheerleading.

"And away we go." Holding on to the wolf's white fur, I transported us through a shadow into Pyotr's cave.

The gargoyle took one look at us and activated a walkie-talkie with a hideous amount of static. "The yellow bird rises at dawn."

Oh, brother. I'd forgotten about this.

There was another burst of static and a garbled response, which Pyotr nodded at. He picked up his potted Chinese evergreen plant, Scarlet, and opened a direct portal to Tatiana's kitchen. "I go visit friends now."

At the last second, he grabbed a bunch of socks, his bottom lip trembling, then he vanished, sealing the portal up behind him.

Assuring myself that Emmett and Sadie would take good care of him, I placed the open Ascendant on the ground. "First channel your Ohrist magic through this," I said to Laurent, "then add Banim Shovavim power."

Laurent balanced his left front paw on both halves of the orb. As he did so, golden light bloomed up from his back paws, his fur illuminated into the blinding white of snow on a crisp sunny day. He flexed his free front paw, the claws glowing white, and all his magic funneled into the orb.

A hum rumbled up from the cave floor. Stalactites and stalagmites vibrated, and the wolf strained forward, his lips bared and his canines dripping saliva.

I remained on edge, positive that Neon Sign Face would appear, but Dumah's ring worked as advertised and we were undisturbed. Unfortunately, while the wolf poured magic into the Ascendant until his flanks were heaving, nothing happened beyond every hair on my body standing on end from the intensity of Laurent's assault.

"Laurent." I waved at him to get his attention. "Stop."

He immediately powered down, breathing heavily.

I picked up the orb and scratched behind his ears. "Good try, Mr. Fluffington."

He headbutted me in the hip.

"You're right." I snickered. "It *is* time for the women to step in and show you how it's done."

Smoky popped into the cave. "I am waiting."

"Sorry," I said. "We need to reset." I glanced up at the ceiling. "All is well?"

It nodded. "But time runs out. If the entity you call Neon Sign does not return to consciousness soon, *they* will sense it."

The ring knocked it out? Good to know. "Gotcha."

Smoky vanished and I hurriedly popped Laurent and me back to Tatiana's where I grabbed my boss.

If Laurent's combined magic driven through the Ascendant felt staticky and made my hair stand up, Tatiana and I created a surge of power that scoured my skin as if scrubbed with molten hot sandpaper. The pain took over my brain, curling inward and flaying me from within.

I bent over, half-twisted, with one hand pressed to my side and the other gripping one half of the open artifact.

Even with my eyes closed, I felt the darkness into which I'd plunged the cave. My shadows battered the walls and ceiling, and I wobbled on rubbery legs.

Pebbles snapped like Pop Rocks, so I cracked one eye open to check on Tatiana. Although her body trembled, the determined set of her jaw reassured me.

The air swirling around us grew wilder under the force of our combined power, plastering dozens of socks against us. My hair lay damp against my skull, and I had a bra-shaped sweat print that felt disgusting, but the Kefitzat Haderech remained intact.

I was spitting an errant sock out of my mouth when suddenly, our magic stuttered. A wash of light swept across the darkness, and the pebbles hung suspended in midair until a second stutter.

The Ascendant cracked—and every part of me went on pause. This couldn't be happening. The artifact was integral to my success. A wash of cold slid over my skin, and my magic fell apart, dripping off the rocks like slime.

A final pile of pebbles snapped into dust at Tatiana's feet and then her magic went silent as well.

"Nonononono!" I shook the orb, opening and shutting the two halves to reboot it, but it was fruitless.

Smoky appeared. "Why do you not start?"

Tatiana shook her head at the fissure running through the orb. "We overloaded it. It's done."

Smoky roared and spat a gust of wind at Tatiana and me, and blowing us backward into a shadow, socks pelting in alongside us.

I knocked into my boss, glancing down at my feet.

Big mistake. The shadows underfoot stretched and thinned, and the sponginess that supported me when I entered the KH disappeared.

There was a moment where my heart dropped into my stomach, just like when I crested the big hill on a roller coaster. I had one final glimpse of the KH, seeing through Smoky to a confused Neon Sign Face, then darkness enveloped us and we plummeted.

13

TATIANA'S WAIL SNAPPED ME INTO ACTION. I gathered the shadows to me to form a net, which caught us, gently bouncing us back up through impenetrable darkness.

"Miriam!"

I fumbled around, feeling for her hand and willing the shadows to open into her living room, but the tiny drop of magic I had left was engaged in keeping us aloft, and the Ascendant was either out of juice or broken.

There was no sense of our environment. Our heavy breathing seemed to both fill a tiny space and be a whisper in a void.

"I should have worn my other outfit," Tatiana said with a bravado belied by her trembling body.

"We're not dying. Give me a minute." This wasn't the conventional way back, but I was Banim Shovavim and these were shadows. They were mine to control. Trying hard not to think about how we were suspended here, I visualized the crochet hook that I used to mend my invisibility mesh, but in reverse. I envisioned it catching hold of the shadows and prying them apart, while maintaining an image of Tatiana's living room firmly in mind.

I squinted. Was that a pinprick of light or wishful thinking?

Tatiana elbowed me sharply, her breathing raspy. "Keep going."

Salty sweat burned my eyes, but I worked at that stubborn shadow like Lady Macbeth doing laundry, until I had a hole the size of my fist. "Hello?"

Unable to see anything beyond light from the other side, I squinted through the hole like it was a telescope.

A large eye popped up, blinking slowly, and I yelped, tripping backward.

Tatiana grabbed my arm to steady me.

"Break with fist."

I almost wept to hear Pyotr's voice, scrambling to do as he commanded.

With a few sharp raps, the shadows crumbled, leaving a gap large enough to climb out.

Emmett and Pyotr helped us, Sadie running to grab a chair before Tatiana's legs gave out.

The elderly artist dabbed her pale skin with a green and black argyle sock. "Never again," she declared.

Sadie bounced anxiously on her toes. "Did it work?"

Shaking my head, I crashed down on another chair, breathing heavily.

Pyotr squeezed my shoulder with a "Better luck next time," and whistling, left with his plant.

Laurent crouched down in front of me.

"No sarcasm," I said.

Emmett mimed twirling a nonexistent lock of hair around his finger. "Like 'Welcome to Failureville, population you three'?"

Sadie glared at him.

"It was a hypothetical statement." The golem humphed.

I jabbed my finger at Laurent. "Don't you start either," I said, then sighed heavily. "How did that not work?"

"It was a good try," he said.

I narrowed my eyes, unable to tell if he was being sincere.

"Just tough luck," he continued. Yup, definitely sarcasm.

"You can stop now," I said.

"Next time send in two men to get the job done."

"I foresee two less people on my payroll." Tatiana gave her shark smile to Emmett and Laurent, who shrugged.

"Eh. I'm loaded."

My daughter leaned across the counter. "Really? Because I have this list of dream items."

Laurent laughed while I hauled my ill-mannered child back.

She squirmed out of my grip. "I'll tell Nav too, just to make it fair."

"Enough," I said. "We failed."

Laurent kissed my forehead. "If you and Tatiana couldn't do it, then it wasn't achievable with the Ascendant. We'll figure out a different method." He placed his hand on the small of my back to brush past me.

It was a mundane gesture, but those were some of the best. They weren't huge romantic statements having to prove something. They were undertaken with the quiet confidence of a person who expected to have a life so filled with them together that one alone didn't have to encompass all the affection you felt for that person. It could just be a simple gesture, and that freedom in itself was even more indicative of the love than a grand gesture would be.

My heart triple stuttered and my brain chanted "Mine." I felt like I was fifteen with a horrible crush again. Geez, I was one step away from doodling our names in hearts.

I shook it off. *Not the time, Feldman.*

"We'll get all the magic brains on the job. Not just magic ones either, because Dad should come." Sadie plucked a fat green grape off a bunch from the fruit bowl and tossed it in her mouth.

Even if Senoi, Sansenoi, and Sammaneglof never discovered what I'd attempted, all I could see was those dead versions of myself from my dream. I'd agreed to this to heal my younger self's wound, but I felt like I'd ripped open the scar tissue that I'd carefully built over decades, trapped back in a chasm of grief and horror.

I *had* focused on the wrong thing. The only fear I'd had going into this was of the celestial trio stopping—or killing—us. The possibility that the plan itself wouldn't work hadn't been a factor. How could it when Dumah had given me both this mission and the means of completing it?

I stared at the floor, twisting my engagement ring around. Angels weren't infallible; Dumah must have been mistaken. If the only way to make it up to my wounded inner child was by forgiving those three angels or some form of closure that didn't involve vengeance, then I wasn't capable of it. I wanted them to suffer so badly that I tasted it. And it was bitter.

I didn't want bitter anymore. Give me sunbeams and rose petals, my world filled with love. Sadly, I wasn't sure how to get there.

"Mom?" Sadie gently shook my shoulder.

"I'm okay." I smiled, even though Tatiana's question of whether I could close the gap and achieve one hundred percent happiness remained unanswered.

The only upside to that disaster was that when I got home, I ripped up the letters I'd written to Jude and Eli.

Dumah and I needed to have a little chat, but the Ascendant still wasn't working. I refused to give up on it, though, so I holed up in my office, giving it time to repower, and threw myself into the file that Tatiana and Emmett had compiled on Dr. Justine Eversol. But first, I erased all the information on my whiteboard, aka my murder board, since I'd solved my parents' and McMurtry's murders.

The comprehensive dossier detailed Dr. Eversol's many professional achievements: an undergraduate degree from Stanford, a doctorate from Yale, her many years working at Johns Hopkins University and various respected clinical laboratories, not to mention all her cutting-edge research and published papers on telomeres.

The information formed the basis of a timeline spanning the whiteboard, complete with locations, and while it was impressive, it didn't yield any new ideas. The private investigator that Gabriel had previously hired had spoken with friends and colleagues, and Tatiana had double-checked his work, proclaiming it thorough.

I added the main points of those interviews to the board as well, though I doubted I'd be following up with any of them. Shaking out my wrists, I glanced at the silver orb that rested on my desk. Had enough time passed for it to power up a bit? If I tried it now, would I use up what little charge the orb had and still get nowhere?

I quit bouncing my leg, forcing my attention back to the file. There was still no bank or credit card activity, nor did Dr. Eversol own any property in her name. However, there wasn't a death certificate either.

Speaking of which, I removed a printout of a newspaper obituary from the folder. Dr. Eversol had lost her only child, Miranda, when her daughter was twelve. Justine was her only surviving parent, the father having passed on when Miranda was little.

Miranda's photo showed a blonde girl with a bubbly smile and dancing green eyes.

I added that fact to the timeline, my heart twisting. I couldn't—didn't want to—imagine Justine's grief, the parallels of a single mom with an only child hitting too close to home. For all I'd lost and survived, I wasn't sure I'd make it through that particular nightmare with my sanity intact.

The cause of death wasn't noted, but the date twigged something. I sorted through the notes on Dr. Eversol's career until I found it. Shortly after Miranda's death, which was about twenty years ago, the geneticist had left a tenured position to work for a small start-up looking at the intersection of technology and genetics with a special focus on cancer.

Had Miranda been afflicted with the disease? Had she endured years of hospital stays, chemo, and hair loss? Did it help to find peace with a child's passing when you had time to move through the stages of grief to acceptance or was it just longer to build a foundation of rage, until she sat at her daughter's deathbed, holding her hand, her sorrow indistinguishable from her fury?

I swiped at my damp eyes with the back of my hand. This was all conjecture anyway.

Tatiana had made a note in red on a sticky tab that although Miranda passed away and was buried in Baltimore, she could find nothing tying Dr. Eversol to that area after the death. However, she'd tracked down the cemetery and provided me with the plot location.

The start-up that the geneticist had gone to work for was in Ohio. Maybe she'd needed to get away from Baltimore, the city that held such sorrowful memories, but wouldn't there have been good ones there as well?

I put myself in her shoes, concluding that I'd still want some form of connection with my child even if a job took me elsewhere. But if Justine no longer lived in Baltimore, then how did she remain connected?

My patience for the Ascendant's re-up ran out, and I flipped the orb open. The crooked smile of light didn't appear, only a series of stuttery blinks. Closing my eyes, I cast my magic into the artifact, rewarded with a tiny flutter deep inside it.

Cupping it in my hands, I coaxed the magic out like a weak flame in a strong wind. Jagged white light streaked across my office but immediately winked out. I took a deep breath and tried again. And again. Each time I managed to widen the rift to Gehenna a little more until it filled the room.

I called out for the angel.

"You here to blow my mind with amazingness, matzoh ball?" Dumah-Goldie said. She wore a knobby yellow sweater that I always secretly thought made my cousin look like a corn cob and those stupid clogs. The scent of orange blossoms competed with rotting onion, but there was still no trace of Goldie's signature tea tree oil smell. Could she not call up scent memories?

"It didn't work," I said. "The Kefitzat Haderech is perfectly intact."

She swatted a couple of dybbuks away from the rift. "Bummer."

"That's it?" The way I held the orb didn't allow me to cross my arms, so I scowled at the angel. "Aren't you desperate for them to pay?"

"You did it wrong, now you'll redo it. I forgive you your incompetence." She made a gesture of benediction. Goldie used to do that, knowing it pissed me off.

It had the same effect now, and angel or no angel, I snapped. "I didn't do it wrong. You gave me the world's most vague instructions to make a magic fire, and I followed them best I could. We funneled Ohrist light and Banim Shovavim light through the Ascendant."

The angel tilted her head. "Nothing?"

"Nada. Zip."

"Well, that part of the formula was an educated guess."

My mouth fell open and I made a sputtering sound.

"But there's no doubt about what light and dark represent." She nodded. "You're still alive, so you didn't alert the schmuck trio, and they'll be caught off guard when you find the correct catalyst to trigger the magical reaction." The angel fired finger guns.

"Excuse me?" I fully intended to unravel the angels, but I hadn't imagined that Dumah-Goldie would wash her hands of me. "You're not going to help?"

"I gave you the formula and two-thirds of the elements involved. I did my part." She planted her hands on her hips. "Now you must do yours." She said it in the same "you're not going to be unreasonable, are you?" tone that Goldie would take with me.

And just like that, I was back to my full-of-resentment teen self. "I did my part too, and I'm not the only one with skin in this game, remember?"

YOU AGREED.

The voice that ripped through me didn't sound like my cousin's. It wasn't even spoken aloud. Each word was dropped into my mind like a knife that was so sharp you didn't even realize it was cutting you until there was blood, so much blood.

I held my hands up to my face, pressing them against my eyes, my ears, my nose, convinced something terrible had shifted in my head.

Nothing.

"Whoops." Dumah-Goldie chuckled. Audibly. "Used my inside voice."

A swirl of dybbuks raced toward my living room, but the angel grabbed them before they escaped the rift and squeezed, the whirling crimson and gray spirits oozing from between her fingers with inhuman wails that sent shivers up my spine.

"What I meant to say." She raised her voice to be heard. "Was that I don't have any further knowledge, and given the restraints of my environment, you're in a better position to figure it out. But you're right. We're partners and I need to buy you time. How about I plant false information? I'll make up some evil plans I'm putting into place to take out all

Banim Shovavim simultaneously when I leave Gehenna so no one can stop me."

I took a step back against the glint in her eyes, almost tripping over the Ascendant, which had fallen on the ground, and she laughed again.

"Kidding. Some of my best friends are Banim Shovavim." She glanced at the dybbuks that she'd reduced to goo, and I swallowed hard. The angel flicked her fingers clean. "Great chat, matzoh ball."

With that she disappeared.

As the rift to Gehenna winked out, the fissure in the orb snapped and a chunk of the Ascendant rolled across my floor. Totally busted.

Although my weird-ass ally hadn't intended to harm me, I couldn't stop shivering, even with three sweaters on and the heat jacked up, and my focus was shit. Sitting cross-legged in meditation made my butt fall asleep and did nothing to quell my racing mind, so I returned to the case. I used Google Earth to sift through images of the cemetery where Miranda was buried, hoping for a quote or something engraved on a tombstone that would shed light on Justine's whereabouts.

The repetitive motions of clicking, scanning, and clicking again soothed my jangled nerves. Sadly, when I found the plot, the plaque contained nothing more than Miranda's name, dates of birth and death, and "beloved daughter."

I swiveled my office chair from side to side, absently scrubbing at a smear of blue dry-erase marker on my index finger. The photo on Google Earth had been snapped when the magnolia tree next to the grave was in full bloom. I pictured Dr. Eversol laying the flowers visible on the well-kept plot, then sitting down on a small bench nearby. She'd inhale the fresh air, taking in the broad, glossy leaves and huge white fragrant blooms, and telling her daughter about her life since their last visit.

Except for this to happen, Justine had to either live nearby or have flown in. No property, no credit card activity. Had she taken on a new name in the past year? I would, if I'd helped create a vampire-targeted virus, but it would make it much harder to find her.

I swiped on some lip balm, relieving the chapping from me gnawing on my lips the past hour, and stared at the photo. My remaining anxiety was tamped down by the tingling of my researcher instincts.

After grabbing a pen and notepad, I noted down every element of the grave and its surroundings, with quick searches on magnolias and Google Earth images. The trees bloomed in the summer, and images were updated anywhere from a month to three months.

I pulled off two sweaters, tossing them on the corner of my desk. It was September now, thus the magnolia would have lost most of its flowers. That put the photo firmly in summer. This past summer, since it wasn't over a year old. Two months ago at most. The timeframe mattered but it took me a while longer to pinpoint why.

The flowers.

Had Justine placed the bouquet herself? When Eli's dad was cremated here in Vancouver, the family paid for a regular floral placement service at his urn in the mausoleum, even though his mom visited her husband all the time.

I texted Tatiana asking if she'd looked into that angle, but she hadn't because Jews don't leave flowers graveside and it hadn't occurred to her. It wouldn't have occurred to me either, since I was only familiar with Jewish cemeteries where we left rocks, which were eternal and didn't die. Or, in the interpretation I liked, we placed stones because the impact the deceased had on us was everlasting.

My parents didn't have a grave or an urn. They were murdered and a fire was set to burn their remains. Even if Jake wasn't hiding me and could have asked for ashes to conduct a memorial, all trace of them was gone in less than two days. My pen tore through the drawing of three angels burning in flames that I'd doodled, and I pushed the pad away. Their time would come.

Besides, Goldie and I had created our own memorial in her backyard under a cherry blossom tree. Anytime we went to the beach or for a walk, we'd find a new special rock to place there. I smiled at the memory. My cousin had gotten custody of a sullen, terrified child and had it not been for her huge heart, I would never have found any happiness at all.

Goldie had built a rock-solid foundation for that emotion, but I had remained cautious and held back from fully embracing it until my magic resurfaced and blew up my life in the best way. Who was I kidding? Even then, it took time.

It's funny how happiness was the thing we all claimed to desire, and yet, it was the scariest thing to try for because the stakes were so high.

My relationships with Eli, Jude, and Sadie were stronger and healthier than ever, I had Laurent, and a circle of friends that I didn't have to hide from, not to mention my amazing magic fixer job. Rather than being laser focused on what I had to do to stay safe in the present, my future remained wide open. I just wanted to swim through the ocean of happiness possibilities that I'd barely waded knee-high into.

But back to the case. It was easy enough to track down the company that supplied the flowers to the cemetery where Miranda was buried. They even had a handy contact form on their website, but they wouldn't give up customer information. Well, not on purpose.

I eyed the shadow in the corner of my room.

Ah, hell with it. Might as well find out if any alarms had been raised by this morning's events. Still, I had to gather my courage to walk into the shadow, part of me certain that I'd be trapped and falling through darkness once more.

The universe cut me a break. Nothing in the KH was amiss, nor did sirens wail or angry celestial beings show up at my appearance. Pyotr glanced up from his video game long enough to nod at me, and sock in hand, I was at the offices of the florist company in Baltimore minutes later.

My cloak-and-dagger—or rather *cloaked*-and-dagger—jaunt was a success. I got into the accounting department unde-tected, and though I had to wait until the overworked employee went for a coffee refill, their well-organized soft-ware made it easy to find the name and address of the person paying for the flower service: one Margaret Beverly on the San Juan Islands in Washington State.

I intended to cross-check that name in the dossier, but when I got home, Sadie urged me to come eat dinner. My stomach growled in agreement, and by the time I finished eating, I was hit with a wave of exhaustion, so I flaked out on my sofa for my Sunday night date with my kid.

Since our *Buffy* rewatch had been my pick, Sadie had chosen *Once Upon a Time* as our next series. I'd caught a few episodes here and there when it had originally aired, but the pilot tonight sucked me in more than I expected it to.

When the end credits rolled, Sadie alternated between thumbs-up and thumbs-down. "Well?"

Our agreement was that if one of us hated the first episode, the person who'd chosen the show had to pick another one.

"Thumbs-up."

"Knew you'd say that," she replied smugly, already playing the second episode.

My team had to be updated about this Margaret Beverly, not to mention Zev and Gabriel, and I should check in with Laurent, since the anniversary of Delphine's death was tomor-row. But curled up on my fabulous sofa with my head on my daughter's hip, enjoying the denizens of Storybrooke, I was ninety percent happy, the feeling dancing inside me like fire-flies caught in a jar.

14

I GOT AN EARLY START ON MONDAY MORNING. MY first task was putting Sadie's brilliant idea of getting our friends to help with the schmuck trio into play. I sent out "dinner and brainstorming" invitations to Ava, Romi, Daya, Eli, and Nav, with a second text buttering Eli up about his excellent grilling skills.

He saw through it, but after he heard the topic of discussion, offered to not only grill but pick up enough meat for everyone, including a hungry shifter. Truly a prince among men.

After a moment's consideration, I invited Marsha as well. She was Ohrist, and despite disliking her for ages, she was becoming a good friend and I'd value any insights she had. I guess fighting a demon together really did bond people. Sadly, she and her husband were going away for a romantic vacation. It was too bad she wasn't ready to share her abilities with him, but good for them for prioritizing their love life over a family holiday with their kids.

I wasn't sure when Jude got back from her yoga retreat but sent her an invite as well. However, I hung off telling my team until I had something concrete to share about Margaret Beverly.

There was no mention of either friends, colleagues, or family with the Beverly surname in Eversol's dossier, and none of the Margaret Beverlys that I found on social media were her. I tossed my phone on the counter. If she'd taken this new identity, there had to be a reason for it, because my love of British crime shows had taught me that most people didn't choose new aliases out of thin air.

I didn't expect much from my online search of the name, but the most common hit I got surprised me. Margaret of Beverly was one of the few women ever to be a warrior in the Holy Crusades, helping to defend a besieged Jerusalem back in the late 1100s during the Third Crusade.

This historical figure snagged my interest for a couple of reasons. First, Gabriel had described Justine as conservative and not someone he'd expect to be intrigued by the existence of vampires. Teasing that out, did it follow she was disgusted to learn of the undead and made it her personal crusade to destroy them? Were that the case, this identity made sense.

The second reason this choice felt likely was due to a quote attributed to Margaret of Beverly. "Though a woman, I seemed a warrior, I threw the weapon; though filled with fear, I learned to conceal my weakness."

Fear, concealing weakness, and still being a warrior: traits I was very familiar with when dealing with vampires.

Excited, I messaged Tatiana, Emmett, and Gabriel that I was going to check out the address I had and that I'd let Zev know. I also gave them the information about the dinner and brainstorming session tomorrow, adding that Juliette was invited as well.

Last, but not least, I phoned Laurent, wanting to hear his voice. Despite the acceptance he'd found regarding Delphine's dybbuk inhabitation and subsequent suicide, it would be understandable if he was feeling blue today. There'd be no point asking him because he'd just answer that he was fine, but I was pretty good at reading my boyfriend.

"Good morning, Mitzi." His coffeepot burbled in the background. "What did you get up to after I left you yesterday? Wait, let me guess. You taught yourself magic welding skills and single-handedly fixed the Ascendant."

I grinned at his teasing but replied with mock sternness. "I'll have you know, smarty-pants, that I successfully used it again."

He groaned. "To do what? No, don't tell me on the phone. Someone should be present when I have a heart attack, so I don't lie here for three days without being found and then Boo gets hungry and eats my corpse."

A snort-laugh burst out of me. "The Feldman love of melodrama is rubbing off on you."

"Yes. I blame you entirely. Are you coming over now?"

"Depends. Are you going to feed and caffeinate me?"

"Mais bien sûr. I don't have a death wish."

"Uh-huh," I said drolly. "See you soon."

I grabbed the dossier, eager to share my findings. We could visit the address in the San Juan Islands together. After throwing a couple key items into a bag in case I stayed over at his place, I did a last sweep of the house to check the stove was off and all the windows were closed before locking up.

Sadie was at school and had switched to her dad's last night for the week, so my day was free and clear to spend with Laurent. Sure, we had this case to investigate, but that counted as a date for us these days. Now, how to ensure his reaction to my visit yesterday to Dumah counted as foreplay?

I grinned. I was a clever woman. Much as I wished to snap my fingers and get to Hotel Terminus, I had a stop to make first.

"Dinner?" Giulia's mouth fell open.

"Yes. I'm inviting friends to help with a magic problem and I'd like you to be there. Careful," I teased when she continued to gape at me. "You're going to catch flies."

She snapped her mouth closed, waving her front paws for a couple of seconds before she regained her composure and tossed her head back haughtily. "Well of course you want me there, bella. I shall try to fit you in."

"Please do," I said somberly. "Uh, what do you eat?" Even though Emmett only drank, that might have been a golem trait, because Pyotr sure did appreciate food.

Her eyes lit up. "Can I have fatty tuna or salmon?"

"Absolutely."

She gave a delighted squeal and leapt back up to the top of the condo tower. Her infectious mood stayed with me all the way to Hotel Terminus, and I blamed that giddy vibe for the three yellow lights I may have run.

Laurent stood on the sidewalk bouncing impatiently in his bare feet, his hands jammed in his jeans' pockets. His curls were rumpled as if he'd been running his fingers through them, and he had a dusting of dark stubble along his jaw.

With him was Ryann Esposito, the head of the Lonestars here in Vancouver. Her electric blue hair was buzzed close to her scalp, she sported tie-dyed leggings and a blue sweater with tiny hearts all over it, and was hands down one of the most magically powerful people I'd ever met. Beside her was a cool electric bicycle.

Boo ran around in the overlong grass behind them.

I wrenched my car into park, snatched my belongings off the passenger seat, and hurried over.

"Hi, Miri," she trilled. "What trouble are you getting up to today?"

"Wow." I shifted my overnight bag to my other hand. "One little interrogation and suddenly I'm a ne'er-do-well."

She winked at me. "I've got to run, but as soon as I get any hits, I'll let you know."

I raised my eyebrows in question.

"Ryann is tracking down my former pack members that Léa can't find," Laurent said.

My heart swelled in admiration. The man when I'd first met him had been running into the arms of death to get away from his past. He'd overcome so much to achieve this self-awareness.

"We're having a community outreach day in two Sundays from now at HQ," Ryann said. "It's a yearly thing. Fun for families. Free BBQ. Swing by."

Provided I hadn't been killed by the trio, it sounded lovely. "I will, though I should warn you that my family is pretty huge now." With Eli dating Nav, Daya and Evani back in my life, and my fixer family, we were a big mishpocha.

"The more the merrier."

I debated inviting her to my brainstorming session, but I hadn't interacted with her outside of her Lonestar role, and I wasn't sure that was the best event to change that. Maybe at the BBQ I could invite her out sometime as friends.

Ryann kicked up the stand and swung a leg over her bicycle. "Talk to you both soon."

After she'd disappeared around the corner, I rose onto tiptoe, fisted Laurent's shirt in my hands, and kissed him.

His arm came around me like a band of steel, hauling me against him, and he deepened the embrace, smelling like cedar and home.

I moaned softly, my hands still resting on his lean torso, pulling away to gaze up at him through half-closed lids. "Hi."

His contented sigh rumbled through me. "Hi yourself. What was that for?"

"Being you. Being awesome."

"I mean, I won't argue with you." He poked my overnight

bag. "I like a woman who comes prepared for any contingency."

"I had a list."

His green eyes twinkled. "I look forward to helping you cross off the other items."

"Great!" I held up the bag. "Will you bring this in?"

He bowed low. "Your wish is my command."

"Reeaaally? Can I get that in writing?"

He tapped his finger against his lips. "Depends whether you brought your thong and corset."

I opened the overnight bag.

Laurent peered inside and grinned wickedly. "You can have anything you want."

"Set me up with coffee and breakfast while I call Zev." I patted the shifter's cheek.

Scowling, he took the bag, and we headed up the walk. "You didn't say this was a threesome," he grumbled.

"It'll be a duo when it counts." I winked, and at the twinkle in his eyes as he mock frowned, I almost blurted out that I loved him.

Oh fuck. My mind reeled. I wanted to run away and sit with this new discovery, trying it on with a quiet delight. But seriously? Of all the times to have this realization. It was the anniversary of his wife's passing.

Besides which, there was no point saying anything until the schmuck trio was dealt with.

I sighed. Luckily, Laurent hadn't noticed that my entire reality had upended.

"Boo." He snapped his fingers. "Come inside."

The cat threw him a disdainful look, and with a flick of her tail, scampered in the other direction.

"No more hunting birds," he called out sternly.

"Says the wolf." I closed the hotel door behind us.

"I don't kill feathery little birdies."

I slipped off my flats. "Have you ever killed a sweet fuzzy rabbit?"

"You mean those little shitting machines?" He flashed a claw. "Snicker snack."

I gasped. "You ate Thumper?"

He stared at me, clueless at my reference, before walking away, shaking his head. "Come in the kitchen when you're done your call."

I admired his tight ass for a moment, then hit Zev's number in my contacts.

The vampire actually answered on the first ring. "Where are you?" he demanded.

"At Laurent's. Why did you own that Dantora painting?" I fired back.

"Hazard. Working or playing house with your boyfriend?"

"Huh?" I shook my head. "To the hazard part. And I'm working."

"It was a dice game popular in the 1800s," Zev said. "Dantora had an unfortunate addiction to it."

"So the seeing...?"

"What seeing?" He sighed. "You have a working knowledge of the English language. I know this, Miriam, because of the sheer number of messages you insist on beleaguering me with."

"That painting contained a magic tracker in the form of a face in the window seen only by Banim Shovavim magic. It was placed there by hunters to locate my kind, and I was attacked outside the speakeasy."

"To quote Oscar Wilde, 'a life crowded with incident,'" Zev said dryly. "Do try to attract less attention on this case."

I shot the phone the finger.

"Speaking of which," he said, "do you have anything worth reporting?"

I filled him in about tracking down Margaret Beverly, the

vampire snorting at my hypothesis on that name as Dr. Eversol's alias. "Pretty clever of me, right?"

"You're already being paid. Accolades cost extra." What a jerk. "Under no circumstances is the scientist to be harmed. I want her brought to Blood Alley where I will get Gabriel all the information that he requires to produce a vaccine."

"Why would I hurt a human?"

"Why you do anything is a morass I'd rather not wade into," he said.

"I liked you better when we were enemies."

"Oh good," he snarked. "I feared I was alone in my sentiments toward you."

I stomped into the kitchen, my phone shoved into the pocket of my red A-line skirt.

Laurent pulled a platter of croissants out of the oven, his cell cradled between his shoulder and cheek. "Oui. Je t'aime, Maman."

I smiled at the sweetness in his tone.

He rolled his eyes, though his expression as he hung up remained affectionate. "She always checks in on me on this day." He didn't mention his father doing the same, and if Jacques hadn't spoken to him, Laurent hadn't sent his love to his father at the end of the call either. "So…" He set the plate on a trivet on his counter next to a butter dish and small pot of jam. "How's Zev?"

"I take it you heard the conversation." I grabbed the mug of coffee he'd already poured and doctored with milk and sugar for me, and took my first sip of ambrosia today. "He's such a dick."

"True, but he's a dick who didn't know about the tracker." He slathered a pastry with jam, his even white teeth flashing when he bit into it.

"No, he's innocent of that charge. I doubt he knows what happened to Hiram and Ephraim either. He just wants Dr. Eversol and a cure." I broke a warm croissant in half, buttery flakes falling onto the plate. Did I dare lick those up once I'd finished eating? Eh. My boyfriend was a wolf. He wouldn't even notice.

"Now then." I swallowed my mouthful. "Do you want the heart attack–inducing update before or after I share my brilliance?"

He hopped up to sit on the counter and took a long swallow of coffee from his large mug. "Brilliance first, since I may not be alive to applaud you after the other."

"Fair. Wait, first, tomorrow night I'm holding a brain-storming session on the unraveling."

Laurent couldn't keep the shock off his face upon hearing how many people I was trusting with this.

"I'm capable of growth," I said lightly.

He saluted me with his mug. "Here's to growth. Now, on to brilliance."

"I'm pretty sure I found Dr. Eversol."

He listened to the details, sipping his coffee. "You deserve a second croissant for that."

"Right?" Even though I hadn't yet finished my first one, I added the second to my plate. "Zev didn't even give me a gold star emoji." I paused. "Is there anything special you want to do today after we visit the San Juan Islands? Any traditions you have to honor Delphine?"

He placed his empty mug in the sink. "Like what?"

"We could find a rock to place somewhere special in her memory, you could share stories of her, or go eat something she loved. Anything." Delphine had wanted to be cremated and Laurent had spread her ashes in the river on pack property.

"I appreciate that, but—" He reached for me, and I imme-diately shielded my plate from wolf theft. His eyebrows shot up. "I was going to take your hand while we had a tender moment."

"Oh." Blushing, I held out my hand.

"Forget it. The moment's ruined."

I smacked my hand against his chest. "Take it and emote, damn you."

"Fine," he growled and caught my hand. "I'll never stop loving Delphine, but I was hoping to make new, happier memories of this day." He said it all in an annoyed voice.

I tugged free. "Nope, it didn't have the same resonance."

"Next time, just jump to the part where I am inevitably right," he said loftily.

"Nah. What fun would that be?" Laughing, I lunged for my plate, which he'd stolen.

He bit into my reward croissant with a smirk.

I narrowed my eyes. He was extremely lucky that wasn't the last one. "Remember how I told you I got the Ascendant to work one last time yesterday? It was to contact Dumah."

Laurent choked on his food.

Smirking, I pounded him on the back.

He finally got his coughing under control. "Tell me you didn't accuse the angel of giving you the wrong instructions."

I crossed my arms. "Like I'm that stupid."

A muscle in his jaw ticked, as did the seconds as he held my gaze, waiting for me to expand.

"We agreed that another method must be found." I fiddled with my coffee mug, very interested in checking the rim for lipstick marks. "Then I may have irritated the angel by implying they step up and do their part."

"Really?" he said with a flat stare. "I'm shocked."

"I only mildly irritated Dumah. They got over it pretty quickly since I'm such a valuable ally and a delight to work with."

Laurent chuckled then he hopped off the counter and tilted my jaw up with his finger. "All of us have your back. We'll unravel the three who killed your parents, and you'll be free of all angels forever."

I pressed my cheek against his chest. "Thank you."

Once I polished off my second croissant, we entered the KH.

My boyfriend tensed and I poked his biceps. "You won't be hurt."

"Uh-huh." He relaxed a fraction, but his expression remained wary. They could throw him a ticker-tape parade in the KH, and he still wouldn't trust his safety here.

Pyotr hurried over and sadly informed me that Big Boss wouldn't come out of the grotto.

Sighing, I rubbed the back of my neck.

Laurent poked my side. "Do not feel guilty. You're doing your best."

I nodded, though I still felt bad when I told Pyotr to pass on that I wasn't giving up. The business with the Leviathan aside, I had to admit it was nice that the KH remained in existence for easy travel. Since Dr. Eversol was a Sapien and could enter without consequence, with any luck, we'd be back at Blood Alley in no time.

I mean, we had only to convince the brilliant scientist who'd helped engineer a virus to wipe out all vampires to come quietly and help a master vamp reverse her work, before she was most probably killed. I rubbed the back of my neck again.

Eh. Compared to unraveling angels, this was going to be a piece of cake.

15

LOCATED JUST NORTH OF SEATTLE, THE SAN JUAN Islands were an archipelago of about 172 islands, the three main populated ones being San Juan, Lopez, and our destination, Orcas Island.

I gave Laurent the rundown as we walked through the KH to the exit, having researched the place before leaving. "Orcas only has about five thousand inhabitants," I said. "It's rural and hilly, with small fishing villages, and one main road." I pointed at the yellow door that had appeared in the rock face up ahead and we stepped up our pace.

"The kind of place where everyone minds their business." Laurent stepped over some loose rocks. "Perfect for someone who wants to disappear."

I opened the door and was hit with a brisk salt-tinged breeze that winged through me, but even on this overcast day, the property was a riot of color. Stately pines and Douglas firs competed with ground cover planted in rich brown earth for the lushest green. A raised bed held flowers with glowing gold and orange blooms, while a creeper vine in vibrant purple had taken over one side of the rustic cabin.

Set atop a bluff, the residence had sweeping views of the

cool blue Salish Sea to the white-capped peaks of the mountains in the distance, but damn was it brisk out here. Wrapping my arms around my green cardigan, I leaned into the wind and jogged up to the front door.

Laurent pressed his hands against it. "Wood veneer over steel. I smell it," he said to my questioning glance. He crouched down. "Reinforced with iron rebar going into the frame. I couldn't break through." He stood up, brushing off his palms. "Without examining the rest of the structure, I'd say someone poured a lot of money into making it look run-down when it's got top-shelf Sapien security, and no easy entry point. A very paranoid person lives here."

"Let's meet her."

The door flew open at my knock.

A fierce older woman with steely blue eyes held a crossbow steady, its end resting on her shoulder.

We put up our hands.

Fuck, those things were big in person. I swallowed down the taste of bile, clenching my bladder tightly. At this close range, the wooden bolt with its metal shaft would fillet us. Scratch that. From the way Laurent had paled, it was probably silver. Crossbows were hardly commonplace, though if someone was worried about their business partner, the weapon would easily stake a vampire at a distance.

A woman prepared for any contingency. I respected that.

"Margaret Beverly?" I said.

"Who's asking?" she said in a gruff voice.

Dr. Eversol also had blue eyes, but that's where the resemblance to the photos I'd seen ended. This woman was gaunt and appeared at least a decade older than the scientist's sixty-five years. Her hair was no longer a vibrant silver but a lank gray.

"I'm Miriam Feldman and this is Laurent Amar."

"And?"

I licked my lips. "Could you lower that, please?"

164

"I could." She didn't.

Laurent nudged me aside to stand directly in front of the weapon. "My brother-in-law, Gabriel Naumovich, speaks highly of you. He needs your help."

"You've got the wrong person." She slammed the door in our faces, bolting it with a series of clicks.

"She's lying," Laurent said. "Her heart sped up and I smell sweat."

I knocked again, raising my voice so she'd hear me. "Dr. Eversol, please. Hear us out. We're trying to save you."

"Don't do me any favors," she sneered through the door.

If Laurent was right, then this place was a fortress, and we weren't getting in without Justine's permission. I glanced at my partner, expecting the same exasperation, but he wore a thoughtful expression.

"Today is the anniversary of my wife's death," he said.

"My condolences," Justine said. "Now leave."

Laurent placed his hand on the door. "Seven years ago she was inhabited by a dybbuk. Do you know what that is? What that means?"

There was a pause and then a soft "Yes."

"My wife knew the outcome as well, and to avoid hurting those she loved, took her own life." He looked up at the heavy, dark clouds. "Some supernaturals don't deserve to exist." His voice hardened. "And I'd be fine if every vampire on earth disappeared, so if that's why you teamed up with Imogine to create the virus, I support your intentions." His shoulders descended and his lips curved up in a sweet smile. "But I do love Gabriel very much. He's asked for our help to put this matter to bed, and I fear for his safety if we fail him. It is a lot to ask, I know. But will you let us speak to you? Please."

This man continued to surprise and amaze me. I rested my hand on his back, happy to be with him, even under these circumstances.

Justine unlatched the bolts and motioned us inside with the crossbow, which was, at least, lowered. "Say your piece and—"

Laurent and I were knocked sideways so hard that he burst through the wooden railings and flew onto the grass below. I teetered on the edge of the broken porch, catching hold of a pillar at the last second and flinging myself backward. I hit my hip with a grunt, flinching as something hit the floor with a loud thud.

Justine had crumpled to her knees just inside the cabin, the crossbow at her feet. She clutched her torn-out throat, blood pouring from the gash and tears shimmering in her eyes.

A hooded figure stood over her, her long, hooked fingernails coated in blood. Imogine? The vampire kicked Justine, savagely knocking her to the ground.

"Noooo!" My scythe slammed into my palm, funnel clouds of shadows swirling around me, and I swung for the vamp's legs, not intending to kill, just incapacitate.

She leapt up and caught an edge of the roof one-handed, the blade whistling under her harmlessly. Before the momentum of my strike had even finished, she'd dropped down, grabbed my arm, and twisted it viciously up my back, her callouses scraping against my wrist.

I cried out, my magic falling apart.

She increased the pressure, driving me to my knees. Her hot, rancid breath tickled the hairs on the back of my neck as she ran a nail along the skin at my nape.

Shuddering, yet unable to escape her grip, I directed Delilah to physically fight back. In my growing distress, it was all the magic I could control.

The vampire took the hits, her breathing growing heavy, but she didn't let up. The pressure on my shoulder increased, and I gritted my teeth, braced for my shoulder blade to snap.

Justine, meantime, gave one last gasp, a bloody, shuddery

exhale, then fell still, staring at us with vacant, lifeless eyes from the doorway.

A Banim Shovavim turned into a void, my parents' deaths, a scientist murdered. Again and again, I was thrust up against the pointlessness of lives cut short. I'd only reclaimed mine; I couldn't die here.

My arm suddenly fell free.

Laurent had his claws around the vamp's throat, slamming the fiend over and over against the exterior wall.

I hadn't heard him or felt a whisper of wind at his arrival. Much like the vampire.

"Don't kill Imogine," I cried. "We need—"

With the next slam, the vamp's hood fell off and I gasped, my heart thundering in my chest. It wasn't Imogine at all. I didn't know what that vengeful once-woman looked like, but I did recognize this face.

She was dirtier now, her blond hair matted, and the bubbly smile replaced by a twisted sneer. I'd recognize this little girl anywhere. She'd been in those pictures with Dr. Eversol, grinning up at the camera like her mom could save the world.

Miranda.

Laurent swung his head my way and the vampire lashed out. She kicked him in the balls, then jerked free and dove in for the kill.

A zeptosecond. That was all it took for reality to shift on its axis. We'd failed Justine, but I wouldn't fail Laurent.

Or Miranda.

Delilah and I dove for the two of them, but with a roar, Laurent tore the vampire's heart out.

He met her eyes, his snarl turning to a horrified cry when in the second before she turned to ash, he saw her young face.

The wind picked up, blowing all trace of Miranda away, and I held my hair out of my face to watch Laurent, who hadn't moved.

"How old was she?" He turned stricken eyes to mine.

"Twelve." He doubled over like he'd been punched, and I touched his shoulder. "But not really. Miranda, um, she was Justine's daughter, was turned years ago. You didn't kill a child."

He gave me a shaky nod, but it was for my benefit, not because he believed it.

I didn't know how to comfort him but sticking around wouldn't help. I tugged on his arm. "Come on. Let's get you home."

I had enough presence of mind to shut the cabin door. Justine had been isolated enough that I doubted anyone would find her before I got a team member out here to search, but the return trip through the KH was a blur. The three angels could have been there with flaming swords and I wouldn't have noticed, intent on getting Laurent home safely.

He didn't speak until we were back at his place, and I'd gotten him to sit on the sofa, placing a blanket around his shoulders.

"April 15," he murmured.

It was September now. "I don't understand." I sat down next to him.

"Delphine's due date. The baby would be six." Laurent took a shuddering breath. It was like an explosive detonated inside him. Vertebrae by vertebrae he crumpled until he was completely hunched over, his forehead pressed to the couch cushion.

My eyes blurred with tears. He'd killed someone else's daughter on the anniversary of his own's death. I pressed my lips together, my fists clenched, forcing my rage at the cruel irony of life down until Laurent had gotten through this.

I stroked his hair.

His body rippled. Once. Twice. Fur burst out along his right arm and his sweater ripped apart, fabric flying as his body changed.

Unwilling to remove my hand and lose contact with him, I

felt the reverberations of the bones breaking and transforming, the increased tempo of his breathing, and his silky curls turning to a bristly fur.

The wolf jumped off the sofa, threw back his head, and howled a dirge of unspeakable loss and sorrow. His desolate lament bounced off the walls and burrowed into the very marrow of my bones, but it wasn't enough for the wolf to mourn.

I sat quietly until the animal had cried himself hoarse. "Laurent, change back." He growled at me, but I didn't budge. "You need to grieve in human form."

He bared his lips, his ears flattened back, and his fur stood on edge.

"You're right. I can't make you, but you have to lance this wound. Not to forget her, never, but you haven't properly mourned your baby girl, have you?"

He gave a soft whine, his muzzle drooping.

"You had to grieve Delphine first. That's understandable. She was the one you knew and loved. You're not a bad person." I rubbed my heart. "Grief sticks you in limbo. You thought you'd gotten free but today was a trigger. It may not feel like you deserve to be unstuck right now, and we both know how scary it is to let yourself fully live again after something so unthinkable has happened, but you want to." I waved my hand around this lovingly refurbished space and noticed for the first time that some of the boards had been taken down from the second floor.

He was expanding his home. I steeled my shoulders because he wouldn't be closing it off again on my watch. "This is you. This beautiful gem that you poured your heart into because you wanted a home. You wanted connection. You have to go through the pain in your human form, sweetheart. And if you want me to, I'll stay by your side for however long you need."

The wolf simply watched me.

I threw my hands up. "Do you want me to go?"

He snapped his teeth at me.

"Then shift." I gave him three minutes. "No?" I walked toward the foyer.

He butted me backward with his muzzle, then slunk off into the back.

I folded his torn clothes, laying them on a chair, then I paced the room, idly perusing the books on his shelf and flipping through the stack of sheet music on the piano.

After wiping my sweaty palms on my poor skirt for the umpteenth time, I called Emmett to see if Pyotr could get him a return trip through the KH without me. I wasn't worried about Smoky's or Neon Sign Face's reactions to the Ohrist power that animated the golem, since Emmett was treated like any object with that magic and basically ignored, but I wasn't sure he could enter and exit without me assisting.

Emmett replied "No sweat" then asked what the mission was. The glee in his voice made me smile, even if it didn't reach my eyes. I gave him Justine's address, explained about the murder, and instructed him to get her laptop and any notes. As an afterthought, I asked Tatiana to tell Zev and Gabriel about the scientist's demise. Imogine was still out there, and we'd concentrate our efforts on finding her, but meantime, better Tatiana deal with Zev's rage at the news of Dr. Eversol's death than me.

I was grateful that it didn't occur to Emmett to question why I was delegating all that, since Laurent's condition wasn't mine to share. The golem assured me he'd get in touch as soon as he had her stuff and hung up.

When Laurent came back, once more dressed, he walked slowly—as if he'd gone ten rounds with a heavyweight champ. His eyes were dry, which wasn't a great sign.

I sat down, patting the cushion.

He rubbed his left ring finger, unable to meet my eyes. "Maybe I should be alone."

If I assured him his grief was nothing to be embarrassed about, that would make things worse. I didn't think he should be by himself, especially after how desperate he'd been for me to stay, but if he required solitude to get through this emotional upheaval, I'd respect that.

For now. But there was no way in hell I was letting him regress back to death-wish dude.

I prayed he didn't want to become that man again either.

"Okay." I gathered up my purse, hugging him on my way out. Same as I would with Jude or Ava or Daya.

He held himself stiffly, then his arms came around me and he held on like his life depended on it, his head buried in the crook of my neck. We stayed that way until a strangled sob tore from his throat and he pressed his fists against his eyes.

I led him back to the sofa, where he slid onto the ground, his face buried on his arms which rested on his bent knees. His cries were silent, his body racked with shudders.

I dropped down beside him, holding him tightly because I recognized that grief.

It was a sorrow so deep that it carved a canyon in your soul, and while it seemed like it existed only for this wave of emotion to batter against, one day his life would expand around that sadness, and as much as it would always hurt, it wouldn't make up the entirety of his reality. Like it had for me and it had for him before, eventually, he'd be able to sit at its edge without wanting to hurl himself off.

He cried himself out until all he had left was deep, raspy breaths, then he rubbed a hand across the back of his neck, a flush creeping across his cheeks.

I brushed my nose against his. "I don't think less of you because you cried."

"No. You are a very good mother."

I pulled away. "Mother? Wow. Okay, so we're never having sex again."

"Merde." Laurent raked his hands through his hair. "I am making a hash of this."

"I'll be honest," I said, "it's not sounding great."

He clasped my hands. "Today, that girl..." He cleared his throat. "That vampire. It was horrible, but it was what I needed. I know it will take time to grieve my baby, but I feel like I've been drained of this poison that clogged my veins. And I'm very glad you were here with me."

No death wish, no regression, no running away, just an adult acknowledgment that this would be hard, from a man who'd broken open that last piece of sorrow.

"I'm glad too," I said, and rested my head on his shoulder.

16

Emmett and I met a couple hours later in Pyotr's cave for the handover. The golem wore a trench coat that was too short and tight and a pair of dark sunglasses, and somehow Pyotr had unearthed one of those pairs of plastic glasses with a fake nose and mustache that made everyone look like Groucho Marx. It kept sliding down his stone nose to hit his chin.

I crossed my arms. "You've got to be kidding me."

They stood together in a shadowy spot, looking furtive. Emmett had a messenger bag tucked under his arm, but when he went to hand it over, Pyotr elbowed him and shook his head.

"Right. Code word, toots."

"Give me the bag, Emmett."

"How we know it's you?" Pyotr reached for my ears. "Could be glamor."

I slapped his hands away. "Drop this nonsense or you won't get an invitation to my dinner tomorrow." I jabbed a finger at Emmett's. "Yours can be revoked too."

They exchanged a look, then turned their backs on me and had a whispered conversation.

Seriously? I'd left Laurent for this?

Emmett gave me the bag. "The laptop was encrypted. Mr. Toledano sent someone for it and as soon as they break in, he'll make sure Gabriel gets it."

"And?" Pyotr prompted.

"Oh yeah. The vamp is taking care of cleanup."

"Good," I said absently, studying the gargoyle. "Pyotr, did you go with Emmett to Dr. Eversol's house?"

Pyotr rocked from one foot to the other, his face lapsing into such a sorrowful expression that the glasses fell off and plopped onto the ground. "Is bad?"

"Not at all. You two make a good team." I made a note to speak to Tatiana about letting Pyotr be an official associate. A gargoyle would be a real asset, especially one who would soon be jobless when I destroyed his workplace.

My guilt was eased by Pyotr hopping up and down, flapping his wings and almost taking out Emmett's eye. "Crime-fighting duo. And we have disguises, so no one knows it's us."

"I'm the senior partner, obviously," Emmett said.

Pyotr waved a dismissive hand at him. "Yes. Yes."

I slung the light bag across my torso. "Not many notes?"

"No notes at all. I got you the only paper I could find." Emmett smacked his fist into his palm. "But don't worry, I did a thorough search."

God, he'd wrecked the place. "Okay, thanks."

Apparently, leaving through the same shadows I'd come from was only an option when Smoky approved it. Or for Emmett, because he didn't register as alive. He had the gall to smirk as he waltzed back into Tatiana's. Meantime, I had to pick a sock and do the obligatory trek through the KH until the exit to Laurent's appeared.

I walked into the hotel and threw the bag on a chair, hearing Laurent speaking French in the kitchen. I didn't bother announcing my presence—he'd both heard and scented me—but I did wait until he was off the phone to join him.

"I've created a monster," I said.

"Emmett?"

"Him too."

Laurent had made good use of our time apart by fixing us sandwiches and more coffee.

I bit into the crunchy sourdough piled high with turkey slices and a cranberry mayo. "You're the best," I said through a mouthful. I swallowed. "Was that Gabriel? How is he?"

Dr. Eversol hadn't been his close friend, but she was still a respected colleague.

"Not great, obviously, but he was glad we made it out unscathed."

We carried our food to the dining room table where I dumped out the contents of the bag.

Laurent picked up the closest page, covered in precise print. "It's a letter to her daughter."

My pulse spiked and I curled my fingers into my palms against my instinct to grab it from him in case the letter upset him, but he read it calmly.

"Quit watching me, Mitzi. I'm not going to wolf out."

"I was waiting for you to read it," I lied.

He shook his head, but under the table, he nudged my foot with his.

I took half the pile, the two of us eating and reading in silence. Occasionally, one or the other made notes on the legal pads that Laurent had produced. By the time we finished the pile, our food was long gone, and daylight had faded. I stood up to stretch out my kinked back and neck.

Laurent rolled his shoulders back. "Twenty years. That's a long time to hang on to hate."

"I'm not sure I'd be any different if my child had been turned. Miranda was a baby." I smoothed out one of the letters that I'd stained with tears. "Justine tried so hard to protect her, but when she couldn't, and Miranda went feral..." I sighed.

"I'm not judging her." He gave me a wry smile. "She trapped, sedated, and experimented on vampires for years before Imogine found her and they perfected the virus. Makes me feel like a slacker for wasting away the best years of my revenge."

"So you should. Taking on Banim Shovavim magic and existing to only kill dybbuks was pretty lazy of you." He'd never explained how he acquired his second set of powers, but given how much pain he was in every time he used them, I didn't need—or want—to ask.

Laurent leaned across the table to catch my hand and stroked my knuckles with his thumb. "She never found any other reason to be happy."

"It's too heartbreaking." I slid my hand free and gathered up the letters. "The number of elements that had to line up for this virus to happen are incredible. Miranda's death, the precise advances in biohacking technology that allowed this vector to not only disseminate the magic virus into vamps' systems but pair with the magic in the first place."

"The luck and timing of meeting Imogine." He frowned. "I'd love to know how that happened."

"Me too." I thrust the letters back into the messenger bag. "Maybe we'll get a chance to ask the vampire when we find her." This couldn't be an "if" scenario. Zev wouldn't accept that, nor would Gabriel.

I fiddled with the zipper. "Laurent?"

"Hmm."

"Do you want kids?" It took all my courage to look at him. "Because I don't, but I also don't want you to miss out on being a dad if that's what you want." Losing him now wouldn't be easier than if I lost him in twenty years. He was tied into the fabric of my life. His friends and family were now mine, hell Nav was dating my ex, and his aunt was my boss.

Was I supposed to cut everyone out to stop the reminders of him?

How would that even work? Change my name? Leave the country and send Sadie cryptic postcards?

"Stop it," Laurent growled.

I blinked at him.

He tapped his head. "You're making lists and not the fun kind."

"How—you— There's no way you could know that." Huffing, I crossed my arms.

His eyes twinkled and his lips quirked. "I don't want children."

"If you say so."

"Mmm." He nodded. "Want to say that again with slightly less skepticism?"

I twisted my fingers together. "I just want you to be sure."

"I am. Believe me. I get to be Uncle Wolf and now I have Sadie in my life as well. Truth be told?" He rubbed his left ring finger. "I would have been overjoyed at Delphine's pregnancy, but if I'm honest, I think she didn't tell me because I also would have been fine never having kids."

"Oh."

He peered at me with a worried look. "Does that upset you? Sadie means everything to you."

I held up my hand. "I don't think everyone should have or even want them. It's a personal choice. Jude doesn't. She loves being Sadie's aunt and that's enough. I was just surprised by that admission. No judgment."

"That's settled then." He rapped the dining room table. "It's been a long day. Will you stay over? I want you here but…" He grimaced. "I'm too exhausted for anything other than sleep."

"Sleep is enough for me tonight. We have all the time in the world for other things."

It was the second time Laurent had missed out on the

thong and corset, but third time was the charm. Besides, when he held me all night, being vulnerable with his body and soul because he trusted me, my night was perfect anyway.

———

I spent the next day running all over the city to get ingredients for dinner, not crashing through my front door with my first load of grocery bags until 3:30 PM. My fingers were turning white from the weight, and I sped into the kitchen to dump everything on the counter and fire off a quick text to Eli to come over and help me.

On the return trip to my car for the rest, I happened to glance in my living room and almost tripped over my feet backtracking.

A sound between a growl and a deflating helium balloon punched out of me as I circled the empty space where my precious sofa had once been.

Correction. It wasn't an entirely empty space, because the beautiful wine-colored velvet masterpiece had been replaced by a dog bed.

I whipped out my phone and called my possibly former boyfriend, but it went straight to voice mail. Well, he wouldn't bail on tonight so he could enjoy the two hours of life he had left.

"Mir?" Eli came inside. "Got an extra bottle of—"

"Did you help?" My teeth were bared.

He saw the dog bed, laughed, then immediately schooled his face to a very neutral expression. "Nope."

Eli hadn't let him in, and Sadie was on her way home from school, which meant Laurent had broken in. "Was Nav part of the heist?"

Eli snickered again and I smacked him. "I don't know," he said, raising his hands. "I swear, but it is pretty funny."

It was. Unless a single velvet fiber had been harmed, in

which case I'd be laughing all the way to Laurent's house like Jack in *The Shining*.

My ex took the meat and some soy sauce to his place and returned with a bunch of folding chairs since I no longer had a sofa for anyone to sit on. I arranged them around the living room before dashing out for one more quick shop. At least there was no danger of my baby getting stained tonight.

By the time I got home, Sadie was waiting to help me prep. I'd opted to save time and effort and bought several fruit and veggie platters along with tons of premade side dishes from a couple of delis.

While I dressed and showered, Sadie put things on serving plates and in bowls and into the fridge until our guests came. Since she didn't ask about the sofa, Eli had filled her in.

I quickly vacuumed and was cutting up cheese for a charcuterie platter when Eli entered holding a couple of glass baking dishes piled high with grilled meat.

Then Jude showed up at the back door, looking calm and refreshed after her yoga retreat, holding a foil-covered cake plate. "Lemon cake."

Sadie peeked under the foil. "Your mom's recipe. You're the best, Aunt Jude."

Jude squeezed her niece in a one-armed hug. "I am. And you're looking much better than the last time I saw you."

"I'm doing better. Mostly." Sadie waved her hand around. "I'm going to keep an eye out for guests." She scurried out.

"What's up with that?" Jude said.

"She owes Ava and Romi an apology. I'll fill you in later." I poured us each a glass of red wine. "Look at you, so pretty and clay-free. My goodness, is that actual color you're wearing instead of the black of your shriveled soul?"

"Don't get used to it." She saluted me with the wineglass. "You clean up real well, sug, wearing clothes I've never seen before and a divine haircut." She sipped the wine. "Did you finally ditch the sadness wardrobe?"

"Okay, first, stop talking to Emmett. Second, yes I did." I tossed my head back. "And I look fabulous."

"Apparently, there's a lot I have to catch up on."

My doorbell rang.

"Yup, but I'll explain some of it when everyone's here." I handed her the charcuterie board. "Put this on the coffee table by the veggies, will you?"

I headed into my foyer to her "Where in tarnation is your sofa?" My cheeks got hot, my skin tight and itchy. My first gathering of family and new friends and I had to entertain them looking like I was a broke university undergrad.

Sadie had already answered the door and was taking coats from Tatiana, Juliette, and Gabriel. Emmett was wearing an old man's cardigan that he didn't want to part with.

Juliette's hair was a wind-tousled mess, and Gabriel looked a bit green.

"You all came with Tatiana, I take it?" I grinned.

My boss muscled past me. "They can take the bus next time. So much kvetching. Oy."

I peered out the door and down the sidewalk.

"Looking for my uncle?" Juliette said. "That's sweet."

"You may not feel that way after I break his legs."

She fumbled the hair elastic that she'd pulled off her wrist. "What? Why?"

"Miriam," Tatiana barked from the living room. "I pay you enough to own proper furniture."

I counted backward from five and took a deep breath. "He stole my couch."

Juliette pressed her lips together, turning away to put her hair in a ponytail.

"Ciao, bella."

I turned to the voice and shrieked, my hand flying to my racing heart because Giulia peered at me upside down from my roof. I ushered her inside, but before I could shut the door, Ava called out, "Two more."

She and Romi had brought another couple bottles of wine.

"My favorite kind of guests." I hugged them, then took their coats.

Sadie hovered in the foyer, nervously bouncing on her toes. "Can I talk to you both, please?"

The women exchanged looks and then Romi answered, "Sure, honey," in a kind voice, and they followed my daughter upstairs.

I watched them until they were out of view, hoping that Sadie's apology was enough to pave the way for Tovah's parents to forgive her, since the dad was Romi's brother.

"Mir?" Eli sounded a bit strained so I hurried into the kitchen. He was plastered against the cupboards, holding himself very still while a large cat gargoyle rubbed herself against his hip.

"He smells nice," Giulia said.

"That's my ex-husband, Eli. Eli, this is Giulia."

Someone knocked on the front door, and Emmett called out that he'd get it.

A large figure lumbered out of the shadows, and Eli sucked in a breath.

"And Pyotr. Glad you made it, buddy," I said. "Pyotr, this is Sadie's dad, Eli, and Giulia."

Pyotr nodded at Eli then waggled his fingers at Giulia. "Hello, most beautiful gargoyle ever."

Giulia beamed at him, still marking Eli. "Ciao, bello."

Pyotr turned to me expectantly. "My bestie is here?"

"Yup. She'll be down in a minute. Emmett's in the living room if you—" I chuckled, the gargoyle having waddled out before I could finish the sentence.

"Bloody hell, Giulia, get off my man." Nav strode into the kitchen, which was now far too crowded, and plonked a bottle of wine on the counter. After shooing the cat away from Eli, Nav draped an arm over his boyfriend's shoulder.

"You get all the pretty ones," Giulia sulked.

Eli quirked an eyebrow at Nav. "*All* the pretty ones? Sounds like a long list."

Nav swept a hand along his body. "My innate charm and dashing good looks make me a magnet, darling. It's a blessing and a curse."

"Eli, get Nav a drink. Giulia, do you want water or are you hungry?" I motioned to a platter laden with plump slices of fatty tuna and salmon with a sign reading "for Giulia" in fancy script.

She purred at the food and licked my hand. "I will visit for now," she said and scampered off.

"Where's Daya?" I said.

"Emergency C-section," he said. "She sends her regrets with strict instructions to call and set up a girl's night."

"Yes, please." I reclaimed my wineglass from the counter. "Where's my sofa, Nav?"

"Are you in the habit of misplacing furniture, poppet?" He sipped the merlot that Eli had poured him.

"I know you helped him."

"Hypothetically." Nav traced a finger along Eli's arm, speaking to my ex. "Would it upset you if I had?"

"I'm staying out of it." Eli helped himself to a cold beer from the fridge. "But hypothetically, return the couch unscathed. It would be a shame to have to replace you."

Nav gasped. "I am irreplaceable."

Eli shrugged. "I mean, I'd mourn you. But I'd move on." He slapped his rock-hard abs. "I'm a catch, man." He laughed as Nav turned and pressed against him, whispering something in my ex's ear that had him blush and smile at his boyfriend sweetly.

"Ugh." After topping up my wineglass, I fled the kitchen, running into Ava and Romi coming down the stairs. "How'd it go?"

Ava smiled in reassurance. "Good."

"She was very contrite and misses Tovah a lot," Romi said.

"And Tovah misses her too. I'll talk to my brother and sister-in-law. Sadie made a mistake, but she's young, and new to magic. She deserves a second chance."

"Thank you so much."

"Now that that's over." Ava adjusted the cute rectangular glasses she wore. "Wine?"

"Absolutely." We caught up for a bit, and then I announced to everyone to come get dinner.

I was waiting my turn to fill up on the buffet-style spread I'd laid out when my front door opened. Trying not to rub my hands like a cartoon villain, I hurried into the foyer to greet my final guest.

"Sorry." Laurent toed off his shoes. "I had bike trouble."

"Well, you're just in time to eat." I threw him a bright smile.

He studied me for a second, almost as if he expected a different reaction, then followed me into the kitchen, greeting Jude, Gabriel, and Juliette on their way back to the living room with their plates, and being introduced to Ava and Romi.

From the lecherous eyebrow waggle Ava threw me, I was in for an interrogation later.

Giulia, on the floor next to Tatiana in the living room, called out to Laurent, blowing him a kiss, which he caught with a wink.

My sofa-missing heart melted. A bit.

Emmett, who was armed with a large plastic bottle of 7UP, and Pyotr, his plate piled high with ribs, barely acknowledged Laurent. They sat at the kitchen table caught in a heated discussion about whether some franchise was better as a television series or movie.

My boyfriend's stomach rumbled when he saw the spread, and he reached for a plate, but I took it away from him.

"I have something special for you." I reached behind the

toaster and pulled out a dog dish with "Mr. Fluffington" written in felt pen.

Laurent chuckled. "Nice one." He reached for another plate, but I stopped him, one eyebrow raised, and held the dish out. "You can't be serious," he said.

"You're in sooooo much trouble," Sadie crowed, heaping potato salad on her dish. "This is nothing compared to everything else Mom's going to do to you for stealing her sofa."

Laurent froze and even Nav choked on the piece of dinner roll he'd stuffed in his mouth. Eli patted his back to help dislodge it.

Bless my child. She was totally lying, since I had nothing else up my sleeve beyond the dog dish, but man, was it fun to watch the culprits squirm.

My boyfriend struck a nonchalant pose. "You didn't like the dog bed?"

Sadie jabbed a large serving fork into a steak to heft it onto her plate. "So. Dead."

"What?" He gave a very Gallic shrug. "It was new and it's much more comfortable than your sofa."

"I'm glad you think so," I said, "since it's the only place you'll ever be sleeping if you stay over."

Sadie covered her ears with a "La la la" and headed out of the room, while Nav snickered.

"Eli," I said, "I'm invoking the 'predated clause.'"

"Miiir," he whined.

I crossed my arms.

"Fine," he groused and smacked Nav, whose eyes widened.

"Did you just hit me and not in a fun way?" The Brit pouted.

"I didn't need to hear that," Laurent muttered.

"No sex until Miri gets her sofa back," Eli said.

Glowering, Nav planted his hands on his hips. "No."

"Sorry, babe. Mir predates you. That's the clause, no way

around it," Eli said. "Plus, she's my baby mama, and she's never invoked it before. Return the sofa."

"But we can't get it out of the storage unit for another two days," Nav protested. "I have needs."

Laurent shook his head. "Didn't need to hear that either."

"Yeah," I agreed. "I'm kind of scarred."

Eli shot me a pleading look, but at my head shake, slumped his shoulders.

Nav jabbed a finger at Laurent. "This is your fault."

"Je ne regrette rien," Laurent said, his emerald eyes glinting. "All right, Mitzi. You'll get your sofa back. Unharmed. Can I have a normal plate now?"

"You'll have a normal plate when I have a normal sofa. In two days." I shoved the dog dish into his chest.

He took it, and with a flourish, loaded it up with chicken and grilled veggies. "I've eaten off worse."

"Wait." Nav held up a hand. "He only has to eat out of a dumb dog dish and I am denied the pleasures of the flesh? It was his idea. How is this fair?"

Eli grimaced. "Call it that again, and it'll be longer than two days."

"That's the rule of the predated clause." Satisfied with the outcome, I finally helped myself to food. "When one party invokes it due to bad behavior from the other party's partner, said partner shall deny their partner sex until the matter is resolved. I'm already the victim here. I'm certainly not going to deny myself sex on top of it."

I'd won this round with Laurent and pissed Nav off, two things that buoyed my mood immeasurably. Conscious of the discussion to come, I bit into a rib. Might as well enjoy myself while I still had an appetite, because if we didn't figure this out and the trio came for me, I doubted I'd be granted a last meal.

17

ONCE EVERYONE HAD EATEN AND THE DISHES WERE stacked in the kitchen for washing later, we decided to hold the brainstorming session while we digested, saving dessert and coffee as a reward—or a pick-me-up.

Given the size of some of my guests, it was too crowded for all of us to fit in the living room, so Pyotr, Emmett, and Giulia got comfortable at the threshold to the foyer. Sadie sat with them, and Giulia laid her head in my daughter's lap to be petted. My kid had begged me for a cat for years, so I figured having a magic one made up for denying her.

Tatiana and Ava had taken the two plush armchairs, with the rest of us using Eli's foldouts.

Although some of the listeners were already aware of the details of the unraveling, having been active participants in it, I recapped the story from the beginning.

"This tale goes back to my childhood, so I'm going to give you the most succinct version I can." I got as comfortable as I could on one of the plastic chairs. "When I was thirteen, my parents were murdered, but I escaped. Their deaths were covered up by the Lonestars in the area, and that same night, a fire burned my home down, destroying all evidence."

I'd kept my voice steady and was surprised when Jude gently placed her hand on mine, making me aware that I was twisting my fingers together. "I hid my magic for years, and that would have been the end of the story had I not been attacked in an alley one night."

Not even those in the know about the angel had heard that part, and there were a lot of angry curses.

"I didn't get hurt," I reassured everyone. "At all. Thanks to my magic."

"I killed him," Laurent said matter-of-factly. "The first night I met Mitzi."

"Good." Eli's voice was hard.

"Nice first date," Pyotr said with approval. "Very romantic."

Wow. My friends were so far from normal.

Thank goodness.

"Moving on," I said. "After some more twists and turns, I started working for Tatiana, who offered to help me find my parents' killer."

Jude raised her hand. "I was both the twist and the turn," she said in her honeyed Southern accent. "I got kidnapped and Miri rescued me."

"Hey," Emmett protested. "I was the twist. She didn't know squat about golems before I showed up."

Eli snorted. "And you said my cop buddies had over-the-top stories."

I smiled. "I was young and innocent. Okay, so a few months ago, Tatiana found the name of the Lonestar who'd covered their deaths up. Fred McMurtry. I also discovered that right around the same time that they died, he'd been infected with a demon parasite that cured his terminal cancer and allowed him to live for thirty more years."

"Which is why you pursued the idea that a demon had killed your parents," Nav said. "Since only demons can travel to the demon realm."

"Right. I was convinced a demon had to be behind this, either on their own or working with someone." The chair creaked as I wriggled to get comfortable. "When I went to confront McMurtry, he was murdered in the same way. His neck was snapped, and then a very controlled fire was set, which burned his place down and nowhere else. Both were done with magic." I shifted my weight from side to side because my ass was falling asleep on this dumb chair. Laurent owed me a dozen massages. "Long story short, I recently switched my prime suspect to Dumah, the angel in charge of torturing dybbuks in Gehenna."

Tatiana gave me a shrewd look, then inclined her head as if in thanks for leaving out the Ascendant and her ties to it. Not to mention the part where she'd tried to kill me.

I returned the gesture. "But I was mistaken about that as well. I know now without a shadow of a doubt that Senoi, Sansenoi, and Sammaneglof, the three angels who attempted to eradicate the original Banim Shovavim, and who created the hunters, were responsible."

"I never thought about it," Nav said, "but angels can enter the demon realm. Good sleuthing, Velma."

"Gee, thanks."

Ava sat forward, her empty wineglass clutched in her hand. "That's one crazy story. But how can we help you?"

"I'll never get justice, not that anything could make up for losing Mom and Dad, but I have an opportunity to unravel those three, forcing them to spend eternity aware—" I held up a finger with a cold smile. "Yet powerless to do anything or hurt anyone ever again."

"I like the sound of this." Giulia flicked the claws of her right forepaw out.

"How?" Gabriel's eyes gleamed with the same intrigue I felt when I had a fascinating puzzle to solve.

Once more I explained the chemical formula around creating fire and how light and dark magic in this case were the equivalents of oxygen and fuel, while the Ascendant was the heat that created the shock wave reaction. At least, that's what we'd initially believed.

"How did you attempt it?" Daya said.

"We sent Ohrist and Banim Shovavim magic through a magic amplifier that was touching the rock in the KH but that wasn't the way to go," I said.

Juliette rocked her chair back onto two legs. "Did you try different variables?"

"Yes," Laurent said. "I attempted it first since I possess both types of powers. Then Tatiana and Mitzi combined their abilities."

"You started with one person who had both types of magic and then tried it with the power separated into two people," Nav said.

"Yeah." Tatiana reapplied her coral lipstick. "Bupkis."

"You haven't slotted in a different variable for the Ascendant," Eli pointed out.

"No." I spread my hands wide. "That's what I'm hoping to brainstorm. No one has attempted to touch the trio in a very long time because of their fearsome reputation, and very few know how closely they're bound to the KH. That gives us first shot at them." I pulled out my phone and opened my notes app. "I've been assured that the magic part of this formula is correct, but I have no idea what else is more powerful than the Ascendant to nuke the KH."

Everyone gave it their best shot, but as soon as one person suggested something, another had a reason why it should be struck off the list. Either because we'd never get hold of the suggested item, or it was *so* powerful that using it in a contained area like the KH would kill the user.

We'd taken a break so I could serve the various desserts, but once we regrouped, Jude spoke up.

"What if it's not about power, it's about weakness?" she said.

Gabriel pointed at her excitedly with his fork. "Finding the Achilles' heel so to speak."

"Exactly." She scooped a spoonful of chocolate mousse out of her glass dish. "There's this thing in glassblowing called a Prince Rupert's drop. You create it by dripping molten glass into cold water, and it forms this toughened bulb that's tadpole-shaped with a long, thin tail. The bulb won't break. You can smash it with a hammer, even fire bullets into it, and that sucker remains intact because of opposing forces. There's a high compressive strength on the outside and high tensile strength on the inside." She licked off her spoon.

"Bullets? Whoa." Emmett slurped up the last of his seventh or eighth soda.

"That's so cool," Sadie agreed, licking lemon frosting off her fingers.

"Are you proposing," I said, "that the angels' magic interacted with the Kefitzat Haderech the way that ice-cold water acts on a drop of molten glass?"

"Yes and no."

Romi blew on the mug of tea that she cradled. "It's more that the magic the angels have poured into the KH is the tail, with the physical space being the bulb, right?

Ava swallowed the espresso she'd fired back. "Thus, using the Ascendant was the equivalent of hitting the head with a hammer."

"Exactly," Jude said. "The cool thing about a Prince Rupert's drop is that you can't smash the bulb, but one tiny snip of the tail, the sensitive part, and the entire thing explodes." She made the motion with her hands. "It disintegrates into sparkles."

Nav forked a large piece of cake from the plate he and Eli were sharing. "The snip is the piece we need."

"What would circumcise the Kefitzat Haderech?" Tatiana mimed scissors and all the men crossed their legs. "So to speak?"

"More like castrate," Ava piped up.

"Nope," Nav said, popping the p.

I snickered.

Laurent nudged my foot. "You think that approach might work?"

"I'm not sure. Could the more experienced magic users weigh in?" I scraped up the last of my chocolate mousse, ready to dive into my slice of the lemon cake Jude had brought that sat nice and ready on a plate by my foot.

"The hypothesis is sound only if the angels represent the end of that tail," Gabriel said, "and aren't effectively another bulb on the opposite end. Plus, they must be completely interconnected with the magic they're driving into the KH."

"But how you snip Kefitzat Haderech?" Pyotr had chocolate smeared on his mouth. "Is stone."

"Stone has weak spots," Giulia said. "Not me, of course."

"Of course," Pyotr murmured admiringly.

I swallowed my first bite of tangy, moist lemon cake. Jude had outdone herself.

"We have to remember that we're talking about destroying the magic, which in turn will rupture the physical material," Juliette said thoughtfully. "Not attacking the stone itself." She drummed her fingers on her mug of hot chocolate. "We want the place where the trio's magic is strung out the thinnest."

"You use pliers to break the glass," Jude said. "But I have no idea what the equivalent is in the magic version of this scenario."

Nav held up his fork. "I might. We're not dealing with a physical object so the analogy of a snip may be off base. Perhaps a disrupter is needed so that the Ohrist and Banim Shovavim magic can do their thing, in which case, may I propose a magic tuning fork?"

Laurent snorted, then at Nav's cool stare, said, "That wasn't a joke?"

"No, that was my brilliance, which, once again, you failed to grasp. Remind me why I keep you around?"

"You don't. I only stay for Daya," Laurent said. "And Evani."

Nav gave an offended huff. "I'll accept my sister—"

"Because she can kick your ass," Laurent said.

His best friend glared at him. "But I will not be outranked by a toddler."

"Back to the tuning fork," Jude interjected.

I shot her a grateful look.

"You're proposing that the vibrations would disturb the magic akin to how a real tuning fork disturbs air molecules?" she said.

"Precisely, love," Nav said. "Tap it against the KH to initially break up the magic stranglehold that the angels have on it, then send light and dark power through to finish the job."

"Not only that," Romi said thoughtfully. She balanced her dessert plate on her lap. "It might be a vessel through which to bring Banim Shovavim and Ohrist magics, very different things, into harmony or balance."

"Good point," Nav agreed.

"It's worth a shot," Jude said.

"Is it a demonic artifact?" Giulia's expression was a little too interested, but she raised a good question. Throwing demon powers into the mix was a bad idea.

Nav shook his head. "We confiscated it a while back when dealing with a demon, but it's Ohrist made."

"Great." I pointed at him. "You get us that fork. Tatiana, are you up for another go-around with me in the KH to use it?" She looked offended that I'd even asked, so I moved on, looking at Pyotr. "My best guess for the thinnest spot to use it is somewhere in the prison that the angels are preparing for Dumah."

The gargoyle nodded. "Yes. Is so, I think."

I scraped my fork across a smear of lemon frosting, catching some final crumbs. "That said, the prison itself is enormous. How do we pinpoint the exact location?"

Juliette and Gabriel bent their heads together, speaking quietly in French. "Papa and I will figure it out," the young woman said. "Tatiana? How about you?"

My boss grunted her agreement, since her mouth was full of cake, and motioned at Pyotr with her fork.

He lit up. "Really?"

She swallowed. "You've got the insider knowledge that we need."

Sadie gave Pyotr a huge grin and clapped him on the shoulder.

The gargoyle waved his hand like a little kid in class who really had to go pee. "But is other problem. Angels not let anyone in there now."

I slumped back against my chair, defeat seeping through the room. "Is it completely fortified already?"

"No, but no one can get in without them knowing."

"Cheer up, peeps." My golem partner set his glass on the floor and got to his feet. "Emmett to the rescue. The KH doesn't detect me. I bet whatever sensor those angels have on the prison won't either."

"No way." I shook my head emphatically.

He glowered at me. "You said you wouldn't mother me."

I dumped my plate on the floor, the fork clattering against it. "This isn't mothering. If we were certain that you were right, that would be one thing, but this assumption could cost you your life. Arlo was this disembodied thing in there. I don't want that to happen to you."

"That makes two of us, toots." Emmett shrugged. "Give me an alternative."

I dropped my stare to the ground as everyone looked my way, the silence growing heavy.

"I don't have one," I admitted.

"I'll be okay," Emmett said, and made the sign of the cross. "Scout's honor."

I gave a half laugh, half sob. Sure he was my partner and I trusted him to do the job properly, but sitting there with Pyotr and Sadie, he was also a kid that I'd adopted into this crazy family. Shit. I *was* mothering him.

Laurent squeezed my leg. "Emmett can do this."

The golem preened at that vote of confidence.

"I know," I said. "Thank you for volunteering, buddy." I shook a finger at him. "At the first sign of any angel or the slightest trouble you abandon ship. Also, you can go into the prison alone, but I'm going with you into the KH. Got it?"

"Got it." Emmett high-fived Sadie.

Pyotr thumped his chest. "As partner, I will keep safe."

Tatiana coughed on the sip of tea she'd taken and glanced at me.

Smiling brightly, I gave her two thumbs up, and she sighed, muttering under her breath about payrolls and overhead.

Even though I insisted Sadie and I would handle the cleanup, my friends all pitched in, although Tatiana took more of a management role, directing us to plates and glasses we'd missed.

I stood at the sink, elbow deep in hot water and suds, scrubbing Jude's cake plate, and letting the laughter and friendly chatter wash over me. Had someone told me six months ago that my home would be full of new friends, both human and not, who I had entrusted my past and future to, I'd have laughed. Then probably drank a lot of wine to combat the very idea of opening myself up like that.

Laurent scraped some bones into the composter on my counter, then brushed my hair away to murmur that Giulia and Pyotr were both leaving. It was such an ordinary, small gesture, but I blinked away the sudden dampness in my eyes, because I hadn't experienced that easy intimacy with anyone since Eli.

The feeling was even more profound since I didn't have to hold part of myself back—with anyone who mattered. For so long, I was certain that the only way to live was to keep myself apart, but I'd been slowly strangling myself. Sure, I'd survived, but I'd been like a scrawny weed stuck between the rocks, instead of the lush, blooming flower I'd become. My friends, my family, my ability to fully trust again were nutrients that I'd been deprived of. Now that I had them, I couldn't get enough, and I was grateful for every single one of these individuals.

I dried off my hands and headed into the foyer.

To my surprise, Giulia and Pyotr weren't just leaving at the same time, they were leaving together. Pyotr was taking her into the KH before going to see where she lived.

While Giulia filled in for Harry as the supernatural intermediary every now and again, they were more work colleagues than friends. That wasn't all that remarkable, given Giulia's natural aloofness, but Pyotr, with his sweet nature and giant heart, had swept her reserve away and made her another bestie. I almost laughed at how stunned Giulia looked, pressed up against Pyotr while my other friends said goodbye to them (though Eli kept a careful distance), but I was happy for her and delighted to have played a role in changing her life for the better.

I cornered Gabriel before he left to inquire whether Dr. Eversol's laptop had been decrypted, and if so, whether her notes mentioned Imogine's magic.

Unfortunately, while he now had access to the computer, and her notes gave some useful insights on how she'd created the vector, the vampire's magic was merely referred to as "the X factor." Gabriel was still stumped, and apparently Zev was getting extremely antsy.

A favorite among the vampire emotion smorgasbord.

It was after midnight by the time Jude, Ava, and Romi left. Sadie had gone back to Eli's and Laurent had returned home a while back, scared either that he'd really have to sleep on the dog bed, or more likely, terrified of being stuck with a group of women who'd been shooting him calculated looks all night.

Yes, I answered all their questions. Yes, there were a lot of them. But there was also a lot of raucous support, and on the whole, I got off pretty lightly.

I'd lost a phenomenal couch (temporarily) but gained a huge family. The trade-off was almost worth it.

18

WEDNESDAY DAWNED AS ONE OF THOSE PERFECT Vancouver late summer days. Leaves were still green, flowers colorful, and it was warm enough to wear a short-sleeved shirt with my lightweight linen pants. I'd just pulled out my makeup kit when the doorbell sounded.

Laurent and Nav stood on the duplex's long front porch with my sofa resting between them.

I leaned against the doorframe. "What happened to being unable to retrieve it for another two days?"

Nav lifted his end, indicating for Laurent to do the same. "Did I or did I not tell you I had needs?"

"Did you break into wherever you'd stashed it?" I shook my head. "Don't tell me. Plausible deniabil—stop!"

The men froze, Laurent all of two steps inside my door, and my sofa wedged in the doorway.

"Tell me you took the door off when you stole it and didn't just shove my baby through."

My possibly former boyfriend looked away.

"Oh my God." I called up my scythe, resting it on my shoulder. "If there is a single smudge or tear on it, you'll be sorry. Now back up, take the door off, and move it inside properly."

The guys exchanged a silent communication. "Do we get a screwdriver?" Laurent said.

"Use your claws," I said sweetly. "I'm going to finish getting ready, and when I come down, I expect my house to be in order." I jabbed the weapon at them. "Got it?"

They nodded meekly.

I stomped upstairs, shaking my head at how two otherwise smart men could be so stupid. Luckily for them, when I did my extremely thorough check of the sofa and my doorframe, all was unmarred.

Once I gave them a terse nod that I was satisfied, Nav planted his hands on his hips. "Do you revoke your stupid predated clause?"

"Yes. Return to your regularly scheduled flesh pleasuring. But not anywhere Sadie can hear you."

"I do live with a toddler with no sense of boundaries and very sharp hearing. I know how to conduct myself."

"Good," I said.

"Good," he returned snippily and left.

Laurent snapped his fingers. "Give me the dog bed."

"But where will you sleep if you stay over?" My words ended in a laughing yelp as he tackled me onto the sofa. God, she was a dream to lie on.

He booped me on the end of my nose. "You're thinking about the furniture, aren't you?"

"No," I said, nodding my head yes.

He grabbed my wrists and pinned them above my head.

"Am I going to be punished now?" I said happily.

"I guess we can call a détente."

"How magnanimous of you." I draped my arms around his neck and leaned up for a kiss.

He complied with enthusiasm. A lot of enthusiasm that was getting me all wriggly as I ground against it.

"We have to stop," I said.

He nuzzled my neck. "Are you sure?"

"No playing dirty. We're in détente mode." I pushed against his chest. "I'm going to visit the Wise Brothers' bookstore again and search for a way into their game show studio in case they're hiding there. Come with me?"

Laurent rolled off me and sat up. "Why yes, that sounds like so much more fun." He heaved a sigh. "D'accord. We do need to learn Imogine's location. Should we get the Dantora painting?"

"Let's find Hiram and Ephraim first." I didn't mention that this was as much about rescuing the Wise Brothers from any dangerous situation they'd found themselves in as the vampire, but given the way Laurent rolled his eyes, he understood.

I patted his cheek. "Good behavior shall be well rewarded."

The bell jangled merrily as we stepped inside the hush of the bookstore. Part of me had hoped to find Hiram or even a scowling Ephraim behind the counter, but it was the same man we'd encountered previously.

The ideal scenario would have been to go in cloaked, but I couldn't hide both of us and check for any ways into the hidden game show space, especially not using both my regular vision and that of Delilah.

Fake Owner was ringing up a large purchase of books on his old-fashioned cash register, looking laid-back with his surfer hair, T-shirt with a curling wave graphic, and a braided black leather bracelet. There was no stack of books on the glass counter this time, but the travel mug and register had been joined by a sleek silver laptop.

Theo the dog lounged on the threadbare rug under the bronze chandelier, once again growling at Laurent.

My partner angled himself so the humans in the store couldn't see anything and let his wolf out, his canines elongated and his eyes changing shape.

The dog whimpered and lay his head down.

Fake Owner looked surprised to see us, but I turned on the charm, gushing about how sorry I'd been not to get to browse last time we were here, and how as a librarian, bookstores were second only to libraries as my favorite places.

Honestly, I had no idea if he bought it, but he told us to enjoy ourselves and to ask if we had any questions.

Laurent and I crowded into the first narrow aisle walking toward the back, where I'd decided to begin the search. Unlike the windows, which displayed books willy-nilly, the books here were categorized by genre and author. It wasn't the Dewey decimal system, but it didn't make me long to pull the books down and reorganize them either.

The store was deeper than expected, and the farther back we went, the dimmer it grew, the smell of old paper growing stronger.

I trailed a fingertip along one of the surprisingly dust-free bookshelves. "Not like I'm a magic detector," I said quietly, "but I don't sense anything off and we haven't hit any wards."

Laurent edged one of the titles off the shelf, rubbing his thumb over the faded gold embossed title of an old noir mystery. "Could be that whatever magic compelled that guy to believe he owns this place would have conflicted with any wards."

"Could be, but does this new magic, whatever it is, override access to their game show studio?" I rapped on the wall.

Laurent shrugged.

We worked quietly but couldn't find a way into the hidden space.

I clicked on my phone's flashlight, which added enough

light back here to animate Delilah and see through her green vision, but whether viewed through her eyes or mine, the results were the same.

The bell on the door chimed, the customer calling out bye.

"You distract the guy, I'll search," I said.

Laurent strode off. "I'm looking for a limited-run hard-boiled crime anthology," he said a moment later, "but I've forgotten the title of it."

"I can definitely help you with that," Fake Owner said.

Keeping one ear turned to their conversation, I slowly trod up and down the other aisles seeking out the hidden entrance, my head pounding from concentrating so hard through both my regular and magic visions.

About three-quarters of the way through my search, Theo joined me, trotting along with his tongue hanging out.

I scratched a tuft of gray fur on his head. "Hey, buddy," I murmured. "Where are Hiram and Ephraim?"

Sadly, Theo didn't answer in the King's English or even with a single bark perfectly conveying their location. *Hiram and Ephraim fell down the well* would have been a great clue at this point. Instead, a long string of drool fell from his mouth to the worn floorboards and that was about it.

Back at the cash register, the owner triumphantly announced he'd found the anthology and could order it in for Laurent.

Our time was running out.

I hurried through the rest of the store, but although I didn't find anything, I remained convinced there had to be a way into that game show studio.

Laurent was giving a PO box address to send the book to when I rounded the last bookshelf and returned to the main open area. Massaging my temples, I squinted at the sun hitting my eyes through the glass door, and quickly turned my head away, having a vertiginous moment where the aftereffects of the sunlight intersected with both Delilah's and my vision.

It caused this weird dissonance, and as I spied the owner out of the corner of my eye, he flickered. I attempted to replicate it but couldn't, nor was there anything strange about him when viewed directly through Delilah's green vision.

Smiling, I approached the counter and slid my arm through Laurent's. "I just found the best coffee table book on Rome." I pointed toward the back.

"Coming," Laurent said.

Fake Owner waved him off, typing in the order on the laptop.

Once our heads were bent over the admittedly stunning black-and-white photos capturing la dolce vita in that city, I told Laurent what I'd seen. Or thought I'd seen.

He flipped the page, looking pensive. "You didn't see anything strange with Delilah's vision or have any sense of a dybbuk?" When I shook my head, he frowned. "If it is a glamour, we'll have to attack the guy to break it."

I stared at a photo of an old man, his wrinkle-lined face lit up as he saluted the camera with a tiny espresso cup. Oh, to be that carefree. "We ruled out Fake Owner being a vamp on our last visit. Or a demon since he didn't react to Delilah. Now, if he's a golem with a human glamor on him, that's one thing, but my gut says he's a real person who was forced into this mess, and I don't want to hurt him."

"You saw him flicker," Laurent said. "Your call."

I slowly perused the rest of the book, weighing my options. Dr. Eversol was dead, and Zev would be furious if we walked away when finding Imogine was of the utmost importance. The clock was ticking on a vaccine for the vamp contagion. The trouble was that not only might we badly injure Fake Owner, but we could also break his perception filter, putting us in violation of the Lonestars' prime directive.

"A small attack." I reshelved the book with a heavy heart.

"Nothing drastic, just enough to startle a change in his appearance."

Laurent brushed his knuckles across my cheek. "You want me to do it?"

I smiled at him. "Thank you, but no. It was my idea to come here today. You lock the door and make sure we're not seen."

He kissed the top of my forehead and followed me up to the front.

Fake Owner looked up. "Do you want expedited shipping or—"

His head snapped back from the punch Delilah had landed, and he crashed into the wall behind him, sliding to the floor. Whoops.

"Nothing drastic, huh?" Laurent locked the door and pulled the shade down over the glass.

Wincing, I ran for the counter to check on the man, but before I made it there, the ground rumbled, and the windows rattled.

"Earthquake!" I cried, and spun around, intending to get Laurent and me back into the KH before we were crushed under books. But I froze because it wasn't an earthquake.

It was Theo. His cloudy eyes were a clear and sharp crimson, his mottled gray and tan fur had turned black as pitch, and his razor-sharp teeth and white-foam flecked jaws were befitting of his monstrous new size.

I craned my head up, my pulse spiking.

Laurent snorted. "I'm still the alpha," he said and charged.

That was his issue? I'd have rolled my eyes except they were shaken like googly stick-ons when I was grabbed from behind, lifted high, and slammed back down. Stumbling forward, I rolled my right ankle when I landed, a sharp shaft of pain firing up from my foot.

"Fuuuuck!" My left side had to take the brunt of my

weight because any attempt to balance on my right side was a hell nope.

A loud series of cracks pulled my attention back to my attacker.

Fake Owner's head sat askew on his neck, his right ear now connected to his shoulder. His eyes narrowed at my gobsmacked expression, then he cracked his head back into position with a snap that made me flinch.

Aw shit. Totally called that wrong. Give this demon an Oscar for his acting chops in pretending to be oblivious to Delilah when he first saw her. I dropped into a fighter's stance, scythe in hand, and limped warily around my opponent.

Meanwhile, Laurent had shifted his hands and teeth to wolf form. Both he and Evil Theo were snarling and tearing at each other, but although my boyfriend had a brutal gash along his shoulder, he was landing more hits.

I feinted left with my scythe, the demon easily avoiding the blow. That was fine, because it was a fake out to distract him from Delilah, who'd popped up behind and nailed him in the back of the knee. His leg buckled, but a millisecond before her follow-up crescent kick, his skin turned into a rock-hard armor.

My shadow pulled the kick in time to avoid bashing into his solid form, but I lost my balance, tumbling over.

"Should have butted out." Fake Owner's shadow fell over me, the demon raising his leg for the final blow.

Delilah jammed the scythe into his left eye and he stumbled sideways.

"Should have seen that coming," I taunted, rolling away.

Howling, the demon tore the scythe free, a black viscous liquid pouring from his eyeless socket.

I scooted away on my butt, flinching every time my sprained ankle got jostled.

Delilah once more had the scythe, but there was no point

in going for his skin, and he dodged her attempts to blind him.

My vision grew fuzzy, my animated shadow beginning to stutter to the point where I resorted to throwing books at the demon to keep him occupied.

Evil Theo bit into Laurent's shoulder.

I screamed almost as loudly as Laurent, but my energy was with Delilah, keeping Fake Owner from getting to me, and she couldn't strike him since his skin was still rock-hard.

His chest heaving, Laurent tore free, his bloody shirt shredded. He gave an enraged howl and barreled into Theo, knocking the evil dog into a bookshelf.

It toppled into the next shelf, setting off a domino-like reaction all the way to the back.

My attacker swatted my animated shadow away like a pesky fly.

Get up, Feldman. Don't let him finish you off.

Using the glass counter for support, I struggled to my feet, my breath coming in raspy pants, and my scythe ready, hoping I could get his other eye.

The demon tackled me, sending my weapon flipping into the air like a majorette's baton.

I grunted, my poor back taking the brunt of the fall, but I didn't have a chance to recover because he jumped to his feet and grabbed my legs, swinging me like a discus into an intact bookcase.

Screaming from the hot agony blazing in my ankle, I crashed into a section of self-help books. A side seam popped as I slid to the ground, my head ringing, and reality heaving while books rained down. Couldn't he have chosen a more dignified section to bury me with? Art or poetry, perhaps, crushed by beauty, not seven ways to burn thigh fat.

The demon ran for Laurent.

Dislodging a bunch of books and wishing the bookstore would quit bobbing like we were at sea in a storm, I mustered up the last of my magic reserves, and sent Delilah into the fray with the shadow scythe.

She ran up a wall, flipped over the back of the demon dog, and swung, decapitating Evil Theo.

Laurent spared a glance from dodging Fake Owner's blows to check on me, his features pinched with worry.

I feebly waved my hand like I was tearing open a portal and slurred, "Gehenna."

Luckily, Laurent understood me. He leapt backward, grabbed the heavy cash register, and bashed the demon in the head.

While Fake Owner staggered in a drunken circle instead of politely falling down unconscious, Laurent tried to shift the rest of the way to his wolf form with the precious seconds he'd bought himself, but beyond his already transformed hands and teeth, nothing happened.

The demon grabbed me by the hair in a lightning-fast move. He'd faked being dazed to get close. "I'll kill her first and make you watch."

My boyfriend shot me a wide-eyed look, shaking his paws like he could reboot his magic.

I whimpered, fighting to keep my scalp from being torn off.

Suddenly, dazzling white light leaked out of Laurent's shoes, twining up his legs.

"No," I whispered.

Deploying his Banim Shovavim magic in human form could kill him. His mouth fell open in a silent scream, the tendons in his neck sticking out, and bloody tears fell from his eyes.

The demon was momentarily transfixed, allowing me to pull free and limp away as quickly as possible.

The radiance consumed Laurent, snaking up his torso, forcing his body to twist and bow. It spilled from the top of his head like a radioactive waterfall, driving him to his knees with a weak mewl.

My desire to get to Laurent was thwarted by one of the fallen bookcases. I couldn't climb over it with my injured ankle.

Fake Owner laughed, striding toward me with a nonchalant air.

There were maybe fifteen steps between us. I slammed my scythe into my palm for a last-ditch stand.

Ten steps.

The air went still and I tilted my head, uncertain if the faint scratching noise was real or not.

Five.

I wrinkled my nose at the stench of rotting onions, my face lighting up.

The demon sniffed and spun around.

Still on his knees, Laurent now swayed like a flag in a gale storm, his eyes covered in a film of blood. With a roar, he slashed his glowing fingers through the air.

A jagged portal opened between the demon and me, a malevolent storm swirling on the other side.

For a brief second, I swear I saw my cousin Goldie roll her eyes at me, then the demon was sucked backward, and the portal vanished.

In the quiet of the destroyed bookstore, hanging on to my consciousness by my fingernails, I heard the thump of a cane.

"What part of 'the Wise Brothers don't exist' was an invitation to come in here, undo all my fine work, and wreak havoc on my bookstore?"

I blinked blearily at Hiram, uncertain which of the three versions I saw was the real one. "A simple thank-you would have been nice," I said, and blacked out.

19

THE SOFT STRAINS OF THE BEE GEES' "HOW DEEP IS
Your Love," as played on an electric keyboard complete with
fake bass line and flute, roused me from the depths of my
slumber. I immediately checked my mouth for signs of dental
surgery. Not finding any, I came to the only conclusion I
could: I was dead. Though whether this afterlife waiting room
was upstairs or down remained to be seen.

I wonder what number I had?

"About time you woke up, Goldilocks." A wrinkly white
face loomed over me, and everything came racing back.
"We're not running a B and B."

"Ephraim." I sat up, but a surge of nausea set me flat on
my back again, the movement jostling a bag of frozen peas off
my ankle and onto the floor.

The elderly Ohrist wore a pair of navy pinstripe pants and
a faded navy shirt, both dusted with the ash from the cigar he
puffed on that had missed the small glass ashtray balanced on
his lap.

I fanned away the clove-scented smoke, retrieving the peas
to put back on my injured foot.

Appropriately enough, I lay on a fainting couch in a small

room lined with overflowing bookshelves and artwork placed haphazardly: paintings sat on the floor propped against furniture, a statue was crammed sideways on a shelf, and a creepy wooden mask with horns and wings sprouting from its head dangled from one end of the curtain rod holding once-grand silk gold curtains, now closed. The worn antique coffee table was littered with dirty china teacups, while the only light came from a single standing Tiffany lamp.

I eased myself onto my elbow at a snail's pace. The world held steady, but the thick tensor bandage wrapped around my foot felt like an anchor. I couldn't get an accurate picture of how swollen it was, but at least the cold bag helped numb the pain.

My boots were on the floor, my shirt was torn, and when I touched the back of my skull, my fingernails came away with dried blood under them. "Where's Laurent?"

A shifty look crossed the Ohrist's face before he glanced away. "Hiram. Good. She's all yours."

Hiram's cane thumped closer. "You were with her for all of five minutes."

"I'm not the chatty type."

Snorting, the Black man eased himself down on a turquoise velvet chair with an art deco sculpted back, careful not to wrinkle his carefully pressed trousers. His cane was made of a rich red wood, which matched the color of his shirt. "So, I imagined the last twenty minutes of your bitching?" he said.

Ephraim jabbed the cigar at him, a clump of ash falling onto his leather slippers. "That wasn't bitching. It was me explaining to you—yet again—why that cockamamie carny story was not a stroke of genius."

Hiram coughed pointedly and Ephraim ground the cigar out in the ashtray, which he dumped on the coffee table.

"It deterred the hunters." Hiram jerked his chin at me.

"How was I supposed to know that Nancy Drew here had a bee in her bonnet about finding us?"

"I was worried about you," I snapped. "A mistake I won't make again."

That Bee Gees atrocity cover tune transitioned to a clarinet-heavy version of "Girls Just Want to Have Fun." Not in this reality we didn't.

The Wise Brothers started in on each other again.

"Enough bickering!" I pressed a hand to my throbbing head. "First Laurent, then we'll bond over our hatred of hunters."

"He's not seeing visitors right now," Ephraim said.

Hiram chuckled.

I narrowed my eyes. "Why is that funny?" Hurriedly, I ran through my memories of recent events. *Laurent, blood streaming from his eyes as Banim Shovavim magic poured off him.* I sat up, ignoring the stabbing pain as my sprained ankle hit the ground. "Is he blind?! You think that's a joke?"

"It's only temporary." Hiram smoothed his neat silver mustache with a finger.

"How can you be sure? Was he checked by a healer?"

"Yeah, we brought in the staff of a major metropolitan hospital to care for you two." Ephraim tapped the bag of frozen peas. "What part of 'we're in hiding' hasn't registered yet?"

"I'm sure because his vision is slowly coming back," Hiram said evenly. "We've made him comfortable. Let him rest. I'll take you to him after we talk."

With my injured foot, sprinting past them was out of the question. There were no nearby shadows to escape into, if this was even the real world and not a hidden space, and I was too exhausted to call up my magic. And woozy. Why was I so woozy?

"Is my foot broken?" I said.

"Sprained," Ephraim said.

"Why is it wrapped in about thirty layers of tensor bandage then?"

"What am I, a Boy Scout?" he said. "I checked it for broken bones and wrapped it. I'd have given you the good drugs, but you have a concussion, so you got the fancy peas. You're welcome."

"Thanks for the stellar bedside manner," I said. "But fine. Let's compare notes on the hunters. Straight trade, fact for new fact. No games."

"Deal," Hiram said. "You first."

I settled myself against the fluffy throw cushions, stretching my legs out and repositioning the frozen peas. "Hunters were created by Senoi, Sansenoi, and Sammaneglof."

Hiram did a double take. "The angels who tried to kill Lilith's progeny?"

"Gold star. Your turn."

Ephraim rubbed his jaw. "There are artifacts out there containing trackers that lead hunters to Banim Shovavim."

"Bzzz. Thanks for playing." I mimed pressing a button. "I already know that." Their twin looks of surprise were a joy to behold. I smirked.

"How?" Hiram narrowed his eyes.

Nope. I'd learned negotiations from some great lawyers, spent the last few months studying under my "paycheck über alles" mentor, Tatiana, and topped it off with close and personal raven shifter time.

I crossed my arms. "New fact first."

"The owner and dog you saw were demons that we'd bound," Hiram said.

"I'd never have guessed," I said dryly. "If you're going to waste my time, then this talk is over." It was a total bluff because I had to bring the conversation around to the Dantora painting and see if they could pinpoint Imogine's location.

"Hush a minute and let me finish." He rubbed his knee

with an arthritic hand. "Ephraim and I aren't the only ones binding demons. Those lower-level fiends are extremely popular with certain Ohrists these days."

"Why?"

"New fact first," Ephraim snarked back. He picked up a teacup, sniffed it, considered drinking from it for far too long in my opinion, and then set it down with a sigh.

"I have the Dantora painting."

Hiram regarded me with a shrewd look. "You want something from us. All right. There's going to be an event and these Ohrists want demon bodyguards."

Cagey bastard. I admired him. "The hunter I met was Banim Shovavim."

Hiram paled and Ephraim swore under his breath.

"He's been dealt with, but don't trust anyone," I said.

"Hardly a problem," Ephraim muttered.

Hiram shook his head. "That's not enough to earn you the details of the event. Pony up, kid."

Time to go in with guns blazing. "You know about the vampire contagion?"

"Yeah." Ephraim seemed to notice the ash on him for the first time and dusted it off. "What of it?"

"It's lab made. A Sapien geneticist scientifically created the vector to transmit a specific Ohrist magic that infects vamps."

"And could be modified to infect humans?" Hiram asked.

"In theory. We have someone who can reverse engineer a cure if we find out what Ohrist magic was involved. Unfortunately, the owner of those powers is also a vampire and does not wish to be found."

Ephraim half shot off his chair, his eyebrows raised. "Hiram."

"I know." The other man seemed to shrink in defeat, his shoulders slumping inward.

A heavy lump formed in my gut. "What?"

"The event is an auction. After what you've just told us," Hiram said, "we're concerned that the item in question is the virus."

I swallowed a couple times to clear the sudden dryness in my throat. "Do these Ohrists want to modify the virus to use on others?"

"Agree to hand over the Dantora painting first," Hiram said.

It was my only card. How should I play it? Use it to get Imogine's location—if they had it—or the details of the auction? Now that Dr. Eversol was dead, could anyone other than Imogine have access to a surplus supply?

I drummed my fingers on the sofa's armrest. Shit. "I'll agree on the condition that you tell me everything you know about the auction."

"Don't go there, Miriam." Ephraim's sincerity made my pulse spike. "You'll be the lone Banim Shovavim lamb walking into a den of lions."

I was about to argue that I was hardly a lamb when the penny dropped. "Hunters?"

"Or those sharing hunter beliefs," Hiram said. "It goes beyond Banim Shovavim. These people go after anyone with power who don't fit their sanctimonious idea of who deserves it."

The schmuck trio's gift that just kept giving.

"That's why we found it expedient to get the hell out of Dodge for a while," Ephraim added.

"I'm still going," I said.

Hiram reluctantly gave me the details of the auction, but unfortunately, we had less than forty-eight hours to find a way in, and the Wise Brothers refused to come out of hiding to help procure us an invitation.

"Take me to Laurent."

Hiram lent me an extra cane to hobble around on until I got to a healer. It wasn't stylish like his, but when I stood and put my weight on it, the cane was sturdy, which was all that mattered.

"Sit down, Mitzi." Laurent stood in the doorway. He was pale and had some nasty gashes, but he was walking under his own power, and his eyes were clear. The blood had been washed away.

I did as he asked.

"The polite thing to do when one has shifter hearing is not eavesdrop," Ephraim scolded.

Laurent shot him a "get real" look and sat down beside me. "How many fingers?"

"Two." I pushed his hand down. "And I think that's supposed to be my question. How's your vision?"

"Better. A bit dark at the edges, but I'll recover."

"Told you," Hiram said.

There was so much more to ask him, but I was conscious of the Wise Brothers watching us, so I hugged my boyfriend tightly, the adrenaline fumes I'd been running on giving way to a shakiness. "You saved me."

His arms tightened around me. "We saved each other."

Ephraim gagged.

After arranging to get the painting, the Wise Brothers escorted us to their front door.

"The only way out is through the bookstore," Hiram said.

I impulsively hugged them both. "You two can be real assholes, but I'm glad you're safe."

Ephraim shrugged it off with a sarcastic comment, but his fingers tightened on my shoulder in his one-armed hug, while Hiram told me he'd be very put out if I died at that auction.

I opened the door, the bookstore now intact. Behind the counter was a slender Black woman, with one of those enormous Maine coon cats taking up most of the glass counter.

Hiram winked at me. "Always have a plan B."

20

THE NEXT COUPLE OF DAYS SAW A FLURRY OF successful activity. Juliette healed Laurent and me, and Tatiana called in a favor from a retired macher to snag two invitations to the highly exclusive auction being held in London, decreeing that I would accompany her.

To say that Laurent was unhappy about being left behind would be like saying King Kong was just some ape. He wasn't worried about our safety since events like this were neutral ground. Staging an attack at one would bring the entire global might of the Lonestars down on you, not to mention any criminals or machers in attendance who'd strike back twice as hard. Plus, he knew we could handle ourselves.

But Gabriel was hitching a ride as well since he was returning to France with Dr. Eversol's notes to work on the vaccine vector and await word on Imogine's magic type, and Laurent wanted more time with him.

However, my boyfriend acknowledged that he wouldn't be the best company on a plane, given how anxious he got being enclosed in one. Instead, Gabriel and he made plans to spend the next couple of days together like two besties devastated at being separated, which made me smile dopily.

That aside, I was pumped to go into the field with just my boss. The fact that she'd chartered a private jet, since people would be watching our every move, wasn't too shabby either. We'd be colossal idiots if we used the KH to go to an auction filled with hunters and the likeminded.

Juliette would come on the flight as well in case we needed a healer.

The last piece of good news was that with Pyotr's help, the crew identified the best location for Emmett to unravel the angels. Or as the golem so eloquently dubbed it: "Operation Suck It, A-Bags."

Branding.

As soon as we got back from London, we'd take the three down and close that chapter for good. It was tough to separate my feelings on that from my combo of nerves and excitement regarding the auction, so I didn't waste energy trying.

Eli was crazy busy with a homicide case, so Jude came to stay with Sadie while I was gone.

Several hours before our departure, my best friend dumped her small suitcase in my bedroom. "So much for joining the Mile High Club."

I cleared some clothes out of a couple drawers for her. "Yeah, I was so hoping that could happen with his aunt, niece, and brother-in-law on the other side of the door. I got hot just fantasizing about it."

Jude hung her jeans in my closet. "Fair point."

"When's that new home décor magazine showcasing your candelabra collection launching? I thought it was this month." I followed her to the bathroom.

"There was a delay." Jude placed her huge toiletries bag on my bathroom counter. My red-haired, fair-skinned, pottery-creating friend didn't go anywhere without a cornucopia of lotions. "Not 'til November now."

"Are you going to the publisher's party in Japan? Schmooze the buyers who'll be there?"

"Oh," she said nonchalantly. "Didn't I tell you? One of my collections was picked up by one of the largest home goods stores in Asia."

I screamed and the two of us hugged, jumping up and down in excitement. "Your pottery is going to be everywhere."

"I know!" She gave a shaky laugh and pinched herself.

"It's not fantasy, baby," I said. "It's years of hard work and all your talent finally getting you everything you deserve."

She dabbed at her eyes, scowling. "Stop it. I'm not wearing waterproof mascara."

"Now you have to go to the party. Let them meet you." I waggled my eyebrows. "See if there are other collaboration possibilities with the editor."

"A) shut up, and b) I'm still debating." She mimed weighing her options with her hands. "On the one hand, party in Tokyo. On the other, I have to pay to get there." She paused. "And the editor is an idiot."

I nudged her with my hip. "They haven't fallen for your womanly wiles yet?"

She tossed her red curls. "Enough about me, sug. You got everything you need for London?"

"Packed and ready by the door."

Since the flight didn't leave until 2AM Vancouver time Sunday morning, I got to hang out with Jude and Sadie, who stayed up to see me off.

Our goodbyes were far less emotionally charged than when I'd bid them farewell to take part in the Human Race, or even when Emmett and I had stolen the Torquemada Gloves. Good to see that my danger quotient trajectory was trending in the right direction.

With all the security precautions that Tatiana had told me about, the only thing that worried us was finding Imogine, since there was no known description of her.

That and the fact we couldn't stop the sale of the virus

because we'd be victims of the same security that we trusted to keep us safe. Neither Tatiana's informants nor any of Zev's connections discovered where these viral samples were currently locked up, how they were being transported to the auction location, or even how many there were, just that we were correct about the goods up for sale.

We'd have to stop the buyers from leaving with their purchases. That would be left to me. I'd find somewhere private to cloak, and when the new owners were arranging payment, steal the samples. Unfortunately, I couldn't remain cloaked for the entire thing because we had no way of ascertaining what wards might be in place. After all, this auction was going to be filled with narrow-minded Ohrists. Who knew what arrangements they'd made to keep out gate-crashers?

After hugs and kisses for Jude and Sadie, I picked Tatiana up and drove out to the private airfield. Laurent was taking Gabriel and Juliette.

My boss had outdone herself on the fashion front in a silver moiré suit whose jacket was cut asymmetrically and featured a row of tiny silver buttons polished to a high gleam. She'd paired her trademark oversize red glasses with two waist-long necklaces of big red beads and matching red bracelets. It was a look designed to turn heads, impart power, and do it all with her own unique style.

I hadn't bothered choosing a special outfit, since Tatiana was bringing a disguise for me. We couldn't risk anyone realizing I was there, and it was too easy for anyone digging into Tatiana's macher business to learn she had a Banim Shovavim on staff. I hoped my outfit was as fabulous as hers.

She was in a chatty mood, gossiping about Emmett's and Marjorie's burgeoning relationship. Apparently, she'd caught them holding hands the other day, but had backed away before they saw her so they wouldn't be embarrassed.

I smiled. This was quite the change from the woman

who'd barked orders at her assistants. It seemed that the combination of having Emmett living with her, the shift in her relationship with Laurent, and making Marjorie cry had softened something in the elderly artist. Not that she'd lost her edge or fire. I'd still put my money on Tatiana in a fight, but the passion and deep love she'd once possessed had dimmed after losing Delphine and died down to a faint spark when Samuel died. She'd been rattling around in that house emotionally alone, and this change was heartwarming to behold.

Tatiana directed me to the small parking lot at the airfield, and we joined the others on the tarmac in front of the plane.

Gabriel and Juliette said goodbye to Laurent first, with much animated French chatter and a big hug between the men that got me misty-eyed. Then the pair boarded.

"Be safe." Laurent met my eyes, all seriousness. He included Tatiana in his gaze. "Both of you."

"Don't get melodramatic, Lolo. We'll be fine," Tatiana snapped, but she squeezed his hands. "Come along, Miriam," she said, sweeping up the stairs like a grand dame on the red carpet.

I rose onto tiptoe, clasped his head in my hands, and kissed him, pouring all my hopes and desires for a long and happy future together into it along with my still-unspoken declaration of love. *Soon*, I assured myself.

When we broke apart, he gave me a crooked grin. "Come back quickly."

"I will." With one final wave, I boarded.

This was my second time flying on a private jet, and I doubted I'd ever become blasé about the lie-flat seats, meals served on real china, or a flight attendant ready to cater to my every need.

After kicking off my heels, I struck the first item off my to-do list soon after takeoff with a delicious chicken curry then got all snuggly to sleep the rest of the way to London.

Juliette and Gabriel were talking quietly on a sofa at the rear of the plane.

Tatiana woke me up with about two hours left in the nine-hour flight to get me into disguise.

I blinked at the scrap of leopard-printed fabric that Tatiana had removed from the garment bag. "No way."

She shoved the dress into my arms. "Yes way."

"I'll look ridiculous," I said. "Mutton dressed as lamb."

"Exactly! No one would expect that of you." She opened a carry-on bag and pulled out item after item of makeup: bronzer, contour, foundation, and a dozen other things I'd never owned in my life. "You won't be recognizable once I'm done."

I got a horrible feeling in the pit of my stomach, my fears justified when ninety minutes later, I stared in the bathroom mirror in horrified fascination. The blond tresses of my wig fell in poufy waves, my lids were dusted with sparkly blue eye shadow, and the ridiculously long fake lashes Tatiana had affixed resembled spider legs. I was stuffed into the short dress with a heavy-duty shapewear undergarment and padding in my bra, upping my boobs by several cup sizes. The final touch was green-colored contact lenses.

I poked my face, because with her contouring job, even the shape of it was different. I hadn't yet slipped on the heels she'd brought along and my feet already hurt. I appreciated her turning me into this visual distraction but oy vey.

The pilot made the announcement to prepare for landing and I exited the bathroom.

"Mon Dieu!" Gabriel pressed his lips together, his shoulders shaking.

Juliette pulled out her phone. "Maman would like a photo of you."

"Don't you dare." I lunged for the camera as she took it.

She nodded happily and turned the screen around to show me. "This will do."

I blanched at the photo. My wide eyes looked crazed with those ridiculous lashes, the giant boobs were lifted as if airborne under their own power, and thanks to the contouring and the light in the plane, it looked like I had a five-o'clock shadow. "I'll pay you a hundred dollars to delete it."

"Non," Gabriel said as Juliette put the phone in her pocket. "A picture like that is priceless. Send it to Laurent and me as well."

"I'm charged extra for cellular communication," Tatiana groused, leaning over the back of her seat to face us.

"There you go," I said. "We can't have extra charges."

"But I think in this case," she said, "the expense is worth it. Send me a copy as well."

I glared at her, taking the seat next to hers and buckling in.

"Done." Juliette fired off a series of texts even though we were in the air because our flight was fancy that way.

"You two are horrible people." I scowled, but Tatiana wasn't even trying to hide her laughter. I poked her arm. "And you're a menace."

That only made her laugh harder.

I tamped my own grin down. The photo was so over-the-top, it was funny. Also, Laurent had already sent Léa a very nice photo of me, so it wasn't like his sister-in-law would see this one and wonder if he'd lost his mind.

My phone pinged. Laurent had sent me a photo of him pretending to pour bleach in his eyes, with the message *You'll have to work that thong and corset hard to make me forget those fish lips.* I laughed and showed the photo to his aunt, though my thumb blocked the message.

Once we'd landed and come to a complete stop, we prepared to disembark.

I hugged Gabriel. "We'll talk soon."

"Stay safe at the auction." He stepped back, still holding my shoulders. "And thank you."

"Just doing my job."

Gabriel shook his head. "No, for bringing Laurent back to all of us."

"Oh. Well." Blushing, I toed at the ground. "That was his decision."

"Yes, but you gave him a reason to choose life again, and for that I will always be grateful." He smiled broadly. "Welcome to the family."

Relief, gratitude, joy, they swirled together into an intoxicating concoction that seemed to stretch my skin two sizes larger. For so long, my family had been Eli, Sadie, Jude, and Goldie, and I'd been fine with that, but now that all these other people had accepted me as one of them, I realized how starved I'd been for more. For someone who'd felt so alone, so hidden for so long, being myself, accepted, and cared about was a rush that I intended to ride for the rest of my life.

"It's good to be here."

On the drive into London, Tatiana grilled me on the backstory she'd had me learn. I was Regina Green, Tatiana's Ohrist cousin by marriage with alt-right views when it came to magic. Regina was a real person, and Tatiana despised everything she stood for. However, when my boss showed me a photo, I agreed that she'd turned me into a dead ringer for the woman. There was no danger of the real Regina showing up, since she was currently in Switzerland undergoing deluxe Botox treatments.

Juliette accompanied us though she was to stay out of sight in the town car. She read on her phone while Tatiana and I talked.

We pulled up to the auction house on a quiet street as dusk fell and the streetlights turned on, spotlighting the large, elegant building. Our Ohrist town car driver, William, opened the door and I stepped into the London twilight, fizzy with excitement.

The interior surpassed all my expectations with its fluted colonnades, recessed ceilings, exquisite antique furniture, and floral arrangements on tables in alcoves. Employees directed us to a gallery at the back showcasing artwork from an upcoming auction.

The four dozen or so other guests in attendance, who'd likely kill me on sight for possessing magic I had no say in choosing, were astoundingly normal. Predominantly white, the men were dressed in everything from plaid shirts to expensive suits, while the women ranged from the church-going pearl and cardigan set to ones as flashy as I was.

No one was as slick as my boss, though.

While Tatiana recognized a couple of criminals—who were the only ones to acknowledge her presence with cool nods—neither of us could tell for sure who the hunters were.

Nor was there any sign of Imogine.

We moved slowly from painting to painting, two of the few people interested in perusing the art. Goosebumps broke out under the thin fabric of my dress. How many times had I stood next to someone who shared the same beliefs as these people and hadn't known it? Would the chatty cashier at the grocery store turn on me if she learned I was Banim Shovavim? Did Sadie's principal come from a hunter family? There was something so unsettling about their very banality. Monsters hiding in plain sight.

About twenty minutes later, a bell chimed, and double doors zoomed out of the far wall.

Next to me, Tatiana stilled. "They have a hidden space?" she murmured.

Warning bells went off in my head. This wasn't her first visit here, and if the macher hadn't known about a hidden space, nothing good would come of entering it.

A male employee in a navy suit and white gloves opened

the doors, revealing a room set up with folding chairs and a podium at the front, and everyone obligingly moved toward it.

"Traps? Wards?" I asked quietly. I gave a bright Southern gal smile to a ruddy-faced man jostling past us to get a good seat. "What should we be prepared for?"

"I don't know." My boss was grim.

"I don't want to bail." Things had taken a more dangerous turn, but this was our best shot to find Imogine, and besides, we couldn't let the virus samples leave this building.

"Me neither, but if trouble begins, do whatever you need to." She gave me a meaningful look and I nodded.

We took seats at the back, away from the doors, the group falling quiet as a statuesque brunette in her early thirties entered with a small metal briefcase chained to her wrist. She took the podium, unlocked the case, and set it on top. Her tan complemented her green eyes.

Navy Suit shut the door, standing with impeccable posture beside it.

"Good evening." Her voice had a melodic Irish lilt. "The host of this private auction welcomes you."

People turned around to find the host but there was no one else there, and the brunette gave a throaty laugh.

"Consider me their proxy," she said. "Tonight is most unusual in that there is only one item for sale." The woman pulled a vial of crimson liquid from the briefcase. "This may look like regular blood, but it contains enough of a contagious virus to decimate the remaining vampire population here on earth."

A ripple of excitement ran through the room.

"What about humans?" a squeaky-voiced woman in a peach twinset piped up. "I was told the virus could be modified."

The brunette hesitated before answering. It wasn't long enough for anyone else to notice, but given my insider knowledge on Dr. Eversol's death, I did.

"Your information is incorrect." She staved off further questions by holding up the sample. "This is the sole sample in existence. That makes this all the more valuable."

"There's only one," I said under my breath in relief. That would make stealing it so much easier.

The ruddy-faced man jumped to his feet with "There's only one up for grabs?"

From the bristling and shifty-eyed looks on those around us, I braced for violence, but the brunette merely quirked an eyebrow.

"If anyone takes issue with what is available, they may leave. But should you do so, or are asked to remove yourself due to poor behavior, do remember the *binding* NDAs you signed."

Uh, what NDAs? And why the emphasis on binding when that's what nondisclosure agreements were by their very nature?

Ruddy-faced man sat down heavily, nodding, leaving me more confused.

Tatiana smoothed out a wrinkle in her trousers. "Amateurs."

I raised an eyebrow.

"With magic auctions," she murmured, "if you leave before it's over, you won't make it out the front door." She sliced a hand across her throat, and I swallowed. "Don't worry," she added. "I signed it for you."

Good. Thanks. Because that was totally my fear, that I wouldn't be able to forge the signature of one Regina Green well enough on my don't-murder-me NDA. I wiped my clammy palms on the synthetic leopard-print fabric of my dress.

The brunette had to be working with Imogine, so where was the vampire? Watching us on a security feed? I unclenched my fists, making sure my benign expression of interest was in place.

Bidding started at one hundred thousand dollars. Tatiana bid on behalf of "Regina," but dropped out when bids rose to 1.5 million. By that point, only about half of the crowd was still bidding, but come on. That left over twenty people with that kind of cash just to wipe out vamps.

Fifteen minutes later the brunette host called out, "Five million. Going once. Going twice." She banged the gavel. "Sold for five million dollars."

That's when the doors burst open, and the vampires poured in.

21

IN THE FIRST MOMENTS OF CONFUSION, I THOUGHT that Zev had somehow arranged for vamps as backup. Then a woman screamed, and chairs were knocked over, and I took a second look at the new arrivals.

My heart leapt into my throat.

Gaunt and ravaged from the contagion that infected them, the vamps were grabbing whomever they could and biting them, but while they were drinking deeply, they weren't killing anyone.

People attempted to flee, but vamps blocked the exit, stopping anyone who tried.

Luck and our position in a far back corner kept us from being attacked, but our best chance was for me to cloak us, which would blow my cover in a room filled with Banim Shovavim haters.

It wasn't much of a choice. Pulling Tatiana to her feet, I slammed my invisibility mesh down over us.

The brunette calmly navigated the carnage, heading for the exit, briefcase in hand. Not a single vampire touched her.

"Oh no you don't," I muttered and kicked off my shoes to

move faster. Holding tightly on to Tatiana, who could haul ass in heels, we followed in hot pursuit.

The cries of pain reverberating through the room were deafening.

One of the diseased vamps we passed bit her own wrist, forcing her victim to drink.

Tatiana swiftly inhaled. "They're turning the Ohrists," she said, fiddling with her long necklace with a shaky hand. Her other necklace had broken off somewhere along the way.

I stumbled. All these people were being changed into infected vampires? Oh fuck. These Ohrists were being changed into *weapons*. They wouldn't be taken in and cared for, they'd be left on their own as rogues.

I knew exactly how much damage a rogue vamp could do. So a rogue *infected* vampire? I swallowed down a scream, panic fueling me to break through a knot of fleeing humans who'd gotten bottlenecked.

"New plan." I held on to Tatiana so hard I was bruising her, but we had to get out of here. The brunette had the vial and was presumably working with Imogine.

The thirty feet to the door back to the real world felt like thirty miles. I shook from the strain of staying on the alert for vampires, while sending Delilah ahead with the scythe to take out vamps in our path.

She killed only a few, but none of the bloodsuckers old or new made it out the door before us.

I stepped into the hallway and cursed because the brunette was gone. I spun back to the fight, slamming the doors shut. "Can you keep the doors to the hidden space in plain view?"

"No problem," Tatiana replied.

I jammed my scythe through the handles to temporarily lock the doors, while Tatiana changed the floral arrangements in our vicinity into a mass of ropy vines that then bound the doors like chains.

Once they were secured, I tore through the shadows into

the KH. I lost precious seconds convincing Pyotr it was me, succeeding only by tearing off the wig and pulling out my fake boob paddings, but I got my sock and dashed down the gloomy path to Eli's garage in record time. I grabbed the jerry can of gasoline he stored in case of emergency and a package of long matches.

Our barricade still held when I returned, panting and perspiring heavily from lugging the gasoline container, but the doors were rattling hard from someone throwing themselves against them from the inside.

Tatiana fed a constant stream of magic into the flowers to keep the chains intact, her arms beginning to tremble. "Hurry it up already."

After tucking the matches under my arm, I opened the lid, waving away the fumes. "On the count of three, drop your magic and stand back. One."

Someone crashed into the doors hard enough for them to bounce open a crack.

I picked up the jerry can. "Two. Three."

The floral bindings vanished, and the door flew open, but I stopped the vampire barreling through with a spray of gasoline to the face. He stumbled back, knocking into a couple other vampires, who turned on each other in a frenzy.

No humans remained unturned.

I edged inside, splashing everything and everyone I could with gasoline. Then I tossed the empty can aside, backed out the door, and lit the match.

A wall of flames burst up in front of me, the heat blasting me in the face. Using my scythe so I didn't get burned touching them, I shut the doors to the hidden space, then backed up a few feet and dropped into a solid fighting stance, weapon in hand. Delilah was next to me, ready to take on anyone who made it through the inferno and into the hallway.

Miraculously, neither the fire alarms nor the sprinklers went off here in the real auction house. In fact, I could neither hear, nor feel the fire, even as the doors to the auction room blackened and withered.

Tatiana took a seat, breathing heavily, and pulled her necklace off, dumping it on the ground like she was ridding herself of an anchor. "Enough excitement for one night."

One of the doors had burned away, the other almost gone as well.

"Just a couple more minutes to make sure we're in the—"

The door opened and an Ohrist stumbled out, wide-eyed and sobbing. "Help me," she cried, her face raw and burned.

I fumbled the scythe, because she still looked human, even though I knew she couldn't be.

She lunged, her lips twisted in a sneer. Her outstretched fingers were gnarled, age spots dotting the papery skin.

I decapitated her with a single strike.

Her head bounced onto the carpet, her mouth in an O. For one horrible second, I was positive that I'd killed an elderly human instead of a diseased vampire, but she crumbled into ash, and I let out a breath.

"We have to go." Tatiana tugged me to the front of the building.

I glanced back, worried about any other vamps getting free, but none followed. In fact, the doors had vanished, all trace of the hidden space gone. Forever, I hoped.

Even though they'd been horrible people and even more dangerous as rogue infected vamps, now that the flight or fight immediacy had passed my mind reeled with the atrocity of what I'd done. Burning them to death was so much more reprehensible than one-at-a-time vamp killings. I exited onto the street on rubbery legs, sucking in the cool night air.

William tossed the cigarette he'd been smoking into the gutter and hurriedly opened the back door for us.

Juliette glanced out. "It went well?"

My attention snagged on the brunette from the auction standing across the street, partially in shadow. Why watch the building like a killer returning to the scene of the crime? Was she supposed to report back to Imogine on the success of the multiple infections?

A second, more nefarious—and simpler—thought occurred to me.

"Imogine," I gasped, and sprinted in my stocking feet into the street.

Wrong move. I'd been so focused on learning what magic she'd used in the virus that I'd forgotten her powers would follow Ohrist rules.

And I'd just given her perfect line of sight.

She flicked her hands at me, and I doubled over as pain ripped through my abdomen. It felt like someone had swung a mallet into my belly button and then left a spike as a lovely parting gift.

"Miri!" Juliette yelled.

Swallowing down the taste of vomit, I stumbled toward a parked car to shield me on tingly weak legs while the world swam dizzyingly. My heart was palpitating, and it was hard to draw in a breath. Then my left leg went numb and useless, being dragged along like dead weight, and my chest constricted, anxiety flooding my system.

I made it to the car, falling forward onto the hood, and screaming as millions of hot pinpricks lit up every nerve ending. My arms and hands were swollen and covered in blisters, and unable to support myself, I slid onto the ground.

Juliette caught me. She rested on her shins, radiating calm. "We have to get you to the town car so I can heal you."

Tatiana stepped into view above me.

"Imogine," I slurred, curling into the fetal position and wishing I was dead.

A cold look slid over my boss's face. "Oh no you don't," she said and stormed off.

The sliver of my brain not trying to keep me from shutting down in the face of all this pain urged me to go after her.

Juliette held me down, telling me to be still, but I shook my head. "Tatiana. Help."

The healer assisted me so I could stand up, balancing on my one functioning, albeit rubbery and tingly leg. However, I was still bent double, my swollen body covered in blisters.

"You are as stubborn as my uncle," Juliette said peevishly, the two of us peering over the roof of the parked car to where the weirdest showdown was happening.

Tatiana stood on the sidewalk with her hands outstretched, her jaw clenched, and her face beaded with perspiration.

Imogine walked jerkily closer, fighting every step, her face contorted in fury. She marched under a streetlamp, the bronzer she'd used to fake her tan streaking along her skin and exposing pale swaths of skin.

My eyes bugged out. There was this one night back when Sadie was a baby that Eli and I had been up fighting. I don't remember what the problem was, but we were sleep-deprived and on the brink of emotionally hurting each other to the point of no return. I was sitting in the kitchen, rocking Sadie against my chest and crying along with her, convinced everything would be shit forever and ever, when the sun came up in. Out of the gloomy gray darkness, the sky ignited into brilliant color. I threw open the back door and breathed it in, bathed in the majesty of something greater than myself that gave me the strength to resolve our fight.

Watching Tatiana puppet Imogine like she was a marionette filled me with that same feeling. There was still danger and a battle to be won, but like the sun, Tatiana had ignited this dark, wet night with her brilliant color.

She'd once confessed to this ability, but the last time she'd done it, my boss had suffered a stroke. My sense of awe and wonder leeched away, leaving only the image of my elderly boss pushing herself to the brink.

"Stop," I begged in a broken voice. "It's not worth it."

When Tatiana didn't listen, I called up my magic, but there was only a single pathetic spurt of shadows, which triggered another wave of agony in my stomach.

"That's it," Juliette said irritably. She put her arm around my shoulders. "William! We need help."

With a roar, Imogine tore free of Tatiana's magic, lifting her arms to the sky as if in wonder that she could.

Tatiana crumpled to the ground like a silk slip. Juliette helped me to limp over, since she wouldn't leave me alone while she took care of her aunt.

Imogine's break from Tatiana's magic cost her as well. Decay crept up from the vampire's feet like a cloak of ashy velvet, turning her limbs into shriveled sticks. Imogine fell over, her torso twisting in on itself like a hollowed-out corpse, but before the rot mottled up her throat and fully claimed her, the vampire bared her teeth. "This isn't over," she hissed. With that, she dissolved into fog and whirled into the sky, lost to view.

"*No!*" I reached out like I could grab her. It wasn't right that she escaped while Tatiana lay unconscious.

William picked up Tatiana, who was as limp as a noodle.

Two silver buttons plinked off her jacket. They rolled along the dirty concrete and disappeared down a sewer grate.

"Get her into the back seat," Juliette ordered.

The artist was white as a corpse, her eyes sunken in her face with black bags around them. Her closed lids twitched but she didn't come to. There wasn't a trace of her vibrancy, and her formerly stunning outfit appeared as diminished as she did.

She'd said she had a death outfit. Had this been it? Had she known?

I pushed that thought away.

"Briefcase." I motioned feebly at the metal container that Imogine had left behind.

Juliette picked it up and then assisted me into the town

car. "This is going to hurt, but it'll keep you until I do a fuller check."

The blast of healing magic she sent into me had teeth and it bit deep. I writhed in agony, made worse by Juliette buckling me into my seat so I didn't throw myself through the window to end the pain.

She stayed in the back with Tatiana while William drove at breakneck speed back to the airfield. Between me screaming and writhing beside him and the eerie quiet from his other passengers, the poor guy must have been terrified and desperate to unload us.

When we got to the private airstrip, he carried my boss up the stairs. I made a note to get him an enormous tip when we got home.

Meanwhile, I dragged myself up. My legs both worked again, and the stomach pain had subsided from "kill me now" to a bad ache, but my skin was still swollen and there remained patches of blisters all over me.

Numb, I buckled in for takeoff. Juliette looked grim, and Tatiana was still unconscious.

I couldn't lose her. This fierce, amazing, stubborn woman was family. She had to meet Goldie when she came back next month and be there for Sadie's graduation in a couple years and see what happened between Marjorie and Emmett.

And what of Laurent? I lay my cheek against the window. He'd only just opened himself up to Tatiana again.

I darted a glance at Tatiana's niece, holding it together like the champ she was.

Once we'd attained our flying altitude, the flight attendant brought me a pillow and blanket, which I gratefully accepted. It was a testament to his professionalism that he didn't even blink at my condition.

Juliette lay her hand on my shoulder. "Let me finish healing you."

"No. Save it for Tatiana."

The Frenchwoman glanced back at her aunt, then shook her head, sorrow in her eyes. "I can't do anything else for her."

My heart caught in my throat. "How bad is it?"

"Bad." Juliette sat down, exhaustion pulling at the corners of her eyes. "I've put her in a magic coma for now. Her pulse and heartbeat are erratic." She wiped a smudge of dirt off her forearm. "Allow me to heal you and then we'll discuss that further."

I tried to get her to eat or drink something first, but she was adamant. I wasn't the only stubborn one on this flight.

Her expression somehow got blanker and blanker the more she worked on me, but my swelling went down, the blisters vanished, and all trace of stomach pain and nausea left me.

Finally, she patted my legs, which were propped in her lap, the two of us having moved to one of the two sofas in the rear lounge area. "All done."

Studiously ignoring Tatiana's stillness on the other couch, I twisted the edge of the blanket I'd kept with me. "What did Imogine do to me? Can you identify her magic and tell your father?"

"Now that I've seen its effect firsthand, yes, but that alone won't get us the vaccine." She blotted her forehead with the back of her hand. "It's a subset of blood magic. Do you know what a porphyrin is?"

"No idea."

"It's a large ring molecule. It does a few different things, one of which is cause your blood to be red."

"Okay," I said, not following. "Imogine gave me this molecule? Took it away?"

Juliette exhaled slowly. "Porphyria is a disease. If the human body has low levels of the enzyme required to create heme, porphyrin can build up in tissues, or the liver and in skin. Porphyria has different symptoms depending on where the low levels are located, but some of the acute effects include severe abdominal pain, nausea, disorientation, muscle tingling, breathing problems, rapid or irregular heartbeat, swelling, and blisters."

"Imogine hit me with the full smorgasbord of symptoms." I pulled the blanket up to my chin. "But I don't understand how this magic porphyria is the cause of the contagion."

"Me neither," she said. "I don't know if this matters, but porphyrin can accumulate not only in tissues, but sometimes even in teeth. It causes this creepy red fluorescence."

"Like blood."

"Like blood. It also makes people sensitive to the sun, causing burning pain." She gave me a wry smile. "Sound familiar?"

"Vampires. But they're created from demons. They don't have porphyria."

"No. However, individuals with this condition were believed to be the origin of vampire legends. Little did people realize that real vampires existed, mirroring the disease in certain aspects."

I adjusted the pillow at my back, shuffling and reshuffling the pieces that Juliette had given me into a single picture. We'd foiled Imogine's plans to amp the spread of the contagion and put it in the hands of people who'd use it on other humans, so what more did Juliette require?

Too bad we didn't have a handy formula like Dumah had given me.

I stilled. "Oh," I breathed.

"What?" Juliette paused, a glass of sparkling water halfway to her mouth.

"If Imogine fired her magic directly into a vampire, what would it do?"

She took a sip, licking a drop of water off her lips. "Not much. Even if she could cause an immediate buildup of porphyrin, which I'm not sure would work on vamps, their accelerated healing would nullify it."

"Good. Okay. We've been assuming there are two parts to this virus," I said. "Imogine's magic and Dr. Eversol's delivery vector, but what if there are three? Magic, vector, and human blood, which combines to trigger a reaction?"

"Papa didn't find any trace of..." In her realization, she jostled the water, which almost sloshed out of the cup. "The blood they're *drinking*."

"Yes." I gestured excitedly as I spoke. "What if the magic and the vector act like a sleeper agent? It's not until they drink human blood that the virus turns on?"

Juliette was already calling her dad. When he answered, she informed him he was on speakerphone with us.

I explained what had happened to me and Juliette and my conclusions. "Could the blood be like the match in a fire? It goes off in the vampires, resulting in this disruption to their innate healing abilities and allowing the contagion to take root?" I crossed my fingers that I was on the right track, fidgeting while Gabriel remained silent.

The only sound was the scritch of a pen.

"Do I have this all wrong?" I said hesitantly.

"No," he said. "I'm writing down my thoughts."

"Oh." A man on my wavelength.

"The virus is airborne," he said. "My hypothesis was that the first vampires were infected by Dr. Eversol."

"Her test subjects," Juliette said.

"Exactly. I still do think it was spread through saliva droplets, however, given this new information, the vampire host would only be able to pass the virus on within a couple hours of drinking human blood while the virus was active. It does make me wonder how the outbreaks occurred in disparate areas."

Juliette leaned forward. "Ohrists aren't harmed by their own magic. Imogine could have injected herself with the virus, drank blood, become infected, and made contact with other vampires. A simple conversation would be enough to infect other vamps, and she could do this over and over again with no injury to herself."

"She could," her father agreed. "While the other vampires would be passing it on none the wiser."

"That's mind-blowing," I said. "And, if I'm right about human blood being the catalyst, then any vamps who drink synthetic blood wouldn't be affected either."

"True," Gabriel said. He clicked a pen several times. "This is tracking," he said slowly.

I high-fived Juliette.

"But," he continued, "it doesn't account for their suppressed healing abilities."

Juliette didn't seem surprised by that, so I guessed it was the missing piece she'd alluded to earlier.

"I'll have to do some more research," he said, "but I suspect that the vector is working faster than their healing. Imogine's Ohrist magic infects the ingested human blood with porphyria, and the vector transmits it to the vampire. Not the way the disease presents in humans, but with symptoms that are consistent across all vampires, nonetheless."

I slumped back against my seat, weak with relief. "We have the last lab sample of the virus and it's all yours."

"I'm incredibly grateful for this information," he said, "but engineering a vaccine is going to be far more difficult than I'd anticipated. The specificity of Imogine's magic..." He sighed heavily. "We need our own magic that's able to counteract the porphyria infecting the human blood."

"Why did estrie blood work?" I said.

"Since estrie magic is foundational to the creation of vampires, the tiniest bit of blood works as a powerful cleansing agent. Sadly, we don't have enough for a vaccine. Zev has barely any left."

I folded my hands in my lap, eyeing the veins at my wrist.

"What about Banim Shovavim blood? It staved off some of the effects of the virus in an ancient vampire for a bit."

"That would only be a stopgap, not a solution," Juliette said.

Too bad.

"Tell me if I've got this right," I said. "Infected vampires don't get sick until they drink blood and the virus is activated. So, any vaccine either has to stop human blood from being contaminated with porphyria or suppress Dr. Eversol's vector, allowing vampire healing to root out the disease."

"That's essentially it," Gabriel said.

Tatiana twitched, and Juliette and I hurried to her side.

Juliette performed a couple tests. "Still unresponsive," she said regretfully. There was a pause, and then we looked at each other in astonishment.

"Tatiana," I said.

"She's the cure," Juliette agreed.

"Explain," Gabriel said sharply from his end of the phone.

"Tatiana can control a vampire's body," I said.

Gabriel whistled. "I knew she could do that to a person but not a vampire."

"She probably didn't know before tonight either," I said sadly.

"If her magic works on their motor cortex and nervous system, presumably it would extend to controlling other parts of the brain and systems as well." His voice became more animated. "I could effectively create a shield against the original virus. If it couldn't take hold, then the healing magic wouldn't be suppressed. This could work. Put her on."

I cursed, prompting Juliette to explain what had gone down tonight.

"Imagine breaking out of Tante Tatiana's hold essentially short-circuited Tatiana's magic, and it's causing physical complications," she said. "The wrong treatment could burn her magic out entirely and send her nervous system into shut-down." She ran a finger around the rim of her empty water glass. "I'm scared that if I wake her, she'll die."

"That shouldn't be on you to decide," Gabriel said angrily.

"Tatiana is always prepared," I said, glancing wistfully at her still-unconscious form. "She must have instructions on what to do in this type of emergency." Give me lists, names of other healers or doctors, or any task I could undertake, and I'd do it.

The attendant brought us hot meals, but not having an appetite, I declined.

"She does. Very specific instructions." Juliette accepted a pasta dish. "There are two other healers I've texted who'll be waiting at the airport when we arrive. If neither of them can improve her condition to where she has full use of both her intellectual and physical faculties, then her power of attorney for personal care makes the final call."

It was a measure of how exhausted and upset I was that I hadn't come up with that in the first place. Of course she'd have designated someone. Eli and Jude were mine since it wasn't fair to put that kind of a decision on one grieving person alone.

I didn't envy the person Tatiana had appointed.

"Do you know who it is?" I said.

"Yes." Juliette shook out her linen napkin. "You."

22

I REMAINED IN A STATE OF SHOCK FOR THE REST OF the flight. If Tatiana couldn't be healed, *I* was supposed to decide her fate? I glanced quickly at Juliette and then away, pretending to be absorbed in the view of the clouds. How did that make her family members feel?

What was the right decision when a person's life was at stake? Intellectual exercises on morality and quality of life were important—and totally different from deciding when looking at a loved one's face and wondering if this would be the last time I saw them. Would I stick to my choice in light of other people, ones who'd known Tatiana longer, begging me to act differently?

How would I find the strength to be the person Tatiana, no, *everyone* in her life, needed me to be?

Her appointing me to this position was either the most absolute sign of her love for me or... I shook my head.

And what the hell? Did vampire salvation rest on my shoulders too? I'd delivered on the job. Gabriel knew what Imogine's magic was. Obviously I'd do anything to wake Tatiana up, but if the worst came to pass, would my decision doom the undead? I hated spiders, but I didn't want to be the cause of their extinction.

I had a hazy memory of calling Laurent because he needed to know about his aunt's condition, but I was scattered, and the conversation played out like a bunch of Charlie Brown "wah wah wahs." I think—I hope—I comforted him.

Two healers whisked Juliette and Tatiana from the airfield within minutes of landing, leaving me blinking stupidly in the overcast afternoon light, on the edge of falling into a rabbit hole of hysteria.

"Mitzi."

I processed Laurent's scent before his words and leaned into his chest. "What are you doing here?"

"You're in no condition to drive," he said gently and held out a hand. "Give me your keys."

"But—" I scrunched up my face, words not working. I was jet-lagged and exhausted, not having slept for an amount of time I couldn't calculate. I hugged him. "I'm glad you're here. I'm sorry."

"You're not to blame." Putting one arm around me, he led me to my car.

I flinched when I caught sight of myself. I was still wearing the leopard-print dress, but without the fake boobs, the front gaped awkwardly. My hair was a disaster from having been under the wig, and my makeup was streaky and I'd lost one of my green contacts.

Laurent got many bonus points for not commenting on my appearance. "Gabriel told me what happened. You and Juliette are amazing for figuring that out."

I appreciated him focusing on our win and not getting upset about my attack. That was huge progress on his part. Yawning, I nudged the briefcase that was stashed by my foot. "We need to courier this to Gabriel ASAP."

"I'll take care of it. You rest."

I opened my mouth to protest, but Laurent shook his head. "It helps to keep busy."

I understood that sentiment all too well, so I nodded. While I wasn't certain I could fall asleep, the motion of the car lulled me under in no time.

Laurent shook me awake. "You're home."

Unbuckling the seat belt, I stretched my legs out. "I needed that."

"I figured. You slept through me stopping at the courier office." He paused. "Nav drove me to the airfield. I can call him if you don't want me to come—"

I grabbed his sleeve. "Please stay."

He nodded and we walked in silence up to the door.

Jude flung it open before we'd made it onto the porch. "Sug?" She held out her arms. "What happened?"

It was the best kind of friend who knew to settle me on my sofa with a fuzzy blanket, my kid, and a strong mocha latte before I told the story.

Sadie had broken out a package of dark chocolate Hob Nob cookies, and all of us ate our way through it while I spoke.

My boyfriend kept his shit together through the replay of my attack and details of Tatiana's condition. When I told them about being power of attorney for her personal care, he took a very deep and controlled breath. "She was right to appoint you. You've got a good head in a crisis."

"She does," Sadie agreed, handing me another cookie.

"Which is important, because Zev will want to change her." Laurent sounded disgusted.

I choked on a bite of cookie. That hadn't even occurred to me. The master vamp was ruthless when he decided upon a specific outcome. Fuck. I didn't have the bandwidth to deal with him. Or fight him off.

I shook my head through my subsiding coughs. "I won't let him."

"Not even if it's the only way to save her?" Jude dunked her cookie in her coffee.

"Can I refuse the position?" I buried my face in my hands.

"No," Jude said. "Tatiana chose you because when push comes to shove, you'll consider all angles before deciding on her fate."

"It's true," Laurent said. "And the rest of us would probably come to blows in the process."

"Please don't make this more complicated than it is." I shot him a level stare.

"Does the vamp even know about Tatiana?" Sadie said. Okay, she still hadn't let go of her anger toward him, but as long as she showed respect in the fiend's presence, she could hate him forever.

Shrugging, I looked to Laurent in question, but he didn't know either.

"Check in with the healers first," Jude said. "If Tatiana is up, then this is all moot."

"Fingers crossed." I gnawed on my thumbnail. "There's more. Gabriel believes that only Tatiana's magic will work in a vaccine."

"Aw, crud," Jude said.

Laurent shook his head, a grim expression on his face.

My hand flew to my mouth. "I didn't tell Emmett."

Jude stood up. "I'll go see him and take care of that."

I walked her to the door. "I love you. Thank you for being there for Sadie and me."

"That's because I'm the very milk of human kindness, hun." She smiled. "Love you too, Mir."

Sadie surprised me soon after by offering to make dinner. She paused then asked Laurent what he liked to eat and if he wanted to watch *Once Upon a Time* with us tonight.

It was so mature and well adjusted, but when I beamed at her, she rolled her eyes.

Laurent was flustered by the invitation, stammering out

244

that he'd eat anything, and yes, he would like to watch, if it was all right to crash our Sunday TV date.

Sadie replied that she wouldn't have invited him if it wasn't and added that she'd catch him up on the previous episodes of the show.

"What are we having?" I said.

She bobbed on her toes a couple times, her forehead screwed up in thought. "Pasta with Bolognese sauce. Easy."

"And salad," I called out after her.

"Whatever," she called back.

I crowded Laurent when he called Juliette for an update, but Tatiana's condition remained the same, and the healers were still debating treatments. Just before he hung up, I had a brilliant idea.

"Tell them to contact Zev about Kian's blood." The estrie blood cured the contagion, maybe it could heal Tatiana.

Laurent muted the phone. "That's a long shot."

"Yeah, I'm totally grasping, but if the healers don't have any other ideas, it'll be up to me, and I just don't know how to make the decision I may have to."

Laurent dutifully passed the message on.

When he hung up, I rested my head on his shoulder. "How are you doing?"

He shrugged, a helpless look on his face. "I was so angry at Tatiana for so long because she wouldn't back off, but I don't know what I would have done all these years without her."

I hugged him tightly. "I wish I could promise you it will all be all right, but I have to believe she'll get through this. She's such a fighter..."

"Just like you."

I raised my head and met his gaze. "Just like *you*."

"A fighter or a weapon?" He laughed bitterly. "I took on Banim Shovavim magic, for fuck's sake."

"To make the world safer after your unimaginable loss."

"That's what I told myself." He spoke quietly, his expression distant.

"Even if you did it because you were furious and just wanted every last dybbuk to die," I said, "you were entitled to that belief. And who cares? The fact is you've used that power for good."

He clasped my hands loosely in his. "The *fact*, ma chérie, is that I abandoned my pack, and single-mindedly, no, obsessively, took on another magic power at incredible cost to my relationships and my physical being, instead of admitting I was hurt and angry and lost."

His bleak expression broke my heart. "You're reaching out to your pack to make amends."

"I shouldn't have done it in the first place. I don't want to be that man anymore. You deserve better."

"We've all done things we wish we could take back, but you are exactly the man I need and want. Besides, this isn't about me. *You* deserve better than to believe you're letting anyone down. Because you aren't. I promise you."

He didn't speak for a long time.

"Is this about your dad?" I asked gently.

He blinked and quickly looked away. "He's never loved me," he said after a moment. "Saying that he did was another lie I told myself. As was thinking that if it wasn't for Zev's presence in his life, he wouldn't be the man he is. But that's not true. He is who he is. I just wasn't the son he wanted. Maybe no one would have been. What an asshole." He gave a sharp exhale. "Merde, that's a hell of a thing to accept."

"It's not one-way," I said. "He was never the father you needed and that's a hell of a thing to accept too. Trust me, I've come to more than a few realizations about my mom's and dad's shortcomings through all of this."

"You're right."

"The only question that matters is, are you the man *you* want to be now?"

"I'm getting there." He kissed my knuckles. "When all this is over, do you want to come to France with me? We could see Gabriel and you'd meet Léa."

"You mean when you visit your former pack members?"

"Oui. We could spend a few days in Paris as well. Perhaps see Maman." He gave me a small, bashful smile, just a hint of sunshine peeking out. "It would be nice to have you there."

Meeting his mom? I was a powerful, self-reliant forty-two-year-old woman, yet this was the most nerve-racking proposition I'd ever heard. And I was about to take down three angels. "It would be nice to be there with you."

Jude called during dinner to say Emmett was shaken up, but Marjorie was with him, and then it was time for our TV date.

Under normal circumstances, I would have enjoyed the next episode of the television show, but I'm not sure any of us were paying attention. It also didn't help that one of the characters was called Regina, because every time I heard that name, I remembered my disguise and the auction would begin to loop in my brain.

One minute I was blinking to fight off sleep during the end credits, the next I was yelling in terror at the giant figure shaking me and screaming gibberish.

Laurent caught my wrist before I could swing my scythe. "It's Pyotr."

"What?" Recalling my magic, I blinked groggily, realizing that Pyotr was so distressed he was speaking in Russian.

"What happened?" Sadie came barreling into the room. She was still dressed, so it couldn't have been that late. "Pyotr?" She placed her hands on his trembling arms, looking directly into his eyes. "Breathe with me."

Slowly she inhaled and exhaled, nodding encouragingly,

just like all the times Eli and I had done when she'd spin out in anxiety.

I was wrong. That last time wasn't the proudest I'd been of her. This was, by a mile.

"Like mother, like daughter," Laurent murmured.

I smiled.

Sadie not only kept her cool, she calmed Pyotr down enough for him to switch to English.

"Emmett went into Kefitzat Haderech."

"Why? He doesn't have the tuning fork." It was all my foggy brain could muster.

"He does," Laurent said grimly. "Nav delivered it yesterday."

Emmett couldn't be that stupid. I sucked in a breath. Please don't let Emmett have been that stupid.

Pyotr wrung his hands. "Is my fault. I bring him to play video games, but he was sad because of boss." He fluttered around in a circle and bashed into an end table.

I caught the lamp before it fell. "You were being a good friend. What happened next?" My voice was pitchy, but it wasn't hysterical, which was good, because if I lost it, Pyotr would never answer our questions.

"He wanted to hurt—"

"Vampire," Laurent snarled. Bristling, he jumped to his feet, his hands shifting to claws and his canines lengthening.

"No," the gargoyle said with exaggerated patience. "Angels. We talk about angels."

My boyfriend growled in a way that was not quite human at something in the foyer.

Something that also wasn't quite human and had 24/7 access to my home.

Pyotr turned, eeped, and jumped back into the KH.

There was no pretense of humanity left in Zev Toledano, not anymore. He was stripped to his most raw, primal form, power radiating off him like cold from a glacier. His eyes shone with fire or blood, his fangs were long and pointed, and he was wreathed in an incandescent rage.

Sadie pressed back against the cushions, Laurent stepping in front of her, while I sat there, oddly disconnected from any terror.

"Should Tatiana fail to rally, you will allow me to change her." Zev's compulsion ripped through my head with the subtlety of a car slamming into a concrete wall.

I felt like I'd snorted vinegar, and the inside of my head burned like brain freeze. The worst itch had settled in my nose like I wanted to sneeze, knew it would hurt, and yet couldn't. Charming combination.

Planting my feet against the floor, I stood up, my eyes watering, and shook the compulsion off. "I won't do anything unless it's best for Tatiana," I said, approaching him steadily. "And if you ever try that on me again, you'll meet the business end of my scythe."

He unclenched his fists, his shoulders slumped. He didn't wear a suit jacket, and his wrinkled shirt was untucked from his trousers. It was as disconcerting as if he'd been naked. "The estrie blood didn't work."

"Are you sure?"

"Unless the healers lied. They wouldn't tell me where she was—one picked it up from me. I was supposed to trust them," he sneered. He'd gripped the top of a folding chair that had been left behind after the brainstorming session, and by the time he finished speaking, the top of it was a twisted ruin.

I hurled a couch cushion across the room. Tatiana was running out of options, but Emmett might be...

"Get out," I ordered the vampire and hurried out of the room to grab Dumah's ring. It wasn't for Emmett since the KH didn't detect him, but for me.

Tatiana was stable in the coma, which gave us time. Zev wouldn't take his anger out on Sadie or Laurent—unless my boyfriend provoked him. Which he wouldn't. Not with Sadie present.

There was the faintest squeak of my sofa being sat upon and then a sharp intake of breath.

I made the mistake of looking.

Zev sat with his head buried in his hands. "I can't lose her. I'm not ready."

Sadie, Laurent—now fully human again—and I stared at each other in helpless confusion. I couldn't stay, but I couldn't leave Zev like this either.

Wearing the same expression that Eli used to when changing Sadie's poopy diaper, Laurent squeezed the vampire's shoulder. "I'm not ready either."

Zev's fangs lengthened at the contact.

I threw my hands up. "Do you always suspect an attack?"

"Yes," the shifter and vampire said in unison.

"Well, it's not. It's comfort. Nothing more. Right, Laurent?"

"I guess," he acknowledged reluctantly.

Zev still looked suspicious—and broken over Tatiana—so I threw my boyfriend a pointed look. "Because..." I prompted.

"You aren't to blame for my father's shortcomings," he muttered. "Also—" He shifted his weight to his other foot like he'd rather have angry hornets shoved up his butt than be saying these things. "I understand loss too, if it came to that. Which it won't. But if it did and you wanted to talk..."

Zev's mouth actually fell open.

"Awww," Sadie said. "That's sweet."

If I wasn't so upset about Emmett, I'd have laughed at the pair's mutual grumpy expressions. "Are we good?" I said.

I crossed my fingers that Laurent didn't go into protective mode, but he surprised me with a nod.

"Go," he said. "You've got this."

I raced upstairs, slid the ring on, and stepped into the KH.

Pyotr almost tore my arm off in his haste to usher me out

the narrow door of the reception cave and onto a path in the KH. He even forgot to make me take a sock, which spurred me to an Olympic burst of speed.

We ran, taking twists and turns too dizzying to track, the already gloomy light growing dimmer and denser, until I could barely see two inches in front of me. At the gargoyle's sudden stop, I crashed into his back.

The magic seeping out through the crack in the rocks almost drove me to my knees. It felt like being walloped in the face with an anvil, except the whole thing was made of feathers. Sticky strands of magic bound me like honey, and the beating of wings roared in my ears as the temperature rose, as if I stood too close to a bonfire.

I scrubbed at my skin, but wiping away that magic was impossible. Gritting my teeth and clenching my hands into tight fists, I put my eye to the crack, my companion holding on to the back of my shirt.

By some miracle, Emmett was upright and unharmed, stretched on tiptoe with his hands pressed to the cave wall. The prison didn't look like it had when Arlo had been tortured here—thank goodness. There were no oozing black and white stripes or giant crazed eyes, because the binding magic on the prison was horrific enough.

Emmett wasn't showboating or going off script. He held the tuning fork with quivering arms against a pitted scar in the rock face, presumably the spot that had been identified by our team.

Unlike the invisible strands that I attributed to the angels, the magic that wafted past my face from inside poor Arlo's old prison had the subtlest difference to it thanks to Emmett's attempts: a silky murmur throbbing through it like a streak of gold in a dark mine.

I laughed softly. That crazy wonderful golem might pull this off. I'd never mother him again.

It hit me that this was really it. The schmuck trio would be unraveled and finally pay for what they'd done to my parents.

To me.

It was surreal, almost incomprehensible, yet I'd never longed more for any single moment. After three decades of hiding, secrets, and anger, closure was finally in my grasp. Dumah was right. The three angels hadn't suspected a mere human would be their undoing, and especially hadn't considered her many and unique friends, including a golem, would help take them down. It hadn't needed to be me who unraveled them, in fact, it felt a million times better this way, because it was my found family who'd come together to have my back and put the pieces into place.

I pictured my parents, wishing them peace, just as Smoky popped into view.

"I feel it." The phantom skeleton face wore a wide-eyed look of wonder. "I shall be free."

All three of us put our faces to the crack, watching Emmett. I was on the bottom, doing my darndest to not scratch my skin off, with Pyotr above me, and Smoky hovering on top.

The silky quality of the magic grew stronger and I sighed. It was a cool splash of relief against the hot, itchy assault of the angels' prison binding magic.

"Just a little more," Smoky said.

Emmett either heard Smoky or sensed us or something, because the golem swung around to face us with his chin up, his shoulders back, and a proud smile.

An icy wind slammed into me from behind, knocking me face-first into the rock, with the gargoyle tripping forward into my back. Luckily, Pyotr didn't crush me, though he did tread on my heels. I stepped away, rubbing my poor nose and calling out for Emmett, but he couldn't hear me, and the gargoyle's grip ensured I didn't try to enter that space.

Emmett wasn't affected by the angels' magic; I was. And

that was from out here, not to mention that they'd detect me if I entered the cell.

Dejected, I quit struggling, though I yelled for Emmett to get out of there until my voice was hoarse.

The wind gusted past with a desolate howl, swirling into the prison designated for Dumah like black ooze, a vast darkness that streamed over every surface like water. It was hypnotically beautiful, yet grotesque, and felt somewhat familiar.

"Nooo!" Smoky roared.

Tears streamed down Pyotr's face and I shook him. "What is that?"

His answer was buried by the continued howl and beating sound, which was growing faster, but I'd read his lips.

They were Banim Shovavim.

My hand flew to my mouth. These were the damned, called forth by Emmett's necromancy Banim Shovavim magic, the same powers that gave him his divination abilities.

I hauled some rocks out to widen the gap, careful to stay on my side, and screamed Emmett's name as loud as I could, but the black ooze had spun up like a tornado to engulf him. I struggled to free myself from Pyotr's grip. "I have to go in."

"Angels will sense!" he cried.

Then they sensed. I wouldn't stand here and watch him die. Not even if it meant losing our shot at unraveling them.

Get in, get out, get us back to my house in the blink of an eye.

But before I could do anything, the KH rumbled so hard that rocks shook loose from the ceiling.

Pyotr shielded me with his stone body, a thundering bang knocking both of us off our feet. I staggered back up, coughing dust, and clambered over the pile of rocks partially blocking my way.

The Leviathan had knocked down part of a wall with its

massive armored head. It thrashed deeper into the space, Smoky flying above it, screaming that it would be free.

Meanwhile the tornado of the damned funneled off the ground, sweeping across the room with a violence that matched the sea monster's rage.

The silky characteristic of the magic was gone, that feather-covered anvil sensation hammering into me so hard that blood streamed from my nose and ears.

I scrambled down the other side of the pile, my scythe in hand, yelling at Pyotr to get to my house and praying that Emmett was inside that tornado, because the angels were coming.

23

AGAIN AND AGAIN, THE LEVIATHAN LAUNCHED itself against the rocks, either trying to help Emmett or just lost in its frenzy to escape. The ground bucked and rolled, every step like surfing an angry sea.

Finally, I caught up to the funnel cloud, which was taller than I was, but I didn't know where to swing and not hit Emmett. Hoping for the best, I sliced across the bottom.

The Banim Shovavim dispersed for a second, as if they were curtains momentarily opening and then settling back into place, but it was enough to find my friend. I hauled him out the way I'd come, waving my scythe to keep that crazed cloud at bay.

Emmett was dazed and pale, mumbling apologies.

"Not your fault," I panted. There was so much destruction that I picked a gaping hole at random and half dragged him out.

We'd just jumped over the collapsed rocks into the rest of the KH when the prison filled with light. Not white and dazzling, luminescent and serene, this light hit my eyes like daggers.

"Don't look!" I screwed my lids shut tight, but even the

after traces burrowed into my brain with the subtlety of a jackhammer.

The Leviathan's rampage, the howl of the Banim Shovavim, and the beating wings all cut out at the same moment, leaving a silence so barren that the hairs on the back of my body stood on end.

A scream rent the air. I'll never forget that high-pitched keening until the day I die, because it was the sound of hope murdered.

I carefully opened my eyes to find that the celestial light had dimmed, allowing me a perfect view of the Leviathan's head crumbling into ash as if it was a cigar that had been tapped against an ashtray.

A large tear made of sooty vapor rolled out of one of Smoky's eyeless sockets and dripped off its face, then the phantom dissolved. Gone forever.

I pressed my fist against my mouth.

The walls of the prison thundered back into place, but the rocks around us shook loose, crashing to the ground.

"Run!" I screamed.

To where? I had no idea. I didn't have a sock, I didn't have Pyotr, and the Leviathan was dead.

A portal flashed open before us. The gargoyle stood in my living room, holding it open, his features creased in concern. I could have kissed him.

Emmett and I dove through, and the portal vanished.

We were alive and we were safe. I held on to that for the time being.

———

We held a wake that night, a strange gathering of Laurent, Sadie, Emmett, Pyotr, me, and Zev—who hadn't left—yet not an unwelcome one. Oh, and Scarlet, whom Pyotr had rescued before he'd fled the KH.

I'd broken out the aged Kentucky Bourbon that I'd been gifted for a couple of years in addition to my bonuses by the partners at my old law firm. Zev took one of the unopened bottles from me, raising his eyebrows at the label before pronouncing it would do.

The adults stood around my quartz-topped kitchen island, with Laurent and Zev on opposite sides, eyeing each other like they expected their nemesis to lunge, or worse, hug them.

Sadie had told me that she and Laurent had recounted my auction story to the vampire, who'd immediately put out the vamp equivalent of an APB on Imogine.

We toasted the memories of the Leviathan and Smoky, as well as Emmett's Banim Shovavim magic, which had been used up in the attempt to unravel the angels. The golem didn't look any different, but he sensed the lack inside him, subdued and uncertain about how being robbed of that power made him feel.

That made two of us. I was delighted that the threat of him being lost to his divination magic was gone, but he'd been created to use it. It was one thing for him to choose not to, and another for that magic to be taken from him. Plus, it had been Banim Shovavim magic, and in a way had kept another of my kind alive. Now all of that person was gone.

Team Gargolem, as Sadie had dubbed Emmett and Pyotr, was a mess. The golem was drunk, repeating loudly that exchanging his magic for booze was a win as if to convince himself, while Pyotr was deep into a sugar high from all the pop he'd consumed, with an ugly crash looming. Every time the gargoyle took a sip, he wriggled his nose at the fizziness of the carbonated drink. It would have been cute had he not been sobbing over the death of his sea monster friend and clutching his plant close. My daughter kept rubbing his back and silently handing him tissues, which he loudly blew into.

My daughter, Emmett, and Pyotr retired to Sadie's room, my awesome kid confiding that she'd cheer the others up.

I'd been jumping at every noise outside, braced for either the schmuck trio or Dumah to suck me into their respective realms, but thanks to the bourbon, I grew more and more languid. The quartz countertop felt so good against my cheek that I rubbed the other one against it as well to even out the sensation because asymmetry sucked.

Laurent pulled me up, placing a glass of water in my hand. "Drink."

"Lightweight," Zev chortled.

I pointed a very steady finger at his chest, not even coming close to his eye, so the big, scary vampire didn't need to flinch. "I hold my booze just fine. You're the one who gets all —" I flapped a hand, Dumah's gold band on my thumb glinting in the light. "You."

Zev shook the first bottle of bourbon over his glass, frowning when nothing came out. "Conversation of the finest order as usual, Miriam."

Laurent cracked the second bottle open. "Since when did you two get so chummy?"

I motioned him close in confidence. "We're besties," I whispered.

Zev grabbed the bottle away and poured himself a healthy five fingers' worth. "I don't do besties," he scoffed.

"Riiiight," I sang. "Because you don't like people." I laughed. "You and Laurent have more in common than you think."

The vamp and the wolf both bristled at my brilliant insight.

I picked up my glass and the second bottle and sashayed into my living room. "Zev has Yoshi, Laurent has Naveen, and you both have Tatiana." I fell onto my sofa, nudging the vampire with my foot as he took the chair next to me, swirling the amber liquid around in his glass with a morose expression. "Quit it," I said. "She's not going to die. I'm the one who's pissed off..." I counted on my fingers under my breath, but that took too much energy. "Angels. Plus, Imogine saw my face so there's that."

"Just because Senoi, Sansenoi, and Sammaneglof caught Emmett in the act doesn't mean we can't try once more." Laurent had sat at the other side of the sofa, which seemed wrong until he pulled my feet into his lap to massage them.

"You make it sound so simple," I said, and groaned. "Ooh. Press there again."

Zev actually gagged. "Must you two be so touchy-feely?"

I snorted. "First, I'm in my own house, so back off. And second, like you and Tatiana were so platonic in public. I heard the love poetry, remember?"

Laurent gentled his touch. "Mitzi, please. That's my aunt."

"Much as I hate to agree with the wolf," Zev said, pointedly moving on, "he's right."

Laurent smirked.

"Tatiana's condition is the far worse problem," the master vamp said. "This magic coma is the only thing keeping her alive, and it cannot be sustained indefinitely."

"You don't think I know that?" It felt wrong to be enjoying a foot massage, so I pulled my knees into my chest. "The healers are stumped, the estrie blood didn't work."

"Changing her would," Zev said darkly.

Laurent slammed his hand on the armrest. "Tatiana chose her humanity."

"No, she chose her humans," Zev snarled. "And now they're mostly dead. Samuel is gone, her friends are gone, and she has no children. Tatiana has so little tethering her to a mortal life that it's laughable. I could give her an eternity of art and purpose. I could save her."

"But at what cost?" I held up my hands because Zev's fangs had descended, causing Laurent to give a wolfy growl.

"Stop it. Both of you. Zev, if Tatiana wished to be changed, she would have asked long before now. You know this."

He crushed his glass in his hand, booze and blood streaming down his arm.

"Stain my furniture or rug and you're paying for it," I warned. "I'm serious. I've had the worst night."

The blood instantly clotted, and the vampire used the tail of his shirt to mop up the alcohol. Yikes.

Leaning back against the cushions, I curled my arms around my legs, resting my chin on my knees. "You know what I want? I want the three unraveled. I want them to pay for what they did to my parents." I sighed. "I can live with it if it doesn't happen, but I can't live with more loss."

Laurent lifted my chin with his finger and met my eyes. "Tatiana isn't going anywhere and you aren't either."

"It's too bad Jude's animation magic only works on inanimate objects." I reached for the bottle of bourbon, then changed my mind. "Maybe I'll move into Blood Alley. I bet the angels wouldn't think to find me there."

"Alas, we're full up," Zev said. "Try the demon realm."

I wagged a finger at him. "Angels can absolutely get into the demon—holy shit!" I sat up too fast and the world swam around me. I clutched the top of the sofa for balance.

"You okay?" Laurent said.

"Yeah. Fine. The demon realm. That's the answer."

"That was a joke," Zev said.

"But it's not. The schmuck trio infected Fred McMurtry with a demon parasite that cured his terminal cancer and let him live for another thirty years." I made a face. "At which point they murdered him, but you get my point. I'll bind a demon, or Nav can, and make them get the parasite."

Laurent's nostrils flared, his eyes turning flinty. "Your solution is for my aunt to be infected by a demon that would play her like a marionette for the rest of her life?"

"She'd still be human." I reached for him, but he stood up, stepping out of range, shaking his head.

"Tatiana would never choose life under those circumstances."

"Why not?" I argued. "At least she'd be alive. McMurtry didn't even know about the parasite. I was the only one who could see it."

Laurent turned his body away from me with a sneer. "Are you even hearing yourself?"

"Again, I find myself in agreement with the wolf," Zev said in a lethal voice. "Tatiana would never accept that." He paused. "Though seeing as how she chose you as her power of attorney, her judgment is open to question."

"If the healers fail, then what would you have me do? Let her die?" I glared at Zev, who'd opened his mouth, likely to push his "turn her" agenda again.

He remained silent, though his glower spoke volumes.

"Be the person Tatiana believed you to be when she chose you as her power of attorney," Laurent said.

I hugged a pillow against my chest. "Oh, wow, thanks. So helpful."

"I'm out of here," he muttered.

One fight and his first reaction was to run away?

"No," he said evenly, "you're drunk and I'm not having this conversation now."

Whoops. I'd said the quiet part loud. Regardless... "I'm not drunk. You're narrow-minded and totally not appreciating my position."

He held up his hands and walked out of the living room.

My front door slammed. I rubbed my breastbone, willing away the hollowness inside. It was just a fight. Not even a fight. Just the wrong time for a conversation. It didn't mean we were over.

Zev smoothed his hands over his trousers. "Don't do anything you're going to regret."

"More threats? Take a number."

"That's not a threat, Miriam," the vampire said, snapping me out of my grim thoughts. "It's a reminder that you've got Tatiana's life in your hands. Choose wisely."

"It's not just her life, though, is it? There's the vaccine to consider. Zev Toledano, the vampire who saved his kind. Don't worry," I said sarcastically, "even if Tatiana doesn't wake up, there must be some way to get her magic for Gabriel to use in the cure."

Zev looked at me for a long moment, his chin tilted down and his lips pressed together. "Whatever happens, I'll distribute the cure to those in need. In the meantime, however, I believe, that I too shall take my leave."

His quiet click of the front door shouldn't have mattered like Laurent's slam, and yet my house felt profoundly empty with them both gone. And did he really have to be the better undead person getting all free with the cure?

After a good five minutes cursing out this evening and most of the people in it, I went to bed, but I spent most of the night tossing and turning in a sweaty ball of anxiety. I almost called Laurent seven times, but before I hit dial, the guilt at my bitchy behavior was overridden by my anger that I'd been placed in an impossible position, and it would have been nice had he understood that.

That didn't stop me from pulling up a photo of him smiling into the camera with a bit of a squint since the sun was in his eyes and tracing my finger over it wistfully. At some point, I must have fallen asleep because I jerked awake at a clang from my back alley, like someone had kicked over one of my metal garbage cans.

Except my trash bins were plastic.

I crept to the window and peered out. It was probably kids. No, it wasn't even dawn yet. Raccoons then. No further noise occurred, and I got back into bed, but I couldn't shake off the sense that something was out there waiting for me.

Too bad for them, nothing could get past my wards. Well, Zev could, but he'd probably had enough of me tonight. Which suited me perfectly. After punching my pillow back to a lovely fluffiness, I pulled the covers up to my chin and shut my eyes.

Thirty seconds later, I threw them off with a huff, getting up to check that all the windows and doors were locked. Which they were because my OCD on that front was stronger than any booze I'd consumed.

A second clang sounded, and I leaned over my kitchen sink, peering out into the darkness to see the culprit. Was it the angels? More hunters? Imogine?

Probably the latter. Angels wouldn't bother rattling around outside and raccoons wouldn't make the hair on the back of my neck stand up.

I shot the finger to whomever or whatever awaited. As I turned from my window, a raven flew off the telephone line in the alley with a quiet caw. It wasn't Poe, and it didn't feel like it was here for me or anything, just a neighborhood bird, but the sight of a lone feather drifting slowly to the ground made me freeze.

I gripped the sink, trying desperately not to think of battlefields, corpses of me, or raven feathers, but it was no use. After getting a glass out of my cupboard, I filled it, and sat at my table in the darkness.

The water was tepid, just like my life had been before I'd reclaimed my magic. Had I misinterpreted what those corpses represented? The second time that I'd been on that battlefield, the one in my dream, the raven had said I was focusing on the wrong things.

Was I so obsessed with the past that I was doomed to repeat it?

I drummed my thumb against the glass, the gold ring from Dumah making a weighty clanking sound.

Tatiana had asked me if I'd even known full happiness. I'd

gotten to ninety percent happy, even ninety-five percent, but that last five percent gap of sorrow was a perverse comfort. It was dangerous to forget about sorrow and strife. Hell, it was a time-honored Jewish belief.

I flicked a drop of water off my finger. What if all those visions of me dead on the battlefield weren't a reminder of what I'd suffered but a warning? I rocked the chair onto its back legs, literally and symbolically feeling like I'd hit a tipping point.

Was my fixation with a demon parasite as the solution to Tatiana's predicament simply because I didn't want to have to pull the plug? How could Laurent and I survive that? He'd lost so much, and now that he and his aunt had restored their relationship, I was supposed to tear it away from him? What about Gabriel and Juliette? They were starting to feel like family to me. Not to mention that Emmett would be devastated. I'd literally be destroying his home.

I set the chair legs down abruptly, stood up, dumped the water down the sink, then nudged my junk drawer closed.

Something inside caught my eye and I opened it once more.

It was the two halves of the ace of spades card that I'd gotten from Poe.

The death card.

I ran a finger over a torn edge. When hunters broke down the door of my childhood home, Dad hadn't had time to understand what was happening before he was killed. What had Mom felt in those final moments after she told me to run? Did she have space to think or was she running on a primal drive to buy me time to live?

Putting myself in her place, as a mother, knocked the breath from my lungs, much like watching her die through the window had. Maybe that's when my love of puzzles had begun because I could sift through pieces and put a picture together.

I was in control, not some outside force, and that extended to my love of facts and lists. How wonderful to be able to strike things out or grasp the shape of an objective truth.

Was I really going to hide and hope the angels never found me? That wasn't plausible. Even if it was, I'd be back to blending in, making sure I was never noticed. Becoming a shadow of myself.

I slammed the junk drawer closed.

Sometimes death was the right answer.

Not literally, though. It was time for my final fears to die so I could be reborn into the future of my choosing. A future that included showing my daughter it was okay to be scared, so long as that didn't stop you from living. A future that might require me to make the worst decision imaginable where Tatiana was concerned, but the right one.

A future that, at this moment, involved killing a vampire. I gave a cold smirk. That sounded fun. First, however, I headed upstairs and stood in my daughter's doorway.

Emmett and Pyotr were sprawled on the floor, the golem snoring away with his head on the gargoyle's stomach. Sadie had given them both blankets. Pyotr clasped his to his cheek like a teddy bear while Emmett had tucked his blanket carefully around his feet.

Smiling fondly at them, I walked over to Sadie's bed. She was tangled up in her covers, with one foot sticking out over the edge of the bed. I leaned over and pressed a kiss to my baby girl's forehead.

She mumbled something unintelligible, and rolled over, burying her head under the covers.

A moment later, I stepped into the alley outside our protective wards, and Imogine peeled herself from the shadows. All the points to me for correctly guessing who my visitor was.

She hadn't bothered to make her skin look human and it

glowed, almost cartoonishly radioactive under the street-lights. "You have something of mine," she said.

"Finders keepers," I replied.

A red haze washed over her eyes and her fangs descended.

I slapped my scythe against my palm.

"Wait for me!" Sadie barreled across the wards in her pajamas, waving her mini flamethrower, Phoebe, her messy dark hair flying out behind her.

My second of shock allowed Imogine to run toward my kid, but her gait was shaky like she was still finding her balance on her newly regenerated legs and couldn't just blur toward her prey as usual.

The wind picked up to the sound of beating wings, and Imogine stumbled in her tracks.

The night sky was drenched in the same mind-blowing (literally) light as in Arlo's prison, making it look like midday in the heat of summer. The moment of perfect brilliance shone like a nightmare; the angels had arrived.

The vampire turned her face to the sky with a look of wonder...

Then crumbled into ash.

24

Sadie yelped, waving Phoebe around.

With a scream stuck in my throat, I hauled my child behind me, but Senoi, Sansenoi, and Sammaneglof didn't show themselves. Instead, their magic light sucked together to form a flaming sword, which shot toward us.

I threw us into the nearest shadow. There was a moment of stickiness where we snagged in the darkness, but I hauled us through into the KH.

Pyotr's table in the reception area was knocked over, his laptop and video game console smashed by a stalactite. The stone slab with the socks had been reduced to rubble.

I picked up one of the few single socks to have survived: a dingy, stretched-out white girl's sock with a droopy yellow happy face on it. Socks didn't have magic to help me travel, but now was no time to buck superstition.

Sadie was wide-eyed, white-knuckling her flamethrower, which she'd had the presence of mind to shut off. "Mom?"

"Shh." The narrow green door hadn't appeared, and stepping back into a shadow didn't get me anywhere.

We were trapped. Every second felt like a minute, time

slowed down conveniently for the angels to torment us at their leisure.

I twisted Dumah's ring around my thumb. Neon Sign was an agent of the KH, and I'd assumed it would be antagonistic toward me because it did whatever was in the best interests of this magic space. I righted Pyotr's rickety table.

How could Neon Sign condone the carnage the angels had wrought?

Acting on a huge leap of faith, I flung the ring into a corner.

"Neon Sign," I whispered. "Help us."

It flicked on, blinking "out of order" in large black letters.

"Fuck!" I scrubbed my hands over my face, conscious of every passing second. All right, no sign, but I had Sadie and her nulling magic. Could that get us out of here and into the rest of the KH to get back home? Bringing us here had been a gut-level action to save our skins, but staying here would get us killed. We were in angel-controlled territory.

Cloaking the two of us, I tugged Sadie over to my best approximation of where the green door always appeared.

"The angels have done something to keep the exit from showing up." I outlined the area she should work on. "Use your nulling magic. If the door appears, then—"

"We've got a shot at unraveling them. Got it."

I blinked at her, about to protest that we didn't have the tuning fork, except Nav's reasoning for the tuning fork was that it would disrupt the magic stronghold, allowing the Ohrist powers to destabilize the KH and the Banim Shovavim magic to shock wave through the angels, unraveling them.

Sadie's nulling magic could theoretically do the same thing.

It was crazy. Crazy enough to work? *Crazy enough to get my child killed.* I shook my head. The tuning fork had also seemed to bring Emmett's Ohrist and Banim Shovavim magic into harmony. Our plan was working, until it was derailed by the tornado of tormented souls when his Banim Shovavim necromancy magic took center stage.

Even if I supported Sadie helping me, the tuning fork—which we didn't currently have with us—was unreliable.

"The only way you're helping unravel the angels is to kill me and step over my dead body."

"Melodramatic much?" she retorted.

I jutted up my chin. "Sorry, stepping over my dead body and looking me in the eyes as you drive the knife in."

"You're being unreasonable." She glared at my incredulous laugh. "You are. I'm powerful and I've been training."

"Are you immortal and unkillable?" I planted my hands on my hips. "Come back to me when you are, and I'll give you my blessing."

"I get you want to protect me, but when the three angels murder you because you didn't get them first, I'll feel so very safe. Stop helicopter parenting me."

I'd been so focused on my daughter's safety that I wasn't letting her fly. Making Sadie face the consequences of sneaking into Blood Alley had been relatively easy because I was sure she wouldn't die. But she was asking me to take her along and trust her on a mission where death was the most likely outcome. It was one thing to make a choice to help Sadie grow and another to make one that could kill her.

Exactly, a voice in my head reminded me. *Arlo wanted to fly and look what happened to him.*

"Way to play the guilt card, kid." I shook my head. "Still not happening, though you are our ticket home. Visualize a narrow green door appearing as you use your nulling magic on the rock face, and let's get out of this place alive." I was loath to drop the cloaking, but we couldn't risk my magic interfering with hers.

Grumbling, Sadie stashed Phoebe at the small of her back under her pajama top and her shadow blossomed to life. I shielded my eyes from the white glow that lit up the cave, squinting as the shadow pressed its hands to the cave wall.

The cave rumbled and part of the stone slab flew into a large stalagmite, crushing it to dust.

Sadie shrieked and ducked.

I called Delilah up to protect us. Well, protect Sadie. Delilah could stop us from being hit, but I'd get injured if any rocks slammed into my animated shadow. I even drew my scythe, just in case, but the angels didn't appear. Not even their flaming sword.

They might not be able to physically manifest here if they'd bound most of their magic into Arlo's old prison in preparation for Dumah, but with their control over the KH, they could kill us nonetheless.

The ground bucked violently. Delilah bounced up and down like a rubber ball, while I clamped hard on Sadie's shoulder and told her to try again.

With a deafening roar, the ceiling in the middle of the reception area caved in.

We were coughing and fanning at the dust in the air, which had dampened Sadie's magic light.

I spat dust out of my mouth, running through our options.

At its heart, the KH was a Banim Shovavim space, existing for our kind to travel through, and Sadie didn't have that magic.

I smiled grimly. "Once more." As Sadie's light filled the cave, I expanded Delilah until she too permeated the space.

Light and dark. Both inherent magics. Mother and daughter. Balance.

No tuning fork needed. I shoved that thought away because still hell no to Sadie facing the three. "Concentrate on the exit!"

With another rumble, the floor collapsed. Sadie teetered backward on the edge of the gap, both of us screaming, but

Delilah caught Sadie's arm and yanked her to safety on the tiny strip of solid ground.

We pressed ourselves against the cave wall and tried again.

To my amazement, the narrow green door shimmered into light.

"Holy shit," Sadie said. "We did—"

Her words were drowned out by the beating of wings.

The air swelled like a wave about to break.

I shoved us out the door a second before it vanished.

Never had I been so happy to see the gloomy path. Unfortunately, I wasn't sure where the exit was. We ran forward, but at the first fork, I hesitated.

A faint neon arrow blinked on, pointing left.

"Is this our way home?" I said.

Its light grew stronger.

I let out a relieved sigh. "Thank you!"

Neon Sign kept us on the right path, but there was no escaping the devastation. The KH was in ruins, its rock cave-ins creating dead ends and piles of rubble, just like my heart felt witnessing the destruction.

In some places, the KH simply fell away into darkness altogether, and I warned Sadie not to stare into those voids.

The angels raged, distant sounds of rocks crashing and wings beating, but they didn't show up.

The arrow's light grew weaker and weaker, until it was barely visible. It blinked insistently three times, and the barest outline of an open door appeared.

Your mission, should you choose to accept it.

Get home safely and regroup with the tuning fork. Got it. I touched the edge of the sign. "The yellow bird rises at dawn."

It switched to its face, flashing us a sad smile, before returning to sign form. *My aunt loved yellow birds.*

"Mom! The door is flickering."

My chest constricting with a heavy sorrow, I held up my

hand in goodbye, then Sadie and I jumped back into our living room.

No, not our living room.

Neon Sign had steered us into the prison. Driven my daughter and me into the hands of the angels. Instead of getting Sadie safely home, I'd brought her to ground zero.

My worst nightmare had come true.

The soccer field–sized space reeked of wet compost, and the walls, ceiling, and floor were once more jagged black and white stripes.

It hadn't looked this way when Emmett was in here, but at least the beating wings sound was a bare hum. What were they waiting for?

Who was I kidding? They had all the time in the world to kill us. I'd even been allowed to retain my magic, that's how negligible a threat I was to them.

Dark viscous liquid drained into the light stripes, tainting them, the entire cell overlaid with a glossy finish, a translucent membrane covering the prison like shrink-wrap.

"Oh my God." Sadie gagged. "What's that?"

"It's the Banim Shovavim who were damned to eternal torment," I said, enveloped by a rush of hot anger. "The three must have trapped them here."

In the center of the room, a cloud of celestial light, which was so bright that bloody tears streamed from my eyes when I looked at it, swished and pulsed.

A figure emerged from it.

Just like Dumah, the trio had taken my cousin's form from my memories—one single image though there were three angels. Unlike Dumah, they didn't care about the details. While this Goldie was also humanoid shaped with fuzzy hair, they hadn't bothered with any other features, coloring her in with a lower wattage of their light.

Shouldn't they have melted our brains with a glance? Smote us with a single word? Had the three angels spent so much of their magic in their self-righteous quest to punish those they deemed abominations that having drained Arlo, all they had left were these Banim Shovavim to draw an external hit of power from?

"Hello, matzoh ball." Each word was a chord, each of the three's voices a note on a scale played on a rusty saw.

"Don't call me that," I snapped.

Sadie wiggled a finger in her ear. "Their magic feels like the pressure of going up in an airplane, but it's not popping. It hurts my head."

I stepped forward to meet the beings who'd been the instruments of my family's destruction and irrevocably changed the course of my life. "All your plans were for nothing. Dumah doesn't want to go free, and now you've wrecked the Kefitzat Haderech like toddlers having a tantrum. Well, it's our turn now." I waved a hand at the shifting stripes. "No more torturing Banim Shovavim. Let them rest in peace."

"There shall be one more," False Goldie said. "And a bonus abomination."

"I am not an abomination," Sadie said, her chin set at a stubborn angle.

Mom yanked me out of the kitchen chair and shoved me toward the back hallway. "Hide," she whispered.

Heavy wings beat at us, each flap battering my daughter and me backward toward a swirling vortex of blacks and purples that had opened in the floor.

My daughter grabbed my arm. "We'll do this together. Remember, you can't put on a play with one person."

"Yes, you can," I fired back, my heels skidding along the ground. "It's literally called a one-person show, Miss Theater Lover."

"Your *life* isn't a one-person show. It's got an ensemble cast. You let Dad and your friends play their roles, now you've got to let me play mine."

The floorboards tilted, speeding up our plummet into the endless void.

The angels' mocking laughter shivered through us.

Your final mission, should you choose to accept it. Neon Sign's last directive.

My mother had never given me the option to face the hunters, and not once in all these years had it ever occurred to me that the outcome of that night could have been different if she had.

The void loomed larger and closer. Sadie squeaked, digging her fingers into my arm.

With a snarl, I dug my heels into the ground, hauling my daughter against me in a hug. I backed us up, and in my mind, embraced my younger self as well. *We're not alone anymore.*

The floor leveled out, our toes dangling over the void.

A furious, discordant cry bounced off the rocks.

I squeezed Sadie's hand. "Let's give them a show to remember. Uh, is it normal to want to vomit before you go on?"

"Totally." She grinned.

For a woman who'd spent most of her life making herself as small as possible, I was about to put on the biggest, loudest show in the history of the universe with my daughter by my side, and I wouldn't have wanted it any other way. "Time to bring down the house."

A rock tumbled from the ceiling past my head, and I shook a fist at it. "I meant metaphorically!"

Delilah swelled to life, filling the prison alongside Sadie's light.

Suddenly time flipped from endless seconds filled with dread to the two of us standing in the middle of a fast-forward blur of light and sound.

False Goldie blew apart with the sound of nails on a chalkboard, and the angels gave a tortuous howl that we felt like a punch to the gut. It was good but not enough.

Balance.

I twined my fingers through Sadie's, and it was as if something snapped into place. Where her magic and my animated shadow had, up until now, coexisted, they merged into a glorious web of pale pinks and oranges, the dawn of a new chapter in our lives.

My breath caught, and a soft sigh escaped my lips.

The angels' flaming sword appeared, tearing through our radiance, the slashes growing faster and more furious, but unlike all the other times Delilah was injured, I remained untouched—as did my daughter.

Our glorious combined magic seeped into the rocks, turning this cavernous prison into a Technicolor kaleidoscope.

A handful of shriveled white feathers careened down as if made of lead and exploded in a puff of dust.

The celestial sword vanished, but the pressure grew until I was positive my brain would pop. We staved it off, our combined magic deepening into the rich gold of the most perfect summer's day.

Sadie high-fived me, then skittered like a high-prancing pony because black ooze rose out of the floorboards. It grew higher and higher, first at our ankles, then our knees, then our chests, ensnaring us in a morass of stinging goo.

More and more feathers hit the liquid, like raindrops on a lake.

My heart was going so fast, I swore I could taste it, but I held tight to Sadie, giving her an encouraging smile.

The sides of her neck and ends of her hair were matted with blood, and welts covered her exposed skin from the ooze, yet the smile she beamed at me was pure confidence.

Our magic transformed into the smudgy blacks, indigos, and deep russets of sunset.

Rocks collapsed all around us—a hurricane to our calm center. Yet not one of them hit us.

The beating wings grew fainter and fainter.

Our fight lasted an eternity and a zeptosecond, that gap in my happiness dwindling to almost nothing.

There was a ferocious rip and reality itself began to cave in.

Time snapped back to normal.

I spat feathers out of my mouth. "We have to get out of here!"

The problem was we had no way of telling if the angels were fully unraveled. How much longer did we need to stick around to make sure they didn't rise back up?

And how were we going to escape?

A crooked portal, a smile with teeth, tore through the prison, and everything fell still. A small tornado of crimson and gray shot toward the opening, only to be caught by a stubby-fingered hand with coral nail polish and squished into oblivion.

Dumah-Goldie stepped into the mouth of the portal and, wiping her hand off on her baggy jeans, nodded in satisfaction. "What are you waiting for?" she said. "An invitation? Get your tuches out of there already." She spied Sadie and shook her head. "Not the little one, though."

With that, she sucked me into the portal, and it winked shut.

25

We blinked into Hazarmavet, the Courtyard of Death.

I pressed my scythe into the angel's neck, holding it with both hands, which shook as much from rage as fear. No victory in the world mattered, not even saving the earth itself, if I lost my daughter. I hadn't finally grieved my own inner child and found closure, found pure true happiness, only to experience the one blow I would never recover from.

My daughter was not expendable. Tonight was not her final curtain.

"Sadie. Here. Now." I was incapable of forming more words through my tight jaw.

Dumah-Goldie wrinkled her nose, and my weapon turned into a bottle of prosecco, which she plucked from my hand. "I'm not a monster. She's waiting for you at home, safe and sound. Erica!"

My relief swept over me in a tidal wave that made my legs buckle, and I crashed onto a chair by the bistro table overlooking the river.

The scabby cube demon appeared, its eyes on stalks bobbing up and down and it beeped several times.

"Champagne flutes," Dumah-Goldie said. "It's a celebration." The angel hummed a few bars of "Celebration" by Kool & the Gang, breaking out Goldie's hip-wiggling, arm-waving dance moves.

I stretched out my legs, glad to see that Erica had survived. She seemed like a good sort. For a demon. I waved at her and she returned the greeting with one of her many stumpy arms, a writhing dybbuk stabbed on the end of its claws like a shish kebab, before she vanished.

Mmm. Maybe I'd do BBQ tonight.

"Is the schmuck trio fully unraveled now?" I said.

Goldie's kind brown eyes changed to those reptilian gold slits that I hated. "Oh yes," she purred. The angel smiled brightly. "Want to listen in?"

One of those old-fashioned hearing trumpets appeared on the bistro table. I picked up the metal horn and held it to my ear, almost dropping it at the lament of unbearable agony and unquenchable rage.

"Catchy." I set the horn down.

"Right? I'm thinking of making a playlist."

Uh-huh. I kept my smile in place and nodded. Then I remembered some of my own friends' peccadillos and figured the angel wasn't any stranger.

Oh, my friends. My expression sobered.

Dumah-Goldie frowned, taking the glasses from Erica, who'd briefly appeared to deliver them, and poured us prosecco. "What's with the long face?"

I had a boyfriend to apologize to and a vampire to make amends with, but there was only one friend that I was grieving. I took a sip of the fizzy alcohol to be polite, then held my glass. "I'm glad this all worked out, but I have to go home. Someone I care about is gravely injured, and if she hasn't been healed from her magic coma, then I'm facing a horrible decision."

That was a lie. I'd already decided that if Tatiana couldn't be saved by healing magic, I'd let her go. Much as I wanted her to live, making that happen by either turning her into a vampire or infecting her with a demon parasite was wrong.

All my triumphant elation turned sour and heavy.

"Is there anything else you want to say?" Dumah-Goldie prompted, one eyebrow raised.

I barely refrained from rolling my eyes, experiencing the same surge of irritation Goldie inspired whenever she insisted that I'd forgotten my manners.

"Yes, of course," I said. "Thank you for helping me get closure on the past. I mean that. I feel like a weight I've been dragging around for almost thirty years is gone."

The angel blew a frizzy curl out of her eyes. "What? Is my magic not good enough for you?"

"Huh?"

Dumah-Goldie spread her hands wide. "Hello. Angel here." My prosecco turned to a black liquid that stank of vinegar. "It's somewhat insulting that you aren't begging me to heal your friend."

"I would have if I knew that was an option." I set my glass down as far from me as possible. "But how? We don't have the Ascendant for you to leave Gehenna, and I'm not sure how safe it would be to bring Tatiana through the rift."

"Obviously I'm not doing either of those things," the angel said with a sniff. "Just give her this." She held out her palm with an unmarked tin on it.

Inside was a single hard lemon candy.

"It's not as good as what I could do if I touched her, but it'll buy her a bit of time."

"This is amazing. Thank you." I clasped the tin to my chest. "What do I tell her and her family about how long she has left? Weeks? Months?"

The angel looked at me with her brows creased like I was stupid. "Twenty or thirty years."

Right. Angel time.

I stood up, suddenly feeling awkward. What was the right way to bid an angel goodbye?

Dumah-Goldie pushed to her feet and held out her arms. "Come here, you."

I hugged her tightly, and when she clasped me back, feathers tickled my spine.

"We won't be seeing each other again," Dumah-Goldie said. "I hope," she added pointedly.

"Nope. I'll be good."

"In that case, matzoh ball." The rift opened up, revealing my living room, with Sadie hovering on the other side. "There you go."

I waved at my kid, who returned the gesture with relief, then turned to the angel. "I'll never forget you."

"Duh." She winked at me.

Once I was home, I glanced back. Dumah-Goldie and Erica were waving at me while dybbuks zoomed into the sky above them to form a heart.

Fuck, was my life weird.

I turned to my kid.

And pretty wonderful.

Sadie was bouncing off the walls, high on our victory. Apparently, Jude had picked Emmett and Pyotr up and taken them back to Tatiana's, but not before Sadie had told them the whole story.

Jude and I were going to have a ton to talk about at our next brunch, and if we didn't fully catch up on all the details, that was okay. We had the rest of our lives.

Sadie had called Tovah too, though she hadn't told her about the angels. The kid was babbling, and her excitement became too much when she saw the lemon candy cure, but thankfully, I heard Eli's door shut so I sent her next door to tell her dad the story.

I stepped into a shadow, confusion when I didn't go anywhere giving way to sadness—and not just for the KH. I was ready to grab hold of my future with both hands, but I took a moment to absorb the enormity of a door once and for all closing on my past.

Then I got in my car and drove to Tatiana's.

Juliette ran outside to meet me, her eyes wet with tears.

"Is Tatiana gone?" I squeezed the candy tin.

"No, but there's nothing left to try."

I put my arm around Juliette's shoulders. "Actually..."

A few minutes later, Emmett, Pyotr, Marjorie, Juliette, and I gathered around Tatiana's bedside. She lay under the covers looking like she had one foot in the grave.

"You're sure this will work?" Emmett said.

"Yes," I said with a confidence I didn't totally feel. Was I supposed to give it to her while she was in the coma? What if she choked on it?

Juliette took the tin. "Let me." She placed it on the side table, and then rested her hands on Tatiana's chest. A warm glow appeared between her palms and my boss's nightgown.

Tatiana's lips parted and the healer fed her aunt the candy.

I swear we all held our breath until she sucked on it.

The room filled with the scent of lemon trees on a warm summer's day and a faint bloom kissed Tatiana's cheeks. Her skin color grew healthier and healthier, her frailty falling away, until she sat up, clear-eyed, and said in a strong voice, "Oy. Who died?"

Juliette and I crushed her in a hug.

Pyotr whooped.

Marjorie jumped up and kissed Emmett, who froze. She stepped away, mortified, but Emmett ducked his head to plant a peck on her lips, and the young woman beamed, slipping her hand into his.

While Emmett, Marjorie, and Juliette stayed by Tatiana to fill her in on everything since the fight with Imogine, including that the vampire was dead, as I'd updated them on all that, I motioned Pyotr into the hallway.

"Neon Sign Face is gone," I said. "I'm sorry."

His bottom lip trembled but he nodded bravely. "Is not your fault. Is angels'. I'm glad they hurt."

"Me too. You have a job with Tatiana's company, but you could go back to Russia if you like. However, if you did want to stay?" I placed a hand on his shoulder. "You could live with me."

He bounced on his toes, his wings fluttering. "With best friend Sadie?"

"Yes." I chuckled.

He thought it over then shook his head. "I stay with partner. Tatiana already had room for me."

"Did she now?" Seems I wasn't the only one who'd expanded her family. "That's great."

"But what about best friend Malorie?"

I sighed. I hadn't thought about other Banim Shovavim suddenly discovering they couldn't travel through the KH, and I certainly hadn't considered Pyotr's other friendship. "How about we get you a phone and find her number? Then you can call her whenever you like."

"Yes." The gargoyle crushed me into a hug that made me oomph, then gentled his hold, patting my head. "Sorry. I tell partner and new best friend Marjorie."

"You do that."

He drew the adorable couple away, babbling excitedly, while I returned to the bedroom.

Tatiana was three minutes into being healed and already sitting up with a regal expression. "Angel magic? You don't do anything by halves, do you, Miriam?"

"Nope."

Juliette excused herself to call her father with the good news, but before she left she told me to do something about her uncle because he'd been a surly bastard, refusing to say goodbye to his aunt until I showed up and announced my decision.

I pulled a brocade chair up to the bed. "Who's the best power of attorney ever?"

"Who's the smartest woman to have chosen her?" Tatiana said archly.

"Can't let me have this one, can you?"

"I suppose, seeing as you just defeated three angels. Just this once." She squeezed my hand. "How's Sadie?"

"Incredible."

Tatiana tapped her lips. "She interested in a part-time job?"

"No way."

"We'll discuss it later."

"No, we won't." I shook a finger, a stern expression on my face. "She may have helped me defeat three angels, but now she is going to live a normal life with her golem uncle and her gargoyle bestie, and oh fuck, my kid is going to end up working for you."

Tatiana smirked. "I do hire the best." She glanced past me, and a shiver of awareness danced down my spine. "What took you so long to get here, Lolo? You missed my death throes. They were magnificent."

He gave her his most charming smile, his eyes briefly darting to me. "I came when I knew I'd be saying welcome back instead of goodbye."

She snorted.

He bowed over her hand and kissed it. His thigh pressed against my shoulder, but I stopped myself from leaning into him.

"Can we talk?" I said.

He glanced at his aunt, who shooed us away.

"Go. I want a bath and then a drink. Maybe several."

"Okay," he said.

"See you tomorrow?" Tatiana said.

I smiled. "And every day thereafter."

Since the house felt overly crowded, we headed into the

backyard, but Emmett stopped me in the kitchen, leaving Laurent to go on ahead.

The golem hugged me tightly, not letting go.

"I'm okay, Emmett," I said gently. "And it's all over now."

He stepped back, his eyes damp. "It's just that Jude brought me to life," he said gruffly, "but you helped me live."

Sniffling, I nodded. "You helped me live too."

Marjorie and Pyotr called him from upstairs, and Emmett shook off the mushiness. "Okay, toots, see ya later."

"See ya later, buddy."

I looked skyward, blinking rapidly so Laurent didn't think I was getting weepy over our situation.

He sat by the small goldfish pond, running his fingers over a reed that he'd plucked.

"I'm sorry for being such a bitch last night," I said, taking the chair next to him.

"I wasn't at my best either. I'm sorry as well." He tore the reed into strips. "You were in an impossible position. I'm just glad the healers cured her."

"Healers schmealers," I scoffed. "That was all me, baby."

My boyfriend's face was a symphony of expressions as I described meeting Imogine, our battle with the angels, and my final visit to Gehenna.

"You fought angels and saved my aunt, and I made myself a peanut butter sandwich and went to bed?"

"Looks that way, huh?" I took the reed from him and tossed it aside.

"Merde, I've got to up my game if I'm going to keep up with you."

"Yeah, about that."

He leaned back, a wary expression on his face. "What?"

"You should know that I love you. I don't expect you to say it back because we just started this relationship, but after the whole angels thing and hiding for almost three decades,

I'm going to say what I think. You'll have to deal with that." I punctuated that statement with a pat to his thigh.

Laurent looked gobsmacked.

A bit too gobsmacked.

There was "I don't expect you to say it back" and then there was "my boyfriend looks like he wants to go furry forever so he never has to reply to what I just said." I pulled my keys out of my purse, eyeing the fastest route back to my car.

Laurent laughed.

I crossed my arms. "What's so funny?"

"Nothing. Thank you for telling me." He waggled his eyebrows. "Want to go back to your place?"

Okay, sure, I'd literally just told him that he didn't have to say it back, but this was the second man who'd said "thank you" to my declaration of love. He could have replied that he cared for me or tossed out a simple "You are an amazing woman, Miriam." Either would have sufficed.

Instead we were jumping to sex? On the other hand, was I really complaining about the prospect of a mind-blowing orgasm? "Let's go to your place."

"You just said you love me and we still can't be together this way at your home?"

"Not because I don't want you there."

"Because of Sadie?"

"Nope. She's at Eli's this week."

"Then what?"

"You have that tub." I made puppy dog eyes at him.

Pouting, Laurent pressed a hand to his heart. "You only want me for my plumbing."

I shrugged. "It's pretty top-notch."

He stood up, shaking his head. "Forget it. The mood is broken."

I yawned, purely for show. It was Monday evening, and I

hadn't slept for two days, but adrenaline was keeping me going. "Guess I'll just go home and sleep."

He caught my wrist. "Or, you could entice me."

I curled my fingers into his belt loops. "That feels like a lot of work for a woman who just unraveled three angels and saved your aunt."

"You did have help," he said.

"Wow."

He grinned rakishly at me, his expression softening out to one of incredible tenderness, and I was helpless in the face of that emotion.

"Well then, you better come over." I paused. "But drive slowly."

26

I LEAD-FOOTED IT HOME AND JUMPED IN THE shower. I was doing a last-minute dash around my house to set up the mood because I'd come up with a great seduction plan on the drive back, when I found a foot-long sword resting on my sofa.

Carefully, I picked it up. Was this a new cosplay prop of Sadie's? I huffed in frustration because she knew better than to leave something like this lying around. Especially on my couch. What was she thinking?

I picked it up by its silver handle, which had a cross-stitch pattern hammered into it. Wow, this thing had a good weight and heft given its size. A single crimson jewel adorned the base of the blade, the weapon narrowing to a sharp point.

Having no idea which fandom this came from, I flipped it over and gasped, my heart melting into a gooey mess at the engraving on the other side.

Snicker snack.

I was so stunned that I almost didn't register the knock at my front door, but when I did, I ran to fling it open, pointing the weapon at Laurent's throat. "This is a vorpal blade," I said stupidly.

"Yes, Mitzi." He lowered the tip and stepped past me.

"A vorpal blade," I said again.

He laughed, slipping off his shoes. "I'm glad you noticed."

"You left it on my sofa."

"I wanted to make sure you saw it."

I tapped the engraving. "It says 'snicker snack.'"

Generally, I was above merely repeating the obvious, but if I didn't stick to facts, I was going to become a blubbering mess, because this was the most romantic thing anyone had ever done for me. As that would totally kill our impending sexytimes, facts it was.

Laurent ran a hand over his jaw, his emerald eyes serious. "I would have etched 'I love you' on it but I thought it was too soon."

My lip trembled. *Facts*, I ordered sternly. "When did you realize you loved me?"

"When I saw you with Hiram and Ephraim, alive." He curled his fingers into his hair, his head tilted and his face screwed up in thought. "Maybe before then? You came into my life huffing and puffing and giving me attitude with your snicker snack and this spark that I thought was gone forever suddenly flamed to life. I tried to write it off as irritation or indigestion—"

I laughed.

"But no, it's love. Miriam Feldman, I snicker snack you like crazy and I plan to tell you that for the rest of our lives so deal with it." He jutted his chin up, his eyes twinkling.

My grand seduction plan flew out the window. After setting the sword on the small table by the front door, I tore off my T-shirt and shorts, flinging them away.

Laurent swallowed. "That's a thong and corset."

"I'm glad you noticed." Goosebumps dotted my skin. I'd taken on vampires, demons, and corrupt angels, but standing in my foyer in the late afternoon light in an admittedly phenomenal corset and matching thong of blues and lilacs like one of Monet's water lilies was the most terrifying thing I'd ever done.

A gleam entered Laurent's eyes, his expression carnal and dangerous. For the first time it really hit me that he had been the alpha of the largest werewolf pack in Europe. One of the largest in the world.

And I was standing here nearly naked, alone with him.

I licked my lips.

"Get upstairs." His voice was iron sheathed in velvet.

I didn't run, but I headed up at a good clip, his eyes boring into my back. Nah, probably my ass. I threw an extra wiggle into my sashay. When I stepped into the bedroom, I grabbed the curtains to draw them shut.

"Did I say to close them?" He dropped into the armchair in the corner of my room, undoing the top button on his shirt to expose a triangle of olive skin. He'd brought the vorpal blade with him.

"No," I said breathily.

"Stand over there." Using the sword as a pointer, he indicated a spot between him and the bed.

My nipples practically poked through the fabric of the corset as I complied. I shivered, my core strung tight.

The shifter casually rested his ankle on his other knee, one arm draped over the back of the chair with the sword dangling from his hand, just watching me.

I closed my eyes against the bolt of desire that thrummed through me.

He tsked. "Look at me, mon amour." He wasn't demanding or growling, but he spoke with the confidence of a man who knew he'd be unquestioningly obeyed.

I clenched my hands into fists, my thong becoming drenched, and a hot flush hitting my cheeks.

His lids flew halfway closed, leaving only a sliver of brilliant green kissing my skin.

My lips parted. I wanted other parts of him kissing me, but I was also a very willing participant in this game.

"Get on the bed." He drew a circle with the sword. "Against the headboard. I want to see you touch yourself."

I moaned, wobbling backward until I hit the mattress. My scooting onto the bed was undignified in my haste to pull the thong off, but I got myself into position. I'd never been so vulnerable with another person, never desired to give myself to them in any way they asked.

"Open your legs, chérie," he drawled.

I was conscious of my belly poking out from under the corset, but all I saw on my boyfriend's face was hunger. Taking a deep breath, I opened my legs.

He quirked an eyebrow.

Gathering up my courage, I stroked my clit. One touch and my body burst into flames. I writhed against the mattress, stroking myself faster and faster, my hips beginning to buck.

I must have closed my eyes again because Laurent called my name, startling me, and I snapped my lids open.

He stood up and prowled toward the bed, still fully clothed, though his erection strained against his trousers. Coming around to the side of the bed, he leaned over me, enough to feel the heat pouring off his body but maintaining a gap between us.

"Laurent," I pleaded, slipping a finger inside myself.

"What is it?" he said tenderly and ghosted the tip of the blade along my naked shoulder.

I moaned again, a second finger joining the first.

"Non." He placed the flat of the blade over my hand, and I stopped, blinking up at him through my fog of lust.

His eyes locked on mine, he very gently dragged the sword's tip up my front, tracing the sweetheart neckline of the corset. Everywhere it touched left goosebumps in its wake.

I whimpered, wanting so badly to chase my orgasm, but I

waited for his next command.

Laurent gave me a piratical smile and set the blade on the bedside table. He straddled me, the mattress depressing with his weight. Covering my hand on my clit with his, he scraped his teeth against the side of my neck and I swallowed. He sat back on his calves with a smirk, studying me like I was a wild territory he sought to conquer.

Very calmly and infuriatingly slowly, he unbuttoned his shirt, then he ducked his head and claimed my mouth in a rough kiss.

My head fell back against the headboard, and I arched my hips with a wanton moan.

He pushed me down onto my back. His mouth scorched my skin as he mapped every inch of me. He teasingly narrowed in on my clit, messily swiping his tongue along it.

I fisted my hands in his hair, swallowing past the dryness in my throat. "Kiss me again."

"But of course." He obliged—but not on my mouth.

Laurent nibbled and sucked, holding my trembling legs apart in his firm grip, until stars danced in my vision and, grabbing his shirt, I begged for release.

His shirt hit the ground and he reached for his belt buckle, before making short work of his pants and stretching out alongside me.

There was no distracting traffic or kids playing. It was as if the world had conspired to give us this hushed bubble as a gift. The desire pulsing through me softened to something no less intense but far sweeter, and I caressed his cheek with my hand. "I love you with all my heart."

He folded a hand over mine, pressing them to his heart, his face awash with wonder and joy. "I..." A frustrated look flashed over his fingers. "English," he said helplessly.

"Snicker snack. It says it all."

"Oui." He laughed, his talented fingers working the hooks on the back of my corset.

"Oh!" I raised my eyebrows in mock surprise. "Is there still mo—" I let out a lusty groan as the corset went flying, the binding replaced by Laurent palming my heavy, aching breasts.

I clasped the nape of his neck and sucked hard on his throat, almost coming from his fierce growl that vibrated from my lips down to my toes.

Laurent rolled me underneath him, his eyes drugged out and his chest rising and falling heavily.

I moved his hand onto my clit, getting myself off against his fingers.

"Fuck." He shuddered and looked around. "Pants. Condom."

"I'm clean," I said. "I was tested, and I haven't been with anyone since we…"

"Yes." The word was a plea. "I haven't been with anyone else in a couple of years."

I smirked. "Then fuck me, Huff 'n' Puff."

He groaned at his nickname, but he was the one smirking when he thrust inside me and my breath caught.

"Je t'aime." His whispered declarations grew faster with his tempo, our kisses messy and the fingers of our free hands intertwined because having found each other, we'd never let go.

My core grew tighter and hotter. I wrapped one leg around his back to draw him even closer. "You're mine," I said.

"Forever."

The promise in that word sent me over the edge, and I shuddered, calling out his name, my head buried in his neck.

Laurent thrust roughly inside me a final time and gave a hoarse shout.

We lay side by side, still holding hands, our heavy breathing filling the air along with the musk of sex and Laurent's cedar scent.

"Not bad," he said.

I nodded. "But we should probably practice."

He propped himself up on one elbow. "You could make a list."

"I already have a list, remember?" I teased.

"That's right. Perhaps you should show me number seven now."

"Hmm. I don't know. Number seven requires a lot of stamina and we just finished."

"Try me."

"When you put it that way," I said and reached for him.

I'd had this fantasy that when Laurent and I got together, we'd hole up at his place on a rainy afternoon with the fire crackling. The two of us would snuggle on his couch, each engrossed in a book while Sadie played with Boo, all to a jazz soundtrack from his 1940s-style radio.

That serenity was nothing like the chaos the next night, with my child stomping back and forth between Eli's place and mine as she looked for a sweater she'd misplaced. A hockey game blared on my television while my ex-husband convinced both his boyfriend and mine why it was the superior sport. For some reason, he had to do it at my place.

Whatever, dude.

Jude and I hung out in my kitchen drinking wine, waiting for the Thai food Eli had ordered for all of us.

"Are we ever going to start our brunches up again?" I twirled my wineglass in my hand. "I miss them. I miss you. Lately we only get to see each other in passing or because there's some grave danger that I want your opinion on. This is the first time in ages we've just chilled."

"I miss you too. Let's start them up this Sunday? Same place, same time? You get the first round of mimosas."

"That sounds perfect." I topped up her Moscato. "I wish

I'd told you about my magic years ago, but I'm glad there won't be any more secrets between us."

"Still not going to tell you if anything juicy happens at the party in Tokyo, sug."

"Yeah, you will."

"Yeah," she sighed. "I will. Brat." She shoved my chair away with her foot, and laughing, I leaned in to kiss her cheek.

Laurent strode into the kitchen with three empty beer bottles, which he set on the counter. "If I have to hear one more time how much more athletic hockey players are over soccer players…" He sneered the word "soccer."

"Don't kill him, Lolo," Nav said, entering with the empty chips bowl. "There are two of us and one of him. We'll convince him of the one true sport eventually." He refilled the bowl from the bag that Jude and I were eating out of and she smacked his hand.

"Bottom cupboard," I said, motioning.

"You're not going to get it for me?"

I sipped my wine, not moving.

"You know," Nav said archly, retrieving an unopened bag, "your ex takes direction."

"That's because I trained him," I said. "You're welcome."

Eli, wearing a Canucks jersey—not his autographed one, which had been reframed and rehung above his mantel—froze in the doorway with a groan. "I liked it better when you hated my boyfriends. Less painful communication."

"Oh." I blinked. "You think I like him?"

"Bless your heart," Jude added.

"Just for that." Nav swiped our chips as well and strode back to the living room.

"Get crumbs on my couch and die," I called out.

He replied with a raspberry sound.

Eli sighed and grabbed a roll of paper towel. "Please don't hurt him. I like this one."

"I'll consider it."

"Promise me and I'll let you be there when I tell my sister about the existence of magic."

"Ooh." Jude leaned forward, her eyes gleaming. "Can I be there too? I've never seen someone's head actually explode."

My bestie hated how Genevieve had treated me—and that was before the divorce.

"As fun as that would be—" I paused, an evil grin breaking free as I played out that scene. Then I sighed. "Prime directive, remember?"

"Nope. Got the all clear from Ryann," Eli said. "Magic is in our family. Genevieve is allowed to know."

Jude clapped her hands. "Her head is totally going to explode."

I pretended to wipe a tear from my eye. "Wishes do come true."

"Hey," Eli said. "Still my sister. But fair."

"And I get to tell Nessa!" Sadie squeaked excitedly, popping her head in before thumping up the stairs.

"Her hearing is so selective," Eli said. I shrugged, then he did too, and headed back to Nav.

Laurent had been hovering the entire time.

"Can I help you find something?" I said. "There's more beer in the fridge."

"Nope. Just waiting for this." He kissed me swiftly and hard, then sauntered back to the game.

"Okay," I said weakly, fanning myself.

"If I have to see that, you better have more chips," Jude grumbled.

The doorbell rang.

"I'll get it," Sadie yelled.

At my daughter's thundering footsteps, Jude grabbed on to her wineglass. "I adore my niece, Mir, but she has the grace of a herd of hippos."

I'd stood up to get plates from the cupboard, expecting the

visitor to be our Thai delivery, when Sadie screeched, "Gramgee!"

I did a double take. Goldie wasn't due home for a visit until next month. Had Dumah shown up at my door? I was sprinting to my foyer before I'd completed the thought.

"What's crackalackin', matzoh ball?" My cousin fired finger guns at me, the scent of tea tree oil drifting off her, and I relaxed.

"Goldie!" I swept her into a huge hug.

Sadie lugged her enormous suitcase in and closed the door.

Goldie shook raindrops out of her gray curls and kicked off a pair of blue plastic clogs that I hadn't seen before. "I left Merle down there to golf to his heart's content for a month because I missed my girls." She slung an arm around Sadie and me. "Nu? Anything exciting happen while I was gone?"

Sadie laughed. "You could say that."

My cousin turned an inquiring expression on me.

"I may have one or two things to tell you," I said, and led her to the kitchen to blow her mind.

Thank you for coming on this crazy journey with Miri and me.

Keep reading for a sneak peek of BIG DEMON ENERGY (Bedeviled AF, #1).

If you enjoyed this book and want to be first in the know about bonus content, reveals, and exclusive giveaways, become a Wilde One by joining my newsletter: http://www.deborahwilde.com/subscribe

Now, are you ready for a funny, sexy urban fantasy with a smart, driven heroine and a second chance vampire romance?

She's just a demon, standing in from of a vampire, trying not to punch him.

Turn the page for a sneak peek of *Big Demon Energy* ...

SNEAK PEEK OF BIG DEMON ENERGY

Sources speculated that the reason Ezra Cardoso was ridiculously photogenic was because he was a Prime. He never exhibited a wonky eye, an unfortunate double chin, or a flat out "burn it" picture like the rest of us mere mortals. Even so, photos failed to capture how the mere quirk of his lips could express ten thousand words of amusement or how when he leaned in, totally intent on whatever you were saying, he made you feel seen in a way no one else ever had.

I braced myself for the force of him live, but the person who strode through the door was so unlike my first love that it was almost like seeing a stranger.

Any softness in Ezra's face was gone, replaced by a ruggedness in his straight nose, full lips, and well-defined jawline that better fit the image of a man raised to be heir to a vampire Mafia.

He'd bulked up, his formerly lean frame now a V shape. The jacket of his blue three-piece suit hugged his ripped biceps and broad shoulders like he was a modern-day conqueror and this was his bespoke armor.

The Ezra I'd known wouldn't have been caught dead in this outfit.

Or undead.

Michael smiled. "Do come in."

I frowned at the way Ezra studied her like a lion determining a threat or prey, every inch the Crimson Prince, then realized it was Ezra's silvery-blue eyes under his thick arched eyebrows that made it both easier and a million times harder to look at him. Where once they'd caught the light, rippling and ever changing, they were now hard crystals promising knifelike edges, despite the easy grin he bestowed on my mother.

"Director," he said.

One word in that smooth, low baritone and my heart exploded against my ribs so hard I was positive it drowned out all other sound in the room.

His gaze lasered on to me and he went stock-still, his eyes never leaving mine.

A shiver ran down my spine. I crossed one leg over the other, blessing the fates for having worn the wine-colored pencil skirt (that I'd bought as an early celebration gift) with my sheer black hose, and high heels with a bright pop of scarlet on the soles. My tailored white shirt with three-quarter sleeves and a teasing hint of cleavage completed the look.

Something flickered in the depths of his gaze, but it was gone in an instant. "Aviva," he said in a bland voice.

I waited for some awkward follow up small talk but got nothing. It was as if he couldn't be bothered to find out how I'd been.

All right. Two could play that game.

"Cardoso," I replied coolly.

I'd have relished his tight expression, but I was busy telling myself his brush-off didn't matter. It was the first exposure and would be the worst. Now, like a virus, I'd been infected and could build my immunity.

He transferred the gift bag he held to his other hand. "Am I interrupting something?"

"Not at all." Michael motioned to a seat.

Ezra took the chair next to mine with no hesitation. My presence didn't disturb him a whit.

I'd have brushed him off just as easily, but I caught a whiff of his cologne with its notes of cardamom, cloves, and bergamot, a spicy orange smell. It was mixed with the fresh, cool scent of a windswept summer breeze that was all him, and I was hurled back to all the times he'd teased me for pressing my nose to his T-shirts to sniff him.

I dug in my skirt pocket for a package of mints, practically huffing the candies before popping one in my mouth.

He raked a wayward lock off his forehead. His black curls had grown out since we were together, now slightly untamed. (Primes could grow their hair, all other vamps were stuck with the length they had at death.) This longer style lent him a rakish air, yet there was a maturity to him that he wore well. Combined with his close-cropped black beard and mustache, he resembled a pirate. Or the physical representation of sin.

Big deal. It had been six years. He changed; I'd changed.

I crunched my mint into dust.

Ezra set his gift bag, with the neck of a wax-sealed wine bottle protruding, on Michael's desk. "I was in the caves of Saint-Marcel for a wine tasting and this one reminded me of you."

"Do tell," she said drolly.

My ex got an impish expression on his face that I recognized from the many "What? Me do something naughty?" pics that kept popping up on my social media feeds despite my best efforts to block them. "Layered and intense."

Michael chuckled.

Ezra didn't wear a tie, that apparently was still a step too far even for him, and the first couple buttons of his crisp white shirt were undone, exposing a triangle of brown skin.

Vamps kept the same skin color they'd had when alive. They looked totally normal in photos, but if you were in the same room and noticed they weren't breathing, or you felt their gaze on your back, your flight response was pinged.

Not that running was a smart idea. Too many of them took it as an invitation.

"It's a token of my gratitude for accommodating my requests at such short notice," Ezra said.

I squelched the memory of running through my apartment, laughing, while he play-hunted me, and shifted in my seat to shake off my squirminess. He'd certainly pinged me in ways that my operative training hadn't prepared me for.

I wasn't the only one. Whether yachting in Saint-Tropez, diving the Great Barrier Reef, or getting together with celeb pals for a charity hockey game, where Ezra Cardoso went, the paparazzi followed. His antics were the definition of clickbait, and his groupies (Ezracurriculars) were rabid, fanning themselves over each scandalous venture.

Michael pulled the bottle out of the gift bag and gave an impressed nod. "Thank you. I'll enjoy a glass tonight. Now, we have much to discuss."

"I can't imagine what's left to work out," Ezra said. "The terms of my assignment here are fairly straightforward."

"Actually," I piped up, meeting his gaze levelly, "it's not so much a discussion as a directive." I tapped my finger against my chin. "You're familiar with those." I paused. Smiled. "From all your work as a Maccabee, of course. I just learned we were fellow operatives, but what exciting assignments you must have had."

"And you, the picture of a legacy princess."

My smile hardened. How dare he throw that at me when I'd shared my fears of never amounting to more than Michael's daughter in this organization, instead of a damn good operative earning my reputation via intelligence and hard work?

"Though I will say." He casually crossed one leg over the other. "A directive saves the trouble of time-wasting repetition when the outcome is a predetermined conclusion."

Sadly, since he was a vamp, I couldn't read him for weakness, and Michael would bitch if I jammed a pen through his throat and messed up her fancy Eames chairs. Not that I would, consummate professional that I was.

"Predetermined conclusions. Right." I picked up her silver pen and danced it over my knuckles. "In that case, it's polite to give the other party a well-reasoned explanation and some processing time." I clicked the pen. "A little tip I've picked up as a clear communicator."

One side of Ezra's mouth quirked up. "You definitely keep talking until your point is conceded. Sometimes, however, people refuse to accept reality, in which case, it's best for one party to lay down the law and move on."

Perhaps my next click of the pen was a bit violent because Michael raised a hand. "Speaking of how it has to be." She shot me a warning look. "You're in my home now, Mr. Cardoso, and regardless of what anyone has led you to believe, you will answer to me."

"I wouldn't have assumed anything else," he said smoothly.

"Good." My mother gave a Cheshire Cat smile. "I'm pleased to put all our chapter resources at your disposal and approve your off-site office rental. In return, you'll work with a team of my choosing."

The vampire draped an arm over the back of the chair. "I'd hate to pull your people away for this. I know how stretched local branches are. I've brought my own man."

I eagerly swung my head back to my mother.

"He's most welcome here," she said, "but the other members are nonnegotiable."

Ezra slid his gaze to me, almost like he was making sure I wouldn't bite before replying. "Having Aviva working for me might distract from the investigation at hand. I'm sure you want to have it resolved as quickly as possible and get me out of your hair."

Michael didn't even blink at his smug look. She nodded at me.

I got to deliver the news? I almost jumped up and punched the air, instead, I tsked Ezra. "You misunderstand. I'm not a team member." I gave him one exquisite moment of relief before driving the knife in. "I'm your co-leader."

ACKNOWLEDGMENTS

Thank you to every single reader who was excited about a heroine in her forties having magic adventures and finding love. It has been a joy to write Miri and bring so many of my own life experiences into this book.

To my phenomenal editor, Dr. Alex Yuschik, one more series down! You make the entire process so much fun and I thank you for coming on all these journeys with me.

Thank you to my husband for always being in my corner, for letting me spew plot ideas at you when you're trying to fall asleep, and for being my biggest cheerleader. You are my best friend and my happily-ever-after.

ABOUT THE AUTHOR

Former screenwriter, global wanderer, and total cynic with a broken edit button, Deborah Wilde writes funny, sexy urban fantasy books and paranormal women's fiction.

Smart, sassy women who can solve a mystery, kick supernatural butt, banter with hot men, and still make time for their best female friend are the cornerstones of Deborah's stories. Her books are beloved by readers craving magic adventures, swoon worthy steamy romances, hilarity, and happily ever after.

"Magic, sparks, and snark!"

www.deborahwilde.com

Made in the USA
Coppell, TX
08 January 2024

27425890R00184